THE MONSTERS OF SAI

C000157650

SAVAGE
SAINTS

NEW YORK TIMES BESTSELLING AUTHOR **JA HUSS** WRITING AS

KC CROSS

SAVAGE
SAINTS
THE MONSTERS OF ST. MARK'S
JA HUSS WRITING AS KC CROSS

Copyright © 2022 by JA Huss writing as KC Cross
ISBN: 978-1-950232-88-8

No part of this book may be reproduced or resold in any form or by any electronic or mechanical means, including information storage and retrieval systems, without written permission from the author, except for the use of brief quotations in a book review.

This is a work of fiction. Names, characters, businesses, places, events and incidents are either the products of the authors' imaginations or used in a fictitious manner. Any resemblance to actual persons, living or dead, or actual events is purely coincidental.

Edited by RJ Locksley
Cover Design by JA Huss

ABOUT THE BOOK

Pell learns to love pants.
Pie learns to love magic.
And Tomas learns to love a woman.

Pie and Pell are like two peas in a pod. Meant for each other, madly in love, and living their best lives as Mr. and Mrs. Monster of Saint Mark's.
Kind of.

Pie is dreading her new job working for the tall, dark, and sleek Modern Minotaur. And the irony that just a few weeks ago she was demanding that Pell allow her to get a job to support the sanctuary, isn't lost. It's like the gods are playing with her on purpose.

Pell is still his grumpy self but he's got a new job as well—babysitting a bag of magic rings that seem to have a mind of their own. No matter where he hides them, they will not stay put. Add in a doorway he can suddenly see and a new power he forgot he had, and well… things are getting interesting.

Tomas is a brand-new man. Literally. His new freedoms are just the beginning of his adventure into modern humanity. Not only can he leave the sanctuary, drive a truck, and spend time with the people in Granite Springs—he also learns how to cheat the rules.

Everything has changed for the better. But when Pie discovers the secrets of magic, Pell uncovers the real purpose of the rings, and Tomas falls in love with a Townie… things change again.

Only this time, they're the ones with all the power.

CHAPTER ONE – PELL

"Good morning, sweet Pie."

Pie grunts and turns over in bed, pulling all the covers with her.

"Sweetie Pie," I sing.

She pulls her pillow over her head. Groans again. "Go. Away."

"It's time to get up, Pie. You can't keep putting this off."

She lifts the pillow just enough to show me one eyeball. "I'm sick." She holds her stomach, winces and moans. "I don't—" She coughs. *Cough. Cough.* "I don't feel good." She makes her voice nice and shaky. "I-I-I think I'm gonna barf."

I sigh and lie back on the bed, covering my face with my forearm. "Pie. He's been patient. But it's been two weeks now. You said you would go in to work today—"

"Work? Is this what we're calling it?"

"It *is* work. He has your debt. He offered you a job as his personal assistant to work it off. It's not *that* bad."

She hits me with her pillow. "Not that *bad*!" Her eyes are wide and wild. She closes them for a moment. Takes a breath, holds it, lets it out slowly. "Pell."

"Pie?"

"It *is* that bad. He's a fucking… minotaur! And not like you're a minotaur, either. You look like…" She sucks in a breath, pauses, stopping long enough for me to wonder what she was gonna say.

"I look like what?"

"You know."

"No. I don't know. How are Tarq and I different?"

"You're all… shaggy, and soft, and blond, and considerate."

I'm picturing all this, wondering if these are good traits or bad traits. "OK."

"And he's all"—she shakes her head, sighs—"all sleek, and polished, and dark, and… huge."

"Huge?"

"Yes. He's just… too much. I can't do it, Pell. I can't. Do it. I cannot go into that tomb every day with my eyes cast down and just pretend like…" Again, she pauses.

"Like?" I prod her.

"Like he doesn't have that huge monster dick hanging between his legs!"

I guffaw. This is truly funny.

"It's not funny! I'm not gonna be able to control myself! It's too hard. Oh, my God." She slaps her forehead. "And the puns, Pell! The *puns*!"

I guffaw again.

She slaps me. "Stop laughing at me!"

"Sorry," I manage between outbursts. "Sorry. But… all this—the past two weeks of you faking every illness under the sun trying to get out of going to this new job—was all about you not being able to handle looking at his giant cock?"

She grabs the pillow she hit me with and pulls it back over her head, mumbling something I can't understand.

I scoot over to her side of the bed, slip my hands under the covers, and caress her velvety ass. Pie, in her human form, is cute. But Pie in her wood nymph form is sexy. And this velvety ass just makes me want to ravish her. "Pie."

"No." She pushes my hand off her. "Don't touch me. It's not funny." She lifts the pillow again so she can look me in the eyes. "I get it. You think I'm slow, or stupid—"

I point at her. "Cute."

"Whatever. You think my aversion to random, hanging dicks is a joke."

"I don't."

"You do! And it's not a joke! I'm not a minotaur! I'm not even a real nymph! I'm a girl, OK? A human girl who got caught up in some stupid ancient curse, or past life, or magic castle-hallway thingy. One who is not used to bull men walking around with their dicks flopping between their legs!"

My God. Why is she so damn cute? I almost can't stand it. I want to ravish her right now.

She points at me. "I can read your mind, ya know."

"What?" I ask, trying to sound innocent.

"You're thinking about sex. No way, buddy. There is no way I'm having sex with you on a work day." She smiles. Laughs. "Yeah. There. That's the new deal. No sex on work days."

I don't think she means it. We've been having sex at least twice a day since the whole... well, we're calling it the Reckoning. Actually, Tomas is calling it the Reckoning. The rest of us—which is really just Pie and me, since the new monsters don't speak Latin—we're just going along with Tomas.

"You think I'm kidding."

I make a serious face and tell her, "I'm taking you very seriously."

"Liar." She narrows her eyes at me. "I don't want to go work for Tarq. I've told you that a million times."

"A *million*, Pie?"

"At least a million. And you refuse to do anything about it."

"Pie." I smile at her, slip my hand back over her velvety ass. This time, when she tries to push me away, I don't let her. I pin her hand to the bed, making her squirm, then pin the other hand to the bed too, making her struggle.

"Stop. Let me go."

"No. Listen to me." I roll over so I'm almost on top of her. She's refusing to look me in the eye. "Tarq isn't gonna hurt you."

"How do you know that?"

"He told me. I made him promise."

Now she does look at me. But it's not a good look. It might be an 'I hate you' look. "Promise? That's so dumb. What did you say? 'Hey, Tarq. I know you're all sleek, dark, and polished and have all this big-dick energy—'"

I guffaw again.

"'—but don't hurt my nymph.' And he what? Just said, 'Cool, cool, cool?'"

I smile at her, lean down and kiss her. She moves her head side to side, childishly trying to avoid my affection. But I just kiss her neck instead. Then let go of her hands and start playing with her breasts though her thin, white nightie.

"That's not going to work," she insists.

But I think it will, so I don't stop. I take my mouth to her breasts. Sucking on her. Caressing her. Slowing her down and relaxing her.

A few seconds later, she sighs and her fingers begin to tangle in my hair, treating me like I'm something precious.

I look up at her and smile. "See. Worked."

"It's nice, I have to admit that. But my rule has been made. No sex on work days."

"We'll see."

Then we both laugh.

"Pie," I say, serious now, because she might really be scared of her new boss and that's not funny. "He's *not* a bad guy."

"You don't know that! You haven't seen him for two thousand years. You didn't see that place. It's... weird. Like... what is it? Another... time? Another world? Another planet? What the hell is it? I don't want to go there every day. I didn't even want to go there once."

I kiss her on the chin, then scoot up and kiss her on the lips. This time she does not wiggle away. She kisses me back. It's a nice, long, slow, open-mouthed kiss. And we both enjoy making out for a couple minutes. Maybe, if I keep going, she might want me to ravish her before work. But just as I think that, she pushes me away and squirms out from under me. And before I know it, she's out of bed. Frowning at me. Pointing at me.

"It's gonna be your fault."

"What is?"

"When I come home tonight, *damaged*."

I decide to give in and own it. I think she's being ridiculous, but she might be right. At least her fears on day one might be justified. I get it. I think. She has a new body, a new life, a new past, new magic, new monsters—and now she has a new job that lives in a new world.

It's kind of a lot.

She's scared. And fear is no fun.

"Pie, if you come home damaged, I will force my way into that tomb, find Tarq and everyone else who dared to hurt you, and kick some monster ass."

She pouts. "No, you won't."

I jump out of bed, grab her by the waist, and push her against the wall, pressing myself up against her, pinning her in place. "I get it. You see me and think… 'He's just my shaggy, soft, blond, considerate satyr chimera.' But you don't know me, Pie. I might be shaggy and blond—and sometimes considerate—but I am not soft." I bare my teeth at her. She pulls away from me. "Tarq is not going to hurt you. But if he does, I will kill him."

"You don't have to *kill* him."

"Oh, I will kill him. I don't like to kill things, but if I have to, I don't feel remorse about it when I'm done."

"But it's not going to come to that, right?" Her blue eyes look up and meet my gaze. She's asking me. This is a real question. She really is afraid. And now I feel terrible that I didn't understand this sooner.

"It's not going to come to that, Pie. You're mine. He's borrowing you on a technicality."

She sighs. Gives in. Drops her head.

"And hey," I say, tipping her chin back up with one clawed finger, "if he found a way to walk through the tombs, he can find a way for *me* to walk through the tombs. Then I can go with you. Wouldn't that be fun? I'd love to see the new world."

Her pouty frown almost tips upside down. "That *would* kinda be fun. I mean, there are humans there, Pell. But there are people like us there too." Her smile grows. "And being there with you? That would be great. Do you think Tarq could get you inside?"

I already asked him about this when he came through with Pie's Book of Debt a couple weeks ago. But he said it was a special one-off spell that only worked from his side of the door and couldn't be transferred to me. But I didn't tell Pie that back then, and I don't tell her now, either. She needs hope to get through this day. So that's what I give her. "I'm sure he could."

And the lie pays off because now, instead of thinking about how afraid she is about starting this new job, in a new world, with a new monster boss, she's thinking about the two of us going to that world and having fun together like normal people.

It's no longer a frightening place—it's now, maybe, a world where we fit in.

And I have to admit, it sounds a little bit nice. After two thousand years of being the only satyr chimera, I can't even imagine what it would be like to be with my own kind again. Not only that, but be in a place where I didn't have to hide or worry about the fucking curse.

A new life. A brand-new life.

It would be a dream come true.

During my pause for inner reflection, Pie has been reflecting on her own. She's thinking very hard about this day. "Listen," I say. "You've turned this job into something much bigger than it is."

"Oh, have I?"

"Yes. It's not a big deal. It's a paycheck, that's it."

"I'm the personal assistant to the Modern Minotaur, Pell. It's kind of a big deal."

"You think that because it's new and you've never done it before. And the longer you put it off, the wilder your imagination gets. You just need to go in and get it over with. I promise. It will be…" I pause here. Because I want to tell her it's gonna be great, but 'great' feels like a strong word.

"It will be what?" Pie asks.

"It's going to be… interesting."

She actually laughs, one eyebrow raised. "Interesting?"

"No. Fascinating."

She sighs. "I guess it could be. Both interesting and fascinating."

"It will be, Pie. How could it not? It's a whole other world. And you won't feel out of place. You have to be tired of being cooped up here at the sanctuary all day. In Tarq's world, you can go out. And I can't wait to hear all about it. Take lots of pics on your pocket phone."

"Hmm. Do you think my phone will work there? Will I get roaming charges? Holy shit." She pauses to stare at me. "I didn't pay my bill this month. I need to pay my phone bill. And my car insurance. Holy shit. I'm late for everything. My credit score—"

I kiss her. Mostly to make her stop, but also just because she's so damn cute.

Her bills. That's adorable.

When we break apart, she sighs a little.

"Good news."

"What good news? There's no good news!"

"There's always good news, Pie. You just have to look for it. And in this case, it wasn't that hard to find. You don't need money to pay your phone bill."

She screws up her face. "I go into debt when I use the money."

"Yeah, but that's 'this world' debt. Which means you erase that debt by making me happy."

She doesn't want to grin, but she grins. "You've got a one-track mind this morning."

"I do. And I'm not going to apologize for it."

"We had sex last night."

"We did. But I want it in the mornings too."

She giggles, then reiterates her threat. "No sex on work days."

"How about this? How about… if you go to work every day I'll be here waiting for you when you get home. And every evening I will pamper you like a goddess. That also pleases me, Pie. So you get to be spoiled and erase debt at the same time."

She sighs again. But this time she also smiles. "OK. Fine. I will go in to work today."

"You will?"

She nods. "I mean…" Now she blushes. "I'm not gonna turn down being spoiled. Do you take requests?"

I nod, grinning wildly.

She points at me. "I will have demands, mister."

"I can't wait."

But her plump mouth makes a little frown again. "Tell me I'm being dumb again."

"What?"

"Just… tell me I'm being dumb. Convince me. This new job is gonna be fine and—"

I put a finger over her lips to hush her up. "Pie. You are gonna kick this job's ass. You are gonna kick it so hard that new world won't see you coming. Won't even know what to do with you. You're gonna go in there, be the best damn… whatever your job title is… and when you come back to me, I will spoil you silly."

This does the trick. "OK." She pouts a little. "I *am* kinda tired of being stuck inside the sanctuary. And you're probably right. I'm making a bigger deal about this than it needs to be. If I get the first day over with, I can reevaluate things."

"Exactly." This pleases me.

"Nothing's gonna happen to me," she continues. "But if something does, you will kick monster ass on my behalf, right?"

I beam a smile, proud of myself for turning this around. "Cross my heart."

Pie places both hands on my bare shoulders, leans up on her tiptoes, and kisses me on the lips. It's a real kiss, too. Nice and slow. Easy and perfect.

When she pulls away, I drift in her direction, wanting that connection to go on forever. I've gotten used to the idea that I have a woman now. But I'm not taking it for granted.

I really would kill anyone who hurt her.

Pie pats my chest and smiles. "I guess it's not gonna be that bad. And I have a new outfit." She walks over to the closet, opens it up, and pulls out some clothes on a hanger. I watch her as she removes the little pieces of fabric and lays them out on the messy bed.

"What is it?"

"What do you mean, what is it? It's a skirt and a blouse."

I tilt my head. "I see the blouse. But that's not a skirt."

"What?" She kinda snorts.

I pick it up with two pinched fingers. "This... this... *this* is a postage stamp."

She snags it away. "Don't be ridiculous. The eyebrow monster made it for me. He measured me and everything. It fits perfect." She demonstrates by pulling the skirt up her legs and buttoning the waist. "See?"

I twirl a finger in the air. "Turn, please."

"What?" She laughs again. But she turns.

"It barely covers your ass. What is wrong with Eyebrow Monster? He's never heard of office-appropriate?"

Pie stretches out one of her extra-long nymph legs. "What are you talking about? It's a miniskirt. That's what I asked for. But it's not a micro-mini. It hits mid-thigh."

"Micro-mini?"

"You know. Those super-short ones that practically show off your hoo-ha." I must appear confused, because she giggles. "Pell. You can't be upset about my skirt."

"Why not?"

"Because wood nymphs don't wear skirts. You should be happy I'm wearing anything."

She's kinda right. But now that I'm seeing her in this skirt, I don't know. I hate the idea that she's wearing it for Tarq.

But of course, I can't say that. Not after winning the battle.

"Hey, be your considerate monster self and throw some wood on the water heater, will ya? I'm gonna take a bath before work. Do I have a starting time? Tarq never gave me one, so I'm assuming I can just show up after breakfast?"

I'm not really listening. I'm still picturing her in this sexy little work outfit, walking around a whole new city filled with men like... well... me. Lecherous satyr chimeras.

I'm just about to surrender, give her the win, maybe even throw the entire war and let her stay home forever, when she claps her hands. "Pell! Are you listening? Water heater? Wood? And what is this? Were you looking at the rings?"

"What?" But then I notice that she's holding up the bag of magic rings we found where the Book of Debt was supposed to be after the Reckoning.

"The rings! They were just sitting out. Did you take them out of the wardrobe?"

"No."

She shoots me a dubious look. "Then how did they get here?"

"I don't know."

"Well, we need to be very careful with them. If the monsters knew we had them..." She shakes her head. "No. We cannot release fifty ancient monsters into the human world. That would be bad."

"Right," I agree. But then again... would it? I mean, there's a whole family of eros living in Granite Springs. What's the big deal?

"Pell? Water? Wood?"

I suck in a deep breath. "On my way." Then I turn and leave. Because she has to do this job. She has debt. She must clear it. And Tarq assured me that the exchange rate between his currency and our currency is in our favor. Which means Pie can work off her debt quicker. And while she's doing that, I will be pushing the new limits of this curse and breaking it.

We're close. I can feel it. Never, in all my two thousand years of being locked up inside Saint Mark's, has freedom ever felt so close.

Once I break it, we will leave this place.

And I need her to be debt-free when that happens.

I leave the bedroom, go downstairs, throw some wood on the smoldering water-heater fire, then leave the cottage.

The monsters all sleep in various places. Some of them sleep out here with the tombs. They sleep at the feet of other monsters, or on top of the tombs, or some of them tucked away under bushes. Others sleep in the sanctuary. I don't keep track of any of them. None of them speak Latin. I don't actually know what they speak, and I'm pretty sure they are speaking several different languages. Perhaps, one day, I will ask Pie to make one of those language spells. But then again, perhaps not.

Tomas understands them. All of them. He's kinda in charge of them.

Which is totally fine with me.

But I'm still stuck on that skirt. So I'm looking for the eyebrow monster as I make my way up towards the cathedral.

I don't find him outside, but once I'm at the top of the central staircase, I make a gesture indicating bushy eyebrows, and another monster points me in the direction of the Pleasure Cave hallway.

"There you are!" Tomas is coming towards me. "I've been looking everywhere for you."

"You have not. I just came from the cottage. It's where I sleep every night."

"It's an expression, Pell. Flow with me, please."

"Well, I'm looking for Eyebrow Monster. He made Pie a skirt—"

"It's lovely, isn't it? She looks so good in taupe."

"Taupe?"

"It's an office-appropriate color, Pell."

"Well, it's not an office-appropriate skirt. It's too short."

"No."

"Yes."

"No!"

I sigh, kinda tired of this day, and it just barely started. "Where—"

"Never mind the skirt, Pell. We need to have a talk about provisions."

"What about them?"

"We need to go shopping today."

"No, we don't. We just went last week."

"We bought all the wrong things."

"What are you talking about? We got everything we need."

"No, you see… some of our new guests don't eat what we eat. And they're tired of pretending. They need their own food."

"What? What kind of food?"

"Hay. And grain. They need hay and grain."

"Hay? What the hell kind of monster eats *hay*?"

Tomas shrugs. "Vegetarians?"

I sigh. "Well, how much does hay cost? And... how much do they need?"

"Yes. This is the tricky part. They need a lot of hay, Pell. We have thirty-two vegetarians, so—"

"Wait. You're telling me that thirty-two of the fifty monsters do not eat meat?"

"That's correct. They've been grazing the sanctuary but the grass is getting too short now, and, well... they need the hay. So we need to go in to town and buy lots and lots of hay and grain."

I drop my head, shaking it.

"Trust me, I understand. You don't want Pie to take on any more debt. But we must feed them, Pell. You agree, right? We can't just let them starve."

At first, I didn't mind all the extra monsters around Saint Mark's. It's kinda nice to be around non-humans. But they're starting to get on my nerves. And I can't help but think, if we just gave them the bag of magic rings, they might be able to leave here. And if they can leave here, they wouldn't be our problem anymore. And Pie would not have to go into debt to feed them.

"Pell?"

"Fine," I growl. "We'll go get some fucking hay. But they owe us for this."

"Understood."

Understood, my ass. It's not like all these stupid new monsters have anything to offer.

They're just sucking us dry.

CHAPTER TWO – PIE

Magic rings.

One of them is a bad thing. But a whole bag? Yeah. That's horrible. Like… this is not going to turn out well. I just know it. They're little tricksters, those rings. This is the second time they've turned up in a place they weren't supposed to be. Last week I found them in the kitchen and they were supposed to be in the Pleasure Cave. Pell has a little hidey hole there and since he made the Pleasure Cave off limits to the new monsters, we figured the bag of rings could be forgotten about. At least for a while.

But then there they were in the kitchen. The entire bag of magic rings was sitting on a shelf behind the flour. The cooking monster—I'm calling him Cookie. Like Cookie Monster. I snort a little. Anyway, Cookie Monster almost found them while he was making cupcakes.

Then I hid the bag in the wardrobe. And just now they were right there on my bedside table.

I'm starting to think that the bag of magic rings is… well… magic. Like the hallways, or something. Or the tombs. The rings might not even be for the monsters, but if they are, they cannot have them. Not in this world. Maybe there's a tomb out there in the cemetery where these monsters belong? I should look into that. But one thing I know for sure—they do not belong here, in this world, where humans live. So it is my responsibility to keep these rings hidden.

Anyway. I go over to the tub and turn the water on. But it's not hot yet. I'm adapting to the whole you-need-to-heat-your-water-with-wood thing. I am.

But do I like it?

No. I'm really starting to get sick of it, actually. And I barely fit in that tub anymore. My wood nymph self is much taller than my old self. I can't even take a shower because the water hits me in the neck.

"Helloooo? Cottage redecorating gods? Can you hear me? I need a redesign!"

I've been asking—nicely, I might add—for this little retrofit project since the whole epic magical dragon-moth-bloodhorn scene several weeks ago, but they're not listening. Or maybe they just don't care.

I sit down on the bed and check out my hooves. They are pretty but… they are starting to crack along the edges. Like… I need a hoof polish. But if I'm the slave caretaker in charge of giving hoof polishes, who will polish my feet?

Holy crap, Pie. That's not a good road to go down. You polish your own feet, princess.

This makes me laugh out loud. But that's short-lived because I picture how much work it will be to make new polishing paste. Pell made me throw out all the herbs. He was gonna make me throw out the crystals too, but luckily, he came to his senses. How would we get new crystals? Those don't grow in the greenhouse.

It wasn't feasible. But every jar filled with magical stuff in this sanctuary is now empty.

Well. Except for one. Of course.

My eyes involuntarily migrate over to the tall jar of tomb tokens the Freckle Monster made me. He's got a ton of freckles, obviously, so I'm calling him Frecks. He's very good with plants—Tomas put him in charge of the greenhouse—so he harvested a shitload of bloodhorn. Then Tomas, unhelpful traitor that he is, went down to the dungeon and gathered up bags and bags and bags—did I mention he found *bags?*—of tiny little dragon scales.

When Tarq first came through the tomb with my Book of Debt and explained that I was his new employee, I was pretty sure this was not gonna happen because you need dragon scales to do that whole portal spell. And we were fresh out because Tomas isn't a dragon anymore. He's a dragon chimera and the scales on his legs don't work. Probably because it's an illusion or something. Because when he walks through the gate, he has no scales on the outside. As far as the outside world is concerned, Tomas is just another hot guy who lives in the rural P woods. So we think his scales don't work because they're not real.

Actually, there's nothing 'we' about that. I wasn't involved in working out the new portal door spell rules. The monsters did it. They are seriously invested in my new job for some reason.

Anyway, after the whole Reckoning thing the monsters went looking for dragon scales in the dungeon and it was empty. *Completely* empty. Like... not even a couple of dust bunnies in the corner kind of empty.

But then when Tomas went down to look, he came back with bags, and bags, and *bags* of tiny fucking dragon scales.

What a little traitor Tomas turned out to be. Why did he go back down there to look?

I get it, the dungeon is probably like the hallways upstairs, or something. And he probably had nothing to do with finding them all down there.

But for fuck's sake. When you go check a dungeon for dragon scales and find none, you do not go back and double-check! Am I right? I'm so right.

Then Freckle Monster made me a whole giant jar of little bloodhorn and dragon scale brooches, and necklaces, and earrings, and bracelets. He even made me hair clips.

So now I have all the keys I need to go to work.

Isn't it wonderful?

I try the water again. Still cold.

"Jeez. Why is this all so hard?" I go downstairs, check the furnace, and find that the entire fire has gone out. Not even a smoldering coal.

"Fuck this," I mutter, then go back upstairs and just get dressed. No bath for me today. Which is just great. My first day at my new job and I have to go in with day-old hair.

But. I do like the outfit. I look down at my skirt again and smile as I take off my t-shirt and slip on the blouse. And when I look at myself in the mirror I have to admit, I'm a damn pretty wood nymph.

My fur is even more golden than Pell's. And my hair is longer. Like much longer. And bouncy. It's like my hair got one of those expensive blowouts at a top-notch salon. Downside, it needs a lot of taming or I just end up looking like… well. Wild. I look wild. Like a true wood nymph.

Which I am, according to Ostanes. But now that time has passed between that little visit to… whatever realm or dreamworld I was in while Ostanes was talking—yeah, the further away I get from that day, the less likely I believe that it was real.

I'm starting to think I made it up. I hallucinated. I mean, I'm kinda known for hallucinating.

But then I think about my new job. Which requires me to step through a tomb portal to get there.

And if that's real, then all of this is real.

But it's still very confusing. And I still miss Pia. Even though Ostanes said she was just another part of me, she didn't feel like just another part of me. She felt like a whole other person. She was always making me feel better, and cautioning me, and making me happy. I miss her opinions, and her little voice, and even though she's still technically here—well, not here *here*, but around here somewhere—it's not even close to being the same.

What good is a bird if she can't talk? What good is a bird who can't caution me when I get bad ideas? What good is a bird who can't offer up fashion advice?

And now I'm thinking… is she cursed? And does she know what she lost? Does she know what she used to be and now she's stuck in this silent bird body? Does she realize she used to be all chatty and shit, and now she can't talk? I've listened for whistles and chirps and stuff. But she doesn't even chirp at me. Sometimes I do see her little beak moving, but no noise comes out.

It's like someone pushed the mute button on her.

I really need to figure this out because I want my friend back. Everything would be much easier if I just had my real Pia.

And now I'm sad. Because she's not even here and I'm about to start a new job. She was always with me when I started a new job. I have to do this whole freaking day alone.

It sucks.

A monster calls up at me from downstairs.

They all know how to talk, but it's not any language I know. And even though Tomas can understand them, he doesn't know what language they're speaking either. He says he gets pictures in his head of what they're saying. I just... have no opinion on that.

But generally, I can kinda tell what the monsters are *trying* to say. Like this one. He's telling me to get my ass in gear and come downstairs.

So I take one more look in the mirror, pluck a bloodhorn-dragon scale necklace out of the portal-pass jar, slip it over my head, and tuck the necklace inside my shirt.

I find Cookie standing in my open front door holding a paper sack.

"What's that?" I ask, pointing to it.

He smiles, showing me all of his super-scary satyr teeth, then pushes the bag towards me.

I take it, open it up, and look inside. Then I chuckle. "You made me lunch?"

He nods and starts talking in his monster language. I'm pretty sure he's telling me to have a nice day.

Which, I'm not gonna lie, brightens me.

"Thank you," I say, patting him on the shoulder. "That was really sweet. And to be honest, I kinda needed this."

He takes the sack back, puts it inside a canvas messenger bag, and then drapes it over my shoulder.

"You're like the mother I never had, Cookie."

He points out the door, one large clawed hand waving towards the path that leads up the hill.

I sigh, resigned to the fact that I have to start my new job today, and then we begin our climb.

I expect Pell to be waiting for me when I get to the top, but he's not.

Frecks is, though. He's talking to another monster who I have not named yet. This guy has wings. Which is nice. Except they are not white and fluffy and look like they belong on an angel. They are black, and rubbery, and look like they belong on a bat. So that's what I decide to call him in my head.

Frecks notices me, directs the conversation to me, then nods as he pans his hand towards Batty.

Then Batty starts talking. And of course, I have no idea what he's going on about, but then he hands me a rock. Not a fancy crystal. Not even a polished rock. It literally looks like he just picked it up on his way out here. It's not even pretty. It's tan and sandy—in fact, it's probably sandstone.

"Nice," I deadpan, accepting the rock. Frecks looks at me with a serious face, points at me. "Uh-huh," I say. "Sure." Then Batty asks for the rock back. "OK." I'm just playing along at this point. I've learned that if I just humor them, they will get tired of me pretty quick. So I give him the rock. He pinches a corner between a leathery black thumb and forefinger, and little bits of sand fall off.

"Ohhh-kaaaay." I smile at him, nod, accept the rock again when he offers it, then drop it into my messenger bag.

Both Frecks and Batty smile at this, seemingly satisfied.

I have no idea what that's about.

I look back at the cathedral, wondering if I should wait here or go find Pell. I'm not going through that tomb without saying goodbye to Pell. For all I know, I will get stuck in there and never see him, or my home, again.

Then I wonder if thinking that is bad luck and start silently praying. *Please, please, please don't get me stuck in this portal, God. Please.*

But Pell doesn't come out of the cathedral. Another monster does. This one is skinny, and a little bit greasy, and creepy, if I'm being honest. But then I notice that Pia is perched on his shoulder.

"What the fuck?" I mutter under my breath. Is Greasy trying to cut in on my magical bird best friend? I'm still thinking about this, pretty sure my resting bitch face is showing because Greasy is eyeing me warily, when they approach. Pia flies away from him and circles over my head. Then she lands on my shoulder and snuggles up to my neck.

"Aww." I smile. "You're coming with me. Thank you, New Pia. You're not the same anymore, but I don't care. We can still be BFF's."

Of course, she doesn't chirp or anything. But it's OK. Things are looking up. And then, just as I'm thinking that, I notice that Pell is walking towards me.

For a moment, he's frowning as he looks me up and down. I'm pretty sure that's about the skirt. But then he rallies and his smile is bright when his yellow eyes meet mine.

"First day." He reaches for me, kisses me, pulls me close. Kind of a caveman move, like he's proclaiming his ownership of me in front of the other monsters. But I don't mind. He's here, and that's all that counts. "Are you ready?"

I nod reluctantly. "Cookie made me lunch, Batty gave me a good-luck rock, and Pia is coming with me."

"Sounds like you've got it all figured out," Pell says.

"I wouldn't go that far, but what choice do I have?"

"It's gonna be fine," Pell says. "In fact, it's gonna be great. You're gonna love your new job. And weren't you just begging me for a job a few weeks ago?"

"Yeah, I get the irony, thanks."

Pell chuckles. "You're gonna kick this job's ass. Don't worry." Then he takes my hand and leads me towards Tarq's tomb. The door doesn't appear, but that's because Pell is too close to it.

I don't understand why the curses around here have to be so damn contradictory. Can't they just do me a solid? Like, for once in my life, just make shit easy for me?

I don't get it.

But then… I have a thought. Maybe I've always been cursed?

"Stop thinking so hard," Pell says, giving me a squeeze. "It's gonna be great."

Yeah. It's not. But I smile anyway. "OK. Well. I guess this is it, then. Better back off so I can go through."

Pell kisses me and just before he pulls away, he whispers, "Great," into my mouth.

And I think that was a bit of magic. A bit of breathy, good-luck magic. Because I suddenly get all tingly and warm.

He holds my hand as he backs away, clinging to my fingertips until the very last moment. Then he and the monsters disappear between the tombs. And when I turn back to Tarq's tomb, there's the black door.

I reach for my dragon scale necklace, hold it in my palm, and walk through.

The other side of the door is pretty much the same as it was the last time I was here. Very, very busy. All humans, no monsters. They glance at me as they bustle around, but generally are not surprised to see a wood nymph appear through a magic door in the middle of an office-building lobby.

I look over my shoulder and the cemetery shimmers for a moment, then disappears into blackness.

And that's it, I guess. Like it or not, I'm here.

"Holy crap!" Pia exclaims. "Thank you, thank you, *thank you*!"

"What? Pia! You can talk again!"

She flutters in front of my face, her little voice chirping excitedly. "Greasy Monster put a spell on me! And he promised that I would be back to normal if I came through the tomb with you!"

"Wait!" I'm still smiling, but—"What spell? I don't—"

"Don't kill my buzz, Pie. I'm serious. Someone pressed my mute button and I've been going crazy for weeks!"

"OK, OK, OK. Fine. We'll talk about that later." Then I regroup. Smile bigger. "Pia!" I squeal it. "You're here! You're back! You can talk! Yay!"

"Oh, my God. Here I am," she squeals back. "I missed you so much, Pie!"

"Me too! Oh, my God, me too. You have no idea how hard life is without you, Pia! It's not the same. But hey, wait. Why doesn't the spell work at home?"

"Greasy said he doesn't have power there. Only here. He says he's from here. That's why it works."

My good mood falls. "Wait. So you can only talk here?"

"Yes. I'm sorry, Pie. It's not the best solution, but it's all we've got right now."

I let out a long sigh. Solid. Can I get one? Anyone got one for me?

"It's OK, Pie. Don't be sad. You'll be here every day, all day long. It's only at night that I won't be my chatty normal self."

"Yeah," I say noncommittally. Because I'm not convinced. "The normal version of you being here with me definitely makes things *better*. But…." I pout and drop my head and my shoulders as my arms go limp, ready to do the monkey walk. That's what Pia calls it when I pout. She says I look like a gorilla. "Why, why, why do the gods hate me?"

"They don't hate you. No one can hate you. You're adorable. And that skirt, Pie. It works."

I look down at myself—which isn't hard because I'm still pouting like a gorilla—but then I smile and look up. "It does work, right? I swear, Eyebrow Monster really knows what he's doing when it comes to wood-nymph fashion."

"I like him," Pia says. "He said he was going to make me a tiny hat and cape set today. So I can look fancy at your work. He says I'm your personal assistant and I should dress for success."

"Huh. That's sweet of him. Hey, wait, can you understand them?"

"Sure. Can't you?"

But before I can answer, Luciano is calling my name from across the crowded lobby. "Miss Vita!" It's an excited call and he's coming towards us at a pretty good clip. "Oh, this is wonderful. I was starting to wonder if I'd have to organize a special trip to collect you."

"Collect me? That doesn't sound ominous."

"Well, who is this little charmer?" He taps Pia on her bright red head. "Aren't you adorable?"

"Thank you," Pia says.

"You're very welcome."

"I'm Pie's personal assistant. Do I need to talk to human resources about my signing bonus?"

"Signing bonus? Pia—wait." I point at Luciano. "You can see her? And hear her?"

"Of course," Luciano says. "Is that weird?"

"Yeah, actually. In my other world, only monsters can see her and hear her."

Luciano smiles at me. It's one of those 'mmmm-hmmmm' smiles. Like he's waiting for me to put two and two together.

"Ohhhhhh. I see. You're a monster."

"Don't we all have a little monster in us, Pie?"

"Sure. Whatever." He's not as charming this time around. In fact, I'm pretty sure that 'special trip' he just mentioned was really gonna be a kidnapping. "So. What should I do now?"

"Now." Luciano clasps his hands together. "I will take you to Tarq and he will definitely put you to work."

"Great," I mutter.

But as I follow Luciano though the magic hallways, Pia is snuggling up against my neck, commenting on everything from the fashion, to the little kiosks selling what looks to be coffee, and the city we occasionally glimpse as we pass by windows.

And I have to admit, it's all pretty fascinating.

Plus, I no longer have to go through my first day alone.

My Pia is back.

CHAPTER THREE – TOMAS

I allow Pell his pouting time after Pie leaves us behind for her first big day on the job. I even sit with him, contemplative and, most importantly, quiet.

The sanctuary comes alive around us as the morning gets started. Monsters, monsters everywhere.

I play with an errant scale on my leg, which is a beautiful shade of fire. Orange, and yellow, and red. With some blues and greens if I turn the right way.

But eventually, I get bored. So after three minutes, I say, "So. Should I drive?"

"What?" Pell is all growly this morning. "Drive? What the fuck are you talking about?"

"We need to buy hay, remember?"

He lets out a long sigh. Clearly he did not remember. "You're not driving, Tomas. Don't be ridiculous."

"But shouldn't I learn? Shouldn't this be something I do?"

Pell looks at me, baring his teeth. "No."

"Surely you have more to say about it than just no."

"Actually, no. I don't. Driving…" He sighs again. "It's not as easy as it looks."

"Well, you can do it. And you're not exactly an intellectual, now are you?"

"I have been driving for a hundred years, Tomas. I was there when Granite Springs got their very first automobile in 1908." His shoulders droop a little. "That was kind of a fun day."

"Are you taking a trip down Memory Lane? Should we go up in the hallways and look for that day?"

He turns his head in my direction and squints his yellow eyes at me. "Why are you bothering me? Can't you see I'm in need of some alone time?"

"I understand. You're one of those broody satyrs. Dark, and grumpy, and mercurial. But monsters are starving, Pell. We don't have time for your self-pity this morning. Maybe we can fit it in later, around lunchtime?"

He sighs. "Why can't I find a way into the tombs? I mean, what the fuck? What is the point now?" He looks me in the eyes. "What the hell are we doing?"

I contemplate this for a moment, then offer, "We're being moody?"

"No, you idiot. Not what are we doing *right now*. What are we doing as in… the big picture?"

"Big picture? I'm not following."

"Of course you're not. You have no idea about anything. You've spent your entire lifetime locked behind a magic gate in that animalistic dragon state."

I ponder this, wondering if I should let it go. Or should I correct him?

But before I can decide, Pell continues. "The world, Tomas. The world is big and twisted. And that's bad enough, but look! Look around? All these tombs could be other worlds. Take that big black one, for instance."

I find the big black tomb with my eyeballs. "What about it?"

"It's new. How did it get here? Why is it here? What is it doing? Who is inside of it?"

"I'm pretty sure it's the statue guy in there, don't you think?"

"Of course the statue guy is inside there. But who is he? And where has he been for the last two thousand years? What has he been doing? And why now? Why appear *now* when things are changing?"

I'm not sure if it is a rhetorical question or a serious one because I feel like the answer to these questions is fairly obvious.

"You have no idea what's really going on."

I look around. Take it all in. "I think I know, Pell."

"Not *here*, you simpleton. In the wide world."

"OK." I put up a hand. He's getting on my nerves. "I understand that you have a superiority complex, Pell. But I'm not simple. In fact, I'm very, very complicated. And I think we should table the self-pity for lunchtime so we can go into town, buy hay and grain, and then come back here and feed the monsters. Shall we vote? All in favor, raise your hands."

I raise both my hands and declare the motion passed.

Meanwhile, Pell has walked away.

CHAPTER FOUR – PELL

I have to admit that I have not really thought about the tombs in the past. Until Pie came, I never questioned why new ones were constantly appearing. It's just always been this way. It was normal for them to appear. In fact, if they had stopped appearing, that would've been unusual.

But after we brought the forest monsters back with us, things about this place didn't make sense anymore. If we're supposed to save monsters, then why are all the tomb monsters still locked up?

And if the curse hasn't been broken, why can I now leave?

Pie tried to explain her visit with Ostanes and how she said the boundaries of the curse had been shifted... but why? Why do we even need this curse? Tarq has had Ostanes' book this entire time. And from what Pie says, he uses it. Has it locked away in some secret safe in his office.

Should he be doing that? Isn't that book too powerful for a mere monster?

No. Something is very wrong here.

"Pell!"

Tomas is calling me. But I keep walking. I go right up to the statue of the monster in front of the new black tomb. At first glance, he pretty much looks like all the other satyr chimeras in the cemetery. In fact, his statue looks a lot like Tarq's with one exception. The obsidian black is complemented by gold accents. His horns are gold. His hooves are gold. And so are his eyes.

Tomas has caught up with me and now we're standing shoulder to shoulder. I ask him, "What do you make of this?"

"Make of what?"

Gods above. Why does my curse partner have to be so fucking clueless? "The statue, Tomas. The fucking statue. Have you ever seen one with gold accents like this?"

"Is it real gold?"

I reach up and scratch a horn with my claw. Little flakes come off. "I think it is."

"Hmm. So. Some sculptor or whatever made this obsidian statue and then added gold leaf to it?"

"Looks that way."

"Well, he must be important."

"Yeah. I'm getting that." I turn to Tomas. "How do we find out who he is?"

"Well, obviously, we ask the hallway gods. They know everything."

I inadvertently glance at the cathedral. "Do you think he's up there? He just got here."

"I'm not sure. I would love to help you figure this out, Pell. It's just… we have duties right now. We need to go into town. And I need driving lessons."

I sigh, then give in. "Fine. We'll go to the feed store. But I'm not teaching you to drive today. I can't think straight about anything right now. I'm worried about Pie, and the tombs, and the curse—"

"All right, all right, all right. We will table the driving lessons. But we agree that I should learn to drive, correct?"

I wave my hand in the air. "Whatever."

"Great. Let's go."

CHAPTER FIVE – PIE

After several hallways, an escalator, and a short set of stairs—none of which I recall from last time—we finally make it to Tarq's glass-walled office. He's on the phone, but he's facing me and a smile appears as we approach. And thank my lucky stars, he's wearing clothes.

In fact, now that I think about it, every monster we passed on the way up here was wearing pants.

They are not the same kind of pants humans wear, though. They are a little bit like the pants Pell wore for a day. Tight—way too tight because his huge package is clearly outlined—and stopping at the knee.

I've worn pants since I've gotten my new legs and I completely understand the cropped look. All the anatomical bits below my knee are just awkward in pants.

Tarq's breeches appear to be made of very fine leather. They are light tan, almost the color of butter. And they remind me of a designer purse. Soft and smooth, begging to be caressed.

He's wearing a vest under his jacket—the word 'waistcoat' appears from the depths of my mind—and it's a very pale robin's-egg blue color. The outer coat is leather, like the pants, and it's the same buttery color. It's not a suit coat or a sports jacket that men wear in my world. It's a bit longer. More dramatic. The cuffs are very wide and a bit of white fabric trails out from underneath the edge near his wrist. Not lace, just cotton, I think. But it's fancy like lace and adds a touch of pirate to his look.

The fur on his legs below the knee is as smooth as the skin on his clean-shaven face and his hooves are so polished and shiny, they are like mirrors.

Tarq holds up a finger, then turns his back to finish his conversation. I study the fine embroidery on the back of his coat. It's tucked into some kind of wide dart at his waist, with buttons on either side.

He looks like something out of the eighteenth century, but the contrast of the modern office surrounding him is a good reminder that I'm in a different world.

A whole other world. And I get it—the mere fact that he's a monster should be enough of a reminder. But I'm a monster now too. It's no longer enough to shock me.

"Well, Miss Vita," Luciano says, "I will leave you to it. But you, my sweet little bird friend"—he lifts his hand up to my shoulder, a signal he wants Pia to hop on—"you must come with me and we'll sort you out with human resources."

"Wait. What? No. She can't leave now. I need her. Can't she do that crap later?"

"You'll be fine," Pia says, settling on Luciano's finger. "It shouldn't take long. And we can use the bonus."

What bonus? I want to say. But before I can object, they turn and walk away.

I deflate again. Sigh. And I'm just about to morph back into my pouting monkey-walk posture when the office door opens behind me.

I turn to face my new boss and get an up-close-and-personal look at the outline of his package underneath those skin-tight leather pants.

When my eyes meet Tarq's, he's grinning wildly. He walks towards me, reaches for my hand, takes it, kisses it, and stares into my eyes. His are yellow, like Pell's. But then again, nothing at all like Pell's.

"Miss Vita. I had almost given up on you." He lets go of my hand, takes a step back—like, is he *trying* to give me a good view of his junk?—and then spreads his arms wide. "You look fantastic. The other nymphs in the office will be insanely jealous of this outfit."

My eyebrows go up. "Other nymphs? There are others?"

"Oh, herds of them."

"Really?" Hmm. This is interesting. I don't know why I thought I was the only one, but I did. And the prospect of meeting more wood nymphs—maybe even making a friend or two—well. Color me intrigued.

"I keep forgetting that your world is so different. You really don't have nymphs or satyrs there?"

"No. Just me as far as wood nymphs go. At least that I know of. Saint Mark's has a lot of new satyrs. But I don't think they're supposed to be there because they're locked behind the walls of the sanctuary. Oh. And we have a Tomas."

"Tomas?"

"He's the dragon chimera."

"Oh, right." Tarq smiles again. It's wider this time. And a little bit… mischievous. "I didn't meet him when I took my trip through the tomb. But maybe one day."

"Oh. This reminds me. Can I ask you a question?"

"Anything, Pie." His voice is low and rumbly. And, I have to admit, when he says my name, it's... sexy.

Focus, Pie. "How did you get through the tomb door? I thought it was supposed to be locked."

"It is. But you left your dragon scale behind on your last visit. It's a key."

Hmm. Did I leave it behind? Did I really? I mean I knew it was missing when I got home, but I didn't *leave it behind.* I think he stole it.

No. It wasn't him. Because the scale was missing before I met Tarq. I remember that clearly. I was scrambling to explain my appearance when we first met and the scale was already missing. At first, I thought that that's just how it is. The scale is not a key, but a token that must be exchanged.

But now I'm not so sure. Because the dragon-scale necklace I put on this morning is still here. I can feel it under my shirt, kinda shifting between my tits.

I think Luciano stole that last scale. I don't know how, but who else had the opportunity?

Tarq is staring at me intently as I think these thoughts. But if he can read my mind, he doesn't show it. Instead he walks up to me, places a huge, clawed hand on my shoulder and says, "Would you like a tour?" His touch makes me shudder. And I'm too busy thinking about my reaction to him to answer, which makes him take control and assume my answer is yes. "Let's see your office first. Shall we?"

I don't care, really. But when he leads me into his office, I can't help but get curious. "I thought you said we were going to my office? This is your office."

"Your office is in my office." And then he closes his office door.

"O-kaaay." He and I are now alone.

Tarq presses a button on the wall and suddenly all the glass turns opaque.

"Well, that's not creepy."

Tarq laughs. "Relax, Pie. I'm not going to jump your bones, if that's what you're worried about. I just want some privacy when I open your office door."

"That's not creepy, either." Except it is.

Then I remember the moving bookshelf that hid his safe room, or whatever it was. He walks over to the bookshelf, presses some mechanism, and it opens. Just like last time. But this time, he looks over his shoulder at me and says, "Stay close. The hallways in here are tricky."

I look down at my cute hooves and pout. *Why? Why, God? Why you gotta make my life so unorthodox? Why can't I just get a boring cubicle like every other assistant in the world? Why you gotta put my office inside a dark, stone hallway that wants to control things?*

"Pie?"

"Hm?" I look up and see Tarq waiting for me.

"Stay close?"

"Right. I'm coming."

I reluctantly follow him into the bookshelf hallway. And it *is* made of stone. A very light-colored stone that reminds me of the Pyramids or something. Oh! Kinda like that stupid rock Batty gave me. I have an urge to take it out and compare, but Tarq is talking, so I force myself to pay attention.

"This is the research and development department." And just as he says that, we come out into a huge room. Like *huge*. I'm talking 30th Street Station kind of huge. It even has the tall, skinny windows and intricate geometric ceiling. In fact, if there weren't a couple dozen monsters sitting at high-tech laboratory stations, I would almost think this *was* the 30th Street Station.

"Holy crap," I say. "What is this?"

"Welcome to Vinca's premier research laboratory."

I just stare at all the… things. There's so much to look at. All the monsters—satyrs, all of them. They are wearing white coats like scientists. And they have a whole bunch of chemistry shit going on. Then I notice the apothecary on the far wall. At first glance, it looks a lot like the one at Saint Mark's. Jars, and jars, and jars on many, many shelves.

But then I notice that it's all very… sterile, or whatever. I'm not that close, so maybe I just need a better look at it, but from where I stand the jars do not appear to be filled with herbs and plants or rocks and crystals. It's all powders and liquids.

The jars in my apothecary are all different sizes. Some of the glass is very thick, like it was handblown hundreds of years ago. And some of my jars are colored. Not amber, like some of these jars. I'm talking real colors. Green, and yellow, and red, and even some purple ones.

These jars come in clear and amber. And they all have stainless-steel lids. In fact, there's a lot of stainless steel in this place. Nothing like the stone counters and leather couches in my apothecary.

Again, there is that same contrast I saw up in Tarq's office.

And that's when it hits me. Tarq is what's out of place, not the world. I get it. I'm no expert on this new world, so maybe I'm wrong. But Tarq's clothes—while very beautiful—don't match up with the rest of the city. And what was that word he just used? I look up at Tarq. "Vinca?"

"Oh, that's where we are. This is Vinca. Welcome." Then his face goes thoughtful. "You really don't know anything."

I scowl at him.

"No," he says, reading my expression. "I don't mean it that way. You really have never travelled outside of your world before, have you?"

"Generally speaking, people don't hop worlds where I come from."

He nods at me. "Right. I have to keep reminding myself of that fact." Then he smiles. "Welcome, Pie Vita. And let me be the first to say that you are an exciting addition to our world."

For some reason this makes me feel good. Little bit warm. Little bit… comforted. Like maybe working for Tarq won't be that bad. I pan my hands wide. "So this is my office?"

"This is the hub. Your bench is private."

"Bench?"

"Your research bench. Work station," he clarifies.

"Wait." I shake my head a little. "What do you mean *research*? I'm not a scientist. And clearly this is a place for scientists."

"Well, you're an alchemist, right?"

"No, not really."

He raises one eyebrow at me.

"I'm serious. I'm not a witch, or whatever. I'm just a regular girl. And I'm definitely not a"—I look around, searching for the right word—"*researcher.*"

"Well." Tarq lets out a breath. "You are now."

"What do you mean? I thought I was your personal assistant?"

"You are. This is my department. Therefore, you will assist me here."

"But what can I do? I don't know anything about this stuff, I swear. I barely got through high school. I'm not qualified."

"And yet…" He smiles big. Kinda like the Big Bad Wolf, if you ask me. "You found your way here using a dragon scale. How do you explain that?"

I point to my chest. "That wasn't me. I didn't do that. Tomas did. I just… wore the damn scale as I passed through the door."

"About that scale."

"What about it?"

"Where did you get it?"

"I just told you. Tomas got it."

"But you said he was a chimera."

This throws me for a moment and I stutter. "W-what?"

"You said he was a chimera." He says these words slowly. Carefully.

"Yeah. He is. But…" I stop. Because something inside me says I should not tell him that Tomas is a real dragon.

"But what?"

"But he has scales."

"He does?"

"Mmm-hmm. On his legs, yes."

"And that's how you get through the door?"

Wow. My instincts were right. Tarq is fishing for info on Tomas. "No," I say quickly. "Those scales don't work." Tarq nods. Like he knew this. Like maybe he's testing me. "You need real dragon scales to make that spell work. And there used to be a dragon at Saint Mark's." Technically, not a lie.

"Used to be?"

"Yeah. It's gone. But there were some scales left in the dungeon. That's what we're using."

He reaches for me, his clawed fingertips gently catching on the chain around my neck. He lifts the dragon scale necklace out from my blouse and holds it in his hand. "This?"

I nod, suddenly feeling weird. He's so close to me. And he's literally got me on a chain.

He must notice that I'm becoming uncomfortable, because he drops my scale back under my blouse, and when the scale and metal hit my skin, I shiver with a sudden chill. "We have some scales," he says. "But they don't open doors. How did you make it work?"

Well, isn't this interesting. In a very scary kind of way, that is. Because Tarq doesn't know about the bloodhorn inside Pell. I almost involuntarily look up at his horns, wondering if he's made of blood the way Pell is, but I catch myself just in time. "What do you mean?"

"I mean, the scales don't work. That's not the whole spell."

I laugh a little. "Oh, that's right. I came here for the banishing spell. Turns out, the portal door spell is the same as the one for banishing."

I expect him to say "Oh!" or something that conveys surprise. But he doesn't. He says, "It doesn't *work*, Pie."

"What?"

"I know that the banishing and portal-door spells are the same. And it works just fine for banishing, but it doesn't open doors. We've tried it."

I pull up my chain and hold my dragon scale in my hand. "Clearly, it does."

"How did you get it to work?"

"I don't know what you mean. A dragon scale plus bloodhorn."

"Doesn't work, Pie." His voice is even lower now. Even more growly. Serious. "So how do you do it?"

"Well, I'm not sure what to say about that." I want to be very careful here. I do not want to lie to this monster. But I don't want him to know about Pell's bloodhorn, either. If Pell is the only one made of blood fire, what would that mean to a monster like Tarq? He clearly wants to walk through the doors, and he can't. I think they stole my dragon scale when I was here. And I think that one trip through the tomb was all he could take. I think he used my scale for that one trip and then it wore off. That's why they never came for me when I didn't show up.

They *can't* walk through the doors.

They need Pell. And they don't even know they need Pell.

"The spell calls for bloodhorn and a dragon scale," I say, shrugging. "I swear, that's all I use."

Tarq lets out a long breath. "Interesting. How do you grow your bloodhorn? Do you add anything special to the soil? Do you feed it?"

"I can't really help you there. I didn't grow it. It was growing when I arrived. I didn't even pick it. I just... used it."

"Intriguing. So the Saint Mark's bloodhorn is the only bloodhorn that works for the portal doors?"

"I have no idea, Tarq. I swear." None of this is a lie, so it comes off as truth. "I wish I knew more about all this stuff, but I just don't. I'm really not an alchemist."

"No," he agrees. "You're not. But don't worry, Pie." His smile is back. "We're gonna turn you into one."

CHAPTER SIX –TOMAS

Pell pulls the Jeep out onto the highway that leads to town and I decide that leaving the sanctuary behind will never get old for as long as I live. I suck in the fresh air, and tilt my head into the sun as we drive, and enjoy every moment of my newfound freedom.

I daydream as we roll along, thinking about a future so different to the one I never much bothered picturing before Pie appeared.

I do not want to waste this new opportunity so I must have a plan of action.

Driving. That is my number one priority.

But number two shall be... Hmm. I don't actually think I have a number two.

What does one do after one learns to drive? I'm not sure. I will have to think about this.

Pell is quiet as we make our way into town. He slows down when he sees the front end of a sheriff's car sticking out from a side street, and we both side-eye the driver as we pass.

"Not him," Pell growls, meaning that pesky Russ Roth.

We've seen him a couple times when we've been in town, but he doesn't acknowledge us. And he never came back to Saint Mark's, so we are all assuming that whatever banishing spell Pie threw at him also wiped his memory.

Pell checks the little mirror in the middle of the windshield as we continue to crawl down Main Street. Then, satisfied that the local authorities aren't going to bother us, he flicks a turn signal and pulls into the feed store.

"OK," Pell says, turning off the Jeep. "We're here to buy hay and grain and that's it. I don't want to add any more to Pie's debt than we need to."

"Got it."

"Do you know what kind we need?"

"What kind of what?"

"What kind of hay and grain, you idiot. What do these monsters eat?"

"Isn't hay… just… grass?"

"I don't know. I have never bought hay in my life."

I pat Pell on the shoulder. "Don't overthink it."

The girl across the counter is young, strawberry-haired, and freckle-faced. She's wearing jeans, a canvas coat, and a black winter beanie that says, 'I Have Issues' in white letters.

Her grin grows as she looks Pell and me up and down and I immediately love her. She is quite the adorable human specimen.

"We need hay," Pell growls.

Issue Girl leans her elbows on the counter and bats her eyelashes up at us. They are long and fair and she is cute, in a fairytale kind of way. "Well. What kind of hay do you boys need?"

Pell side-eyes me. And I can practically hear his thoughts. *Don't overthink it, he says.* But I rise to the occasion and proclaim, "We need… grass hay."

"OK." Issue Girl pulls out a dirty binder filled with pages in plastic covers and starts flipping through it. "I have brome, I have timothy, I have rye, I have half-and-half, and I have fescue, Bermuda, orchard… what's your fancy, boys?"

"What's the difference?" Pell asks. "I mean, isn't it all just grass?"

"Oh, no," Issue Girl says. "It's all very different in digestibility, and sugars, and proteins. What kind of animals are you feeding? Let's start there."

Pell side-eyes me again.

"Bulls," I say.

"Bulls. OK. Well. Are you going straight to auction, sending them to the feed lot or—"

"What's your cheapest hay?" Pell interjects.

"Oh, you don't want the cheapest," she says.

"Why not?" he asks.

"It's cheap for a reason. If you want nice bulls, you have to feed them well. You are what you eat."

I can tell Pell is getting frustrated, so I decide to take over. "Give us something in the middle."

"OK. Let's go with half-and-half. That way you get your protein and—"

"We'll take it," Pell says.

Issue Girl smiles. "How much do you boys need?"

"How much, do you think?" Pell ask me.

I just shrug. I have no idea.

"How many bulls are you feeding?" Issue Girl asks.

"Fifty or so."

"Thirty-two," I pipe up. "Not all of them want hay."

Pell glances at me with a shut-the-fuck-up look on his face.

Issue Girl appears confused. "What do you mean not all of them *want* hay?"

"Don't listen to him," Pell says. "He's been drinking."

The girl chuckles. Winks at me.

I blink at her, wondering if that was intentional, or maybe she has something in her eye.

"Well," she says, "depending on how often you want to do this little dance, you can buy fifty or five hundred."

"Five hundred?" Pell looks at me, about to lose his shit. "How much would that cost? And how long would it last?"

"A bale might last you three or four days per bull. So five hundred might get you... six weeks? Half-and-half is going for about twelve dollars a bale right now, so that would come to..." Her eyeballs roll up a little as she does some arithmetic in her head. "About seven thousand dollars."

Pell turns and walks out.

Issue Girl looks at me with surprised eyes.

"Don't mind him," I say. "He's always moody like that."

"I get it," she says. "Times are tight, right? Everybody's broke these days. And feeding cows is never cheap, even when it's eight dollars a bale."

I want to agree with her, but times are not tight with us. We're not even using real money. But the more we spend, the longer Pie will have to work for Tarq. "How long would a hundred last?"

"About a week. And that would come to about fifteen hundred with tax. Do you need it delivered? That's an extra hundred or so, depending on where you boys live. And if you want it stacked, that's an extra two hundred."

I suck in a deep breath as I hold up a finger. "Can you give me a moment?"

She closes her book and smiles. "Sure. I'll be here all day."

Pell is pacing the parking lot when I go outside.

"Seven thousand dollars?" he growls. "Every six weeks? No." He stops pacing and shakes his head. "No. No way. There has to be another answer to this problem."

"We have to feed them, Pell. They can eat the hay or we can make them food, but either way, it will cost money."

"Why are they here?" he demands.

"Well, Saint Mark's is a sanctuary. And they are orphan monsters. So. I'm not sure what you're asking."

"What are we supposed to do with them? We are not a charity! Shouldn't we be finding them a real home? This isn't even their world! We need to find them a new home. A place where they can... be free to wander. To live."

"What makes you think this is not their world?"

"Look around, Tomas. Do you see any other monsters here? They don't belong here."

"Well, this town is filled with wayward eros, isn't it? Maybe they *do* belong here."

"They don't," Pell growls.

"Let's table that conversation for another time. Right now, we have to decide how much hay to buy and how we will get it home."

"Get it *home*?" Obviously, Pell didn't think this through, either.

"They have delivery," I offer, holding up a finger.

"Delivery? We can't have a delivery, Tomas."

He turns his back to me and paces again, angry now.

"Perhaps we should buy a truck," I say. "Then we could haul it home ourselves."

Pell turns back to me. "Where the hell are we going to get a truck?"

CHAPTER SEVEN – PELL

Tomas points over my shoulder, and when I turn, I see the sign. "Used cars?"

"Look," Tomas says. "There's a truck. Right there in the back of the lot."

My gaze skims over the cars and lands on a flatbed in the corner. Even from here, I can see the price tag in bright yellow windshield paint. "Great. So not only do we have to buy thousands of dollars' worth of hay, we have to spend fifteen thousand dollars on a fucking truck? Are you insane? Pie is going to kill me. And how will we get it home? I can't drive two cars. I'll have to drive the truck, drop it all off, then… what? Walk twenty miles back into town to pick up the Jeep?"

I'm so mad.

"I can drive it."

"You don't know how to drive."

"I don't think it's that hard."

"It is."

Tomas narrows his eyes at me, fed up with my dark mood. "Then I guess it will be a long walk. You can stay here and pout or not. But I'm going to buy the truck and then I'm going to buy the hay, and then I'm going to drive it all home."

And with that, he walks off.

I stand there for a moment, unable to make a commitment about any of this. But… what choice do I have?

I follow him across the street.

By the time I get there he's already sitting in the driver's seat chatting up the salesman.

"It's an automatic," Tomas exclaims as I approach. "Driving it home will be no problem at all."

"I wash my hands of this. All of it. I will not be responsible for any of it."

"Good. You do that," Tomas says. "Go home then, I will take care of everything else." The he grabs a piece of scrap paper and a pen off the truck's dashboard, writes down the word 'money,' and hands it over to the salesman.

The salesman beams a smile because even though it's just a piece of paper with the word 'money' on it, it's magic money. So he thinks it's real. "Very good, sir! It's been a pleasure doing business with you!" And then he drops the truck keys into Tomas' waiting hand and walks off, looking down at the piece of paper in his hand, grinning at his good luck.

"We're really doing this?" I ask.

"We need to feed them, Pell. We need the truck. I know this will make Pie angry, but she will understand."

I know he's right, I just don't want him to be right. Pie hates that she has to work for Tarq. She's probably having a terrible day and the moment she gets home tonight I will have to break the bad news that she's now even further in debt than ever. Magic money. It always comes with strings. And the strings right now are not acceptable.

And where does it end?

Will it end?

How?

We will always need more things. We will always have more debt. And now that we have fifty new monsters to take care of, there is no end in sight.

She's a slave.

Not only that, she's worse off than any other slave in the history of Saint Mark's. No other caretaker had to provide so much.

Tomas jumps down out of the truck and places a hand on my shoulder. And he must read my mind because he says, "She'll understand."

"I know that, Tomas. Pie isn't going to complain about taking care of the new monsters. She will see it as her duty. Not as a slave caretaker, but as a human. Which is almost funny, since she's not even human anymore."

And now everything that has happened over the past month sinks in.

Nothing is the same.

Everything is different.

And life as I know it—as *we* know it—will be different forever from this point on.

Thirty minutes later Tomas waves to the strawberry-haired girl as he climbs into the truck, the bed now fully loaded up with a hundred bales of hay. We didn't even get grain. That was out of the budget, even for Tomas. "See you next week!" he calls to her. Then he smiles at me and yells, "I'll follow you!"

This is going to be a disaster.

CHAPTER EIGHT – PIE

Tarq leads me through the bustling room towards a large staircase. I want to ask all the questions but he's very focused on our destination. We climb up the stairs, turn left and then we're facing a set of translucent glass double doors. They are open, so beyond the doors I can see a large laboratory with windows on the far side that overlook the city outside.

He walks forward and I follow. Once inside, he turns to look at me. "This is your space."

I eyeball the room. It's a *very* serious room, filled with scientific shit I've never seen before. "This is not an apothecary."

"No," Tarq agrees. "It's not. Like I said, we don't do herbs and spells here, Pie. We do science."

I press my lips together. "Mmm-hmm. Well. I'm not sure what part of this you're failing to understand, but I'm not capable of"—I don't even have a word for what happens in laboratories, so I land on—"any of this."

"You say that, and yet you come here with a magic talking bird."

"I don't know why people automatically assume that my magic bird means I can do witchcraft—"

"Science," he corrects me.

I point at Tarq. "You do realize that expecting me to do science is even more ridiculous than expecting me to do magic?"

"So you've said. I'm sure there will be a learning curve, but it's fine. We have lots of time."

I sigh, frustrated. "Can you just please explain to me what you want? What am I supposed to do in this room?"

I stare at the laboratory and try to make sense of it. It's set up in a circle with a round conference table in the center and stainless-steel counters with cupboards below and shelves above surrounding the table. Lots of jars, but again, they are not whimsical and hand-blown, like my jars at home. They are all very sterile and cold.

"Come this way," Tarq says. "This is our laboratory bloodhorn."

I follow him around the laboratory counters to a small grow room set up in the corner. There are lots of lights hanging from the ceiling and an intricate set of pipes that must be a watering system. I've never seen the actual bloodhorn plant since Pell still hasn't let me past the front entrance of the greenhouse—and we have monsters who know far more than I do—so I study it for a moment. It doesn't really look the way I pictured it. In my mind it was… like a poinsettia. Big, red flowers. Because, of course, all I've ever seen were the big red flowers.

But it's nothing at all like a poinsettia. It's more like a palm tree with long spikes. The red flowers only grow from the top. And it's super tall. Like… ten feet tall.

"Why are you looking at it that way?"

I glance up at Tarq. "Huh?"

"You're looking at it funny. What's wrong with it?"

"Nothing. I don't think. I've just never seen the whole plant. Pell won't let me inside the greenhouse. He says some of the plants are dangerous so he just brings me the flowers."

I get the idea that my explanation—even though it's the truth—makes Tarq suspicious.

In fact, I'm pretty sure that's why I'm here.

He thinks we've got a secret. And we can't blame him for that, because I now know that we do.

The scary part is that Tarq thinks that I will give him that secret.

But I won't. And I think he's starting to realize this.

But you know who might give him that secret?

"You should invite Pell along tomorrow," Tarq says. Like he's reading my mind.

Yep. Him. Pell's whole opinion of Tarq is based on some ancient friendship. He clings to the idea that he and Tarq are the most amazing BFF's of all time. He thinks that they're on the same side and that they have each other's backs.

If Pell was here and Tarq asked him how we got through the portal, Pell would tell him. I know he would. He's... *loyal*. Yep, that's the perfect word for Pell. Loyal.

"Pell can't see the doors," I say. "If he's with me when I approach the tombs, the portal disappears."

"I think we can fix that."

"Oh?" I try not to sound disturbed by this, but I'm not entirely sure I succeed. "How would we do that?"

"I have Ostanes' book. Remember?"

"Right. The book. So there's a spell in there that can make Pell see the tomb doors?"

"I'll check it out. In the meantime, you should make yourself at home here."

And then he turns, like he's going to just leave me here in this place. "Wait! What do I do?"

Tarq calls over his shoulder as he walks away, "Learn how to open the portals using things we have here, Pie. That's how you cancel your debt." And then he disappears around one of the lab stations.

I follow him, practically running to keep up. "But how do I do that? And how much is it worth? I need to see the Book of Debt!"

"Later, Pie. We'll meet at the end of the day before you go home. If you have something good to tell me, we'll talk about erasing some debt."

"Talk about it?" What the fuck? "That's not how this works!" I yell. "There's a menu of… tasks and what everything is worth! You can't just change the rules!"

Tarq stops at the glass door and turns. Smiles. "It's cute how clueless you are. Ya know that?"

"What?" And then he turns to leave again. But I grab his arm before he can escape. "Wait. What are you talking about?"

He laughs at me. It's not a mean laugh, but it's still a laugh. "You really have no idea about anything." He taps my nose with a clawed fingertip. "But you'll understand soon." Then he turns away, and really does leave.

I just stand there with my mouth open, unable to process all the many confusing things that just happened. And I've only been here like ten minutes.

"What. The actual. Fuck?" I mutter.

"Don't let him get you down. He's always gruff and growly in the mornings."

I turn, looking for the source of the voice, and find a lovely wood nymph chimera peeking out at me from across the lab.

"Hi." She waves at me, then steps out from behind a tall shelf. "I'm Talina. Your assistant."

"Assistant?"

And then I relax a little. Because she is a wood nymph, just like me.

Only she doesn't look anything like me. She is wearing a white lab coat that is buttoned all the way up to her neck and dropping all the way down to her... hock, or whatever it's called. The fur on her face, hands, and lower legs is all a rich, chocolate brown, but with a patch of white over her right eye. That matches her white hair piled up on top of her head in a bun that sits between two gazelle-like horns.

Her smile is warm and bright as she walks towards me, her hooves clip-clopping across the polished tile floor. She has huge green eyes set in a petite and sweet face and she is very tall and slim— like a ballerina, if ballerinas had hind legs and hooves. She points at me and I notice her fingernails are long, white, and glittering with clear, tiny stones. I think I could look at her for ages and never run out of things to marvel at. "Where did you get those lovely clothes?" she asks.

I look down at myself, then back up at her. "Oh. I have a monster—a... satyr chimera—at home. He's really into fashion design. He made this for me."

"It's really nice. Like the stuff you find in the mall."

"You have a mall here?"

This makes Talina giggle. "Of course. This is Vinca City. We have everything here. Where are you from?"

"I'm from…" Hm. What do I say? Earth? Did I leave the planet? Or is this just some alternate reality? I'm not sure, so I just say, "Pennsylvania."

"Oh." Her eyes widen until they are big saucers. "Where's that? I've never heard of it."

"It's, um… between New York and Ohio."

"Oh," she says again, her eyes still huge. "I'd love to travel one day."

"Well. Yeah. OK."

We stare at each other for a few awkward seconds, then she says, "What should I help you with?"

"I wish I knew. I'm supposed to make the bloodhorn open the portals. But—"

"Oh, good! I've been working on that."

"You have? Any luck?"

"Unfortunately, no. I have run hundreds of experiments and none of them work."

"Whew. Thank God."

"What?"

"Oh." I smile at her. "Nothing." But I'm secretly happy that she's not having any luck.

"Personally," she says, "I think we're missing something critical."

My relief disappears. "What do you mean?"

"I don't think we have the right kind of bloodhorn."

Shit. "Are there other types of bloodhorn?"

"Several subspecies. But I've tried them all. So I'm thinking… maybe the missing ingredient is not bloodhorn?"

"What else could it be?"

Talina shrugs. "You tell me. You're the expert. You're the one who can walk through portals. No one else in this place can do that."

"Really? No one?"

"Just you. Well, Tarq did it that one time. But I was told he used your leftover key."

"What happened to it?" I ask. "That… key?"

"It fell apart when Tarq returned."

Well, that's good news. For a moment I was thinking that maybe he still had it and they might do some sort of chemical analysis on the scale and figure out the secret.

"I'm researching this, though," Talina says. "I just started looking at alternative interpretations for the protocol. I'm on it. So you don't have to worry. I'll figure out what the problem is."

"Great," I mutter.

"So." Talina smiles brightly at me. "What should we do?"

"Hell if I know. I'm not an alchemist, Talina. I'm not a chemist, I'm not a witch, and I'm one hundred percent not qualified for this position."

She giggles. "Stop it."

"I'm serious."

She sighs and frowns. "I know how you're feeling."

"You do?"

"Yes. Imposter syndrome."

"What?"

"You know. When you start something new and you feel inadequate. Like you're an imposter. I know it's all very weird, but you're here for a reason, Pie."

She pauses, then holds up a finger. "I know what we should do. We should go get coffee."

"Oh, my God. *Yes*. I really need a coffee."

"Perfect." Talina hooks her arm in mine, then steers me towards the door. "Let's have a break."

"Won't Tarq get mad?"

"About what?"

"Slacking off, or whatever?"

"This is science, Pie. People don't really expect *results*." She giggles as she removes my messenger bag from my shoulder and places it on a large central table. "They only expect *progress*. And progress is relative. I've got my progress mapped out for the next two years. I'll share it with you."

"You will?"

She smiles at me. She's a very pretty wood nymph. And I'm a little bit weirded out that my new co-worker isn't human, but at the same time, I'm also a little bit relieved to be around others like me. "Of course," she says. "We're best friends now."

I mull over the idea that I have a new best friend—and that she's a magical creature—while I let Talina lead me through the building. Which, once again, looks nothing like the place I walked through to get up here.

"This building does not make sense," I say. "It's like the hallways back in my sanctuary's second floor. Always changing."

"Yes. All Tarq's buildings are variable. But don't worry, it's not like that outside."

"How do you find your way around? Don't you get lost on your way to work every day?"

"No, there's an entry portal we go through. Two, actually. Well, I'm sure there are a lot more than two. But I only have access to two. They kick you out in the Grand Laboratory regardless of which door you come through. And here one is." Talina and I both stop in front of a large metal door. It looks like something you'd find in a medieval castle—or a dungeon—and stands much taller than either her or I. Talina pauses as I take it in, then dramatically presents the exit portal to me with a wave of her hand. "Once we go through the portal, we'll be kicked out into the Lesser Lobby. That's the only exit I have access to, but it's also the easiest way to get outside the building."

"There's so much magic here. It's weird."

"It's not magic." She giggles. "It's just the laws of nature."

"Right."

Talina's arm is still hooked in mine, so we pass through the portal doors as a team and end up in the same lobby where I came in from the sanctuary. I look around for my door, but it's not there.

"Do you know how I get home?" I ask her. "Because this is where I came in and my door isn't there." I point to the place where it should be.

"Oh, portals are tightly regulated here in Vinca. What time do you get off work?"

"I don't know."

"Didn't you sign a contract?"

"No." I say this emphatically, and maybe a little bit too loud, but I feel the need to make this point clear. "I did not. I didn't sign anything. Tarq just appeared one day saying he now owns my debt and—"

"Wait." Talina squints her eyes at me as she holds up a hand, which is very feminine and not monsterish at all. I really love her sparkling white nails. I wonder if I can get my nails done here? "What?" she says.

"He owns my debt." I sigh. "It's a long story. I'm stuck in a stupid curse in my world and this whole Book of Debt thing is part of it."

"Wow," Talina breathes. "That's so fascinating. I want to hear everything about your curse and your home. But let's get coffee first."

I agree. I need an immediate infusion of caffeine.

Talina leads me across the lobby and then heaves open a heavy glass door, holding it for me as I pass through.

And even though this isn't a portal, I feel like I enter an entirely new world as I step outside and take in the city around me.

The buildings are all made of glass, and steel, and mirrors. A sleek train slithers by atop a monorail above me. Airships in the sky, huge birds gliding between the tippy-top architectural spires, and a river! A calm, wide river of light-blue water burbles down the middle of everything. Like it's part of the transportation system.

There are fat houseboats that sit low on the water anchored to docks. Slim gondolas filled with people skimming the surface in a hurry like taxis. And long flat ships carrying large wooden crates and metal containers.

I sniff the air as a waft of bakery smell invades my senses. Then other smells—mostly food, which makes my stomach grumble, but sweet floral scents, too. A row of flowering trees lines the edge of the road running alongside the river. Butterflies float around them in a cloud, stirring up the smell with their soft, fluttery wings.

Tiny birds have an argument in a nearby bush, but it's a melodic one. Sweet tweets and crisp chirps.

Then I see the… castle. At least, that's what I think it is. It's modern, but still has a very castle feel about it. Hard, cold towers of silver and steel jutting out from some central cathedral. The blackish-silver clashes with the soft light blue sky dotted with puffy cotton-candy clouds.

"Wow," I whisper.

"Nice, huh?" Talina says. "You don't have cities like this in your world, I take it."

"We do," I say absently, still trying to take in the city. "But then again, no. We don't. Not like this."

Aside from the tall, tall buildings that look like something out of a futuristic—much, *much* cleaner—New York City, there are so many people! I mean, I grew up in Philly and I've been to my share of cities. So I've seen crowds, but this. *This* is something altogether different.

There are so many people. And they are not all monsters, but they're not all human, either. They're a splendid amalgamation of the two. Everywhere I look are men, and women, and wood nymphs, and satyrs.

But there is so much more than that too! Monsters of every different kind. So many different kinds, I don't even have names for them.

But here's something almost everyone has in common—they are wearing spectacular clothes. Silks, and velvets, and chiffons in pale colors, contrasting against the silver background of the skyscrapers.

Just like the contrast of Tarq and his building.

All of the satyrs are wearing pants. Which seems odd after living with them *au naturel* at the sanctuary. A shiver runs through my body as I take them all in.

I finally look over at Talina, who has been waiting patiently for me to get my fill. "Impressive."

"Isn't it?" She beams. "Welcome to Vinca City. The hub of the entire universe."

I have a lot of questions, but before I can ask a single one, Talina takes hold of my hand and tugs me into a moving crowd. She smiles at me over her shoulder, and says, "Coffee first!" And then we become part of the pedestrian river that flows on sidewalks next to the real river below, ebbing and flowing at the whims of people and creatures, until Talina tugs me again and we ease over to the front of a coffeeshop.

"This is my favorite spot," she says with a smile. Then she swings the door open and we go inside.

CHAPTER NINE – TOMAS

I would never admit this out loud, but driving is a tiny bit more challenging than it looks.

Pell is not talking to me. He is barking orders at a group of monsters, telling them to unload the hay and stack it behind Pie's cottage. But every once in a while, he will shoot me a look. A look that says, *I told you so, you incompetent fill-in-the-blank.*

We had a few small mishaps on the way home. And by we, I mean me.

First, there was that telephone pole. Then the flattened stop sign. And I didn't realize that last turn into the woods was so sharp and cut a little corner, almost got stuck in the ditch, but pulled it out in the end like a champion.

All in all, I feel very proud of my first driving experience. And now, after more than two thousand years, I have my own transportation. Which is going to come in handy tomorrow night when I meet Freckle Face from the feedstore for a date in town.

Her name is not really Freckle Face, nor is it Issue Girl, but Madeline. She is a twenty-two-year-old baby with a mouth like a trucker. Her family owns that feed store, so she's an expert in an abundance of useful things like how to properly strap hay to the back of a flatbed truck so when you run into a ditch, the bales don't slide off.

And they did not!

I think she is a genius. A delightful, lovely genius.

And I have a date.

I really like that word so I say it over and over in my head.

Date, date, date. I have a date.

"What the—"

I glance up at Pell and find him walking over to Pie's kitchen window. He plucks a velvet bag off the sill and looks around until his eyes find mine. "What the fuck, Tomas?"

I walk over to him, because that velvet bag is filled with all those magic rings. Rings we're trying to hide from the new monsters, just in case they are a get-out-of-sanctuary-free card and they can actually get out of the sanctuary for free.

"What's that doing there?" I ask.

Pell narrows his eyes, looking at all the monsters. "Were they inside our cottage? Did they take this bag and put it on the window sill? Pie and I hid this bag this morning. Are they going through our stuff?"

"Hmm." I consider this. "I very much doubt it, Pell. They're not that kind of monster."

"Then why is this bag of magic rings suddenly turning up in places it shouldn't be?"

"Perhaps because it's a bag of *magic* rings?" I feel like this is obvious.

He lets out a long breath. "I do not have the patience for this right now. If the magic in this bag is doing its best to be seen by these monsters, then I need better magic to contain it." He turns away and starts walking towards the gate.

"Where are you going?"

"To find a spell to tame this bag."

"Do you need help?" I yell.

But he's gone through the gate, and I'm relieved.

My day is going swimmingly. I have purchased myself a truck—a flatbed, no less—found a girlfriend, and mastered the art of driving.

And it's not even noon.

I feel like celebrating. So I go inside the cottage, pour myself a drink from one of the many liquor bottles Pie keeps stocked in her kitchen, and kick my feet up on the table.

I think I'm going to like my new life as a human-dragon chimera.

I see nothing but bright, shiny things in my cursed future.

Brand-new, bright, shiny, good things.

CHAPTER TEN – PELL

I ignore all the monsters inside *my* sanctuary. I don't like them. I don't want them here. And while I do understand the irony that this place is called a sanctuary and for thousands of years it has been a place for monsters, they were *dead* monsters. Not living, breathing, eating, annoying monsters with opinions.

The only opinion around here that matters is mine.

The apothecary door is open and even from the top of the stairs, I can see half a dozen monsters inside. It's a mess. We're in the middle of restocking and labeling everything in the jars. Not a job I want—not a job Pie is even capable of doing—so the monsters in there are very necessary.

But that doesn't mean I want them there. As soon as I cross the threshold, I growl at them. "Get out."

There are seven. All ancient-looking satyr chimeras. They look like they came from a time before me. They wear clothes, which is unusual from my perspective. And those clothes are not Roman. They are something else. Obviously, I'm not a world traveler, so where these clothes come from, I have no idea. But I don't have the desire, or the time, to be worrying about where this group comes from.

All seven of them smile at me, then bow low—this is another thing they do which I don't really understand—and they put down all their jars and meekly make their exit.

I do, however, enjoy their obedience.

I slam the door behind them with a flick of my finger, then turn to the shelves, looking up and along the walls. All the books are still here after the big Reckoning, but there are a lot of them and even if I had an index of each title—which, if I do, I'm not aware of it—I doubt it would be useful, because they don't appear to be in any kind of order.

So there is only one option. I must pull each book out and see what it is.

I decide to start at the top and work my way across and down. So I climb the sketchy ladder all the way up to the third level, and begin.

I'm barely one third of the way across the top set of shelves when I find one that might do. The book is called *The Magic and Mischief of Bags*.

I never thought about the bag being the problem. I just assumed it was the rings. So I take the book with me as I descend the ladder, then fall into the soft couch in the corner and open it up.

There is a forward by an alchemist called Pressia. There is even a sketch of her likeness. She is a market nymph, which is a cross between a city nymph and a traveling nymph. They are wandering spirits, never staying in one place for very long. They are known for stealing—and selling things, of course. She's quite cute, even though she is not a chimera, so she has no horns, or hooves, or fur for me to appreciate.

Her hair is light and long, but not thick and lustrous, the way Pie's is. She's wearing a beaded headband and a peasant dress that probably has nothing to do with her status in life. She looks young in the image. Maybe a teenager.

But in my experience, looks are always deceiving.

Books don't get written by teenage peasant nymphs. Books get written by educated people. People who can afford paper, and ink, and binding supplies. I flip through the thick, handmade pages and find that they have been illustrated in the same style as the author's picture. They are even in color—and some of them are illuminated with gold leaf.

Very unusual.

Pressia. I search my memory for this name, but if I ever knew about her, I don't remember.

This book is old. The leather cover, which was probably a very high quality when it was made, is cracked and worn. And it's all handwritten.

"All right, Pressia," I mutter. "Let's see what you know about magic bags."

I skim through the contents, trying to figure out how things are organized in the world of magic bags, and discover that it is more about the contents, and the magic required to contain them, than the bag itself.

I flip through, looking for anything about rings, but pause about a third of the way through when I get to the one about breath.

"Huh," I say out loud. "I didn't realize magic breath was a thing."

It's *my* thing, obviously. But I have always been under the impression that I was unique. I've used it on occasion over the centuries. But to be honest, I never thought that magic was very reliable. Who knew that the container mattered?

This makes me think about the little amulet Pie made to protect her from Sheriff Roth and how I breathed into it. I page through, looking for leather in this section on breath, and realize that you can't capture magic breaths inside a leather pouch.

No wonder it didn't work. You have to contain it inside glass tubes or jars with corks and wax or attach it to letters stamped into metals like silver, or pewter, or gold.

Which is kind of obvious, now that I think about it. Leather pouches aren't airtight.

"Never mind this shit, Pell. Stay focused," I chastise myself.

Right. I'm looking for rings.

I page through again, skimming the pictures, get momentarily distracted by the section on moths, but force myself to keep going. Rings are the very last chapter and it comes with a poem.

Rings and bags are hard to tame
They must be sealed with dragon's flame
Blackened iron, ammolite
Nuts and bolts and smote and smite.

Fuck, I hate poem spells. They're the worst. If someone takes the time to hide a recipe inside a poem, it's a sure sign that shit is about to go sideways. I mean, what the fuck? Sealed with dragon's flame? Which is wonderful, by the way. Since my personal dragon has suddenly turned into a human chimera. And what the hell do you do with the iron and ammolite? Smite and smote it with nuts and bolts?

How is iron, and stone, and nuts, and bolts a *bag*?

I fucking hate cryptic people.

But. As annoying as this little poem is, I did get a partial answer.

The velvet bag isn't enough to keep the rings hidden.

Apparently, I need to make something of iron—which I have plenty of around here. You can't take two steps in this place without running into some iron. But ammolite? I scan the room, squinting my eyes to see into jars. There might be some ammolite in here somewhere. I don't know much about it, but I do know this. It's not easy to get. Even though it's flashy and colorful it's not actually a crystal. It's a fossil.

Nuts and bolts I can do, and smite, in this context, probably means to pound.

I read the poem again and again, letting my mind wander with ideas. I guess I could make a bag of chainmail. And even though I actually do know how to do that, picturing the amount of work involved kinda pisses me off. I will have to cut wood. Lots of it. And go looking for the forge and other blacksmithing tools, which I have not even seen in several hundred years.

Stupid bag of rings.

Then I get an idea. This can't be the only way to deal with magic rings. There must be something else. That's when I see the footnote at the bottom of the page. *Ring lore is ancient magic and is presided over by the god, Portunus.*

Portunus. Portunus. Why don't I recall a god named Portunus?

"OK." I get up with a sigh and walk back over to the shelves. There are dozens of books about ancient Roman gods in here, that I know for sure. I scan the shelves, find one with a gold-leaf spine, and pull it down.

I go back to my couch and flip through to the P's until I find Portunus.

"Ah, yeah." I remember him. He was an asshole. There's a full-page illustration, but… no. That's not a great likeness. He had dark hair, I know that for sure. And a crooked eye he often covered with a patch. In fact, he was downright ugly.

Reluctantly, I have to accept the idea that I might need Portunus to take care of my little ring problem. Which means I will require a trip to the upstairs hallways.

I could go now, but I imagine Pie might like to come along. So I'll just keep the bag of rings on my person. Which means I will require pants.

This thought makes me smile and miss Pie terribly. But how delighted will she be when she gets home from her hard day's work and she finds me in pants?

I picture her face and smile at the thought.

Where did I leave those pants?

Oh! I snap my fingers as the memory comes back. In the Pleasure Cave.

I leave the apothecary, make my way to the cave, and find the pants exactly where I left them weeks ago. In a little pile next to the hot spring. They are stiff and a little bit smelly, but they have pockets and that's all I need. When we go to the hallways, I will pick up a new pair. For now, they'll do.

I spend the rest of the morning going through jars in the apothecary. The ancient satyrs wander in and get busy, but I don't stop them. They are intent on reorganizing this place. Tomas appears around lunchtime—not because he needs me, he's calling the monsters to eat. And that's when I see it! A small glass jar filled with red and gold ammolite. I hold it up to the light, mesmerized by their sparkle.

"What's that?" Tomas asks. He comes over to me and leans in to see the little pieces of fossilized shell.

"Ammolite."

"Oh," he says, smiling. "Like the scales on my legs."

We both look down at his legs and then I actually laugh. "Forgot about that. I guess I should've just come to you in the first place."

"Really?" He's excited at the prospect of me needing him. "What for?"

"A spell, Tomas. I looked up magic rings and the only way to properly contain them is with a special dragon spell."

"Really?" he exclaims again, this time louder. "What kind of dragon spell?"

"I need iron and ammolite." I hold up the jar. "And dragon's fire."

Tomas squints his eyes. "You can have as many scales as you like. But I no longer have dragon fire. So I don't know what you'll do about that."

"Oh, come on," I huff. "Surely you have one more puff inside you."

"No. I don't."

I sigh. I want to argue with him—make him admit that he could, technically, breathe a little fire for me if he really wanted to—but it's not worth the effort right now. First, I need to find the forge and brush up on my chainmail-making abilities. So I say, "Whatever. I'll be in the blacksmith building."

"We have a blacksmith building?"

"Well... we used to. It's only been about two hundred years since I was last in there. I'm sure it's around somewhere."

CHAPTER ELEVEN – PIE

Talina and I basically walk into Starbucks, but it's not called Starbucks. It's called Dragonbucks. And I gotta say… that's kinda weird. Starbucks. Dragonbucks. I dunno. Maybe I'm just seeing connections where there aren't any because I have a dragon friend and a buck friend in my new life now, plus there are a lot of other buck-like people walking around this place, but the whole thing reminds me of Bizarro World.

The logo isn't green and white and the inside doesn't look like a Starbucks. It's not hipster, it's actually very formal. Kinda Victorian. Which doesn't make sense, either, because this is another world and that means there was no Victorian-era Europe to emulate. Also, there's that clash again. The lacy, old-fashioned monster stuff and the flashy, gleaming modern stuff.

But this place does have a Victorian look to it. I mean, I'm no expert on eras or anything. But it's all very… period piece, but with a modern twist. I feel like I just stepped into that over-the-top Marie Antoinette movie with Kirsten Dunst where all the royal women are trying on shoes and eating cakes.

The colors aren't washed-out pastels—they are crisp, bright pinks, and spring-grass greens, and eye-popping lavenders.

It's all very feminine, but somehow radiates power, too.

The tablecloths are made of thick silks and luxurious lace. Glass cases in the front are filled with elaborately decorated pastries. The coffee is served in fine porcelain. And the low, whispering chatter in combination with the delicate clinking of tea cups on saucers is a warm and welcoming kind of white noise.

"Wow." I'm looking up at an intricately painted ceiling covered in naked satyrs and nymphs having sex. "That's..." But I don't have words for it, so I give up.

Talina elbows me with a giggle. "It's a reimagining of a famous painting from hundreds of years ago. In the original, they were all prim and proper, having a very formal and boring dinner. The nymphs were buttoned up to their necks in fashion and it was against the law for the satyrs to"—she giggles again—"let it all hang out, so to speak."

I'm still looking up at the ceiling when she says this, but then I quickly glance at her. "Wait. What do you mean it was *illegal?* They were forced to wear pants?" I almost can't contain my snort.

"Yep. That's why now—this is their excuse, anyway"—she rolls her eyes—"now they wear those pants so tight, they might as well be naked."

I point at her. "Right?"

Talina covers her mouth, hiding her laugh as the line we're in moves forward. The place is packed full and I'm starting to wonder how long it will take to get a table when someone calls Talina's name.

We both look over to a corner near the front window where a group of smartly-dressed nymphs are waving. "Oooo!" Talina exclaims, waving back. "My friends are here." She hooks her arm in mine and starts tugging me in that direction. "They're gonna love you."

My heart flutters as we weave our way through tables and people. I'm going to meet her friends. And now I feel like this is a first date that suddenly turned into a meet-the-parents kind of moment and my stomach fills up with butterflies.

Or… moths, maybe.

Gross.

There is a lot of squealing as we approach and the entire table of females gets up and starts hugging Talina. She lets go of me to reciprocate, and now I feel like the wallflower at a junior-high dance. So I stand there awkwardly while they all say hello.

Talina notices and pulls me towards her. "Girls. This is Pie. She's my new boss."

"Oh—" I'm just about to correct her. I'm nobody's boss. But I don't get a chance. All the squealing begins anew, only this time, it's directed at me.

"I love your outfit," one says. Her horns are short and stubby, barely peeking up from her luxurious honey-brown waves of thick hair piled on top of her head.

"Your hair is so pretty!" another exclaims. She's wearing a pale-blue bodice embroidered with silver threads that glimmer and glint in the warm light.

"Wow. I'd kill for those legs." This one is wearing a cream-colored jacket with a lacy top underneath. She's got a sweet, round face with pink cheeks.

"And your horns!" This one has the greenest eyes I've ever seen. Almost chartreuse. And she's wearing a black robe of sorts.

It's like I was dropped in to a let's-make-Pie-feel-special party. And I blush.

"You're embarrassing her," Talina says. "Stop it. We just came in for coffee. We're super-busy working on secret projects, girls. We can't be bothered with gossips such as yourselves."

They all burst out laughing as Talina directs me to the side of the table with two empty chairs.

"Right," Green Eyes says. Then she rolls those gorgeous green eyes and snorts. "Super-secret projects."

"Talina has been telling us that for ages," Sweet Face says. Her voice matches her looks. It's very soft and feminine.

"And she has yet to provide even a single detail," Blue Bodice exclaims.

"Don't mind us, Pie." Stubby Horns reaches across the table and taps my hand. "We're incorrigible."

"Always," Talina sighs. "But I wouldn't have it any other way. Now let me do introductions."

She goes around the table, introducing them one by one. Green Eyes is called Esmah. She's a freaking judge in the law courts.

Mikayla is the one with stubby horns and pretty hair. She owns a bakery and proudly proclaims all those elaborately decorated pastries in the glass cases up front were made by her bakers.

Blue Bodice is a fashion designer and she is called Akkaline. She beams a wild, devious smile at me and announces she has an upcoming show, and would I like to be one of her models?

This offer must make me blush, or something, because Talina skillfully redirects my attention to Sweet Face, who is really called Zantha. She's a healer.

I say hello to each of them and settle a little bit as Talina, once again, tells them I am her boss.

I want to interject, say that's not really true. I'm not boss material. But they are chattering and happy and I don't want to be the center of attention. So I let it go.

We order coffee, and a box of pastries at Mikayla's insistence, and then we leave under the pretense that we have important work to do.

Once outside in the sunshine, I let out a long breath.

"I know," Talina says. "They are a bit much. And overpowering. But they are really great people, I promise."

"Oh, I find them all completely fascinating."

"They showed a lot of self-control this time, Pie. But next time we meet up, you will not be the brand-new girl anymore and they will pepper you with questions. So get ready for that."

"Do they go there every day?" I ask. "And wow. That place. It was pretty great."

"Not a regular date or anything. We all have different schedules and lives these days. We met in boarding school ages ago and never lost touch. And now, they are like family to me. But we all work around the Royal Court, so we frequently bump in to each other."

"Royal Court?"

Talina smiles at me, pulling open the door to Tarq's building. "You work in the most powerful, fascinating district in all of Vinca, Pie. I don't know what your life was like before today, but I do know this—it's never going to be the same again."

I think about Talina's words all the way back up to our laboratory, forgetting to pay attention to the route we take. My world has just completely flipped. And I'm not sure what to make of it.

I think back on this morning, waking up in my cottage with Pell. My sanctuary, and my monsters, and my curse. It seems so far away. Almost... fictional. Like this is the real world now and the one I came from is the fantasy place.

So weird.

Once we're back in the lab Talina breathes out a sigh. "Well, I suppose we should put up a pretense of working, don't you think?"

My coffee is gone—it was the most delicious drink I've ever tasted. But I barely had the chance to think about it because my mind is all ablur with new things. "Yeah," I finally answer. "I guess. But, like I've already said, I'm not what Tarq thinks I am. I don't do any of this." I pan my arms wide to indicate absolutely everything in the lab. "I don't have the first clue where to start."

Talina points to the corner where the bloodhorn is growing. "There. Obviously."

"But what do we do with it? And even if we do manage to concoct a potion—"

"Serum," Talina corrects me.

"Whatever. Even if we do get a freaking serum, how do we know it will work?"

"We test it."

"Test it how?"

"We make one of those." Talina is pointing to my necklace. "And then we walk through a door."

I let out a sigh. "OK. if you say so. But I'm—" I stop talking because this is the moment when I notice something on the center conference table. "What the…" I walk over to the table and pick up the book, just staring at the cover. "This is my debt! What's it doing here?"

Talina comes over to me and studies the massive book in my hands. "Your what?"

"My Book of Debt. This is why I'm here." I let out a frustrated breath because Talina is looking at me with confusion. "It's a long story. But look." I open the book and yep, there's my name. "See?" I point to it. "I'm in debt. At first, I was in debt to Pell." But then I pause. "Hmm. That's probably not right. I think I was in debt to Saint Mark's. But anyway. I came here asking Tarq for help. I needed to banish the sheriff of Granite Springs from the sanctuary and I needed a spell from the Big Important Book he's got. Which he gave me, never telling me what it would cost, and once it was over, he was the new proud owner of my debt. That's why I have to work for him."

Talina is just looking at me with squinty eyes.

"What?" I ask.

"The Big Important Book?"

"Yeah. You know. Ostanes' spellbook. The…" What did Tarq call it that day? "Oh!" I snap my fingers. "The source code. The source code book."

Talina's mouth drops open.

"What?" I ask again.

"He showed you the source code?"

"No. Not really. But he gave me a page from it."

"From the source code?" Her mouth is still open.

"Yeah. Why? What's the big deal?"

"So it's... *real?*"

"What?"

Talina just blinks at me, mouth still open.

"*What?*" I exclaim.

"You're... *her!*"

"Who?"

"Oh. My. Gods." Talina places a hand over her heart and then almost falls over. I catch her just in time and lead her over to a chair. She sinks into it, breathless.

"What's wrong?"

But she can't speak. In fact, she's panting really hard. She might be hyperventilating.

"Talina! Talk to me! What's happening here?"

She looks up at me, eyes wide, then she slips down to her knees and bows at my feet.

"What the hell are you doing?"

She doesn't get up. She's pressing her freaking face to the cold tile floor. "Forgive me. Forgive me, Your Highness! I didn't know! He never told me!"

"What. The actual fuck! Are you talking about!" I yell it. Loud.

She looks up at me. "Your Highness?"

"Stop calling me that! I'm Pie! I'm not a highness anything, I'm just Pie!"

"Pie." She wilts, then bows her head back to the floor again.

"Stop it! Right now!"

"I'm sorry!" She looks up. "I'm sorry!"

"What are you doing?"

"You don't know, do you? You really don't know."

"I don't know shit! I've been telling you people that all freaking day!"

She gets to her feet, grabs my hand, kisses my fucking fingers, and says, "Princess Pianna! Welcome home!"

I slap her. Right across the face. So hard it makes a smacking noise that echoes up to the ceiling. And then I yell, "Snap out of it!"

I saw this in a movie once. It was effective.

But today, it makes Talina cry.

Shit. "Oh, my God. I'm so sorry, Talina. I just want you to stop acting weird. I'm not a princess. I'm a freaking... schizophrenic nobody! My name isn't Pianna!"

Like... gross, right? Pie is cute. Pianna is just... no. Gross.

"Your Highness!"

"Stop calling me that." And then I add, "That's an order!" Just to see if it works.

It does. Talina snaps to attention and wipes her eyes. Breath still hitching, but she is suddenly stoic.

Better. I think. But still not good. "OK. Let's be calm here. I think you're jumping to a lot of conclusions and—"

"What is going on?"

Talina and I both whirl around to find Tarq looming in the doorway, his deep, rough voice still echoing through the room.

Talina falls to her knees again, bowing her head to the floor, mumbling, "I'm sorry! I'm sorry!"

I squint my eyes at Tarq. "Great. That's just great," I snap at him. "Look what you did! I just got her to stop doing that!"

"Talina," Tarq barks. "Leave us."

She scrambles to her feet and scurries out of the lab. Tarq closes the doors behind her and points to the Book of Debt, which I am still holding in my hands. "You wanted to know how the debt works. I'm here to explain that."

"How about you explain *her*," I say, nodding my head at the doors. "She thinks I'm some freaking princess. Some bitch called Pianna. What the actual fuck is happening here, Tarq?"

He seems… confused for a moment. No. Not confused. Conflicted. I'm familiar with this look. It's the look people give me when they're coming to a conclusion. Usually that conclusion is something along the lines of… *Yeah. I thought she was normal, but she's not. I need to end this relationship as gracefully as possible, then get the hell away from her.*

This reaction is so common in my experience, it makes me tired. So I sigh. Loudly. "What aren't you telling me?"

Tarq points to a conference table chair. "Sit down, Pie. We need to have a talk."

"No. I don't want to sit. I want to stand."

"Fine. But trust me, you will need that chair."

I turn away from him, place my hands over my face, and try my best not to melt down. I am so sick of being the weirdo. So damn tired of being the freak. I was having such a nice, normal experience for once. Coffee, and work, and girlfriends. I was having a *Sex and the City* moment. I was pretty, successful, confident Carrie for like ten minutes. Someone who fit in.

And now I have no idea what's happening. The only thing I do know is this:

I am not normal.

I will never be normal.

Tarq takes the Book of Debt from my hands and drops it down on the table, the thump of thick bound pages crashing my pity party. He says, "Luciano mentioned that you left the building today."

"What?" I turn to look at him.

"You left work."

Shit. "Yeah. To get coffee. If that wasn't allowed—"

"It's fine. Did you run into any trouble?"

"Trouble?" It's a weird word choice. But then again, maybe it's not. "You knew."

"What are you talking about?"

"Whatever this princess shit is all about. You knew, didn't you? Talina thinks I'm some princess. Some missing princess. And you do too. That's why I'm here, isn't it? And that's why you're asking if I ran into trouble."

He points to the chair again. "Take a seat."

This time I do. He's right. I need this chair.

Tarq walks around the table and sits across from me. We stare at each other for a moment. He steeples his fingers under his chin. "Forget about Talina—"

"No." I say it loudly. "No." Then again, softer. "I want to know what's going on."

"It's a long story. Filled with nuances and—"

"Cut the crap, OK? Do you think I'm this princess?"

He nods. "I do."

I look away. Stare across the room. Barely seeing what's all around me. My face suddenly goes hot and

I think I might cry, but I don't have the faintest idea of *why* I might cry, which just makes me want to cry more.

Tarq lets out a sigh. "But about the book…"

"Forget the book, Tarq. If you know things"—I force myself to look him in the eyes—"if you know things *about me,* then I need that information and I need it right now. Because I have been wandering through this fucking life clueless!" That last word comes out as a shout. "And I'm fucking sick of it!"

There are several long moments of agonizing silence in which I begin to squirm. He doesn't scare me. Not really. He hasn't been mean to me and I really don't think he's going to hurt me. So that's not why I squirm. I squirm because he's looking at me with such intensity, such focused consideration, his gaze almost comes off as heat.

I can *feel* him.

"OK," he finally says. "But I have one question first." I open my mouth to protest, but he puts up a hand, silencing me. "Just one. That's all."

"Fine."

"Who is your father?"

"What?"

"You heard me. Who is he?"

"I don't know. I never met him."

He nods, like he was expecting this. And I suddenly feel like I'm trapped in a stupid fairy tale and my whole life is a storybook of lies. "Well, *I* think I know him."

"My father?"

"Yes. I think you are this missing princess and I think you being here is going to change everything."

I just blink at him the same way that Talina blinked at me earlier. It's a blink of utter confusion with a healthy sprinkling of instantaneous understanding. Because Ostanes' words come back to me in this moment. *The curse has not been lifted, but the boundaries have shifted.*

She wanted me to tell Pell that. And I did. And we both thought it was about him. How he could now leave the sanctuary as a man instead of a monster. Which is super-handy and nice, especially since I grew hooves and horns.

So we thought that little remark was all about him.

But what if it was about both of us?

I can leave too. I can live in a whole other world. Be a whole other person. I might not even have to go back. I could stay here and be this princess.

It's a wild thought.

But it's confirmed when Tarq says, "You belong here, Pie. You were made *here*. In this world. Not back there in that world. And if you want to stay here, there is a life for you. A very nice life for you."

I'm shaking my head as he talks. "I don't know what that means. What life?" I pan my hands to the room. "I'm not this person. I can't do this stuff, Tarq. And as far as this princess shit goes—" I have to stop and scoff. "I'm no princess."

"Regardless. The offer is real and so is the choice."

"Who the fuck are you? Huh? Who are you, Tarq? What is your business in all of this? Why did you buy my debt? And, furthermore, who the hell did you buy it *from?*"

"All good questions. But the story is so complicated—"

"No! It's not. And I want to hear the bullet points right the hell now!"

"Bullet points." His mouth forms a crooked smile. "Cute."

"Stop it."

"Fine. You want bullet points? I'll give you bullet points. One." He holds up a clawed finger. "Two thousand years ago a princess was born in the Sanctuary of Ostanes. You are that princess. Two." He holds up a second clawed finger. "I was there and so was Pell. Three." Another finger goes up. "We are all royalty. Spawn of the gods, if you will. But from different families. Four. We were there as collateral. A way to ensure these families all got along. If one started trouble, their collateral would be killed. And it worked, for a while. You and I, though?" He pauses to suck in a deep breath.

"You and I what?" I ask the question, but I'm not really sure I want the answer.

"If all conditions were met, the three of us would be released and you and I were to be mated." He throws up his hands. "There. I said it. I should've told you that first time we met, but I didn't know for sure until I came out of the tomb and you seemed…"

I look up at him. "I seemed what?"

"Uneasy." He points to himself. "With me."

With *him*.

I close my eyes. Kinda shake my head a little.

"Pie?"

"What?"

"Did you hear me?"

"Of course I heard you." I open my eyes again, force myself to be calm. "What does any of this have to do with my debt?"

"I didn't *buy* it. It was given to me."

"By who? Who the hell is in charge of all this?"

He holds up his hands. Like he's having a moment of 'isn't it obvious'? "Ostanes, Pie. Ostanes is in charge of all this. She made us on the direct order of the gods. And we all have a purpose. Yours and mine is to... well, you can fill that blank in, I'm sure."

I get up from the chair, turn my back on him, and walk over to the window. I force myself to breathe as I stare out at the weird, yet oddly familiar, city.

He waits me out, I guess wondering if I will say more. And I do have lots of questions, I just can't seem to form words at the moment. Everything is changing. And it's all happening very fast. I suddenly feel dizzy and reach out, placing my palm flat against the window. The glass is hot from the sun outside. And that's when all kinds of other questions start popping into my head. Questions like... is this the same sun as the one I know? Or is it a different sun? Is this a planet? I mean, of course it must be, right? The universe is made up of round, spinning balls of rock or whatever. This has to be one of them. So the tomb doors are like...

"Pie?"

"What?" I turn to answer him because I'm not entirely sure I'm ready to go down the rabbit hole I'm staring into.

He studies me for a moment. "You look pale."

I nod, pressing my lips together. "I'm a little disoriented at the moment."

"I get it. It's weird." He smiles at me. "I'm trying to think back on my first day here, but it was so long ago, ya know? I only get bits and pieces of it really. I sorta remember being confused. But I was a kid. I adapted, I guess. Same way you adapted to your new world. Same way Pell adapted to his new world."

"The sanctuary?"

Tarq nods.

I want to ask how it all fits together, but I don't think it makes a difference right now. So I don't say anything.

"You wanted the bullet points. And now you have them. Would you like the details too?"

"No." My answer comes out automatically.

Tarq lets out a huff of frustration. "Why not?"

I'm suddenly breathing heavy. Like I can't seem to get enough oxygen.

"Pie? Fuck," he says. Then he drags the chair over to me. "Here. Sit down."

I do, because if I don't, I might faint.

Tarq kneels down in front of me so we're eye to eye. He takes my hand in his claws.

I look away, unable to meet his gaze.

I don't want to be here anymore. And if I had a clear idea of how to get home, I'd jump up and head that direction.

Tarq squeezes my hand. Not hard though. He is surprisingly gentle. "There is a plan, Pie. And everything we know is based on the plan."

He stops. Like he's waiting for me to ask the obvious question, *What plan?* But I don't want to know the plan. It feels very wrong to know the plan. And once you know the plan, it's kinda hard to unknow the plan. So… then what?

"What plan?" Tarq asks.

I turn my head to look at him. "What?"

"You want to ask these questions, you just don't want to know the answers. Yet. But you will, Pie."

He's probably right.

"So I'm gonna ask the questions for you. All you have to do is listen."

Again, he waits. But this time I think he's waiting for an objection. And I really do want to object, but it feels like a lot of effort. So I don't.

Tarq lets out a sigh. "I actually do remember this part."

"What part?"

"The part where I learned the truth about what it means."

I stare at him, holding my breath, waiting for that truth to fall out of his mouth.

But he stands back up and says something else instead. "It was a pretty bad time for me. I remember a dark room. And sleeping a lot. And an utter feeling of…" He pauses, searching for the right word. "Helplessness, I suppose. So I'm not gonna say anymore today. Because once you learn the truth, you will never be the same. And I don't know where you've been for the last two thousand years, but you obviously think you're human, so I'm gonna let you lead. We should be allowed to understand ourselves in our own good time, don't you think?"

I nod, because my mouth is so dry I don't think I could speak even if I wanted to.

"It all makes sense once you know the facts. It won't be confusing, or disorienting, or…" He shrugs. "Feel like a curse, I guess."

I scoff. "I doubt that."

"I did too. Have, actually, this whole time. There is a lot to say about me, and I'm sure there is a lot to say about you, too. But enough for today. Let's talk about something else. How was your first day? Satisfactory?"

Satisfactory? That's a weird, sterile word. I just shrug.

"Good. Well. I think that's enough for now. We can have breakfast tomorrow morning and talk a little more. But if you're not ready to learn the truth, that's fine too, Pie. Don't go home dwelling on it, OK? I won't force you."

Force me… to do *what*?

"Oh," he says, snapping my attention back to him. "But do have a good look at the book before you leave. Because there are quite a few new debts in there now and I want you to know, it wasn't me."

I look up at him, suddenly eager to ask questions. But he's already turned his back. He's already walking out the door. His last words to me are, "See Luciano in the main lobby when you're ready. He'll open the portal for you."

Then he's gone and I'm alone with all these new, conflicting feelings. And all these unsettling truths bouncing around in my brain. And all the uncertainty that I've spent my whole life trying to outrun.

Because that's what I've been doing. All those years of wandering weren't about looking for something, or someone, or somewhere to fit in.

I understand it now. My endless uncertainty was about running away.

From the truth about myself.

Because I am sitting here with hooves, and horns, and fur, in a place that should not exist, with a sun that might not be my sun, and I am someone I do not recognize anymore.

I am someone else.

Maybe a princess.

I just sit there for a while, my head in my hands, my mind spinning. Wondering why my life has to be so freaking stupid and complicated.

"Pie!" I turn and find Pia flying towards me, chirping. She lands on my shoulder, then climbs her way down the front of my blouse until I take her in my hands, her tiny feathered body warm against my skin. "Did you have a good morning?" she says, her sweet voice like a long-forgotten melody that brings back memories of much better times.

I don't know what to say, so I say nothing. But it's fine. Pia is talking enough for the both of us.

"I negotiated us a huge signing bonus."

"You did?" At first, I'm just pretending to perk up to hide all the depressing thoughts inside my head. But after I say these words, I find that I really am excited to hear what she's been up to.

"Yes! I got us perks! We have season tickets to the Royal Court Ballet, the Royal Court Orchestra, and the Royal Court Theatre. How fun is that?"

"High five, bitch." She taps her tiny foot on my palm. "Good job."

"And… they gave me a house."

"They gave you a house?"

"A bird house."

"Oh. Nice."

"Yep. So I'm gonna stay here."

"What?" My heart cracks again. "What do you mean?"

"I can't talk in the other world, Pie. It's not fun. I think I belong here. And you're gonna be here every day, anyway. When you're at home, you're with Pell. So this is better."

I want to object. Wildly. Like… I want to throw a freaking tantrum over this. Stomp my feet, and ball my fists, and scream.

Because what the actual fuck?

Why does the universe hate me? Why must it always pull the rug out from under me at every turn? Why can't it ever just let me be happy?

Why can't it ever let me feel safe?

"Pie? Are you OK?"

I want to tell her everything Tarq just said. I want to complain, and make her come home with me, and force her to be by my side.

But I don't.

Because she's happy. And if I ruin her happiness, then I'm the terrible universe that wants to pull the rug out from under her at every turn. And that's not fair.

So I make myself smile. I force the corners of my lips to go up. I make my eyes bright. I show just the right amount of teeth. "That's a great idea, Pia. Tomorrow I want to see your little house and hear all about your first night in your new place."

She doesn't have lips, so she doesn't smile. But she makes a happy chirp. "I knew you'd understand. You have all these great things happening to you, and now we get to be normal. I love it here. I want to stay forever and ever."

Then she flies off and disappears through the laboratory doors.

CHAPTER TWELVE – PELL

It takes me a good while to find the blacksmith shop because the sanctuary is so full of tombs, the entire property is like a giant maze. I haven't been out in the thick of the tombs for decades—probably more than a hundred years, if I'm being honest—so I had no idea how crowded it had become.

There are so many tombs. So many statues of monsters. And Pie's innocent questions from those first days come back to me now.

Who are they and why are they here?

I'm both confused, and slightly embarrassed, that I never asked these questions myself. I know the answers I gave Pie. There were always tombs inside the sanctuary and the new ones appeared gradually over thousands of years.

And on the surface, this does make sense. One becomes accustomed to the way things work. One just accepts these things as normal. It's just the way of the world.

But now that I'm able to see it from an outside perspective, I see how unnatural it really is.

Because these tombs have to have a purpose. And, of course, the main purpose is to hold the bodies—or, at the very least, some kind of essence—

of the monsters depicted by each of the statues outside.

But why do they need to be contained?

The obvious answer to this question is that they are dead and the tombs simply contain bodies.

But if that's true, why are they kept behind walls? Why must Saint Mark's exist in the first place?

Again, I have an answer for this. It's about the battle—the Great Divorce. And Ostanes' desire to hide her powerful book of magic.

But the tombs keep coming.

Where are they coming from?

I'm currently up on the roof of the blacksmith shop, kicking back, getting some air, and waiting for the forge to get hot enough to work some iron. So I have a pretty good view of the tombs right now and that brand-new black one catches my eye from across the compound. It's slightly elevated. On a bit of a hill up near the cathedral. A pretty nice spot, if you ask me. One that was absolutely not empty before this new tomb appeared.

Which tomb is missing? And where did it go?

Did it just move backward into the maze?

Or did it disappear altogether?

Even though I have probably walked past the now-missing tomb a thousand times, I can't even begin to imagine what it might look like. Or the monster contained inside, for that matter.

Was it that guy with the long mane and tail?

Or was it the one with the goat beard and tattooed horns?

Maybe it was that guy with the alabaster marble inlay on his hooves?

I make a mental note to take a closer look at this when I go back tonight.

I look down at the pipe in my hand, then puff on it for a moment, wondering how I forgot I used to love smoking this pipe. I must've left it behind the last time I was in the smithy shop. And it's funny—before this morning I hadn't thought about my blacksmithing days for centuries. But I was a pretty damn good blacksmith when I was younger. I made complete sets of chainmail in the Dark Ages of the Old World. And during the American Revolution, I made muskets. My caretaker was a French arms supplier for the Colonists in his former life and he wasn't inclined to let a little curse stop him from making a profit.

Another memory hits me—shoes. I used to make horseshoes for the horses we kept back then. And once I made a pair for me. Heavy, iron shoes that made a thundering clop when I walked.

I made a lot of things in this shop, now that I think about it. I smile a little, still puffing on my pipe, enjoying the memories of crafty, skilled younger me.

The shop wasn't anywhere close to where I last left it. It's on the very edge of the property now, almost overrun with trees. I didn't notice it before, but all the original buildings are on the perimeter—almost pushed up against the wall.

The old kitchen is out here too, a big outdoor oven made of bricks and stone. Something that was quite nice back in semi-arid and hot Italy, but serves no purpose here in Pennsylvania. It's crumbling, anyway.

There's an old stone barn with a thatched roof as well. The first caretaker I had here in the New World was a shepherd and kept sheep. He loved those stupid sheep and used to make a very fine wool that he traded for meat at the local market—trying to keep his debt down, probably. There was no Granite Springs back then. That place popped up sometime in the late nineteenth century. But there were small clusters of farms and an outpost where people gathered for trade.

The stone walls of the sheep barn are also crumbling and the roof has almost disintegrated.

But the smithy shop—it looks exactly the way I left it.

Magic. That's how that happens. The smithy is filled with magic because it's mine. And I think I knew this, but had forgotten.

I casually wonder what else I've forgotten.

But then I remember why I'm here. The forge has been going for a couple hours now. It's time to get to work.

I leave the roof by a set of circular stairs that dump me out into the main room of the shop, then go over to the forge and stoke the yellow-hot coals in the center, piling them up into a slightly bigger mound.

As I do this, another memory hits me. Bloodhorn. I used to put bloodhorn in my chainmail to make it stronger. That was so long ago—way, way before anyone ever heard of the Americas.

This makes me think of the spell in the book. Dragon fire. I wonder what kind of magic I can put in this bag by using bloodhorn fire. It's my magic, after all. It's always better to use your own magic, when you can. I'm not going to leave out the dragon fire—I'm absolutely positive I can convince Tomas to belch up a little flame for me—but if you're a monster made of hellfire, you might as well use that too.

I look at my neatly hanging set of tools on the wall, choose a rasp, and then lean over the fire and file off a good portion of the tip of one horn. It's an awkward thing to do, but the fire sparks and sputters with each sprinkle of horn powder, turning it a bright and beautiful shade of royal purple.

Satisfied, I walk over to a barrel in the corner where there are dozens of iron rods waiting to be forged into something useful. I'm just about to grab one when I spot a cup of copper rods hiding in the back. They are very thin rods. The perfect diameter for chainmail rings, actually.

But it would be too soft. Copper is a decoration when it's this thin, not what you would use for protection. An iron bag with copper accents, though. Now that sounds nice. Something I could even be proud of.

I grab the cup of copper, plus a few iron rods, and take it all over to the forge. I do the iron work first. Heat it up, and then start cutting small strips to make rings. It only takes me a few minutes to realize I will be here for days making enough rings for a small chainmail bag. But oddly, this doesn't bother me. In fact, I settle into the work, my muscles remembering what to do. Automatically reaching for the right hammer, chisel, tongs, and cone to bend the iron just the way I want it.

I lose myself in time. Enjoying the work. Wondering why I ever stopped doing this.

By the time I look up to find a winged monster in my doorway, it's late afternoon. He says something to me, his bat wings lifting up and falling down with his speech patterns. Of course, I don't understand his words, but I think I get the gist of it.

It's time to stop. He wants me to go back to the cathedral.

At first, I'm disappointed that I have to leave. I'm into it. I want to keep going. I was always that way with projects. Once I get started, I'm super-focused on finishing. In the old days I used to sleep in the shop, sometimes working until morning and only taking breaks when I was too exhausted to continue. But Pie will probably be home soon and I don't care how much I like the blacksmithing—I won't be sleeping out here. I can't wait to get in bed with her tonight.

So I nod at him, point at my forge, and say, "I'll be up in a minute. I have to close the fire."

The monster is satisfied with this answer and leaves.

For all the dozens and dozens of years between this day and the last time I was in this shop, none of what I've done today required much thought. It was all instinct. And closing the fire—without fully putting it out so it will be easier to start back up tomorrow— is also done on instinct.

I like this. It allows my mind to wander. To ponder. To think.

And I did a lot of thinking today. Mostly about the past and how, even though I have been cursed practically my entire life, it hasn't been all bad. It's been a while since I had a sense of purpose. But being here in the smithy was a good reminder that I have value. I can do things. I can contribute.

In fact, before Grant, I was a very active participant in the whole curse-breaking goal. Things changed when he got here. And now that I find myself on the other side of Grant's influence, I wonder if he didn't do that to me—didn't make me this apathetic asshole waiting to be freed—on purpose.

To keep me out of the way.

I take off my heavy leather apron, smile down at my pants—because even though they are dirty, and sweaty, and now black with charcoal dust, they are going to make Pie smile too—and then pat my pocket for the bag of rings.

It's gone.

My head whips around. But that fear subsides when I see the bag sitting on the edge of the water barrel in the corner. I walk over, pluck it up in my hand, then go over to a set of leather straps hanging on the far side of the shop, fashion a tether, and tie the stupid bag to my belt loop before shoving it back into my pocket.

Just a few days. That's how long it will take me to finish this magical bag if I work diligently. And then I can stop worrying about magic rings.

I stop at Tarq's tomb on my way back to the cathedral and find the winged monster. He says something to me, which I interpret as *Pie isn't back yet.* And I nod at him, suddenly getting an idea.

Her first day of work. She was so strung out about it this morning, and while I'm sure it wasn't entirely terrible—Tarq is a really good guy, despite her misgivings—she deserves a special evening.

A celebration of sorts. To commemorate her first work day as a magical being.

I was just planning on taking her back to the cottage, throwing her down on the bed, and fucking her brains out, but I suddenly have a better idea.

A romantic idea.

I point to the monster. "I have something to do real quick. If Pie comes home before I get back, tell her to meet me in the cathedral."

The monster nods and I start up the hill.

The little patio space directly outside the back of the cathedral is bustling with monsters doing various things. I don't pay any attention to them, but that's mostly because the black tomb is suddenly right in my face and I remember that I was going to check it out.

I don't have time right now, so I just slip past everyone, go inside, up the stairs, and pretend I don't hear Tomas calling me from the front hall when I enter the hallway leading to the Pleasure Cave.

Pie needs a hoof massage after a long day of work. Maybe a hornjob, too. This makes me chuckle. And I want to get the place all romantic and shit before I bring her up here.

"Pell!" Tomas is following me.

"I'm busy."

"That's fine, but the monsters want you to join them for dinner. There's a huge feast to celebrate the arrival of hay."

"No," I growl. "I'm spending this evening with Pie."

"Pie's coming too."

"No, she's not. She'll be with me."

"Don't be absurd. Batty is already waiting for her at the tomb door so he can invite her. She won't say no."

I'm plucking candles out of a wooden box when he says this. I pause. Because he's right. If that bat monster gets to her before I do, and invites her to dinner, we'll have to go. Because she will say yes.

And it's not even like I *can* see her first because I can't be at the tomb when she comes back. The door spells won't allow it.

"Fuck." I sigh.

"It's a nice dinner," Tomas proclaims. "Baked lasagna with a green salad and garlic bread."

"Hmm."

"Sounds good, doesn't it?"

I won't admit it, but it does sound good. Pie is kind of a terrible cook. But this Cookie Monster, he's like a fucking five-star chef. "All right," I growl again. "We'll go to dinner. But afterward, you will leave us alone."

"Oh, don't worry about me. I have a date tonight."

I'm placing the candles on various rock ledges when he says this, but I pause again. "What?"

"Madeline and I have a date."

"Who the fuck is Madeline?"

"The girl from the feed store."

I let out a long breath. "What the hell is wrong with you?"

"What?" He truly looks perplexed.

"You can't date someone from Granite Springs. That whole town is a bunch of clandestine eros."

"Don't be ridiculous. She's not an eros. Neither of us fell in love with her at first sight."

"Hello? You're going on a date with her tonight."

"But I'm not in love with her. I just need to start somewhere."

I make a face at him. "You know what? Whatever. You're not my responsibility, Tomas. Do whatever you want."

"Thank you. I will." He pauses, watching me place candles. "What are you doing?"

"Creating a romantic atmosphere."

"Oh, that's lovely. Pie is going to adore this. She makes you a better monster. You know that, right?"

I do know this. But I'm not going to admit it to Tomas. "Light candles or go away. I'm busy here."

"I'll leave you to it." And he disappears.

But a few moments later, when I'm looking through our box of pastes, the eyebrow monster appears. I'm just about to growl a fuck-off warning at him when I notice he's got two fluffy, white robes in his hands. He holds them up for my inspection with a wild grin on his face.

I force myself to be polite. "Are those for us?"

He nods.

"Thank you."

He nods again. Then hangs them from a hook and walks out.

No sooner is he gone than another monster appears.

"Now what?" My growl is even more growly than usual. Because at this point, I'm more than annoyed. I'm starting to get pissed off.

This is one of the apothecary monsters. He's holding two jars of paste. He thrusts them at me and I take them.

"What is this?" I ask. He lifts the lid off one and the smell escapes, filling the entire cave with the scent of honeysuckle. "Oh," I say. "That's kind of nice. Pie will love it."

He caps that jar, then lifts the lid on the other. Immediately the scent changes to eucalyptus. Then he points a finger at me and winks.

I can't help myself. I smile. Because I see what he's done here. The honeysuckle paste is for Pie, to ease her tension and relax her after a long day. But the eucalyptus is for me. Well, for Pie too. It's so she can polish my horns without burning her hands.

He puts the lid back on and nods.

"Thanks," I say, holding up both jars. "That was nice." He doesn't leave though. He waits. Like he needs something from me. "What?"

He makes a motion of eating.

"Oh. Fine. I told Tomas we'd come. So we will."

This satisfies him. Because he turns on his hoof and leaves.

Once he's gone, I take the pastes over to the wooden box and set them inside. It's a good thing he brought them because the box was empty. Those apothecary monsters were thorough. They threw out everything.

I guess maybe I should reluctantly admit that they are not all bad.

In fact, the sanctuary is starting to run like a well-oiled machine these days. And as far as my life goes—yeah. I smile big thinking about how my life has changed in the last month.

It's good.

No. It's… nearly perfect.

I can leave whenever I want and even though I don't like looking like a human on the outside, it does make things a whole lot easier.

And Pie. Yeah, it sucks that she has to work for Tarq. And the Book of Debt, of course. Everything about her slave status is horrible.

But she's here and she's mine.

All mine.

And even though I would prefer it if we could spend our days together, everyone knows that absence makes the heart grow fonder. So every night she will come home to me, excited about her day, wanting to know about mine, and we will take the nightly meal together, and sleep in our little cottage, and wake up in each other's arms each morning.

Just like a real couple.

Yeah. My life is going pretty damn good.

I light up the rest of the candles, then walk to the door and turn around, taking in the scene.

It's nice.

Pie's going to love it.

CHAPTER THIRTEEN – PIE

I turn away from the lab door and look out the window again, trying not to cry. I'm happy for Pia. I am. She's been living in the wrong world her entire life and it's great that she now feels at home.

I love it.

I want this for her.

But. Am I not allowed to want things for me too?

There are good things in this new life. Pell, for one. Just thinking about him makes me relax a little. He feels like my home base now. And I miss him. I wish he could be here with me because, to be honest, I could get used to this place too. I could be happy here, I think. I fit in, at least. But without Pell I'm adrift again. And I know that it's only been weeks since I first stumbled into Saint Mark's, and a lot of that was really stressful, but Pell was there. He was grumpy in the beginning, but after I went on the date with Russ Roth and came home crying, I saw that other side to him. The protective side. The hidden side. There's a lot more to him than meets the eye. And I barely know anything about his past. But I want to know. I want to know all of it. I think I love him. Like… for real love him.

And now stupid Tarq comes in and lays all this princess shit on me, telling me I'm his?

And ya know what the worst thing is? He's really not a dick. He was pretty understanding today. He could've gotten aggressive and possessive about his side of the story, but he didn't. He backed away. He gave me space. And maybe it's an act. It could be. Maybe tomorrow he'll change his mind about slowly unraveling my part in things and lay all kinds of disturbing new things on me.

But he didn't do that today so it's kinda hard to hate him even if he does own my debt and I am, technically speaking, his slave.

"Oooo!" I look over at the table. "The book!" I had forgotten about it. But Tarq said there were new debts in there and I should look it over before I leave.

That's not ominous at all.

And just as I was beginning to find a bright side, the dark desperation is back. I slump, ready to monkey-walk. But thinking those words makes me smile and then I actually chuckle.

"Pie," I tell myself. "You need to grow up now."

And my internal monologue is right. I do. I've been a scatterbrained weirdo for far too long. It's time to settle into whoever I am and deal with it.

So I walk over to the table, flip open the book, and find my debt.

I have a lot of it now, so I have to flip three pages to get to the new stuff.

"A truck?" I can't help it, I laugh. It's so absurd. Someone at home bought a truck. Then I see the hay and it makes sense.

I flip the book closed and then just kind of stand there in the middle of the lab, looking around, but not really seeing anything. I should go home. I think I was dismissed and I need to be back with my people.

But I can't seem to muster up the energy to go into the hallways and find my way to the lobby where the door is. It all sounds so… exhausting.

"Excuse me."

I turn around and find Luciano standing in the doorway. "Oh. Hey."

"Tarq mentioned that you'd come looking for the door soon. And I waited, but you didn't show up."

"Yeah. I wasn't sure how to get there."

"You don't need to know how to get there, Pie."

"What do you mean?"

"It's magic. You just think where you want to go and the hallways will get you there."

"Who controls them, Luciano? How does it work?"

Luciano shrugs. "Who knows? How does anything work?"

"So that's it, then? This world is just filled with… what, magic thoughts?"

"Most people aren't like you, Pie. Or me. Or Tarq. Or… anyone else who works in this building. Most people are normal."

"What do you mean? What's normal here?"

"You know. People who go about their lives mostly doing what they want."

"I don't get it."

"People who…" He pauses to think. "People who don't have a destination."

"Destination? You mean destiny?"

"No. A destination. A place to be."

"Doesn't everyone have a place to be?" I still don't get it.

"Of course. Normal places. They need to be at work. Or home. They need to meet friends, or pick up children, or attend school. But you don't have those destinations. You have other destinations."

All right. I've had enough. So I put up a hand to stop him. "Ya know what, Luciano? I'm done for today. Can you please take me to the door? I'd like to go home."

"Sure." He smiles. I like him, I guess. He's kind of a cliché mobster type, but whatever. "Follow me."

I grab my bag, sling it over my shoulder, then follow him into the hallway. It's not an elevator or a long corridor this time. It's a few steps to another massive double door and that's it. Luciano opens them both at the same time in a very dramatic fashion, and then there I am. In the reception area. Right where I'm supposed to be.

"You have your key?" Luciano asks.

I pull my necklace out of my shirt and hold it up. "I do." Then I look around. "But there's no door, Luciano. Where do I go?"

He points to the spot where I came in this morning. "Right over there. I have to go back to my desk to open the portal. Then you can step through."

I know I shouldn't ask because this question will just lead me to a hundred more, but I do anyway. "How does it work?"

"The portal?"

I nod.

"Well, normally we can't just open them. Anything could come through."

"What?" I don't like the sound of that.

"But," Luciano continues without acknowledging my question, "if someone has a key, then I can unlock it, and it will open."

"So you can only open it if I'm standing nearby?"

"Correct."

"Interesting."

"Sure," Luciano says. Then he turns towards his reception desk, but stops and looks over his shoulder. "You're coming back tomorrow, right?"

"Why wouldn't I?"

He shoots me a grin, which is kind of smarmy and not really charming. But it's not a bad grin. "Because I'm sure you've figured out by now that we can't come get you. You're on the honor system."

I knew he was lying earlier when he made that veiled threat to organize a kidnapping. But I don't bother with that. What's the point? Instead, I ask a new question. "What happens to my debt if I never come back?"

"I wouldn't know," he admits. "But I don't think it would be anything good."

"No. Of course it wouldn't."

"So... I'll see you tomorrow." Then he really does walk off.

And I do too. Turning in the opposite direction. I walk to the far corner where I came in to this world two times already. And just as I approach, the tomb door appears.

And waiting on the other side is...

Well.

Everyone.

My bad day falls away and I practically run through with a huge smile on my face.

Pell is there, grinning at me from a rooftop several tombs back, looking even more charming and handsome than when I left him. And all the monsters—like... *all* the monsters. Eyebrows, and Cookie, and Batty—are right up front. They rush up to me, like I missed a big day of happenings and they want to tell me all the things, even though I can't understand a word they say.

But as soon as I'm home, Pell jumps across the rooftops separating us, leaps down to the ground, pushes them away, and takes me in his arms. "How was it? Did you see Tarq? Did you eat? Are you hungry? The monsters made dinner. They want us to eat with them tonight. I have a surprise for you."

I just lean up on my tiptoes and kiss him.

He kisses me back like there isn't a mob of monsters around us and when we pull apart, I sigh. "I missed you too."

His yellow eyes brighten and the bloodfire inside his horns glows a little. His body is blackened with soot and he smells like smoke. "I like reunions."

"Why are you all black? And why do you smell like smoke?"

"Oh." He snaps his fingers and shakes his head. Then his eyes go all sneaky as they sweep across all the monsters. "We had another… incident."

"Incident?" My eyebrows go up.

"The r-i-n-g-s."

"I think they can spell, Pell."

"Right." He looks at the monsters again. "Well, she's home. Thank you for coming. We'll meet you in the dining room."

None of the monsters move. In fact, Batty comes right up to me with his hand out, talking in his monster language.

"What's he saying?" I ask. "Where's Tomas?"

That's when I hear the rumble of a truck on the other side of the wall. And when I look down the hill towards the parking lot, I see it drive away.

"Oh, that." Pell sighs. "We bought a truck today."

"I saw. It showed up in the Book of Debt."

"It's a long story, but Tomas learned how to drive and found a girlfriend."

"What?" I laugh this word out.

"Yep. He's got a date tonight."

"Well, look at him being all grown up and shit."

Batty is still talking.

"I'm sorry, Batty. I don't understand you and Tomas isn't here to translate."

He holds out his palm and makes a little circle with his thumb and forefinger with the other, then points to my bag.

"Oh. The rock?"

He nods enthusiastically.

I fish through my bag, find the sandstone rock, and plunk it into his outstretched palm. Several other monsters rush up to him, chatting excitedly.

"What's that about?" Pell asks.

"Hell if I know." I turn to him and smile again, so happy to be home. Then I notice something. "Pell! You're wearing pants!"

He beams a smile at me, like he's been waiting all day to show me his pants. "I needed pockets. For the bag of r-i-n-g-s."

I sigh. And giggle. "I'm so happy to be home."

He grins back at me as he takes my hand and starts leading me towards the cathedral. "Tell me all about your day." But then he stops. "Hey. Where's Pia? She went with you, right?"

"She did," I nod. "But she's staying there. She can talk again. But only when she's there, so…"

"Huh. That's good, I guess."

"It's great!" But my enthusiasm is fake and it shows.

"Aww," Pell says. "You're sad about that."

"Yeah. It was kinda fun in the beginning. Pia could talk, I made a friend—a whole group of them, actually. I got coffee. I saw the city. But—" I stop. Because it feels like a long story and I don't want to tell it now. "You know what? Never mind that place. It's a job. That's all. This is home. I want to know what happened here today. You didn't really explain the soot."

He proceeds to tell me about the bag of rings and how he went looking for a spell. Then his idea to make a bag of chainmail.

"You're a blacksmith?"

"Yeah. I'm pretty good at it too. It was kind of nice to work again after all these centuries."

I am already holding his arm with both hands, but I lean in to his shoulder and sigh. "I missed you. Did I mention that?"

I'm not looking at his face but I know this made him smile. "You did." And then we're at the cathedral doors and he opens them for me. We step through together and the smell of cooking food is strong, wafting down from the center staircase like a siren song.

My stomach grumbles and I'm suddenly starving.

All the monsters crowd us as we ascend the stairs as a mob, but when we get to the upper level, I have to stop to take it all in. Gone is the empty space and in its place is a collection of massive dining tables. Each one seats eight, or ten, or twelve. And each one is covered with platters of food. Lots of green stuff that looks like hay, but then again, doesn't look like hay at all. It's like a professional chef cooked the hay with spices and arranged the platters with herbs and vegetables. There are side dishes of potatoes, and radishes, and turnips. There's meat too. And breads, and cakes, and fruit.

"Wow," Pell says.

"I take it you didn't know about this?"

"Tomas mentioned we were having dinner with them tonight, but I didn't imagine it would be this big of a production."

Production is the right word, too. Cookie is now clapping his hands, directing other monsters to do things. And every one is taking a seat. Pell and I start towards two chairs, planning on sitting together, but a couple of monsters gently lead us in opposite directions.

We are taken to the largest table that seats twelve. Pell at one end, me at the other. Not very far apart— maybe fifteen feet—but it feels way too far away.

We sit, and drinks are poured while everyone else finds their seats.

Pell lifts up a golden goblet twinkling with jewels. He winks at me. Grins, too.

Man, I missed him. I don't care what kind of stuff is in that other world. He is my new home.

I lift my goblet up too and we do a mock 'cheers'. The other monsters join in, and goblets clink against each other. But my eyes are locked with Pell's as we drink.

Pell is my home.

CHAPTER FOURTEEN – TOMAS

My second driving experience starts out only marginally better than the first, but once again I thwart the ditch's attempt at snaring me and my vehicle and arrive in town on time.

This pleases me to no end. In fact, I'm very proud of myself.

They said it would be hard.

Liars.

I have conquered the driving demons like a dragon warrior.

Which I am. So that makes sense.

The feed store is closed when I arrive, but Madeline is standing out in the parking lot. I pull in— nervously, I do admit. But not because I'm a terrible parker. I've just never been on a date before.

My palms are sweaty and my heart is beating curiously fast.

But I am a dragon. I might not look like one on the outside, but it's what's on the inside that counts. So I take a deep breath, get out of the truck, and meet Madeline in the middle of the parking lot with booming confidence.

"Hey," she says, smiling at me in that way she does. "Aren't you going to turn your truck off?"

She points to my truck. Which is still running. Oops. I hold up a finger, trot back over, snatch the keys out, and return to my waiting love.

All better.

Madeline giggles at me. "You're getting the hang of it, I see."

"I am. Learning to drive was not a formidable opponent."

"What?" She giggles again. "You just learned to drive? How old are you, Tomas?"

Shit. I did not plan on probing questions. But I am nothing if not clever. So I deflect. "How old are you?"

She twirls a piece of her long, strawberry hair between her fingers and swivels her hips as she grins wildly. "How old do I look?"

Damn. She's a good deflector as well. I put on my confident face. "Sixty-two."

My lovely Madeline guffaws. "You're fun, Tomas."

"Thank you. I do my best."

"Are you hungry?"

Finally. A question I can answer with certainty. "Famished."

She grabs my hand and tugs. "Come on then. Let's go eat at the diner. I skipped lunch today." And then she starts telling me all about her day. Things I don't really care about, or understand, but I've always been very good at pretending to be interested in people. Maybe I haven't gotten out much in the past few thousand years, but I've practiced being social with a plethora of slave caretakers. Plus, Pell. He counts. And all the new monsters have been interesting.

When we arrive at the diner we are seated at a booth and handed menus. Pell took me out to dinner a couple weeks ago, so I have actually been here before and understand that a menu is something with food on it. And you are to pick what you want from the list.

"I will have the Fun Burger with a strawberry milkshake," I tell the waitress.

She giggles at me. "That your usual now, Tomas?"

Oooh. She remembers me. I am pleased. "Yes," I tell her. They serve the burger open-faced and there are eyeballs and a smile drawn on the top in ketchup and mustard. "I find it delightful."

The waitress, who is wearing a name badge declaring her to be called Sassy, giggles again. Then pushes my dear Madeline in the shoulder. "Be nice to him, Mad Dog. Or I'll snatch him up when you're not looking."

Madeline chuckles.

"Mad Dog?" I ask.

"Oh, that's what we called Madeline in school. She was Mad Dog Madeline on the boys' wrestling team."

"Really?" I am impressed. "You're a rough-and-tumble girl, are you?" Both females snicker at me. "What? What did I miss?"

"Nothing," Madeline says. "I'll have the fried chicken, Sassy. Make it extra crispy. And fries on the side."

"Do I get fries, Sassy?"

They snicker at me again.

Sassy pats my shoulder. "Kids' meals come with the fries, sweetie." Then she walks off, shaking her head.

"She's nice," I say.

Madeline sighs. "You know why I like you, Tomas?"

"Tell me. I'm dying to know what people think of me."

"You're not afraid to be yourself, are you?"

"Why would I be?"

"See?" She points at me. "That. That right there. You're very confident."

I puff up my chest a little, which is filling out this tight t-shirt spectacularly. All those years of working out have suddenly paid off now that I've gotten my hands on some real human clothes.

"You're not from here, though, are you?"

"How do you know that?"

"Your accent. It's... what? English?"

"English?" I make a face. "Do I sound like a Saxon?"

Madeline snorts. "A what?"

"I'm..." But I have to stop here. I'm not actually sure what I am or what this accent is. In fact... "Do I have an accent?"

Madeline reaches over the table to playfully slap me on the shoulder. "You're too funny."

I smile. "Thank you."

"But seriously, who are you and where did you come from? I've never seen you in town before today."

"Oh, I've been here before. But I don't get here much."

"You don't live in town, though. Right?"

"No. I live..." I point in some random direction. "Out that way."

"And that guy you were with today? Who was he?"

"Oh. That's Pell. He's my… friend."

"You don't sound very sure of yourself."

"Oh, I am. We're friends. Best friends, actually."

"Well, he might be your friend, but he's definitely not friendly."

"No." Now it's my turn to chuckle. "He's not. He's a grumpy monster. But he has a good heart and he loves Pie."

"What kind of pie?"

"What? Oh, no. My other friend. She is called Pie."

Madeline lets out a long breath and leans back into the booth, grinning at me like a salacious flirt. "You have two friends and they are called Pie and Pell. That's amazing. Where have you been all my life, Tomas?"

"Oh. I've been in the same place. Just down that way a bit." I point in that random direction again.

"Well, I'm very glad you came in to the feed store this morning. I like you."

I grin, feeling very successful. It's not that hard to be human, now is it? Pell could take lessons from me.

"I need to get your number before I forget," she says. And then she pulls out a pocket phone like the one Pie carries around. "What is it?"

"What is what?"

"Your number."

"What number?"

"Your phone number."

"I don't have one."

"What?" She blinks at me. "What do you mean? You don't have a phone?"

"No."

"Um. OK. How come?"

"Well. I've never needed one."

"But you live outside town, right?"

"Yes. About twenty miles."

"And you don't carry a phone. What if you break down?"

"Break down?"

"You know. That old truck you have can't be that reliable. If you break down, then what? You can't call anyone without a phone."

"So… I *need* a phone?"

"Everybody needs a phone. It's like… having a TV or a car. You just… need one."

"A TV?"

Her mouth drops open. "You don't have a TV?"

I don't really know what a TV is, but I'm fairly sure we do not have one. "We don't have electricity," I tell her. "At the… at home."

Her eyes go wide with excitement. "You live off-grid?"

I nod, not really sure what that means, either.

"Wow. That's kinda cool. It's very trendy to live off-grid these days. How do you cook?"

"We have a stove. It eats wood and makes fire."

"Wow," she says again. Only this time, she sighs the word out. "And what about lights? No lights, then?"

"Fire."

She snaps her fingers. "Oh. They have those cool solar lanterns now. You just set them in the sun and they light up at night."

"Really?"

"Oh, yeah. They have a ton of solar shit these days. They even have solar generators. We have three of them for camping. My brothers are always getting new gadgets for camping like that. They're big into the survival scene. And my uncle owns the Kitchen Sink down on the edge of town."

"The Kitchen Sink?"

"It's like a... like a military surplus store? For Shit Hits the Fan types."

I have no idea what she's going on about. But she's excited about it, so I pretend to be as well. "That's amazing."

"We could go there and check it out if you want."

"Go..."

"To the Kitchen Sink."

"For..."

"I can get you a discount. He sells phones, and generators, and solar panels."

I'm lost now. Completely lost. I will have to quiz Pie on all these things when I get home.

Thankfully, this conversation is cut short when the waitress appears with our food.

"We can go after we're done eating," Madeline says.

Or not.

"OK?"

I nod, clueless.

I hold out hope that Madeline will forget about the kitchen sink and we will take a romantic walk to the park. But after we're done eating, she directs me outside to my truck.

"It's not really walking distance from here. We should drive," she says.

So I have no choice but to go along.

It's only a few miles down the highway. And I only make one driving mistake, something Madeline calls 'blowing through a stop sign,' and in just a few minutes we're in the parking lot of an old mechanic shop with a huge, hand-painted sign that says, 'Kitchen Sink'.

I point at the sign. "I don't understand this name."

"Oh." Madeline laughs. "You know that saying, 'Everything and the kitchen sink?' It's like a junk drawer in a building."

"Oh." I still don't understand. But once we're out of the truck and standing in the parking lot, Madeline takes my hand in hers and I feel like this is the real beginning of our romantic evening.

I smile at her and she smiles back. "I like you, Tomas."

I feel a swell of happiness when these words come out. "I like you too, Madeline."

She shrugs up her shoulders, grinning wide, and then leads me into the store.

"Big Jim!" she yells, once we're inside. "Big Jim!"

"Who is Big Jim?"

"My uncle," she says, then belts out, "I brought you a customer!"

No one answers.

"He's probably on the shitter," Madeline says. I make a face and she laughs. "You're not used to people like us, are you?"

"I'm more of a loner," I say, not wanting to hurt her feelings. But she's right. I'm not used to people like her at all. It's nothing personal. The only humans I've ever had contact with were all slave caretakers.

"Well, if I get too crude for you, just poke me and I'll settle down. I have five brothers so I'm not really a girly-girl. But"—she holds up a finger—"I do like men. You know. In *that* way."

I smile at her. Placating. Secretly wishing that we were somewhere else. But she starts looking around, then points to an aisle filled with large black box things.

"There. Those are the solar generators. Wanna check one out?"

I hesitate, not sure what a solar generator is or why I need one.

"Oh. I'm so stupid," she says. "They're super-expensive. I'm sorry. I'm not trying to pressure you into spending money you don't have."

"Oh, I have plenty of money. That's not it."

She brightens. "Oh, good. But…" Then her face falls again. "Then what is it?"

I want to come up with a lie that will explain my confusion at all these new, modern contraptions. But I can't think of anything. So I just blurt out the truth. "I don't know what any of this stuff is. Or what it does. Or why I would need it."

"Oh." Once again, she brightens. "Well. I can explain it all, if you want."

I would much rather be taking a much-fantasized-about romantic walk in the town park while holding her hand and dreaming about my first real kiss—because that kiss with Pie doesn't count. But I agree. "OK. Please do."

And thirty minutes later my world is... *transformed*.

Electricity can be mined from the sun and captured in one of these black boxes. And if one owns a black box, one can plug things in.

Things like... radios. And computers. And phones. And toasters, and heating pads, and kettles.

Big Jim finally appears once I have all my things on the counter, ready to pay.

"Is this all for you?" he says. His voice is gruff and rustic, like his person. And he talks the same way the sheriff does. He is a massive man. Much taller than me, and I'm very tall. But he is wide, too, and has a gray beard that stretches down to his chest. His bib overalls are light denim and one of the straps is undone and hanging down the side of his pot belly, allowing me to glimpse a picture of an eagle printed in white on a black t-shirt and the letters 'SHTF' over the top of it.

I look around the store, wondering if I should buy more things. I can't wait to get it all home. We have attempted to wire in electricity at the sanctuary in the past, and it would work for a short period of time. But then, of course, the curse would break it.

I tried explaining this to Madeline, but she said there are no wires to power the generator. It's all energy from the sun. Which has not been tried yet at our sanctuary, and we do have sun, so I'm taking a chance.

I'm also racking up a considerable amount of debt in Pie's book. The generator is not cheap—I chose the biggest, bestest one. Plus, two solar panels. This is a new word for me, but apparently, they are the prison that captures the sun's light and puts it into the black box.

I will find a way to pay Pie back. I will.

"I see you are a radio fan," Big Jim says, pointing at my new radio.

I nod, unsure what to say. There are tiny musicians inside this little box. Madeline says all you have to do is fiddle with the dials and music comes out of it.

"Well," Big Jim continues, "I just so happen to have a public access radio show every night from midnight to three in the morning on 623 AM." He points at me. "You should tune in. An off-gridder like yourself will find my topics of discussion *veeeeeeer*-ry enlightening."

I point back at him. "I will do that." Even though I have no idea what 623 AM means. But that's OK. I am thinking about how I will serve tea made in an electric kettle and peanut butter toast made in a toaster tonight when I tell my new monster friends all about my night on the town.

I hand over my slip of paper that says 'money' on it, and then Big Jim helps me put all my new things in the cab of the truck.

Once that's done, he goes back inside. So Madeline and I are alone.

"So." She smiles at me.

"So, indeed," I reply back.

"It was kind of a weird first date, I guess. But that's OK, right?"

"I do admit, it didn't happen the way I pictured it."

She blushes a little, uses the tip of her boot to trace a line in the dirt as she hides her face from me. "How did you picture it?"

"Oh. Hand-holding," I say. "And we did that, so that was nice." Madeline looks up from her feet, grinning. "And a walk through the park. And then, maybe…"

She blinks at me.

And I decide that Madeline, while maybe not completely my type, is very pretty in her own, wild way. She doesn't paint her face, her jeans are old and worn, her boots are dusty, and she never even took off her work jacket while we ate, but I find myself *wanting* to look at her.

"Maybe what?" she says.

"Maybe a kiss good night would complete this first attempt at romance."

"You have a nice way with words." Then she grins. And shrugs. "We still have time for that." Her cheeks go even pinker. "Right now, if you want."

My heart begins to flutter. My palms become sweaty. But I take a few steps towards her, until we are so close, she has to tip her head up to look me in the eyes.

And then… then something magical happens. Cold, wet flakes begin to fall from the sky.

I look up and Madeline giggles. "The first snow of the year."

Snow. I've heard the word, of course. And I've seen it before too. But it doesn't snow inside the gates of Saint Mark's. The sun always shines when it's daytime and the temperature doesn't deviate much.

I look back down at Madeline. "It's a sign."

Her eyes are bright. Almost mischievous. "A sign of what?"

"A new beginning, I think."

She must like this answer because she places both her hands on my shoulders and leans up on her tiptoes.

I lean down to meet her. And when our lips touch it's nothing at all like the kiss I had with Pie.

It's so. Much. Better.

A soft and gentle kiss. So contrary to the wild and rugged girl on the outside. Madeline's mouth opens a little, her lips parting just enough to let the tip of her tongue sweep against mine.

Immediately heat floods my body and when she pulls back, I am breathless.

Madeline sighs. "I like you, Tomas. You're not like other guys I know."

I crinkle up my eyebrows, wondering what that means. Does she know? Can she tell I'm not human? "What do you mean by that?"

"You're…" She sighs again. "*Very* good-looking. Ya know? I'm sure you know that. But you don't act like one of those very good-looking guys, Tomas."

"Thank you for the compliment. But how do these good-looking men act?"

"You know. Like they *know* they're good-looking. All stuck up. Way too good for a girl like me."

I am bewildered. "Too good for a girl like *you*? You seem like a very good girl to me."

"Oh"—she chuckles—"I *am* a good girl. That's the problem. They want to do a lot more than kissing."

"Oh." I nod. "I see. It's a lot of pressure?"

"Kinda." She shrugs. "But that's not really what I meant. I'm not against"—she shakes her head a little—"you know. *Sex*." She whispers that word. And I find this entire conversation adorable. "It's just. I'm an old-fashioned girl. I want something real. And all the guys I know from growing up, they want something fake."

I don't understand. Isn't everything real? How could things be fake? But I can ask Pie about this later. And I don't want to spoil the moment. So I say, "I think I understand."

"Yeah. So." She points to the store. "Our house is actually through the woods there. So you don't need to take me home. I'm just gonna stay here and help my uncle close up."

"The date is over?" I ask.

She nods. "I think so. It was kinda boring?"

"Not at all."

"You're just saying that."

I take her hand. Because she has gone from a confident, wild and rugged girl to a shy, uncertain one. And I don't want to leave her this way. "Madeline," I say, looking her in the eyes. "Nothing about this date was boring. I have enjoyed it. Immensely. And would love to do it again."

"Yeah?"

"Yes."

"Only next time, I won't take you shopping at my uncle's stupid store."

I have a sudden urge to kiss her again. And I think she's thinking the same thing, because when I lean down, she leans up, and this time our mouths are open when our lips touch.

It's a long kiss, too. A passionate one. A kiss filled with promises of more to come.

And when we break away, we're both breathing heavy.

She backs away from me, but doesn't turn. "How about tomorrow? Dinner again? I get off at seven."

I point at her. "It's a date."

"It's a date," she echoes. Then she turns and disappears into the store.

CHAPTER FIFTEEN – PELL

Even though Pie and I can't understand the monsters without Tomas, it's an enjoyable meal. The room is loud with foreign conversation and the monsters at our table make an effort to include us in their dialogue. They point at us. They nudge us. They have a good laugh at our expense.

But it's all fun. Their eyes are bright, their smiles wide, and the food is very good.

Even though I don't eat hay, the dishes that Cookie whipped up using those dry, dusty bales we found at the feed store are appetizing enough to tempt even me.

Though I don't try them.

He made me a roast with tiny potatoes on the side and a sauce that I might dream about tonight.

I'm sipping wine, looking down the length of the table at Pie—who is nodding, and smiling, and paying close attention to a story the monster to her right is telling—when I suddenly realize this meal might be magic.

Then I realize I don't think I care if it is.

Grant's magic food, that makes me sick to think about. Whatever spells he was working on me with the food could not have been good.

But if Cookie is working magic into his meals, it's good magic. It makes people happy. And anyway, it's not really the food that has lifted my mood today. It's everything. The blacksmithing, and Pie, and even Tomas's date tonight.

We're building something here and it's good.

I finish my wine, dab my mouth with a napkin, and catch Pie's eye from the other end of the table.

She scoots her chair back and rises.

I do the same.

There is some protesting from a few of the monsters. And I don't need to understand their language to know what they're saying. *Stay. Don't leave. Be with us.*

But Pie and I have been apart the entire day, so their good-natured objections have no chance.

I meet Pie in the middle of the table. I take her hand without a word and lead her out of the dining room. But instead of going down the stairs to the lower level, I lead her into the Pleasure Cave hallway.

"Where are we going?"

I glance over my shoulder at her, grinning. "In about ten seconds you'll know."

She chuckles. "Pleasure Cave it is."

We enter the cave together, but she stops short. "Holy crap, Pell." Her eyes sweep up to mine, bright and blue. "This is… romantic."

I glance around the room. There are dozens and dozens of wax pillars, still lit, but melting. Drips of wax slide down the columns. The flickering glow of firelight bounces off the cave walls. Just the right amount of shadows to play with our imaginations.

It *is* romantic.

"There's more," I say, walking over to the tray of pots. "Look. The apothecary geniuses made us new salves. One for you." I hold the honeysuckle pot up to her nose.

She sniffs and sighs. "Mmm, that smells good."

"And one for me. Well, they're both for you, I guess. This one will protect your hands from my fire."

Pie giggles. "I guess there's a hornjob in your future."

"I guess there is." I waggle my eyebrows at her. "But first you."

The little buttons on her blouse are made of opals. They shimmer when I unfasten them. Pie blushes furiously as I slip the blouse down her arms and let it fall to the floor. And when I reach around her waist and unzip her skirt, she sucks in a deep breath of air.

I like how she acts when we get intimate. She's so cool and confident most of the time. But when I take off her clothes like this, she always gets shy.

I let the skirt fall to her feet, take her hand, and help her step out of it. Then I arrange her hair so it falls over her breasts.

She watches me closely, holding my gaze when I reach down to unbutton my own pants and they fall to the floor. Then I lead her over to the makeshift rock that is shaped like a bench and dramatically wave my hand at the seat.

Pie curtseys, which is delightful. Then she straddles the seat and leans her forearms onto the rock ledge while I take a seat behind her, slipping my hands around her waist as I scoot forward until my hips are pressed against her ass.

"You put a lot of thought into this," Pie says. Her voice is low and a little bit husky.

"I dreamed about you all day." I take the pot of honeysuckle paste, dip my fingers in, and then begin massaging her shoulders.

"Oh, fuck, Pell. That feels wonderful."

I grin as I press the pads of my thumbs into her muscles. "Tell me about your day. Was it exciting?"

"You want to talk? Now?"

"Trust me, Pie. We're just getting started. We won't be talking later."

"OK." She giggles. And she begins. Telling me about Pia and how she can talk. She describes the building where she works and the laboratory. Her new assistant, Talina. And I love the fact that Tarq made her a boss and gave her an assistant, even though Pie complains that she's not really qualified.

She can't even imagine the power she's hiding inside her.

But I don't interrupt. I'm rather enthralled by her descriptions of the city, and the people, and the clothes. Who knew? She tells me about the coffee shop, and the women she met, describing each one of them as she lists their names.

I make a point to remember these names since they are now her new friends.

Esmah, the judge with the bright green eyes. Mikayla, the baker with the stubby horns and gorgeous hair. A well-dressed fashion designer called Akkaline, a sweet-faced healer called Zantha, and Talina, her nerdy but cheerful assistant.

"Sounds like you have a whole new crew," I say.

"Right? It's a little bit cool."

"Sounds a lot cool to me. I wish I could see it. It would be nice to fit in like that."

"I know," Pie sighs. Then she turns all the way around, moving her legs so that she's still straddling the rock seat, but now she's facing me.

I want to ravish her right now. And as soon as that thought hits my brain, I grab her hips and slide her forward until our lower bodies are touching in a very intimate way.

Pie places her hands on my cheeks, then leans forward for a kiss. It's a nice, long, slow kiss. Open-mouthed and with a little bit of tongue. When she pulls back, I miss her immediately.

"Maybe you *can* see it."

"What?" I've lost track of the conversation.

"The city. Turns out that my assignment from Tarq is to find a way to allow others through the portals."

"They have more than one tomb there?"

"No."

"Then what portals?"

Pie appears confused for a moment. "Oh. I guess I didn't think about that. Is it weird that they have portals without tombs?"

"You're asking a man who has been locked in a sanctuary filled with tombs for two thousand years."

She chuckles. "We don't really know what we're doing, do we?"

I shake my head, agreeing. But I'm playing with her hair, my fingertips lightly brushing up against her breasts.

"Do you think it's dangerous to give Tarq that kind of power? He can't open the portals by himself. He used the spell he gave me, but he knows it doesn't work. He knows there's something missing and that something is you, Pell. Your bloodhorn."

"Do you want to talk about this right now?"

"Do you have better things to do?" She tries to say this with a straight face, but can't. Her giggle is unstoppable.

I stand up, pick her up in my arms—which makes her squeal—and then carry her over to the hot springs.

She kicks her feet in mock protest. "What are you doing? You didn't get your hornjob yet!"

"Hornjob." I laugh. "I can get one of those later. But right now—" I jump into the pool, Pie still in my arms, and she squeals and thrashes, splashing me.

But then I carry her over to the far side, sit down on a rock ledge, and place her in my lap so we are facing each other. She places both her hands on my face again. I love it when she does this. When she gazes into my eyes and holds me in this way. I feel like the center of her world.

And I'm so hard right now, I just want to be inside her.

But she leans forward, softly placing her lips against my mouth. We kiss and take it slow. Taking our time. No more words necessary.

Her hands fall to my shoulders, then slide down my arms. I'm still holding her hips, but my hands slide around to grip her ass, the velvety soft fur there such a turn-on.

Her hand grips my cock and I pull her even closer to me. Then she lifts her hips up and settles until I'm pushing up inside her.

We close our eyes at the same time, a little moan escaping her lips, a louder one escaping mine. These sounds mingle with our kiss and then she begins to move, gently rocking back and forth in my lap.

It feels so good, I can't remember a single other time in my life that has made me so happy.

"Pie." I moan into her mouth.

She lifts up, then down. Our movements becoming faster. Harder. Her breasts bouncing in the water, just under my chin. I grab one, grip it hard enough to make her moan, then bring it up to my mouth and suck on her nipple.

Her fingernails dig into my shoulders, her forehead pressed against my head. I grip her tight with one hand, urging her to move faster. And she responds until our movements are no longer slow and soft.

I let her nipple fall out of my mouth and grip her two-handed now, sliding her back and forth across my lap so I can hit that sweet spot between her legs.

She stares down at me, mouth open. And I picture all kinds of dirty things I want to do with that mouth. I bring my hand up, trace her lips with my thumb, and then slide it inside. She closes her lips around it, sucking. And I about die as I picture her doing this to my cock.

She pulls it out, moans, "Pell," just one time, and then I feel her pussy contract around my shaft.

I take that thumb, thrust it into the water, and play with that sweet spot between her legs.

She comes. Loudly. Her moans echoing off the cave walls. Her heavy breath in my ear as she bites my shoulder.

And that's it for me. I explode inside her, my arms wrapping around her whole body like a vice, holding her so close, we are just one person.

She collapses into me, soft and pliable now. And I lean back, gently sliding my fingertips up and down her ribcage.

We stay like that for a few minutes, at least, her head on my shoulder as our rapidly-beating hearts begin to slow.

Then she sits up, takes my face in her hands again, and kisses me sweetly. "You're my home now, Pell. You know that, right?"

"I do. And even though this place has been my prison for two thousand years, now that you're here, Pie, neither the walls nor the curse feel like punishment."

Her face is flushed pink and her blue eyes are bright and wide. "I'm going to find a way to get you through the tomb doors. I'm going to find a way for us to do everything together."

Then she rests her head on my shoulder again and we stay like that until we're at risk of falling asleep.

The water feels so good. But there are fluffy white robes hanging on hooks and a warm bed in the cottage waiting for us.

I get up out of the hot spring, holding Pie in my arms, and take her over to the robes.

"What about your hornjob?" she asks, once I set her back on her feet.

"Another time, Pie," I say, taking one of the robes off the hook and holding it open for her. She slides her arms into it, and I tie the front closed.

Then I put on my own robe, not bothering to tie it, and lead her out of the cave.

The tables in the great hall have been cleared of dishes and all of the candles save for a few pillars in the corners have been put out. It's empty of monsters. And quiet.

But we find a few of them downstairs when we exit the cathedral. They are getting ready for the night to end, I suppose. I don't know where they all sleep, but a good number of them sleep on the tomb roofs.

They call out to us as we pass and I actually recognize a few words. *Good night*, they are saying.

I want to learn their language, so I imitate the word and say it back to them.

This makes them roar with laughter.

Maybe I said it wrong. Hell, who knows what I said. But there's no time to think about it, because we come to the top of the hill and literally almost knock Tomas over.

"Oh, sorry!" He sidesteps us. "I didn't see you."

"Did you have a nice date?" I ask.

"I did," Tomas says. "It was actually very lovely. My first time ever. We had dinner, and went for a walk." He hesitates.

"And?" I ask.

"She introduced me to her uncle."

"Meeting the fam on the first date," Pie jokes. "That's a big deal."

"He was a very enlightening man."

Tomas is acting weird. So I narrow my eyes at him. "What else did you do?"

He holds up a finger. And this is when I notice he's carrying something in his other hand. "I kissed her."

"You did!" Pie exclaims.

"I did. And she kissed me back. It was nice." He sighs. I roll my eyes, but there is a little part of me that is jealous of Tomas right now. Not because of his kiss—but his date. He went out somewhere with a female he likes.

I would like to take Pie out, but I can't because she's still a wood nymph chimera when she leaves Saint Mark's. The only way to go somewhere on a date without the fear of her being discovered would be to wander the hallways upstairs. And that's just not the same. The hallways are for people who are stuck. They are good for finding pants and wasting time. Or reliving memories.

They are not for making new ones.

So yeah. I'm jealous of his date. Because Pie deserves a night out like that. Dinner in a restaurant. Walks in the town. Or even a trip into a real city—like Pittsburgh—to see a play, or an orchestra, or a ballet.

And I will never be able to give her that.

"What's that?" Pie jostles me out of my thoughts with her question, pointing to a large black box that Tomas is carrying by a handle.

"This?" He squirms a little. I know that look. It means he's done something he doesn't want me to know about.

"Tomas," I say sternly. "What did you do?"

"Well." He pauses, looks at Pie. "I don't want you to be angry, but—" He pauses again.

"But. What?" I snarl.

"I bought something in town." He holds up the big black box. "A solar generator."

"What the hell is that?" I say.

But at the same time, Pie says, "Holy fucking shit."

"What?" I ask. "What's going on?"

"Tomas." Pie ignores me. "Does that do what I think it does?"

"What are we talking about?" I ask.

"It does!" Tomas beams.

"Tell me what we're talking about!" I roar.

Tomas turns to me. "It's a generator, Pell. It imprisons the sun, puts that energy into this box, and then…" His eyes are bright with excitement. "We can plug things in!"

Pie claps her hands. "You're a fucking genius, Tomas."

"I don't get it."

Pie turns to me. "We can have electricity! It's a solar generator."

"And I got this too!" Tomas holds up another black box, this time much smaller.

"A radio!" Pie says.

"Do you know what 632 AM is?" Tomas asks her.

"Not really." Pie laughs. "But it's a radio station. You just point the dial to those numbers." She takes the radio from Tomas's hands and starts fiddling with one of the knobs on the front. "There. I think that's close. You might have to tune it a little once you plug it in." Then she points at him. "You should get batteries. Then you won't have to plug it in. Oh!" She looks up at me. "Holy crap! Why didn't I ever think of batteries?"

"What are we talking about?" I ask, feeling completely lost.

"Oh, I have lots of batteries," Tomas says. "I bought bags and bags of stuff from the Kitchen Sink in town."

"The Kitchen Sink?" I ask.

Tomas looks at me like I'm the dumbest creature around. "It's a survival store in town. Madeline's uncle runs it. And he has a show on the radio every night called *SHTF*."

Pie laughs.

"What's funny?" I ask her.

"I've heard of that show. It's kind of famous. Well." She considers this. "Infamous. Big Jim, that's the host of the show—"

"That's him!" Tomas exclaims. "Big Uncle Jim!"

"Anyway," Pie says, "he's kind of a nutjob."

"Define nutjob," I say.

"You know. One of those crazy conspiracy guys. His shows are about Bigfoot, and the Mothman, and other urban legends like that."

"I don't get it," I say.

"Monsters," Tomas says.

Pie points at him. "Yes. Exactly. Monsters. He believes in all that crap." Then she snorts. "Well. Joke's on me, I guess. Because monsters are real. But he totally thinks aliens are real too, and they're not. So he's still crazy."

"Aliens," Tomas breathes. "I don't know what that means, but I like the way it sounds."

"Anyway," I growl. "We're going to bed." I take Pie's hand and lead her down the hill.

"Good night!" Tomas calls.

Pie says good night back, but I ignore him.

Fucking Tomas.

Pie is pleased. "I should've thought of a solar generator. That's such a great idea."

"You do understand that he used your debt to buy that stuff, right?"

Pie shrugs. "Whatever. The whole thing is pointless, Pell. I'm never getting out of debt. We're feeding fifty monsters now. And anyway, I'm not sure I mind being stuck here for all eternity."

I grin big, liking this new development.

We get to the cottage, go upstairs, take off our robes, and then I climb on top of Pie and ravish her all over again.

CHAPTER SIXTEEN – TOMAS

"That's perfect. Put it right there." I point to the spot in front of the cathedral where Batty should place the toaster. We're turning the patio into our gathering place where we will assemble nightly for Big Jim's radio show. "What time is it? Cookie?"

He barks out a few grumbly words.

"Good. We have twenty minutes before the show starts. Did you slice the bread?"

Cookie points to the carving board where bread and peanut butter is laid out.

"And the tea?" I direct this to the apothecary monsters. They are gathered around in a circle near one of the pop-up solar lanterns that Madeline—my genius of a girlfriend—suggested I purchase. One of them, a large monster with a long beard and pointy horns, looks over his shoulder at me and gives me a thumbs up as he steps aside to reveal the humming stainless-steel kettle that has been placed on the electricity table where we're keeping the generator.

"Good, good. Let's get that toast made and don't be skimpy with the peanut butter." I really like peanut butter. Especially on toast. "Who's in charge of the radio?"

Eyebrows raises his hand, then turns one of the knobs on the front so I can hear the music. They like the music.

"Is that 623 AM?" I ask, with a stern face. Cookie shakes his head. "No. Didn't think so. Find our show, Cookie. I don't want to miss a single minute of Big Jim's monsters."

They are like children. All of them. Always up to something nefarious and sneaky.

But they are as intrigued about the monster show as I am, so Cookie quickly turns the dial and a commercial for car insurance comes on.

"Better," I say.

I'm new to commercials. But we've been out here messing with the radio and various gadgets for over an hour now, and I've come to appreciate them as an educational opportunity. A small window to the world outside of Saint Mark's. Also, there's something called a monster truck show coming up on the weekend that seems like a critical bit of information I should know about. I had no idea one could get insurance on cars, nor did I ever imagine that monsters and trucks got together for shows.

I am a monster and I own a truck. So this monster truck show feels like something I should look into.

I never knew there were so many monsters out in the real world. Pell has been keeping things from me. On purpose, maybe.

Which means I will keep things from him as well. On purpose.

The radio crackles and then horns begin blaring, and dogs start barking, and sirens are going off. All the monsters—myself included—gasp with surprise at the noise coming from the little box.

We gather around it as peanut butter toast and tea are passed out.

I take a bite of my snack as Big Jim's voice booms into the night.

"Welcome to the Hour of Monster Power. The Eastern Seaboard's only serious AM radio show that pulls back the curtain of conspiracy and reveals the dark truth behind it."

We gasp in unison again. Leaning in towards the little box, chomping on our toast, riveted by his words.

"We have a very special guest tonight, folks. Very special guest. Sheriff Russ Roth from my very own home town of Granite Springs, PA. Welcome, Sheriff."

This time I'm the only one who gasps. All the monsters look at me, questioning looks on their faces. "He's local," I say. "I know him."

"Oooooooh," all my monsters say.

"We banished him from the sanctuary. He's an eros."

"Ooooooh," they say again. But this time it's a negative 'ooooooh.'

"Pie opened her palm and flung him into the ether with her magic moths!"

"Ahhhhh," they say, happy now.

"And I breathed fire!"

They clap.

"Oh! We missed something. What did he say?"

None of the monsters know because we were too busy oooohing and aaaahing.

"Shh," I hush them. "Listen."

And that's what we do. We all sit down on various tombs and stone walls that surround the back patio, and we listen as Big Jim and the sheriff of Granite

Springs entertain us with a story about monsters that live in the hills above the town.

"Big Jim," Russ Roth says, "I know you've heard stories of the squonk."

"Of course," Big Jim replies. "Everyone in PA knows about the squonk. They are gruesome, and gross, and covered with warts and blemishes so terrifying, they weep over their own ugliness!"

"Ahhh!" us monsters say. How sad to be an ugly squonk!

"But there is another creature up there, Big Jim. A new one!"

"Something new?" Big Jim laughs. "I doubt that, Sheriff. I've seen it all around these parts."

"It's like a squonk. Terrible and ugly. Fire-breathing, even."

"What?" Jim exclaims. "You're joking with me now."

"No, sir. It's a squonk all right. Gruesome enough to turn you to stone like a medusa! But it's got horns and hooves and it's called the Buckhead Squonk!"

"Oooooh," we all say again, my fellow monsters chattering about what this new monster could be.

I ponder this as well, still listening to Russ Roth and Big Jim. And I'm a little bit embarrassed to say that it takes me several minutes of this storytelling to realize… they are talking about us.

"I'm leading an expedition up there this weekend," Russ says.

"No!" Big Jim replies.

"Hell yes, I am. I've rounded up a posse, we're making our final plans tomorrow night, and in a couple of days we're gonna get to the bottom of these monsters, once and for all."

"Oh, shit," I mutter.

Pell is not going to like this. Not one bit.

But... he can't freak out if he doesn't know about it.

I shall make sure he does not know about it.

CHAPTER SEVENTEEN – PIE

When I open my eyes the next morning, Pell is standing at the window.

I watch him for a few moments. He's naked, of course. So it's a nice view. His upper body is all muscle and in the slanted morning light the shadows cut hills and valleys across his upper arms and shoulders.

He raises his hands above his head, stretching as he yawns, then drops them and sighs.

"What are you so deep in thought about?" I ask.

He turns, smiling, his dick hanging between his legs. I guess I'm getting used to that, but it's still jarring. "It's snowing," he says.

"It is?"

"Not here. Out there." He points in the direction of the lake. "The weather doesn't change here much. It gets a little cool around February and a little bit hotter than usual in August, but mostly it's always the same."

I sit up, leaning on my elbow. "Yeah. I think I noticed that the very first day. The grass was still green even though it was November."

"It must have been a big storm last night."

"Why do you say that?" I ask.

Pell walks over to the bed, leans down, and kisses me. I smile up at him, wondering for like the millionth time how I got here. He straightens up and says, "Because there's a little bit of ice on the lake and snow on the shore. That part of the forest is part of the curse, so the storm must've been bad for it to leak through."

"Huh. Does that mean anything?"

Pell shrugs. "Not sure. But we should keep an eye on it."

I get out of bed and drape my arms casually over his shoulders. I like being taller than before. We're not eye to eye, but at least I don't only come up to his chest anymore. "What are you gonna do today?"

"Work on the bag."

"Blacksmithing." I shoot him a teasing smile. "It's very sexy, Pell."

"Is it?"

"Mmm-hmm." I kiss him again and when he kisses me back, all I want to do is slip back under the covers and stay in bed all day.

But a monster calls for me from below.

"Dammit," I mutter.

"It's Eyebrows. He's been waiting for you to wake up for twenty minutes."

"What's he want?"

"I think he brought you clothes."

"Ohhh." This perks me up. Pell hands me a satin robe and I slip it on. "Well, I wouldn't want to keep him waiting."

Pell pats my butt as I pass by, then follows me downstairs.

Eyebrows is sitting at the kitchen table drinking a mug of something. Maybe coffee. Next to him is an entire rack of clothes. He points to it, says something I don't understand, then gets up and walks out.

"Well," Pell says, "that was enlightening."

I chuckle and walk over to the rack of clothes, dragging my fingertips across the various garments.

"No skirts," Pell says.

I tsk my tongue at him. "Stop it. That skirt was not that short. And anyway, no one was looking at me. I was frumpy compared to the other women in Vinca City."

"Vinca?"

"Yeah." I pull a gorgeous purple silk wraparound blouse out of the rack and hold it up. "That's the name of the city where I work." Then I place it in front of me and turn to get Pell's opinion. "Have you ever heard of it?"

Pell shakes his head, pulls another hanger off the rack—a sweater with long sleeves and a very high cowl-neck collar—and trades me for the silk. "Nope."

I turn back to the clothes, hang the sweater back up, and pull out a tank top. When I turn back to Pell, I'm grinning.

"Why are you doing this to me?"

I blink at him. "Doing what?"

"Teasing me with these clothes? It's December, Pie. Sweaters are appropriate."

"It must be tropical in Vinca City because it didn't look like December there. The sun was high and hot. I'm not wearing that sweater."

He huffs air, then pulls the silk blouse back out. "This is fine, then."

I take the silk and trade him the tank top. "But don't worry, I won't wear a skirt." I pull out a pair of tan trousers that only go to my knee. "How's this?"

He nods his approval. Then his eye catches something else on the rack. "What the hell?" He pulls out another hanger and holds it up.

"Oh. That's nice," I say. "Eyebrows made you some pants."

He chuckles. "Well, I guess you get your way."

"And I guess you get yours too."

Now we both grin at each other, then laugh.

"Anyway," Pell says. "I need to wear clothes when I'm smithing. It's too easy to light myself on fire if I don't."

"Please don't light yourself on fire while I'm at work, Pell. I'll be pissed."

He chuckles as he pulls the pants off the hanger and steps into them. I watch as he arranges his giant dick into a huge bulge, then buttons them up.

"Holy hell. You cannot go out in public like that."

Pell practically guffaws. "Now you know how I felt yesterday with your gorgeous legs all over the place."

I let out a breath. "Fine. I understand your point of view. But... those pants?"

"You don't want me to wear them?" He's grinning like a boy.

"Of course I want you to wear pants, Pell. Just... do you have to bunch your dick up like that?"

He guffaws, reaches into his pants, rearranges his dick so it's lying flat down the length of his thigh, then looks up at me, ready to burst with laughter.

"Fine." I giggle. "Bunch it up, then." I turn away because the sight of his giant dick underneath those tight pants is starting to turn me on.

"Shit," Pell says. "I'll meet you up the hill. I forgot the fucking bag of rings in the Pleasure Cave last night."

"Oh, shit."

"Don't worry. I'm sure it's still there." Then he heads for the door.

I'm sure it's not, but I don't say anything. He's in charge of the bag of rings, I guess. He can deal with it. I go back upstairs and get ready.

I think about work as I brush my teeth and hair. But my mind wanders to my makeshift curling iron sitting on a shelf above the vanity. Then I remember that Tomas brought home a solar generator last night.

I need one for the cottage. I could have a coffeemaker. The kind that uses those the little single-serving cups. And a microwave. I could even have a little electric stove. Or... holy shit! I could get something to heat the water! I have been a pretty big girl about the whole wood stove thing but life would get considerably better if I just had instant hot water.

I might need two of those things. Hell, I might need an entire array of solar panels. I wonder how handy Pell is. Could he install them?

This makes me snort. Because if you had asked me last week if Pell could install solar panels, I would've had a good long laugh at that thought.

But he's a blacksmith. That's the definition of handy.

Anyway. I finish up, grab a bloodhorn dragon scale bracelet, leave the cottage, and head up the hill. Once again, there is a little group of monsters waiting for me. Cookie gives me a bagged lunch and Batty hands me a sandy rock. I tuck both these things into my messenger bag and turn to Tomas. "Where's Pell?"

"Last I saw him he was cursing his way up the steps. But he said not to leave. He'll be right out."

"OK. Hey, are you going into town today?"

"I will be tonight."

"Another date?"

Tomas puffs up with pride.

"Well, I think you should get more of those solar generators."

"You do?" His eyebrows are raised in surprise.

"Yep. We need them. It worked OK?"

Tomas gets a faraway look in his eyes, but nods. I'm suspicious, but not really sure what of. "It worked great. We made toast, tea from a kettle, and listened to the radio last night." He gets that look again. And I'm just about to ask what he's thinking when he says, "But they're very pricey, Pie. A few thousand dollars when you add in the solar panels."

I sigh, then throw up my hands. "Well, who cares. We need them, right? I mean, it's no fun living without electricity. Everything's harder. So, whatever. Get two of them. No. Get *five* of them."

"Pie!"

"I want them, Tomas. It's OK. I'll work the debt off. Don't worry."

"Don't worry about what?"

Tomas and I both turn to see Pell walking towards us. "The shopping list I just gave Tomas. I want some generators."

"And they're very expensive," Tomas adds.

Pell looks at me. But I put up my hand. "It's OK. I'm fine with the debt. I'll look at the book today and make sure I complete tasks that wipe out a lot at one time."

Pell shoots me another look.

"Stop it," I say. "I doubt there's any sexy stuff on the new list. Tarq wants me to do magic."

This earns me yet another look from Pell. "Do you do magic, Pie?"

"No," I laugh.

"Then how are you gonna pay this off?"

I kind of want to tell him about the whole princess thing. But one, I don't want to worry him. And two, I'm not sure how it works. But if I'm a princess, I think this will change things. I might be rich in this other world. It could happen.

Instead, I tell a half-truth. "Pia got us bonuses yesterday. I'll trade my bonus in for debt points."

"Does it work that way?" Pell asks.

"Let me worry about the debt, Pell. You worry about..." I nod my head towards the monsters. Then I whisper, "Did you find it?"

He nods, then whispers back. "Yes. But it was in the great hall this time. Not the Pleasure Cave."

"You worry about *that*," I say. "And I'll worry about the debt, agreed?"

"All right," Pell sighs. "I guess it's better if we divvy up the problems so we don't both have to stress out about everything. No point in that."

"Exactly." I smile at him. "Now. I've got to go to work. You have a great day in the smithy shop." I pat his chest, lean up and kiss him on the lips, then turn and walk into the tombs.

Tomas says, "Bye, Pie." Then I catch him saying, "Divvy up what problems?" as I walk away. But I don't catch Pell's answer. Because my doorway appears and I walk through.

This time, things are different when I arrive. The great hall that is normally super busy and filled with people is absolutely quiet and empty.

Except for Luciano. Who is standing just a few feet away, like he was waiting for me.

"Hi," I say, looking around.

"Good morning, Miss Vita."

I look at him funny. Mostly because he's looking at me funny. "What's up?"

He pans his hands wide. "What do you mean?"

"Why is everything so quiet and empty this morning? And why are you looking at me that way?"

"What way?"

"OK. Whatever. Can you point me in the direction of my lab? I have no idea where to go."

"I'm going to walk you today," Luciano says. "In fact, I'm going to walk you every day. But we need to decide on a starting time so I know when to expect you."

"What time is it now?"

Luciano glances at his expensive wristwatch. "Seven fifty-two."

"OK. So eight o'clock every day?"

He holds up his wrist. "Does your clock at home look like this?"

I study his watch and quickly realize it does not. "You only have ten hours on your watch."

"How many do you have?"

"Twelve."

Luciano makes a face. "Twelve? Nothing is divisible by twelve."

"It's an even number, Luciano. Lots of things are divisible by twelve."

"Well, we run on a ten-hour clock and a twenty-hour day. Which means your time… and our time… well, I'm not smart enough to do that math."

"Me either," I chuckle.

"You should buy a watch today. Then you'll have our time, as well as yours, when you are at home. And we'll meet every morning at eight."

"Sounds good." But then I reconsider. "Wait. Not *every* morning. I get weekends off, right?"

"I don't think that was in your contract."

"What contract? I didn't sign a contract. This entire thing was forced upon me."

"I'm sure Tarq will explain."

"Can't you explain?"

Luciano just smiles at me, waving his hand towards a hallway. "Shall we?"

I sigh, and follow him into the hallway. This time we only walk through two doors before we arrive at the lab. Talina is already there, busily working at her bench. She turns when we enter, her eyes wide behind her safety goggles.

"Have a nice day, Miss Vita," Luciano says. Then he backs out of the lab, pulling the double glass doors closed behind him.

That whole thing was just weird. But… whatever. Nothing I can do about it. So I turn to Talina and smile. "Good morning—"

But that's as far as I get before she drops to her knees, presses her forehead against the stone floor, and just… stays like that.

I walk over to her and look down. "What the hell are you doing?"

She peeks up at me, then quickly hides her face again, and whispers, "I can't talk to you."

"Says who?"

"The rules, my lady."

"My lady?" I snort. "No. I'm not anyone's lady. And get up, Talina. That's dumb."

She doesn't move. "I can't. It's protocol." She peeks up at me again. "You're royalty, miss."

"OK." I tap the toe of my hoof on the tiles. "That's enough. If I'm royalty, then you have to obey me." I'm not actually sure this is true, but this is how royalty usually works, so I say it anyway. "And I want you to get up right now."

Talina immediately pops to her feet, head cast down.

"And look me in the eyes."

She gasps, but follows the order, her eyes glazing over, like she's trying not to focus on me.

"I command you to treat me like I'm not royalty. In fact, I would specifically like you to treat me the same way you did yesterday, before this whole princess thing happened. And that includes looking at me, and talking to me, and generally not acting like I'm special."

Talina lets out a breath. "Are you sure?"

"Of course I'm sure. I'm not this princess, Talina. I'm a girl named Pie. I'm really not anything special." She's about to protest, but I point at her. "And you know what? I like not being special. I want nothing more than to be… unspecial. Just a girl. A regular girl. So if you treat me special, I will hate it, Talina. Hate it. Does that make sense?"

She looks both confused and panicked.

So I elaborate. "See, back where I come from, I was never normal. I was kind of a freak. So I don't want to stand out, Talina. I want to fit in."

"Oh," she says, finally focusing on me. Finally *seeing* me. "I guess when you put it that way…"

"Yes. See? It makes sense. So. We're good?"

Talina reluctantly nods. "OK."

"Great. Now I need your help. I need to knock a considerable amount of debt off my list because I have needs in my other world, and they are expensive. Tarq wants me to do spells and shit. Open portals. Use… that." I point at the bloodhorn tree in the corner of the lab. "Do you know anything about this kind of stuff?"

Talina nods. "Oh, yes. I went to school for years to learn. I'm a certified expert in spelling."

"Spelling?" My face crinkles up. "Like… ABC's?"

"No." Talina laughs. "Spelling. Like… casting spells."

"Ohhhhh. Gotcha. OK. So, can you teach me?"

"Yes. I will teach you how to spell."

"Wait, we're still talking about magic, right? Not Dick and Jane books?"

"Dick and who?"

"You're not going to teach me how to spell words, right? I already know how to do that."

"Well… that's how you do magic. Spelling is magic."

"Stop. Spelling like… my name is Pie. P-i-e. That kind of spelling?"

"Yes."

I let out a long breath. "I don't understand. In my world spelling is just… you know. Academic. It's just writing."

"Oh. But isn't writing… magic?"

"Nnnnnooooo."

"Interesting."

"I mean, I don't think it is. As far as I know, spelling words is just... well. I guess I've never thought about it before. It's not really something that *is*. It's something you *do*."

"Right."

I blink at her.

She blinks back. "OK. Let me explain because I think we are talking about the same thing, but we view it in two very different ways."

So she explains.

Spelling—i.e. the stringing together of letters to make words, and paragraphs, and whatever—is how they write spells.

"See?" Talina says. "Spells. Spelling? Hmm?"

"I get it," I say. "The root words are the same. But they don't mean the same thing. I think this is called a homonym, if my memory of third-grade education is correct."

"All magic is done through writing."

"All of it?" I ask. Because I don't think that's true. "Then why do we need herbs and crystals?"

"We don't."

"We don't?" I want to laugh. But my confusion is real. "Then why the fuck am I here? Tarq wants me to use the bloodhorn to open the portals. If we only need words, why the bloodhorn?"

"Without the right words," Talina, "the bloodhorn is useless. But words can work on their own."

"Hmm. Even if you just say them out loud?"

"A very powerful alchemist can use speech instead of writing. But most cannot."

This makes me think back to the day I had to expel Grant and the sheriff from the sanctuary. I did have my magic moths, and fire-breathing Tomas was there, of course. And Pell's super-powerful horn blood. But the real banishing happened when I yelled, *Get out!*

"Want me to show you, Princess?"

"Yes. But please don't call me that." She starts to protest, but I put up a hand. "Talina. For real. Even if I am this princess, I do not want to be called princess. I don't like it. Just call me Pie like everyone else."

She deflates a little, her shoulders dropping, her face sullen.

"Please. I'm begging you. My greatest wish is to be... invisible, Talina."

Now she looks confused. "Why would anyone want to be invisible?"

"If you had grown up being known as the weird girl, or the crazy girl, or the scary girl—you'd get it."

She sighs. "I understand that part. Maybe better than you realize."

I scoff. "You were the weird girl? Please. Weird girls don't grow up and still have childhood friends, OK? Perhaps you were quirky, or eccentric, or whimsical. But there is no way you were the weird one."

She doesn't say anything, so I know I'm right.

It would've been nice to meet another weird girl though. Perhaps if there were two of us, we could be a team. We could celebrate our weirdness, and prop each other up when we got the oh-so-familiar strange looks. And neither of us would have to feel so uncomfortable in our own skin.

But apparently, I am one of a kind.

I hate it.

Talina must see that I'm serious because she says, "Fine. I will call you Pie."

I brighten. "Thank you. Now show me how the spelling works."

She goes over to a cabinet on the long end of the room, takes out a fresh notebook, grabs some pencils, and comes back to the center table. "Here. This is what I use. These are charcoal pencils because I like thick lines and I like to draw my spells before I compose them."

We each take a seat and she opens the notebook, then pushes it towards me. "This one can be yours, so I won't write in it. I'll just tell you how to do it, OK?"

"OK. I'm ready. Teach me how to spell."

"OK. The first letter of the alphabet is the most powerful."

"Why?"

"Why? I don't know why. It just is."

"Isn't there some kind of… like… science to this?"

"Yes. That's why it's number one."

OK, then.

"Take the pencil and draw the A."

I do that, but Talina points to it. "What is that?"

"What do you mean? It's an A."

"In what language?"

"What language? English. Hello? The same one we're speaking."

"I don't know that language."

I just blink at her. Then it hits me. It's like I'm having that conversation with Pell all over again. "What language do you think we're speaking?"

"Um. Vincan."

"Huh. Well, I'm hearing English."

"That's your language?"

"Yes. And this is my A." I point to it. "Is it gonna mess things up with the spelling?"

"Unknown. But it's very curious. You don't seem surprised that I think you're speaking another language."

"I'm not. Pell said the same thing. He thinks I'm always speaking Latin. But the very first spells I did back in my own world were about understanding languages. So maybe that's why I didn't notice things were off."

"Maybe." But it's a tenuous maybe. I don't think she believes that. "OK. Well, I can only work with what we have. So each letter has a point assigned to it. This is the chart that tells you the value of each letter." She points to the inside cover of the notebook, which is like a pre-printed cheat sheet. And sure enough, there are all the letters of the English alphabet and they all have a point value assigned.

"Huh," Talina says.

"What now?"

"That's not Vincan." She taps the pre-printed page.

"Nope."

"Weird," she mutters.

And see? *See?* This is what I mean. I'm always the weird one.

"Only the first letter counts. And don't ask me why. I'm not a philosopher. That's just how it is. So when you compose a poem you try to get the highest value in your first and last lines."

"How many words per line? Is it like a haiku?"

"I don't know what that is, but maybe. Keep it under ten. Otherwise, it's confusing. And you need to make two different rhymes in each spelling. So you can't rhyme all the last words of each line, that muddies things."

"Hmm. I'm not the greatest rhymer."

"Do your best. Now give it a go."

"Wait. What kind of spell am I composing?"

"Ask for something you need."

"Don't I have to pay for that?" I've learned my lesson about free shit. Nothing is free. It all evens out in the wash, as Tarq would put it.

"No. Your goddess pays for it."

"Whoa. What goddess?"

"The one you were born under?"

I let out a long breath. "I don't have one."

Once again, I have succeeded in perplexing Talina. "If you do magic, you have one."

"Yeah, well, I don't have one."

"Weird," she mutters again. "Then who do you ask for help?"

"No one. I just… mix up a bunch of shit and call it good."

"But you've used words before? In spells?"

"Yeah. Once. But then I just…" I shrug. "Like— I dunno—yelled the words real loud and commanded things to work."

"What did you say exactly?"

"'Get out.'"

"'Get out?'" She whispers something and counts on her fingers. "But that's not enough points to do a spell."

"I don't know what to tell ya, Talina. I don't have a goddess, and I don't want one, either. I'm not asking anyone for help. When people do you favors, they always want something in return. That's the whole reason I'm here."

Talina sighs. I think my newness is wearing off quick. "As I said, just do your best. Now." She places her hands on the table and stands up. "While you're doing that, I'll go get us coffee. Be back soon."

I watch her leave and the understanding creeps in.

Yesterday she was all, *Let's go get coffee together!*

And now that she knows I'm just the weird girl, she's done with me.

CHAPTER EIGHTEEN – PELL

When Pie disappears through the tomb door, I get an overwhelming feeling of heaviness. I'm getting used to her. I'm becoming accustomed to having her next to me. I was busy most of yesterday and concentrating on my current ring problems, so I didn't really notice the heaviness. But when she came back, yeah. The lightness was there. The feeling of a great burden being lifted.

Today though, I sense that heaviness the moment she's gone and I don't like it.

"Divvy up what problems?" Tomas asks.

I turn him, still distracted by these new feelings. "What?"

"What problems are we divvying up?"

I don't want to discuss any of this with him, so I turn away and call out over my shoulder, "I'll be in the blacksmith shop."

I weave my way through the maze of tombs, searching for the forest's edge. Of course, it takes me almost as long to find the shop today as it did yesterday because I'm pretty sure some of these tombs have moved. But once I'm there, I feel better. I put on my apron, light my forge, and pass the time waiting for it to heat up by weaving the rings from yesterday into a small section of mail by connecting and closing the rings.

Then I study that, absently fanning my fire with the bellows. The rings are far from perfect. It has been too long since I last forged for them to look anything but amateur. But it's good practice and I take notes of where I need to improve.

I will do better today.

Eventually the fire is ready so I start fabricating new rings. I get lost in the work. My mind wanders to Pie, of course. I can't imagine a life without her now. She's part of me. And she's perfect. I liked her as a human but I love her as a wood nymph. As upsetting as it initially was for Pie, it felt like the gods blessed me when she came back from Tarq's with hooves and horns. It's like they finally decided I deserved more than a curse.

I also like that she can't really leave the sanctuary anymore. Not easily, anyway. Not without chancing discovery by the outside world. But she's not a prisoner because she has Tarq's world now.

If only I could travel through tomb doors. Then we could do these things together.

I would like to see Tarq's world. I would like to go to that city. Take Pie out for coffee at that place she mentioned. To dinner, or concerts, or festivals.

It would be the closest thing to a normal life I've had since I was a boy and went to the Roman parties. Even if we never break this curse, we could live like that.

We could live within it.

My mind wanders through thoughts of a new life with Pie. A long life. Years would go by. Decades, then centuries. And we could spend them all together.

Partners.

When I pull back from the fantasy I'm imagining in my head I realize I have made hundreds of rings and the sunlight outside is different. It's noon, I think. Time just flew by and I am thirsty and hot.

I put my tongs down, wipe the sweat from my brow, and walk over to the water pump to grab a drink. Then I take it up onto the roof and let a light breeze cool me down.

I stand there, overlooking the sanctuary, and ponder what it all really means.

Is it what I've been told?

Or might there be more to the world than petty gods and prison walls?

Pie started questioning things immediately. Why are the tombs here? Where did they come from? Who's inside them?

And I have to admit, it's a little bit embarrassing that I haven't spent all of my two thousand years of imprisonment trying to get to the bottom of these things.

I just didn't care, I guess.

No. I just didn't *want* to care.

The whole thing is odd and reeks of programming. Did Ostanes—or Saturn, or maybe even someone else—put some kind of ignorance curse on me? Why wouldn't I question things?

Or did I? And I just forgot?

I sigh loudly and let my eyes wander over the tomb rooftops. The monsters seem to like being on the roofs. I can count about a dozen of them up there right now. One group even has a fire going, like they are cooking lunch or something. I squint my eyes to try to make out who they might be, but all I see is the vague shape of wings. Not too many of the monsters have wings, so it's got to be Batty or one of his friends.

I scan again, but then stop abruptly. "What the—" I walk over to the edge of the roof, trying to get closer. "Is that a…"

Holy shit. I think it is.

I think that's a *door*.

And not just any door, it's a door on the side of the black tomb.

I go back downstairs, take off my apron, rake my coals to spread out the fire and cool it down, then leave. I walk quickly, trying to weave my way through the maze of tombs as efficiently as I can, while still heading towards the looming cathedral spires. But it still takes me a very long time and when I finally make it to the cathedral's back patio, I fully expect the door to be gone.

An illusion or maybe a hallucination.

But it's still there and monsters are walking by it like they don't see it, or they don't care.

I grab one by the shoulder as he's passing by, turn him to face the tomb, and say, "Do you see that door?"

He turns to look at me, shrugs and shakes his head.

I let go of him and he walks off.

But I'm not satisfied with this answer. So I grab another monster passing by. "Do you see that door?"

This monster gives me the same answer and walks off.

Is it real? Is this even what a door looks like? It's been so long since I've seen one, other than the opening to my own tomb. But this isn't an opening. It's an actual *door*. Made of metal. Iron or steel. With an intricate trim, accented with rivets, around the perimeter. And a knocker near the top. A knocker with a face on it.

I walk closer, trying to get a better look, and realize the face is of the monster standing guard outside. The one with the gold horns and hooves.

The next thing I know I'm right up next to the door and my fingertips are brushing along the green copper patina of the unknown monster. "Who are you? And why are you here?"

Of course, there is no answer.

But the better question is—what will I do now? Knock?

It feels like a bad idea. I mean, knocking is like an invitation in the magical world. You knock because you want someone to answer.

I reach for the door handle. It's not the kind that turns. It's the kind we have on the front doors of the cathedral. You press a trigger lever and push.

So that's what I do and the door inches open with a loud creak.

I look over my shoulder, wondering if any of the monsters are watching me, but there's a fog lifting up from the ground—like a shield—and even though I can see plenty of monsters, they are passing by without even a glance.

Huh. It's almost like the magic that keeps the outside world at bay when I'm in between slave caretakers.

I pause here because it's the prudent thing to do. If I'm inside a gray fog wouldn't that mean I'm a slave caretaker? One who has not yet accepted his new role?

Makes sense to me. But you know what they say about curiosity.

I press the door and it opens a few more inches. It's dark inside, so the only way to see what's in there is to open the door all the way and let the sun shine in.

I pause and take a deep breath. It's not a good idea to go around opening strange doors. I know this. But wasn't I just standing on the rooftop thinking I had been programmed to not ask questions?

So wouldn't this new door, and a sense of curiosity, be the first step in breaking that programming?

Yeah. It's not a very good argument. But that's because I'm not really interested in talking myself into this. Or out of it, for that matter.

I want to know what's in here.

I'm awake now and there's no way I'm going back to sleep. I want to ask all the questions. I want to know all the answers. And yes. It's a risk. But the alternative is just... accepting my life.

And maybe I've had my moments of apathy about this curse, but I have always looked forward to the day when the curse would be broken.

Maybe it's time to stop expecting the slave caretaker to save me?

Maybe it's time I took a little responsibility for saving myself.

I push the door all the way open. It swings easily and then bangs against the inside wall. I don't do the obvious and call out, "Hello," or anything. If that monster is in here, and doesn't already know that I've opened his door, I don't want to be the warning bell.

My upper body leans inside as one foot eases past the threshold and I wait until my predator eyes adjust to the darkness.

It only takes a few moments before shadows become shapes. Walls, of course. They have architectural design to them that I do not have a word to describe. But it looks a lot like the outline on the door.

On one end there is a darkness that dissolves into nothing and I deduce that is a passageway.

I take a step back, close the door, and turn around. The fog is gone now and the monsters nearby notice me with a start. Like I was not there, and then I was.

Like I had not yet accepted the curse, and now I have.

Half a footstep inside was all it took?

Not much room for indecision, is there?

I call to the closest monster. "Do you know where Tomas is?" Because I feel like he needs to know about this.

The monster points to a pathway leading into the tombs. Just a general direction, but now that I know Tomas is that way, I think I can hear chatter.

So I follow that chatter and find Tomas and his little group of friends gathered around the radio he brought home last night.

"Tomas," I call. "I need to talk to you."

"Shhhh," he says. "Dr. Love is talking. We're just about to get kissing advice!"

"What?"

"Shhhh," he hisses at me again.

I walk over to the radio, pick it up, and turn it off. There is a cacophony of protests, but I turn on the little group, bare my teeth, and growl, "Get out."

They scurry away.

"Pell," Tomas protests. "What is your problem?"

"My problem is that I just found a door in a tomb, Tomas."

He screws up his face. "*What?*"

"Not just any tomb, either. The new black one."

"Are you crazy?"

"No. I'm not. I saw a door, Tomas. I opened it. I almost went inside."

"Now you really are crazy. You don't know what's in there!"

"I know. I backed out, closed the door, and came to you for advice."

He brightens. "You came to me? For advice?"

"Yes. What do we do about it?"

His face scrunches up. "What do you mean? We should ignore it."

"But what if it's a clue?"

"A clue to what?" Now he's looking at me in a different way, confused.

"This place, Tomas. Haven't you ever wondered what the fuck is actually going on here? I mean, we've been here for thousands of years so the time for questioning things is long gone, right? We just accepted this place. We just... assumed that we are prisoners and this is our prison." I spread my arms wide to encompass the entire sanctuary.

"Isn't it?" Tomas asks.

"I don't know. Maybe. But maybe not. We don't know what's in those tombs."

"Well, not true. We know what's in Tarq's tomb."

"Exactly." I point at him. "If there's one world hiding behind a door, wouldn't all the doors be hiding worlds?"

Tomas shrugs. "I suppose it's the logical conclusion. Do you want to walk through this door?"

"Do you think I should?"

"Should? No." He laughs. "But not much happens if you always do the things you should."

"That's a good point."

He puffs up with pride. "Thank you."

"Do you want to come with me?"

"Through the door?" He almost guffaws. "No."

"Why not? It'll be an adventure."

"I'm already in the middle of an adventure. Dr. Love is on. And after her, there is a show called *Conspiracy Hour*. I'm really looking forward to that one. Then, of course, I need to go into town to get Pie her own solar generators and have dinner with Madeline. I have a girlfriend now, Pell. I can't run off for a crazy, spur-of-the-moment adventure."

"Hmmm," I growl.

"I think you should table your adventure until Pie gets home."

"But she'll just tell me not to do it."

"Exactly. This door has 'bad idea' written all over it. Go back to your smithy shop and forget you ever saw that door. In fact, you should not tell Pie about it. All the monsters are worried about her."

"What do you mean?"

"It's clear that her job is stressing her out."

"She's been there one day. How stressful could it be?"

"The monsters say she is, Pell. They know what they're talking about. Most of them said they've been to that world."

"What?"

"Batty has been going on and on about it for weeks. That's why he gives Pie rocks to take."

"What?" I feel very confused right now. "What rocks? What are you talking about?"

"He's a stonemason. His magic is in stone. And he comes from that world. His rocks ran out of power centuries ago. But when Pie takes them through the door and brings them back, they are recharged. He can fly again."

"Does Pie know she's doing this?"

"Probably not. But that's beside the point. Batty has been through many worlds. He's told me that we're the nicest monsters he's ever met and he's going to be staying here forever."

"Wonderful," I grumble. I was holding out hope that the monsters would move on to another place. I never worked out any of the details of that hope, but if they're attached to Saint Mark's it probably doesn't matter.

"Oh, and he said one more thing. He said the saints were all bad. Very, very bad."

"What saints?"

"The Saints of Saint Mark?"

"Who the hell are they?"

"Honestly, Pell." Tomas laughs. "You're joking, right?"

"No. I'm serious. I have no idea who Saint Mark is. Pie looked him up on her pocket phone once, but all she said was that we might've lived in the real world at the same time."

"Well, first of all, he's not a he. It's an organization. And the members are all called saints."

"OK. So what?"

"They're like…" He pauses to pick his words carefully. "Very bad people. They are a group of assassins. And you—well, not you. But you"—he spreads his arms wide, like this 'you' means the entire sanctuary—"you are all their weapons. But not you, Pell. You're the caretaker of the weapons."

One of the monsters offers up an opinion I don't understand and Tomas smiles and points to him. "Yes. Exactly. You are the quartermaster, Pell."

I just stare at him for a moment. Because that word—'quartermaster'—it knocks me back in time and I suddenly feel like I'm falling. The next thing I know, Tomas is all up in my face snapping his fingers at me.

"Pell? Hello? Are you with us?"

I push his hand away. "What are you doing?"

"You... went somewhere for a moment."

"What do you mean?"

"You went stiff, Pell. And silent. And your eyes glazed over. What happened?"

"Nothing happened. I didn't do that. I was thinking about that word 'quartermaster.' But only for like half a second."

Tomas makes a face that says, *No, Pell. That's not what happened.* But out loud he says, "I think you might need some lunch. Go eat something."

I'm about to take him up on that, because now that he mentions it my stomach is rumbling, but then Tomas grabs my arm and points to a broken bit of tomb. "Have a seat and listen to the good doctor give out kissing pointers, Pell. Cookie will bring it to you."

And it's nice, this caretaking.

Even though I have technically been being taken care of for centuries, this time and place. These monsters. Tomas. Pie. It all feels very different in a whole new way.

CHAPTER NINETEEN – PIE

A girl and herself.
No friends and no fun for her.
She is used to it.
A spelling haiku, by Pie Vita.

I write it down in the notebook with a satisfied smile. And ya know what? I was just about to do the sitting monkey walk when it occurred to me that I don't need friends here. I have tons of friends at my real home. I have Pell and Tomas, of course. But I also have Eyebrows, and Cookie, and Batty is a little bit weird, but he shows up to see me off to work every day. I don't know why he gives me rocks, but even if he turns out to be even weirder than I am, there are forty-seven other monsters who probably want to be my friend.

So fuck it.

I can dream up spelling haikus. And it did start with A. So. Yeah.

I wilt. And my shoulders drop. And yep, I do the sitting monkey walk. Because who am I kidding? My spell is stupid and doesn't even have a purpose—except maybe to bring me down.

"Shit. Is that a thing?" I quickly rub my arm across the page, smudging the charcoal words. "Pie, you need to be more careful. If intentions are the mother of outcomes—or something—then you should not be writing negative thoughts in this notebook."

I don't want to be the girl with no friends who is used to it.

And just as I think that, Pia flies into the room and lands on the table in front of me. "Pie," she squeaks. "Good morning! Did you have a nice sleep?"

"Hmmm." I get a warm, dreamy feeling as I think about last night with Pell. That was nice. "Yes," I say. "I did. How about you? How's your new place?"

"I love it. Love, love, love it. My neighbors are amazing. We were up to the wee hours of the night chittering and chattering about this and that."

"That's great. I'm so glad you're happy here."

She hops up onto my arm, then walks up it. "You're sad about something?"

"Nope. I'm not. I have nothing to be sad about. I have a great man, I have a great job, and I have a great home. Not to mention dozens of friends. I don't need Talina and her amazing in-girl group."

"Aww," Pia sighs. "It's happening again, isn't it?"

"*Yeeesss,*" I whine. I let out a long breath too. Because it's no use lying to Pia. She's me. And even though she's less me than she used to be, she's been with me since I was a tiny girl and understands perfectly well that I am the oddball weirdo who always gets shunned. "It's happening, Pia. Talina was so cool yesterday. But today, I dunno. She sees the weird in me. No matter how hard I try, I can't ever completely cover it up."

"Well, if she's gonna be a bitch like that, then she's not the friend for you. She's a coworker and nothing else."

"Yeah." I try to sound like I'm OK with this, but I can't really muster up the enthusiasm to pull it off. "It's just... her little group of friends seemed perfect for me."

"If they don't like you, Pie, they're not the perfect group of friends for you."

"I know." I resume my sitting monkey walk.

"Anyway. I came here to invite you to a party."

"A party!" I perk up a little.

"Yes. There is a very big-deal party happening at the palace in a couple days."

"Oh." I moan again. "No. I'm not going to the stupid palace. These people think I'm some sort of princess, Pia. I don't want to encourage that line of thinking."

"Yes. I've heard the chatter."

"What chatter?"

"There's a rumor going around that the long-lost princess has returned. I was hoping it wasn't you, but... it's you, isn't it?"

I apathetically raise my hand. "It's me."

"Well, then I agree. You should not come to the palace party." She hops off my arm and lands on my notebook. "What are you working on?"

"Spelling poems. Talina says you do magic with words and I'm supposed to write one."

"What will your spell do?"

"I have no idea." I'm still pouting. And Pia can tell. So now she's trying to take my mind off it.

"Well, what do you want it to do?"

"What do I want it to do? I want it to take me home so I can spend my day with Pell. But I can't because I'm in debt and have to be here every day."

"So maybe you should make a spell so Pell can come here with you?"

"That would be great. In fact, that would probably erase my entire debt because that's exactly what Tarq wants too. Well, not Pell. He wants me to open the portal doors. And if I can bring Pell here, then I'd be opening portals, wouldn't I? And if it were as easy as writing a haiku starting with the letter A, then wouldn't he just do it himself?"

"Hmm. I dunno. Doesn't hurt to try."

"I guess."

"Well, I have things to do and people to see. But I'll come back and check on you later."

"No." I'm still moaning. And it's starting to irritate me. So I stop. "No, Pia. Go do your thing. I'm fine. And you're right. It doesn't hurt to try. Maybe I will write the best haiku spell ever and all the freaking portal doors will open at the same time."

"That's the spirit! And if you're sure…"

"I'm sure. Go."

"OK. I'll be back tomorrow."

"OK," I say. And I do my very best to be bright and happy.

"Have fuuuun!" She flits off and disappears through the doors.

Even though I have every intention of writing the best spelling poem ever, only a few minutes after Pia leaves, I'm slinking back into the sitting monkey-walk posture. I flip the page in the notebook and just stare at the utter blankness of it. "Why does it always seem like the world is working against me?"

"Maybe you read too much into things?"

I turn with a start and find Tarq standing in the doorway holding my Book of Debt.

"I don't think so."

He offers me a small smile, then opens the Book of Debt. "It appears you've made some progress." His perfectly manicured clawed finger is pointing to something on the page.

"What do you mean?"

"You've erased some debt. A significant portion, actually."

"Really?" I perk up. "How much?"

"From yesterday's total? Four thousand six hundred and seven vinlomeons."

"Vinlomeons?"

"It's our standard of money."

I sigh. Because no matter what, I'm always going to be a step behind. "What's the exchange rate for dollars?"

"I don't even know what a dollar is, Pie."

"Of course you don't."

"If you want to take the book home tonight to see, you can."

I dunno. I've already lost interest. "With my luck, it's probably equal to like ten cents."

Tarq stares at me for a moment. He's very… dapper today. Stylish. His polished horns are so ebony black, I can see myself in them. And his beard—well, it's not scruffy like Pell's. It's all manscaped. His chest hairs too. The ones I can see, at least. He's wearing a deep scarlet vest with one pocket over his heart made of royal purple velvet that matches the piping along the edges. The whole garment is embroidered in gold thread. His pants are a mahogany brown, made of a more rustic fabric, like canvas. And of course, they only go to the knee. His lower legs are smooth black hide and his hooves are as shiny as his horns.

He reminds me of a stallion. Even his black hair is like a mane.

He walks over to the table, takes a seat, and opens the book. "What were you doing last night?" When he starts this sentence, he's looking down at my debt. But when he finishes it, his normally orange eyes are locked on mine. Only they are dark. Like empty pits.

I should take note of this. His eyes change color. It reminds me of Pell's horns and Pell's horns do magic, so it might be possible that Tarq's eyes do magic too.

"Pie?"

"What?"

"What were you doing last night? That erased this debt? Magic?"

I snort. "No. I was not doing magic."

"Then how did you erase the debt?"

"How should I know? I haven't the first clue how any of this shit works, Tarq. I'm as surprised as—" But then I abruptly stop. Because I do know how the Book of Debt works.

"You're as surprised as what?" Tarq prods.

I look at him and blush. "I… I think I know how the debt got erased."

"I can't wait to hear it."

"It's… well. Pell, Tarq. It's all about Pell."

"What is?"

"My debt."

"No. Your debt was given to me."

"Be that as it may, when I got stuck in this curse my job was to take care of Pell. And whenever I made him happy, debt was erased. Perhaps the two of you both own the debt? Because I made him *very* happy last night and"—I reach across the table and tap my finger on the book—"this just proves it."

Tarq is frowning at me. "You made him happy *how?*"

I almost blush again, but you know what? No. I'm not a child. I'm not a little girl. And while I would never call myself slutty, and I prefer the men around me to be clothed instead of hanging out all over the place, I'm definitely not a prude. "How do women usually make men happy, Tarq?"

He just stares at me for a moment. Then his eyebrows crunch together. "You and Pell are—"

"Of course. We're like… soulmates. And I'm not just tossing that word around, either. We have connection."

Tarq lets out a long, tired breath. Like perhaps he's been through some shit as well, and this is just yet another bump in his long and winding road of despair. "I'm not ready to talk about that."

"Not ready to talk about… Pell and me?"

He closes the book and pushes it towards me. "Take it home, figure out the exchange rate, and bring it back tomorrow."

"Speaking of tomorrow, what day of the week is it? Please don't say Monday. Actually, what I'm really asking is… when's the weekend?"

"The weekend? As in…" He appears confused.

"The end of the workweek? You know, Saturday and Sunday? Those days all people working professional jobs with the title 'researcher' get off?"

"I have no idea what you're talking about."

"The weekend. Holy magic worlds, Tarq! The freaking weekend!"

"Why are you getting upset?"

"Because you're acting like you've never heard of Friday!"

"Fireday? Is that what you're asking about?"

Did he just say *Fire*day? Or did I hear that wrong? *Focus, Pie.* "Friday?"

"Fryday?"

"Oh, my God." I'm about to lose my shit when Tarq puts up a hand.

"Hold on. You're asking about rest days?"

"Yes! Thank you! When do I get my two days off?"

"You just started two days ago. You haven't even earned one rest day, let alone two. I don't know how it works in your world, but here you work eight days, then you get two days off."

"That's a weird number of days. I mean, I'd never get the same days off because there's seven days in a week and—"

"Ten."

"What?"

"Ten days in a week, Pie. Sunday, Moonday, Airday, Waterday, Earthday, Fireday, Charmday, Godsday, Sisterday, Nullday, and Noday."

"No."

"Yes."

"No, it doesn't work that way."

"I'm afraid it does."

"So let me get this straight. You have ten days in a week. And you get two of them off."

"If you work the prior eight."

"If I work eight days in a row I get two days off? That's... bullshit."

"How do you mean?"

"Eight days in a row with no rest? How is that *not* bullshit? In my world we work five and get two. In a seven-day week."

His eyes narrow, like he's thinking about this. "That's a nice schedule. Five days instead of eight."

"Yeah, it's not bad. Four and three would be better"—Tarq snorts—"but eight and two! Tarq!"

"I'm not in charge of the calendar, Pie. It's just how it is."

"I might as well be a slave." Then I'm the one who snorts. Because... that's actually my title back home. "I'm sick of this place."

"That's because you're fighting it."

This pisses me off. Because Pell told me the same thing about Saint Mark's. *It gets easier if you don't fight it, Pie.* "So I'm supposed to what? Just accept that I'm your slave?"

Tarq presses his lips together. Like he wants to say something, but he's not sure if he should.

He shouldn't. Because I'm not even done whining yet. "So how long is the work day? Ten hours?"

"Fourteen."

"Fourteen! So I get six hours off a night? That's criminal!" Again, he holds his tongue as I continue my freakout. "Ten-day weeks and twenty-hour days! The timekeeping here is confusing and complete bullshit!"

"Our timekeeping is very simple, Pie. It's all based on tens."

"Well, there are supposed to be twenty-four hours in a day and I should only have to work eight!"

Tarq guffaws. "Eight. That's a good one." Then he stops laughing and looks at me. "You're serious?"

"Yes, I'm serious! Eight hours in a work day, Tarq. Eight out of twenty-four. Five days in a workweek. Five out of seven. What you people are doing here is... slavery!"

There, I said it.

"Twenty-four," he says. "That's a weird number."

"Not really. Twelve hours on the clock face, twenty-four in the day. It goes around twice. Twelve is a perfectly normal way to count things. It's divisible by lots of numbers. Threes, and fours, and twos."

His eyes roll up a little, like he's doing mental math. "Yeah, but that system breaks down pretty quick."

"Not to mention sixes," I add.

He frowns. "Oh. I get it. You're on a hex system."

"I guess. Who cares? Not the point. The point is—"

He puts up a hand to shut me up. "Stop, OK? If you want to work eight hours a day, then... fine. I won't tell anyone."

And I find this to be an odd answer. He won't *tell* anyone? Who would care if he let me go home early? Isn't he my boss?

"But the five-day workweek, Pie? No. I can't do anything for you there. It's eight days out of ten. It's law."

Yes. This is definitely something I need to ask questions about. The law? There is a minimum workday law? That's weird, right?

But before I can start asking questions, Tarq says, "This hex system your world is based on. Now that is very interesting. Your world must be overflowing with magic."

"No." I snort. "It's not. It's actually very mundane and boring. We don't have magic. Like at all. We have science."

"Science is powerful magic."

"Yeah. But it's not magic. It's just logic."

"Right. I've heard of it."

"What do you mean you've heard of it?"

"There are parts of Vinca that do the logic. But…" He pauses for a few too seconds too long. Like his mind is a whirlwind of ideas. "Anyway," he says. "We can talk about what that means later. You're telling me that your world does not believe in magical science?"

"Well." I shrug. He's throwing me with these terms. Magical science? It's one or the other, isn't it? "There are people in my world who *claim* to do magic. I see them on Insta with their crystals and shit."

"I don't even know what you're talking about."

"Right. Instagram. It's a… a… a place online—do you have the internet here?"

"Internet?"

"You know. Computers and shit. That big invisible realm that holds all the world's data in some fucking imaginary 'cloud.' The World Wide Web? Does anyone call it that anymore? You know what I never understood? Why do people say interwebs? I don't get it. It's so freaking pretentious. I'll find you on the interwebs. Just say internet, ya freak. Am I right?"

Tarq stares at me for a moment. Confused isn't a strong enough word to describe his expression.

"What?" I ask.

"Your world has the Field? But you call it the internet?"

"Field?" I consider this word. Mental images of Star Wars and the Force come to mind, which kinda makes sense. So I say, "Yeah. Sure. We have a Field and we call it the internet."

"I would really like to visit your world."

I chuckle. "Oh, I'm sure you would."

"What's that mean?"

I look up at him and smirk. "I know what you're up to."

"What would that be?"

"You want me to open portal doors so you can go through them. You're gonna take over or something, right? Start wars and shit. Become the next Attila the Hun or whatever. I get it. I'm on to you."

For the first time since he entered the lab, Tarq relaxes and leans back in the chair. He even smiles. And it's not a predatory smile, either. I'm amusing him.

"What?" I ask.

"You think I want you to open portal doors so I can conquer worlds?"

"Of course. What other reason is there?"

"Wow. Your world…" He shakes his head. "It must be a tough place if that's really what you think."

"What do you mean?"

"War, Pie?" And now he gives me a look that I have seen before. On the face of almost every man I've ever met. Including Pell. Including Russ Roth. Including every single temporary boyfriend I've ever had. The look is amusement, but it's got a healthy dose of 'you're simple' added to it.

She is so simple, it's cute. In other words, *She's is not that bright, but it's more naïve innocence than stupidity, so it's OK.*

"We don't go to war here, Pie. We talk like men. We discuss things and come to agreements. We make contracts." He taps a fingertip on the Book of Debt. "But thank you for letting me know your world is less civilized. It's good information."

OK. Fine. Us humans, we're a bunch of heathens. Don't we all kinda know that? We do. But I don't want him to think disparaging things about us, so the fact that we are considered... unrefined, I guess—well, it bothers me. And I'm only questionably human, so why I'm so put off by his tone and assumptions about me, and my world, the race I identify with, I don't quite understand. I just know that I am.

"Anyway," I say. "In my world, we believe in science."

"Right." He pushes his chair away from the table and stands up. "Got it." Then his eyes travel down to my notebook. "Oh, good. Talina gave you a notebook. Are you working on some spells?"

I look down at the empty page and deflate a little. "Not yet. But I'm thinking about them."

"You gotta start somewhere, right?" He turns and walks across the room, stands in front of the large window so he's backlit by the bright sun outside. "I didn't just come to ask about the book and your debt. Though it does intrigue me that pleasing Pell is still part of your obligations. I came to ask if you'd like to go to the palace with me Fireday evening."

"The palace party?"

"You've heard about it?"

"Pia invited me."

"Did you accept?"

"No. I'm not going to your palace, Tarq. I don't want to encourage the people here to think of me as something I'm not. I don't belong here. I belong at home. And as soon as I repay my debt, I'm going there and I'm never coming back."

"Because Pell is your soulmate." He deadpans this. Doesn't phrase it as a question.

"Yes. Because I have a life there." And this is a weird thing to say. For me, at least. Because I've never had much of a life. And if you had asked me a few weeks ago if being cursed inside the walls of Saint Mark's was my idea of a life, I'd have laughed. But that place feels like home now. And the people there— even though the monsters are new—feel like, well, if not family yet, at the very least friends.

Tarq lets out another long breath. "Well. If that's how you feel." He turns his back on me. And as he walks out of the lab he calls over his shoulder, "See you tomorrow."

Just as he's leaving, Talina is entering. "Hi, Tarq," she chirps. "Bye, Tarq," she snickers.

She kicks the doors closed with her foot and walks over to me with a carry-tray of coffee cups and little glycine bags of pastries. "I bumped in to Mikayla and she started forcing pastries on me." Talina sets the tray down on the table and hands me a coffee, then slides two pastry bags over to my side. She sits down in the same chair where Tarq was just a few moments ago and takes a long sip of coffee. When she comes up for air, she smiles and sighs. "I needed that. Oh." She points at me. "Before I forget, the girls want me to invite you to come to the party with us on Fireday. We're meeting up around seven and—"

"No." I put up a hand to stop her. "I can't."

Talina blinks at me. "But Pie, it's a big deal."

"I'm sure it is." I'm not really sure of that at all, but three invites to the same party in the span of an hour has to have meaning. "I only work here, OK? I don't live here, I don't party here, I don't… do anything here, apparently. Except exist. I can't stay and party, Talina. I have people at home."

"Right." She forces a smile. "I knew that. The girls were just really excited about meeting you and want to get to know you better." She puts on a serious face. "Don't worry though. I didn't say anything. They have no idea you're Princess Pianna."

Oh, God. That name again. "I'm really not her, Talina."

Talina nods at me. "Got it." But it's all very conspiratorial. Like it should come with a wink.

"I just can't go. And it's not a joke. I'm walking between worlds, Talina. And this is not how life works, OK? It's weird. And disconcerting. And, frankly, I'm surprised you even want me to go. And if this is just some… polite gesture, well—"

"Pie." Talina reaches across the table and takes both my hands in hers. "No. It's not a polite gesture. We like you."

"Why would you like me? I'm just a freak. This body?" I scoot my chair back and stand up. "This isn't even me! It's part of my curse. In my real body, I don't have horns, or hooves, or fur. I'm human. I drive a run-down piece-of-shit Jeep. I have an imaginary bird friend called Pia. And I'm stuck in the woods in rural PA."

Talina gets up from her chair and walks across the lab to her bench. Then she turns and looks me straight in the eye. "That might all be true."

"Might?"

"Might. But then again, Pie, it might not. Did you ever consider that you don't belong in *that* world? That you were born in *this one* and put there so we could not find you?"

I don't know what to say. Because, of course, I had that whole convo with Ostanes when I was hovering between life and death during the banishing. But that feels like a dream. Even this place feels like a dream. Every second I'm here I'm on edge. And I think it's because I'm afraid that I will jerk awake and when I open my eyes, I'll be sleeping in the backseat of my Jeep in a random gas station parking lot while on my way to Toledo.

And even though that doesn't have to be a bad thing in all ways, it would be a bad thing in the ways that count.

Because Pell and Tomas, they feel real. I feel like Pell and Tomas and I are meant to be. The hallways proved it, right? We were children together. We ran in the woods. We lived in a realm of ancient gods. We were made by a great alchemist. Little drone moths live in my palm and give me eyes for days and days.

I'm not ready to rewrite my history once again and that's what this place is trying to do.

"Listen." Talina's voice is softer now. And I realize that she probably read my thoughts just by the expression on my face. At the very least, she understands my confusion. "There will be more parties, Pie. Hell, there's another one on Charmday. Maybe you could let Pell and your friends know you'll be late that night so they don't worry? And it's smaller than this palace thing. Zantha has earned another certification, so we always celebrate afterward. It's very casual, though."

I don't know what to say, so I say nothing.

"Or not," Talina chirps. "Forget it. It's no big deal. We can just have coffee and lunch with the girls during work hours, if that's better. They just really liked you. And it's funny."

"Why is it funny?" My voice has a little edge to it.

"Because we've been a tight-knit group since we were children. It's been just the five of us for so long. And even though plenty of girls have tried to infiltrate our little pack, none have ever passed the first test. Until you, that is."

"First test? What's that mean?"

"We all have to like the new girl equally. And no one has ever been liked by all of us equally. There were a few who got the majority vote. But none before you who got the unanimous one." She shrugs. "It's dumb, I guess. But we're family. I feel about them the same way you probably feel about your friends back in your world. And that's why I wanted to go get coffee alone this morning. We took our vote and we all agreed. We like you, Pie. We want you to be part of our little group."

They want to be my friends.

This offer is so foreign to me, I'm suddenly confused and overwhelmed.

On the one hand, isn't this what I wanted? Didn't I just write a haiku about being lonely and friendless?

Good God, that was like thirty minutes ago. How could so much happen in thirty minutes?

I feel a little upended. But for some reason, it's not upsetting. It's a little bit exciting. A whole group of girlfriends. I would never even dare to dream of such riches in my other life. It's so out of the realm of possibilities.

But here, it's different.

I'm someone else, that's true. But maybe it doesn't have to be a bad thing?

"OK," I finally say. "Charmday. That's the one after Fireday?"

"Yes!" Talina looks ecstatic. "Two days from now."

"I would love to be a part of Zantha's ceremony. She's the healer with the sweet face, right?"

Talina laughs. "Oh, she will hate you for saying that, but yes. We've been calling her Sweetface since she was seven."

I smile too, then laugh. "I will let Pell know I'll be a little late that night. He won't mind. And I would love to be part of your group, Talina. It's... it's like a dream come true."

CHAPTER TWENTY – TOMAS

I end up missing the rest of Dr. Love and all of *Conspiracy Hour* because I had to go tell Cookie to make Pell something to eat. Pell's so helpless at times. And his memory is not the best. He's forgotten more than I realized. So high-maintenance.

But he's worth it.

Or he will be one day.

By the time all that is over I'm craving Madeline's attention, so I take the truck into town and stop by the feed store before I pay Big Jim a visit.

Madeline is helping a customer at the hay counter, so I browse the shelves as I wait, picking up various farm tools and accessories and giving them curious looks.

Finally, the annoying customers are all gone and Madeline makes her way over to me. "Need a new ax today, Tomas?"

"No." I look at her and smile, wondering how I got so lucky. "I'm sure we have dozens of axes lying around the place."

"Did you come in for something specific or…" She lets that sentence hang there.

"I came in to see you."

She blushes at this attention. "We're still on for dinner, right?"

"Absolutely. I was just on my way to Big Jim's to pick up another generator for one of my friends and decided to stop in so I could see your face."

"Aww. That's sweet." She blushes again. And I feel a peculiar excitement building inside me. "If you want to wait around, we could have lunch in a little bit."

I would like to have lunch with her. I would like to take all meals with her. But Pell's memory issues, plus the news of a new door, not the mention my errand, keep me focused. "I can't stay. But I will be back for dinner. I just have a few things going on at home at the moment."

She's staring up into my eyes. Like she can penetrate my soul. "That's fine. I brought a sandwich for lunch, anyway. But dinner…" She winks at me. "We should go out of town for dinner."

"Out of town? How far out of town?"

"Oh, we could go in to Latrobe. They have a new brewery there."

"How many miles is that?"

Madeline looks surprised. "I'm not sure." She takes out her phone and begins tapping it. Then she shows it to me. "From here, it's thirty-five miles. But it's a quick drive. I go there a lot. Maybe… thirty minutes."

I squint at the map, trying to figure out where Saint Mark's is.

"What are you thinking?" Madeline asks.

And I realize I've been silent for an awkward number of moments. "I'm just wondering how far away it is from Saint Mark's."

"Will you turn into a pumpkin if you get too far away?"

"A pumpkin? I don't think so. But I don't like to stray too far."

"O-kaaay. What's the address? I'll check."

"Check how?"

She holds the phone up again. "See, you put your starting destination here and your ending destination here, and then it tells you how far away it is. You've seriously never had a phone?"

"Never."

"Well. That is a first. Back in the old days, I guess that was common. But kids these days, they get phones as soon as they go to school."

"Little children have these gadgets?"

"Oh, yeah. Parents go nuts keeping track of kids these days. How come your family won't let you have one?"

"My family? Oh, no. I don't live with family. Well, I take that back. They are *like* family. But they're not in charge of me or what I do."

"So you could get a phone if you wanted one? And had the money, of course."

"Yes, I suppose I could."

"So why don't you?"

"I don't know. Maybe I will look into it."

"Well, if you want one that can't be tracked, don't get one like mine. Get a burner from Big Jim. He's got them behind the counter."

"A burner?"

"Yeah. You know. The kind you can throw away if you have to?"

"Why would someone throw away a phone?"

She shrugs. "There are thousands of reasons, Tomas. But if you don't know what they are, I refuse to spoil your innocence."

I chuckle. Because I think she's flirting with me. "Well, it's an interesting idea, Madeline. I shall consider getting a burner when I see your uncle today."

"See you at seven?"

"I will meet you right here at seven."

"And we can go to dinner in Latrobe?"

"Sure. Why not?"

Then she does the most surprising thing. She leans up on her tiptoes, places her hands on my shoulders, and kisses me on the cheek. When she pulls back, she's blushing again. "See you then."

And then she whirls around and disappears in the feed store aisles.

I walk out of the store in a daze, trying to memorize the light touch of her lips on my cheek. And when I get to Big Jim's and walk inside, my entire body is tingling.

"Well, well, well. Look who it is." Big Jim is behind the counter, cleaning a gun. "If you came in to see my niece, she's down the street."

"Oh, no. I just saw her." My fingertips come up to my cheek and I sigh.

"Oh, for fuck's sake. Snap out of it, boy. Madeline does not deserve your stupid look of swooning."

"What?" I'm confused. By both his tone and his words. Is he disparaging Madeline?

"What do you need, son? I'm busy."

"Yes." I shake the confusion off so I can get down to business. "I need more generators."

"How many more?"

"Well. One for Pie's bathroom, one for Pie's kitchen, one for my room, one for the main kitchen… how about seven?"

Big Jim blinks at me. "Seven? With or without solar panels?"

"Oh, definitely with."

"Boy, you do realize these generators are twenty-five hundred dollars each?"

I pause. It does sound like a lot of money. And I don't want to keep adding to Pie's debt. But she's the one who told me to come get them. So I nod. "Yes. I realize that. It's a lot. But we have decided they are necessary."

"Welp. More money for me, I guess. I'm gonna have to go in the back. I don't keep that many stocked out front."

"Oh, one more thing. Madeline mentioned you sell burners."

One of his bushy white eyebrows slides up his forehead. "You need a burner phone?"

"Madeline suggested I get one, yes."

"What kind of shit you wrapped up in, boy?"

"I don't understand."

"What you got goin' on up there in the woods that you need seven solar generators and a burner phone? You making drugs or somethin'?"

My face scrunches up. "Drugs? No. We just want power in the kitchens."

"The kitchens, huh?"

"And Pie's bathroom. And I want another radio, while I'm here. One for my room."

He puts up a hand. "I get all kinds in here, son. So I'm not gonna ask no more questions. But if you need a gun, you're gonna have to get that somewhere else. I don't need that kind of heat."

I have no clue what he's talking about now. "I don't need a gun."

"Good. I'll be right back with your seven generators and your burner phone."

I smile at him, but he's frowning when he turns and disappears into the back room.

I browse the glass case in front of me as I wait and find there's a gadget in there with the same kind of map I saw on Madeline's phone. Maybe I should get one of those? So I can keep track of how far away from the sanctuary I go.

I've asked Pell what happens when you venture too far away and he says it gets foggy and everything disappears. Then you wake up back at home. I've even tried to get him to drive me to the edge of the boundary, but he refused. Said we'd lose the car if he did that and it wasn't worth showing me if we lost the Jeep.

But now we have two vehicles, so I might ask him again.

"Here's the burner." Big Jim returns, setting a phone down wrapped up in tight, hard plastic. "You'll need some minutes, too, I expect?"

"Minutes?"

"To use the phone?"

"The phone runs on minutes?"

Big Jim turns and points to a line of plastic cards hanging from a rack behind him. "How many do you want?"

I'm still trying to figure out how a phone might run on minutes when he plucks a few from the rack and sets them on the glass counter. "One twenty is usually enough. But if you've got a lot of business to attend to, you might get two and save yourself a trip to the store when you run out."

"Very well, I shall take two cards."

"This one here has data. This phone has internet, maps, and—"

"Did you say maps?"

"Yes. It's got maps."

I point to the map gadget in the glass case. "So I don't need one of these?"

"Those are for hunting—" And just as he says that, the bell over the door jingles and we both turn to find Sheriff Russ Roth entering the store. "Well, look who it is!" Big Jim greets the sheriff with bright and friendly interest. "I've got your gun almost ready, Sheriff."

I try not to look at the man, but he's big, and handsome, and… just very hard not to look at. He levels his gaze at me, his mirrored sunglasses shining with a glint of sunlight. Then he looks me up and down with keen interest, and I wait for the spark of recognition. I am the one who burned him with fire several weeks ago. Though he can't really hold that against me. He doesn't appear to have any marks on him.

"Well, who's this?" Russ Roth asks.

"This is—what did you say your name was again?"

"Tomas," I offer.

"Right," Big Jim chuckles. "Toe-mas. Pretentious name to go with that pretentious accent." I look at Big Jim, wondering if he's being hostile. "He's dating my niece," Big Jim tells Russ.

Russ looks me over a little harder. "Haven't seen you around these parts. Where did you say you were from?"

I didn't say, and I don't say now, either. But I don't have to because Big Jim does that for me. "He lives off grid up in the woods."

Russ Roth slides his mirrored sunglasses down his nose and looks me over even harder. "You don't say."

I, again, do not say.

"Well," Russ says. "That's very interesting. I'm leading an expedition up into the woods this weekend, in fact."

"We both are," Jim says.

"You're going too?" I ask. "Because I didn't get that impression from the radio show last night."

"You were listening to my show?" Big Jim asks.

"Oh, yes. It was grand."

"Grand." Russ chuckles. "Anyway. How about you come along? We could use a guide. The woods are weird up that way."

"A guide? To find the squonk?"

"Not just any squonk," Russ says. "Buckhead Squonk. He's different. Mean and nasty. Not all like the regular squonk that inhabits these parts."

"You've seen him?" I ask.

Russ nods his head slowly. "I have. The memory of that beast is burned into my brain forever. I will never forget the ugliness and stench of that beast."

Ugly and smelly. I would not describe Pell as either of those things. But clearly the sheriff is just making things up because he didn't recognize me.

"So how about it?" Big Jim asks. "You wanna get in on this hunt?"

I spend a moment critically thinking about this offer. If I go with them, I could lead them astray. I could make sure they never find Saint Mark's. I could do other things to them as well, if necessary. But I could also slip up and give myself away. I don't understand why Russ Roth doesn't know what he is, and therefore what we are. It's like he's in a fog or something. Perhaps due to the banishing spell that Pie worked on him.

But even if he doesn't realize he's an eros, he's still dangerous. So I say, "I would love to come on your hunt." Because I need to keep my eye on this man. And make sure he can't ever find his way back to Saint Mark's.

Russ repositions his glasses in front of his eyes and cracks a grin. "Excellent."

And when he says this word a shiver runs up my spine and I have doubts.

Maybe he does know who I am.

I wait patiently as Big Jim reassembles Russ's gun, puts it in a case, and then rings him up and says good day.

Then I hand over my piece of paper with the word 'money' on it, and load the truck up with seven more generators and a new phone with plenty of plastic minutes.

CHAPTER TWENTY-ONE – PELL

By the end of the morning, I have woven enough rings together to start the tricky part of actually fashioning the mail into a bag. That takes a couple hours because I have to clamp the edges together. Then I am stumped as to how to close it up tight enough that the rings can't slip through. So I think about this, coming up with a couple ideas. I could make a button. I could make hooks. I could try to fashion a leather drawstring.

But I can't decide, so I take a break and go up to the roof.

The sun is hitting the edge of the cathedral in a way that makes it appear to glow. I take in the tall spires and the Gothic architecture. The intricate beauty of the cathedral has always amazed me. It's so massive, I can't imagine humans building it.

But, of course, humans didn't build it. It's magic. Made by the gods, or something.

I didn't wear my new pants this morning. I didn't want to ruin them. So I'm still wearing the same pants from weeks ago and they are becoming stiff and caked with soot and sweat. So I decide to take a longer break for lunch and a trip into the hallways to find something else to wear that is clean, but not fancy.

Pie is loving the pants. She says everyone in Vinca wears clothes. Even the satyr chimeras. And once she can open the portal for me, she will take me shopping.

I picture this new world she's in. I'm not exactly jealous, but... I can't deny that my heart longs to see it. I would love to be there with her.

I go back downstairs, take off my apron, rake the coals and cover them with ash so they will cool, and then head up towards the cathedral for some food before I go tripping through history looking for work pants.

The sanctuary is surprisingly quiet when I get to the path that leads up the hill. Not a single monster in sight. They are probably up to something. Something not good. And I should find them and figure out what that not-good thing is, but then my gaze lands on the black tomb.

And the door, which is visible.

Why now? That's what I ask myself. Why does this door appear now? There has to be a reason and it must involve me, because I'm the only one who sees it.

I know I shouldn't let it tempt me—I should wait for Pie to learn her magic so she can see it too, and then I could take her with me when I enter—but I *am* tempted. Also, that curiosity I had earlier is back. Like a cold chill creeping up my spine. Something between a warning and a revelation. And before I even make a decision I'm walking towards the imposing black statue.

I stop at his feet and look up into his eyes. He's only a little bit taller than me, but he seems very imposing. Those gold horns don't help, either. It gives him the look of royalty.

"Who are you?"

I don't expect an answer, of course. But I do kind of get one. Because the metal door to the tomb opens a crack with a loud squeak.

An invitation.

Now the question is, should I accept?

There are a hundred reasons to walk away and practically none to go inside, but I take a few steps in that direction anyway. And then I guess the decision is made because I'm standing in front of it. Fingertips touching the metal. Gently pushing it open.

It's the same view as earlier with one difference. There is a lit torch on the wall just to the right of the dark passageway.

"Hello?" I say. Then I shake my head and let out a huff. Didn't I just say I wouldn't do that a few hours ago?

When I look over my shoulder to see if any of the monsters are watching, they aren't. The entire place is quiet. Then I hear small voices from somewhere deep in the maze of tombs. The radio. I think they must all be gathered around that radio.

I turn back to the tomb. "Is anyone in here?"

I sniff the air inside the black tomb, trying to catch the scent of the monster inside. But instead, I catch the scent of woods.

The woods in my tomb aren't very interesting. Just trees, and dirt, and a stream or two every now and then. One of the trees is massive and dead. There's a large hole in the side, and when I'm in there, that's my home base. But there are no comforts.

I haven't been in my tomb in weeks. Pie can't go in there—she can't see the door. Just like this tomb. So I've just been staying in the cottage. But when this woodsy scent hits me, I have an immediate pang of nostalgia for it.

The moment I think this thought, the earthy scent increases. Like it's beckoning me. Which is a warning sign if ever there was one. When a magic tomb reads your thoughts and adjusts the atmosphere around you into something more tempting, the smart thing to do is walk away.

But I'm not sure anyone has ever called me smart.

So I take another step.

And another.

And then yet another.

Until I am all the way inside.

Until I am standing in the center of the small antechamber.

Somewhere, far down that dark passageway, I hear a laugh. The sweet laugh of a wood nymph. And my heart skips inside my chest. Because that laugh belongs to Pie.

"Pie?" I call it out, and I call it out loud. "Pie?" I say it again and then I'm grabbing the torch off the wall and heading down the dark passageway.

As I walk the footing under my hooves changes from stone to gravel to dirt. And then I am in a forest.

The laughter is off to my left. "Pie?"

It's light in here. Maybe... midday, like it is outside. So I pound the end of the torch into the dirt until it goes out, then toss the wood aside.

"Pie!" I yell for her. I'm certain it's her.

I run forward into the woods, but instead of finding a nymph, I find a door with a view of the woods. And for a moment I feel like I'm in a funhouse. One of those mirror mazes where you can't tell which is the real path forward.

I walked through a door, into the woods, and in the woods I see a door with a view of the woods.

On the other side of the door a flitter of movement passes through the trees at an incredible speed and I catch a flash of antlers and fur. "Can't catch me now!" a young wood nymph yells, running and leaping over logs, deeper into the forest.

"Pie!"

"Come on, Pell! Catch me!" Her voice floats through the leaves and around tree trunks. Her invitation spurs something inside of me. Something that makes me want to chase her.

"It's a trick, Pell." My voice is calm, and rational, and low. And I know this is a trick. It's just like the hallways upstairs. None of it is real.

But knowing things and accepting things are often on opposite ends of the knowledge spectrum.

"Pie!" I yell again.

"I'm getting away! You better catch me!"

And she does sound far away. She really might get away if I don't move now.

I'm just about to leap through the door and chase after her when I see myself running after her.

I stop. Stand still, almost afraid to move as I watch him leap over logs and weave his way through the leaves and tree trunks. There is giggling off to my left. Then more, off to the right.

Then the scene through the door changes to a clearing with a large pool of ice-blue water, a waterfall on the opposite edge. Pie is standing on a rock at the very top of the falls. "Can't catch me now," she teases other Pell.

She is young. Very young. Barely a teenager. No breasts to speak of hidden behind her long, blonde hair. No hips. Nothing remotely woman about her, actually. And when I look down at myself, standing on a rock at the bottom of the waterfall, I am the same age. A boy.

The moment I recognize this, thousands of years melt away.

The memory of my time in the sanctuary slips and becomes the life of someone else. Some other Pell, not this one.

"There." Pie is pointing to the rocks below her. "Start right there," she yells over the roaring water. Then she turns and runs.

Young me dives into the pool of water. When he surfaces, he swims towards the rock where she was pointing. Then he is climbing up the ragged cliff and leaping onto the rock where she was standing moments ago.

"Pell!"

I glance to my right and find Pie in the tall grass on the other side of the door. Only now, she's not a child, but a teenager, her round breasts not entirely hidden behind her silky hair. "Pie?"

Teenage me appears from the trees. She smirks at him, her eyes travelling down the length of his body, pausing where the Pie of this world would stop to pause. "Come on." She holds out her hand, beckoning him.

"Where are we going?" he asks.

"You'll see."

I want to be him. I want to take her hand, and go with her, and stay here, in this world where I *know* I belong, for the rest of my life. It's such a strong urge, I almost step through the door and do it.

But this is not real. And whoever this woman is, she is not Pie.

She is a trick.

I turn my back to the door and find a whole line of them before me.

How many? A hundred? A thousand?

I can't count. But each one is open and on the other side is a view of the sanctuary.

These are my doors, I realize. I am inside… what? A key to Saint Mark's? A portal that leads here? A stop on the way through to other worlds?

I realize I'm holding my breath and let it out. Then I turn my back on those doors too, and I run.

All the way back.

When I hit the antechamber, I pause.

Because I hear her laughing again.

The very same giggle I heard when I first entered.

You can come back, that laugh says. *You can come back and stay here with me.*

And then, a whispered voice in the dark—*This is how you break the curse.*

It's Grant's voice.

And I can't help myself, I turn back to face him.

CHAPTER TWENTY- TWO – PIE

I'm just staring at my notebook, making no progress at all, when Talina says, "You should aim small."

"What?" I turn to look at her.

"For your first try," she clarifies. "Something easy."

"Like what?"

"Well, for my first spelling lesson I gave myself the ability to make the perfect cup of tea."

"Tea?" I smile at her.

She rolls her eyes. "Tea-making was the biggest, stupidest deal back when we were in school, Pie. It was so dumb. But the girls who could make the best tea ruled the school."

I laugh, I can't help myself.

"And I sucked at it."

"It's tea," I say. "How hard could it be?"

She points at me. "You're right, but you'd be surprised at how easy it is to fuck up tea. I over-brewed. I under-brewed. My water was the wrong temperature. I used the wrong leaves. I added sugar and milk. I didn't add sugar and milk. I used the wrong honey. I used the wrong mint. I used the wrong lemon."

"Wow. I had no idea it was so complicated."

"I mean, I guess it's not. But when you have a whole school of competitive pre-teen girls trying their best to brew up the perfect cup of tea, it gets intense."

"They were all magical teas?"

"No. They didn't need magic to make perfect teas. And we were too young, anyway. We were supposed to use science. And I would follow the same recipes, and the same steps, and use the same ingredients, but they always tasted awful. Bitter, or too sweet, or too cold. So my proctor gave me permission to do a spelling."

"How old were you?"

"Nine."

"And it worked?"

Talina smiles. Like she's reliving the memory. Then she snickers.

I point at her. "What did you do?"

She shrugs her shoulders all the way up to her ears. "I didn't mean to make it so powerful. But let's just say... from that day on I was no longer the girl who failed."

"You were good at it?"

"I kinda kick ass at spelling. And no one was ever allowed to do a tea-making spelling after me." She giggles. "It was a mind-control tea. Oh, what a fun week that was."

"You devious little witch."

She peers at me through hooded eyes. "Guilty."

I let out a long sigh. "I don't really kick ass at anything."

"I heard you called up a dragon, and a swarm of moths, and banished some powerful wizard from your home."

Savage Saints - JA Huss Writing as KC Cross

I'm just about to say, *He wasn't a powerful wizard.* But then I realize she's not talking about Russ Roth. She's talking about Grant. I hold up my palm and point to the center. "I have moths inside here. They come out, sometimes, and they do things."

Talina pulls up a chair, props her elbows on the table, and leans her chin on her hands. "Continue."

"I don't really know how it happens. Stress, maybe? Desperation? I'm not sure. But sometimes a whole swarm of moths just flies out of my palms and I can see through their eyes. And if I'm in danger they can overpower my enemy."

"I wish I could see that," Talina says.

I look at the spot on my palm where the moths appear and wish for them now. But nothing happens. I look back up at Talina and shrug. "I wish I knew how to control it."

She sits up straight again. "See? This is why you need spelling. That's how you control them."

"With *poems*?" It comes out snarky.

"Yep." And she's just about to say more when the phone on the bench across the room rings. "One sec," she says. Then she rushes over to it and picks up the handset. I can't really hear what she's saying, but it's a short conversation. And just a couple seconds later, she's back. "I have to step out for a moment. A colleague needs my help."

"But what about my spelling? Should I try a moth spell?"

Talina shakes her head. "That sounds like some pretty powerful shit, Pie. Ask for something easy. Something you really want, but also something you know you deserve."

"Ask?" I say. "I'm not asking anyone for anything. I need to be able to use my own power."

"Then make it super, *super*-easy. Even easier than tea. I'll be back as soon as I can." And then she gathers up her bag and a few notebooks and pushes her way through the doors.

I sit there thinking for a while. What could I do that is super-easy and something I deserve?

I want to open portal doors, but that seems like big magic. I want to get Pell through the doors, but that seems even bigger.

But I don't want to waste time on stupid tea spells. So it has to have *something* to do with portals.

"Oh!" I say it out loud. I even hold up a pointed finger. "I could open Pell's door. The door to his tomb!"

This seems so right. It's an easy task, because Pell already has access to that door. And I can already walk through doors with the bloodhorn scales, so all I have to do is give myself the ability to see this particular door.

I pick up my charcoal pencil and draw his tomb from memory so I can get a clear picture of it in my mind. It's not a perfect drawing because I haven't paid much attention to it, but it's close enough. Then I write the letter A to start.

A horn, a hoof, an eye, a bone.

"No." I laugh. "Not that poem, Pie. Oh!" I say it again. Holy shit. That poem above the doors was a spelling poem!

Oh. My God.

Could this be the way to break the curse?

Break the spelling poem or replace it with a new one?

"Whoa, whoa, whoa, Pie. Calm down." I take a deep breath. "Talina said *easy*."

Right. I will think about that later. After I successfully write my first magic spelling on how to enter Pell's tomb.

So I begin. And by the time Talina gets back, this is what I have:

A wood, a buck, a nymph, and stone.
A way into a satyr's home.
A door appears, the nymph walks through,
And now their lives begin anew.

"Holy crap, Pie. This is… wow!"

"Really?" I'm making one of those all-teeth smiles and holding my hands in front of me like I'm praying. "You really think it will work?"

"There's only one way to find out."

"I know. I can't wait to go home!"

"You should leave early. Like now, if you want."

"It's not time to go home yet. I'm sure Tarq would object."

"Object to you actually doing big magic?" She snorts. "He'll be thrilled. Go ask him, if you want. But this is your job."

She's right. It is my job. And I could go ask Tarq, and he'd probably be fine with it. But he would ask what the spell is for and then I'd have to tell him it's to get inside Pell's bedroom. Because that's basically what his tomb was before we started sleeping together in my cottage. And I don't want to have that conversation.

"I'm sure you're right. But I don't want to mess up my debt repayment. So I'll stay for a little longer."

"Well, the girls are coming to pick me up early. We have pampering this afternoon and then book club."

My eyebrows shoot up. "You have a book club here?" I wonder what monster fiction is like?

"Yep. You wanna join in?"

I would, actually. "What time does it run?"

"Four to six. Happy hour. We do talk about the book, but we do it in a bar." She whispers that last part. And then we both laugh.

"Well, I can't go this time. I didn't read the book. And I have to do magic at home tonight."

"Next week though, I'm holding you to it. I'll get you a copy of the book. Then you can plan ahead for it."

For only being here in this world for two days, I feel like I'm making an awful lot of after-work plans with my brand-new friends.

I like this world though. I like these people. I feel like I fit in. But I need to figure out how to open these freaking portals so Pell can come with me. And this easy portal spelling is my first step.

"Yeah," I tell Talina. "I'll plan for next week."

I'm sure I will be able to come up with a portal spelling for Pell by next week.

Talina is busy for the rest of the morning. Like... incredibly busy. She's running some tests that involve little glass trays, a bunch of chemistry shit, and lots of mumbling to herself. When I ask her about it, she wipes her brow and sighs out something science-y that I have no hope of understanding. So I leave her to it.

I try to write another version of my Invade Pell's Bedroom spell, but I don't get far. Nothing sounds as good. Nothing feels as right. And just as Talina is done cleaning up her space and getting ready to head out, she says, "You can't rewrite them, Pie."

"What?"

"The spells. Once they're done, they're done. The perfect version already exists. So you will spin your wheels if you keep trying."

"But how do I know it's the right version?"

"Because it's perfect, isn't it?" She winks at me. "Now. I hate to leave you like this, but the girls are meeting me downstairs. We're getting our horns and hooves polished for the party tomorrow. Oh, and by the by. Tomorrow? I'll only be in to check on my tests." She points to the little glass trays, which are now resting comfortably in a small, glass-fronted refrigerator. "Then we're off to get our hair done and get dressed for the gala."

"This party sounds like a big deal."

"The biggest." She winks at me again. "Maybe you'll change your mind and come with us?"

"Nope. I have things to do at home. And while they might not be glamorous and worthy of all this primping, I actually prefer it that way."

"Very well. But you won't back out of Zantha's little ceremony on Charmday, right?"

"I'll be there. Oh, hey." I suddenly think of something. "Do you guys have phones here?"

"Phones?" Talina points to the phone on the lab bench.

"Yeah. I see that landline. But do you have cell phones? Is there a mobile way to communicate with each other?"

"Oh, you mean the Grapevine?" She holds up her left hand and pulls her lab coat sleeve down to reveal a thick cuff of a bracelet. "Yeah. Do you have one?"

"No. But if I'm going to spend half my life in this world, maybe I need one."

"You do. We'll sort that out on Charmday morning, if you like."

"OK."

"And don't forget to eat, Pie. It's lunchtime. There's a café in the building. Just think foody thoughts and the hallways will direct you there." Talina smiles at me, then with a final wave leaves through the double doors.

I sit at the conference table for a moment, wondering what I should do now. If my new spelling poem is perfect—and I think it is—then... now what?

Should I write another one?

It's tempting. Especially after my success with the first one. But I don't even know if this one works, so it seems better to wait, test it out tonight with Pell, and then take it from there.

So instead, I reach for the Book of Debt, which is still sitting where Tarq left it, and slide it over to me. I open it to the front and when I see my name, I get a weird feeling in my stomach.

It's unsettling to know that the universe is keeping track of you.

But then... "Holy cow!" I blink my eyes, then rub them. Because I can't be seeing this correctly. The entire first page of debt has been wiped away. "What the fuck?"

How is this possible? I've barely done anything.

Is sex with Pell worth *that* much?

This makes me giggle. Well, if that's the case this bedroom spell will kill two birds with one stone. Three, actually. I will have my fun time with my man,

I will finally get to see his bedroom, and I will wipe away a shitload of debt.

In fact... I have an idea. I should totally rock Pell's world tonight. Last night was fun, but it wasn't like out-of-this-world fun. I could spice things up and get a bigger payout.

I flip the pages. There are still quite a few of them. Five, to be exact. But if I can wipe out a page a day, then I'll only come here for a week. Hell, half a week according to this world's calendar!

Yeah, I can work with this.

In fact, maybe I *should* leave early and get a head start on my debt-erasing goal.

I stuff the Book of Debt into my bag, add my new spelling notebook, and then leave the lab. Talina said I could picture food in my head and be led to the café. So it stands to reason that if I picture the exit portal in my head, I will be taken to the lobby.

So that's what I do.

But for some stupid reason, the hallways don't lead me to the door, they lead me straight to Tarq's office.

Thanks a lot, hallways.

Assholes.

Tarq is pacing his office like he's deep in thought. And I'm hurriedly picturing the café, trying to get the hell out of here before he notices me, when we suddenly lock eyes.

He comes through his door. "Pie. I was just thinking about you."

That can't be good. "Well, I was just leaving, but I can't find the door."

"Oh." He gets one of those crestfallen looks on his face. "I was just going to ask you to lunch. Have you eaten?"

"No. But I was going to *leave*."

"Eat with me first. I need to tell you something."

My shoulders drop, my arms go limp, and suddenly I'm doing the standing monkey walk.

"What is that for?"

"What?"

"That posture? You look... very disappointed."

"Well, when someone says 'I need to tell you something,' it's never good. And I'm feeling pretty good about today, so I don't know if I need this news."

"Oh." He thinks about this for a moment. "Well. I don't think it's bad news. It's just... new news."

"I've had a lot of new things added to my plate lately, Tarq. Can't it wait?"

"It can't. It's about tomorrow."

I narrow my eyes. "What about tomorrow?"

"The queen has heard the rumors."

"Queen?"

"We have a queen, we don't have a king, but we do have... me. And now that she has learned about you, we also have you."

I close my eyes and pray for an intervention. *God. I get it. I'm kinda fun to fuck with. And sometimes even I think it's hilarious. But I'm tired of this right now. I just want to go home. Please, please, please let me just go home.*

"The queen is insisting that you come to the palace this afternoon. In fact, she is expecting us for lunch right now."

I open my eyes and stare right into his. "No. I'm not going. I'm not meeting this queen. I will not get stuck pretending I'm some stupid missing princess. I'm going home, Tarq. Point me to the door right now." I stomp a hoof.

He smiles at me. But it's one of those humoring smiles. The kind of smile that says, *I get it. You're about to lose your shit and I don't want to be here when that happens, so I'm placating you.*

And this is fine with me.

"OK."

"OK?" I ask. "That's it?"

"I know what you're thinking. You're thinking... 'Tarq wants to trap me. He wants me to be his princess.' And you're cute, Pie. I really think you're cute. And if, by some chance, we did get stuck together—say, in a curse of some kind—I wouldn't mind getting stuck with you."

"Um. Thanks?"

"But the truth is, I have a woman. She's..." He hesitates.

"Why are you hesitating?"

"I'm just trying to find the right way to say everything. I don't want to overwhelm you."

I think about this. I'm not sure I believe him. But I'm already tired of this conversation and I just want to get it over with. "She's what? Just tell me."

"She's trapped. That's why I want you to open the portals. I'm not trying to invade anything. I'm trying to save my woman. So whatever. Go home. I will tell the queen you slipped out early. But this isn't going to change anything. She wants to meet you. And that means she *will* meet you."

"What if I don't come back?"

"You owe me. You can try to stay away. And it might even work, for a while. But you *owe* me. The universe keeps track of debts, Pie. And we struck a deal. You sealed that deal when you showed up yesterday. You can't get out of it. If you don't come back, your debt will pile up. And one day it will catch up with you in a very unpleasant way." He pauses, perhaps sensing the building rage inside me, then hurriedly adds, "But you found a way to wipe away a considerable amount of debt in just one night. Perhaps it's the exchange rate, perhaps it's something else. But either way, the universe is helping you right now. Do not. Piss it off."

I sigh and throw up my arms. "Fine. What do I need to do tomorrow?"

"Just let me take you to the palace and introduce you."

"That's it? Just an introduction? There's no special... Princess and the Pea test happening?"

"I don't understand the details of that question, but I understand what you're asking. And my answer is no, but..." He shrugs. "I don't know for certain how she will determine you are the real deal, so to speak."

"But you're some kind of prince, right? Shouldn't you know that? Didn't you have to prove who you were?"

"No. I was sent here by—"

"Ostanes," I say for him. "I already know that."

"Exactly. I was sent here as a... gift. I'm not related to her by blood. I'm not actual royalty. I'm just... powerful. It's more of an honorary title. She owes me."

"Surprise, surprise. Seems like everyone owes you."

And at this statement, he grins. "They do. It's that fucking book."

"Ostanes' book?"

"Yes. It's the source code."

"What does that mean?"

"It's the... hidden rules of the universe. But not just the rules, it's the ability to—not really change them. More like circumvent them."

"Like a cheat."

"Yeah. Sure. Like a cheat."

"Huh. Interesting."

"It is."

"So the rules don't apply to you."

"They do, but they don't have to."

"And yet... you cannot walk through portals, but I can."

"Correct."

"Hmm. Well, I'm not gonna lie, Tarq. This is not looking good."

"How do you figure?"

"You are the ghost in the machine and I'm like... the super-hacker who has control of the machine." Tarq looks confused. "Fine. It's kind of a specific analogy, but still a fitting one. Basically, you and I together are like some... powerful super-team that can bend the will of the universe."

"Yes. I think that sums it up."

"And this queen. She wants us to be together so we can do powerful super-team shit for her."

"Pretty much."

"And what do you think of that, Tarq?"

He walks over to me, places his hands on my shoulders, looks me in the eyes. "I want. To get. My woman back."

I let out a long breath. "Fine. I will cooperate and meet her tomorrow. But I want to leave early today. I'm overwhelmed. I need to go home and chill."

He smiles. "Thank you, Pie. Really. I truly appreciate this. I'll even walk you to the door."

We don't talk on the way to the lobby where my portal door is, but I can sense Tarq's happiness. He's very satisfied.

I'm not really sure what I'm feeling.

It's not a terrible sense of dread, but I'm definitely not as content as I was before I bumped into him.

Nonetheless, he does take me to the lobby and when I approach the space where the door should be and the portal appears, no one tries to stop me from going home, so I count this as a win.

"Bye," I say, rushing towards the now-waiting door.

"See you tomorrow! And it's Fireday. Don't forget!"

"Yep." And I step through thinking I have no idea what the significance of Fireday is.

But then there I am. Home.

I step into my sanctuary and the afternoon sun is shining bright overhead. It's neither hot, nor cold, and there's a little bit of wind.

Somewhere deep inside the maze of tombs, I catch the crackling of an AM radio station and the chatter of monster language. And I swear, I have never been so happy to be in a place in all my life.

No one is waiting to greet me. Probably because I'm home early. So I just start walking in the direction of the cathedral. When I come out on the main path and look to my left, I see Pell.

He's standing in front of the black tomb.

"Hey!" I call, still walking in his direction. "I'm home early!" But he doesn't move. "Pell?"

Something is wrong.

I run up to him, grab his shoulder, and try to turn him, but he won't budge. "Pell?"

I slip around to his front side and when we are facing each other I realize... he's in some kind of trance. I shake him, panic rising inside me.

But then he blinks and smiles. "Pie? What are you doing home?"

"What are you doing here? You were in a trance or something. What's going on?"

"What?"

"I was calling your name. You didn't even see me! What's going on?"

He looks at the tomb, studies it for a moment, then looks down at me. "I went inside."

"What?"

"Well, in my head, I did. I don't think I really went inside. But do you know who I saw in there?"

I don't know. And I don't think I want to know.

But before I can say that, Pell says, "You, Pie. I saw you in there."

CHAPTER TWENTY-THREE – PELL

My balance is off, my head is swimming with visions, and the world beyond Pie is foggy. I hear myself talking and I realize I'm standing outside the tomb. Did I ever go in?

"You don't look good, Pell. Come on. Let's go home and sit down. Can you make it down the hill?"

I feel dumb and weak that she even has to ask me this question. And then the fogginess disappears, the visions recede, and I can concentrate again. "I'm fine."

"I don't think you're fine, Pell. What just happened?"

I point at my favorite broken tomb on the top of the hill and Pie tugs me over there. We sit and I take a moment, then try to explain. "I was working on the bag—shit." I pat my pocket, fully expecting the stupid bag of rings to be missing, but no. It's still there. Thank the gods. I pull it out. "This fucking bag."

"Never mind the bag, Pell. Tell me what happened."

"I was heading up to the hallways to find a new pair of pants—"

"Aww." Pie leans into me, nudging me playfully with her shoulder. "You were looking for pants."

I smile at her. "I knew you'd like that. Anyway. I was passing by the black tomb and I saw a door."

"A door?"

"Yep. I saw it, Pie. And then… I thought I went in. I thought I followed a passageway into a forest. And found another door. You were on the other side of that door, but it wasn't you, not the way you are now. It was some other you. A little you. Then a more grownup version. And I was there too. You were calling me to you. Well, you calling other me."

"Oh, man. If the universe made two of me, and I'm just finding this out now, I'm gonna be pissed." Her words are teasing and mischievous. Like she's deliberately trying to keep the conversation light.

"And then after that I turned back and there was a whole line of doors. Like… all the doors." I spread my arms wide. "Thousands of doors. They were all open and on the other side was a view of… here."

Her perky expression falls and turns into concern. "The sanctuary?"

"Yes. Like… that black tomb is the key to opening all the other tombs."

"But wait." Pie puts up a hand. "Why would they lead to the sanctuary? What's the point of opening those doors only to find yourself back in the sanctuary?"

"No. I agree. That makes no sense. But you know what does make sense? I wasn't in the sanctuary when I saw the doors. I was somewhere else. I think when you're here, and you step into the tombs, you don't see the sanctuary—you see whatever world is on the other side."

"Oh, I get it. You were on the other side looking back."

"Yes!" I point at her. "Yes. I think I was seeing the doors from the other side."

"Weird."

"That's not all. Grant was there."

"Grant? But I thought we decided he was Saturn, or whatever?"

"Yeah. We did. But maybe he wasn't always Saturn. Maybe... maybe Saturn did something to him. It's not like Grant was pressuring me for anything during his time at the sanctuary. It's not like Grant ever cared what I was up to. Why would Saturn spend fifty years cooped up with me?"

"Good question. Why would he?"

"I think Grant was a real person. Maybe he was real the whole time he was here, but when he left the sanctuary Saturn got a hold of him?"

"Well, that does make sense from a sanctuary perspective."

"He told me how to break the curse."

"What? How?"

I shrug with my hands. "I didn't catch the answer. I don't even think I was really inside the tomb. I wasn't, was I?"

"Well. No. Not when I came up to you."

"I think the whole thing was a vision. I can't walk through doors." This makes me sigh heavily.

"Well." Pie holds up a finger. "Not true. You *can* walk through one door."

"A lot of good walking into my own tomb does me."

Pie angles her body into mine. "I had a very interesting day as well. And most of it pertains to that one door you can walk through."

"What about it?"

She claps her hands and wiggles her butt—like she's settling in to the stone. Her jovial nature is back now, her face lit up with a smile. Like she's about to deliver some really great news. This girl. She is so damn cute. "I can spell now, Pell! I wrote a good one too. Like… the perfect spell. And that's not all! Holy shit! Sex with you last night erased an entire page of debt. Let me show you!" She shuffles through her messenger bag, pulls out the Book of Debt, and opens it up. Look!" She points to a blank page.

"I don't get it. What am I looking at?"

"My debt! It's gone! And it's because we had that sexy sex last night."

There is no way to stop my grin. Or the chuckle that follows.

"Right?" Pie nudges me with her shoulder.

"Who knew erasing debt could be so fun?"

"And lucrative!"

"So…" I look at her. She's bright with happiness. And whatever that was—whatever happened to me just a few minutes ago with the tomb—the uneasiness melts away. And Pie's enthusiasm replaces it with a sense of warmth and belonging.

"Yep." She giggles. "We can sex our way out of debt. I could be done with this whole thing in a week, Pell."

I let out a sigh. "That's a nice thought. Not that I mind you having a job. But I like the idea that this would be over."

"Me too. But I have another surprise for you. An even better one."

"I can't wait."

"I wrote a spell to get into your tomb."

"What?"

"Yep. Talina, she's my assistant, she taught me how to spell today. And I wrote one that should"—she once again holds up a finger—"technically allow me to walk into your tomb. And if this works, then I can spell my way to a whole bunch of other things! Specifically, a spell that will let you walk through the portal door with me!"

"Wow. Really?" I picture what it would be like to go there. To be in Tarq's world with her.

"Right?" Pie says. "I think I can do it, too. I think I'm just good at this spelling stuff. I mean, I did banish the sheriff with just the words 'Get out.' And I have the moths, Pell. We don't even know what they really do yet. But if I spell my way into a moth poem, maybe I can figure it out. *Maybe...*" Her blue eyes sparkle. "Maybe I can do big magic too."

She's so excited. I love it. And I can't help myself. I reach for her. I slide my palm around her neck and pull her towards me. And I kiss her. A long, slow, passionate I-really-missed-you-today kiss.

And when we pull apart, we're both panting. I forget about the black tomb, and the fake Pie, and the words from Grant.

None of that was real.

But this girl? She's right here in front of me.

"Do you want to try it out?"

"Do I want to take you into my tomb? Fuck yeah, I do."

She claps again. "Yay! Let's do it. Let's do it right now."

I stand up and offer her my hand. She blushes, then accepts my offer and allows me to pull her to her feet. I stare at her for a long moment, just taking her in. Those long legs, and her sleek blonde fur. The curve of her hips under her pants and the swell of her breasts under the blouse.

"Does everyone wear clothes in this other world, Pie?"

She knows I'm staring at her, lets me appreciate her, but slowly nods her head. "Yeah. They do. I mean, I guess there were a few satyrs with no clothes around the city when we were talking to get coffee yesterday, but for the most part, no dicks were swinging."

I chuckle. "I'm glad to hear it." I like Tarq, but I don't want his swinging dick to be on my Pie's mind all day while she's at work.

We hold hands as I lead her into the maze of tombs towards the only one I have access to. My footsteps are heavy and thudding on the stone, while Pie's are light and tapping. Her gait is bouncy, almost prancing. Like she's got energy to burn and wants to run. The way a racehorse is just before it walks out onto the track.

I stop in front of my tomb. "Here we are."

"This one?" Pie's eyes slowly migrate up the five imposing Roman columns that guard the stoa. I can't see past them right now because Pie is here with me, but usually the inner portico is visible.

"This is the one."

"It's really nice, Pell. It reminds me of those ancient temples. Like… the Sanctuary of Zeus, or whatever."

These words conjure up a memory of a time so long ago, only the edges of it remain. "Yeah. I guess it kinda does."

"Hey. How come there's no statue of you out here?"

"My statue is on the inside. Just past the columns. You can't see it, but it's in the center of the inner chamber."

"How do you get inside?"

"Well, if you weren't here, this black shadowy part"—I wave my hand at the black shadow just beyond the columns—"that would actually be a stoa or portico."

"What's a stoa portico?"

"Oh. It's a walkway. The space between the columns and the inner chamber, which is called a naos."

"Wow." She looks back up at the columns. "It's all very… interesting. But what is all that up there?" She points to the space above the columns.

"That's called the entablature. It's a scene carved in stone. Which, now that I think about it, I actually haven't noticed in centuries."

"A lot of it is broken. What was it a scene of?"

I look up at the carved marble. She's right. A lot of it is broken. I'm the one who broke it. "It's my banishment day."

"Oh. Like those scenes that are carved over the doors and stuff inside the cathedral?"

"Yep. But most of that is lies. And unlike this tomb, they were carved by the hands of a mortal slave caretaker. I hope you don't believe the stories."

"The carvings tell a story?"

I chuckle as I look down at Pie. "God, I love you."

She beams back up at me. "Thanks. But…" She squints and directs her eyes at the entablature. "I think that might be what we need."

"What do you mean?"

"See, from what I can gather the spells for portals probably go over the doorways. Like that poem over the doors all around the sanctuary. And isn't it weird that it changed after I banished the sheriff and Grant—err, Saturn?" I must look confused because she goes on. "'A horn, a hoof'... blah, blah, blah? That poem? Did there used to be words up there?" She points to the broken scene above the columns.

I rub a hand over my scruffy chin. "Maybe."

Pie looks around. "Well. I don't know how to carve words into marble. But ya know what the next best thing is?"

"What?"

"A Sharpie. I have one in the Jeep's glovebox. BRB."

Before I can object, she bounds off, leaping and running in the direction of the cottage, like she couldn't wait to release all that pent-up energy. And while I wait, I look back up at my tomb, which is now open and accessible.

Even though it is late afternoon out here, it is always night in my tomb. But a bit of moonlight is filtering its way through the stoa. Enough so I can see the inner chamber where the stone version of me sits on a stone throne.

I have never liked that statue. It's not a true representation of me. It's not even done in the Roman style. It's got an Egyptian look to it. My head is in profile but the rest of my body is facing forward, rigid and stiff, like I really am made of stone. And I'm wearing clothes. None of the other satyr statues in this sanctuary are wearing clothes. Some might have an armband or a bit of jewelry. A few have a simple loincloth. But the statue of me is fully dressed in the most ridiculous attire.

Furs, of all things. What kind of beast wears the skin of another beast? It's kinda gross. And definitely wrong.

"I got it!" I turn to find Pie leaping over a stone bench and I study her lithe body as she trots up to me. "This should do." A black Sharpie is pinched between her fingers. She holds it up for me as she pants from her run, her cheeks flushed red and the heat coming off her in waves. Her eyes are bright and inquisitive. Like she's on the verge of a great discovery.

I used to wonder if she was stupid, but Pie Vita is not stupid. In fact, I bet she's some kind of genius when she's in her element.

I really hope she can open the portal to Tarq's world. I can't wait to see her at work.

"Now what?"

"Well." She tips her head up so she can study the entablature. "I need to get up there. We need a ladder."

"No, we don't." I kneel down in front of her and tap my bare shoulder. "Get on. I'll lift you up."

"Are you sure?"

I peek up at her and grin. "I'm sure."

She climbs on, I stand up, and she squeals a little, her fingers gripping my head and partially covering my eyes.

I laugh as I step forward. "I hope you're not afraid of heights." Then I reach up and tap the bottom lip of the architrave. "Grab onto the carving, put your hoof in my hand, and I'll lift you up so you can stand on this ledge."

"Oh, shit. What if I fall?"

"Those hooves of yours will know what to do. You won't fall."

"OK." She reaches up, grabs onto a piece of stone, and puts her hoof in my hand. I lift her, easily, and she rises up with a laugh. I grip her ankles tight and lift again, until she steps onto the ledge and lets out a breath. "That was easier than I thought it would be."

She has no idea what that new body of hers can do yet. But it's good to see her push the limits a little.

"OK. I'm gonna do it. If I fall—"

"You won't fall. But don't worry. I'm right here."

She looks down at me and smiles. "My spelling is really good. I think this is gonna work."

"I'm busy looking at your ass, Pie. You've got like three minutes before I yank you down, press you up against a column, and fuck your brains out."

She snorts, then leans up on her tiptoes—her split hooves splaying wide to grip the stone—and begins to write.

I read along as she does this. And I have to admit, her spell is more than good. It's excellent.

She reads it out loud when she's done:

"A wood, a buck, a nymph, and stone.

A way into a satyr's home.

A door appears, the nymph walks through,

And now their lives begin anew."

Then Pie turns, back pressed against the broken carvings, and jumps with a wild grin on her face.

I catch her out of instinct, and she laughs into my ear as she buries her face in my neck, her long legs entwining around my waist.

And that's when I notice... "Holy shit, Pie. You did it!"

Savage Saints - JA Huss Writing as KC Cross

She squirms and I set her down. Then she turns back to my tomb with a gasp. "Ho-lee. Shit."

We just stand there for a few moments, staring dumbly at the sunlight shining into the stoa. "Oh, my God, that's you!" She looks at me, mouth open and face awash in wonderment.

"That's me," I agree. Then I offer her my hand. "Wanna go inside?"

She lets out a breath. Like she's emptying herself out so this new experience can fill her back up. Then she places her hand in mine and we walk up the steps that lead into my tomb.

Two seconds later, we're inside.

And I have to pause for a moment to fully appreciate how important this moment is. No one has ever set foot inside this building besides me.

Until now.

Pie is gravitating towards my statue, but I pull her back and lead her around the other side of the inner chamber. "This is where I go when I'm in here."

And as we get to the back of the statue, everything in front of us becomes forest.

"How big is it?" Pie asks, her voice a hushed whisper now.

"There is no end to these woods. It might actually be some kind of circle, because if you run for long enough, you'll end up right back here. But then again, maybe that's just magic."

"Wow." Her voice is still low. Almost reverent. "It's so dark."

"Yeah. It's always dark in here. But I don't mind it much. And if you're worried about tripping—"

"After all that climbing?" She laughs. "No. I get it. My new hooves are pretty good at keeping me upright. Where do you go when you come here? Do you have a house?"

"No. Not a house, but I do stay in a little clearing. And there's a huge hollowed-out tree. But I mostly sleep outside. I hope it's not too rustic for you. That cottage of yours is downright luxurious compared to my home."

She takes my hand and entwines her fingers with mine. Her eyes are lit up a little. Kind of... smoky blue now, like a fog or the glow from lights at night. "Sleep?" She looks up and around. Even though there's not a lot to see at the moment, the sense of wonderment is all over her face. "I don't think I'll get a single wink of sleep tonight." Then she looks at me, shoulders shrugged up to her ears. "I can't believe I did it. I can't believe how easy it was."

"I'm worried about that too."

"Worried? Oh, I'm not worried. Today might be the first day in my entire life that I feel..." She lets out a long breath. "That I feel... powerful."

This statement is both sad and uplifting. I hate that she spent her life feeling inadequate. And if she's not human, then that's even worse. Because someone trapped her inside that human body and just... left her there. To be abandoned.

"I think I'm really good at this spelling stuff, Pell. I think I really can break your curse. I think... I think all I have to do is rewrite the poem over the doors and then—"

I place a fingertip on her lips and she stops talking immediately. "Tomorrow, Pie. It's been a long day. And maybe you won't be able to sleep—I'll stay up with you, if that's the case—but maybe, after I'm done with you, you'll be so exhausted you'll pass out and have the best sleep of your life."

She reaches up, takes my hand, kisses the tip of my finger, and pushes her body into mine. "Take me there. Take me to your little clearing right now or I won't be able to stop myself."

There's a part of me that wants to keep the banter going. I like that about us. I like teasing a blush out of her, and I like the way her innocent reactions heat me up from the inside out.

But instead, I take her hand and lead her deeper into the forest. My hooves follow a path carved out after thousands of years of travel. It is well worn, and smooth, and comforting as it weaves its way around giant trees and through cracks in ancient slabs of granite.

Finally, the clearing is in front of us.

"I can't see anything, Pell." Pie whispers this. Like she's afraid we might wake something up.

"It's OK. Just follow me." I've still got a hold of her hand, so I tug her a little. Being her eyes.

"Can you see in the dark?" Pie asks.

I stop and turn, then look her up and down. I don't really know what darkness looks like because I've never seen it. Not the way others describe it—a void. A blackness. Utterly empty.

I don't see blackness in the dark, I see a faint lavender glow. It's just a touch of light. And I'm not even sure it is light. It feels like smoke. Like air. Like mist. But it's not any of those things. It's just a tiny bit of glow.

But to my eyes, it might as well be the sun. That's how well I see in the dark.

Right now, Pie looks like an ethereal being. Some kind of fairy, maybe. Not the human-sized ones that walk between worlds. The tiny, sweet kind that live inside the cups of blooming flowers or the dip down the middle of a broad leaf.

Not for the first time, I wonder what kind of chimera she really is. Because she seems like so much more than the woods.

"What?" she says. "Why did we stop?" She probably can't see me, but we've been standing here for several seconds in silence, so it's getting awkward.

"Fairy blood," I say.

"What?" She laughs this word out.

"I think you have fairy blood in you."

"What's that got to do with anything?"

Then I remember her question. "Yes. I see in the dark."

"Oh. Well, that's handy."

I smile at her, still unable to believe that she's mine. And I mean 'mine' in the very literal sense of the word. "Come on," I say, pulling her towards me. "It's right over here."

We enter the clearing and the smooth path under our hooves turns into a mass of grass. Not the kind that stands up and tickles your legs as you walk through it, but the heavy kind that flops over and makes a soft cushion to lie upon.

"Mmm," Pie moans. "The ground is so soft."

I stop and kneel down, still holding her hand, so she kneels with me.

"Are we here?" she asks.

We're facing each other, her eyes trying to find me in the dark. "We're here." I reach down to find a candle inside a lantern, take it out, light it with a flint, then put it back inside the lantern.

Pie's face flickers with the dim glow of candlelight as I reach for the tiny buttons on her silk blouse. She takes a deep breath, like this excites her and makes her nervous in the same instant. We've had sex at least once a day for weeks now. But this time feels different.

This time feels like a first.

So I go slow. Taking my time. Undoing each button carefully. And when that's done, I slide the silk down her arms and let the blouse float to the ground.

Pie smiles at me, the lavender glow gone now, replaced by an almost unearthly golden radiance. We study each other for a moment. I'm caught in the spell of her eyes and maybe she is caught in mine too, because it's a long moment of just... nothing.

But it's so much more than nothing. I reach out and cup her breasts in my hands. Pie responds by closing her eyes and reaching for me. Her hand sliding up against the hard bulge beneath my pants.

I close my eyes as well. Wanting to enjoy every moment. I don't want to miss a single feeling.

She pops the button on my pants, slides her hand inside, and wraps her warm palm around my shaft.

"Fuck." She has no idea what she's doing to me now.

Or maybe she does. Because she scoots closer—still on her knees—and then she presses her breasts up against my bare chest and leans into my neck to whisper, "I want to do things to you, Pell."

My hands slip down from her firm, soft breasts until they find the waist of her pants. They are unzipped and open in a moment. She giggles and pulls away, but I push her back into the spongy grass, hook my fingers around the waistband of her pants, and pull them down her legs.

Then I plant my hands on either side of her shoulders and slowly ease my body down on top of hers. Pie's hands grip my upper arms as my cock—still trapped inside these fucking pants—throbs against her lower belly.

Pie leans up to kiss me, her full, soft lips fitting against mine so perfectly. And just as her tongue slips in to tantalize me, she opens her legs, inviting me in.

"Take off those pants," she whispers into my mouth.

I pull back from the kiss and almost guffaw. "After all these weeks trying to make me cover myself, now you're suddenly eager—"

"Oh, shut up and take off the pants!"

I don't want to. I mean, I *do* want to. But I don't want to be away from her for the few seconds it will take for me to stand up and pull them down my legs.

Still, it has to be done. I need to be inside her.

I stand up—but to my surprise, Pie swats my hands away and unzips my zipper.

She looks up at me, still on her knees. And now... now this position is something else. I hold my breath, not even daring to dream about her intentions.

Once my zipper is down, she hooks her fingers into the belt loops and tugs until the tight pants slide down my legs and my dick springs up, finally free.

Pie is still looking up at me. She licks her lips, opens her mouth and—

"Holy fuck," I mutter, my hands immediately gripping her head as her lips seal over my shaft and I slide deep into the back of her throat. For a moment I'm lost in the ecstasy. My eyes close and my head tips back as she works magic with her tongue. Her hand slides up and down my shaft as she plays with the tip of my cock and even though I want this to go on forever, if it goes on much longer it will take all the fun out of what comes next. Because I will explode inside her mouth.

So I kneel down, forcing my cock to slide from between her lips, and even though she moans a protest, I cut it off with a kiss as I push her back onto the soft mat of long grass.

She squirms and wriggles underneath me, giggling a little as I pin her down with the weight of my body, then nudge her legs open with my knee.

Pie responds without hesitation, her hands gripping the muscles of my shoulders, her nails digging into my flesh just a little. I reach down, slide my hand between us, and slip my fingers into the waiting pool of wetness between her legs.

Pie bucks her back a little, biting her lip and moaning. Her eyes open now, looking straight at me. She flickers in the candlelight—dark, then light. Dark, then light.

Her hands come up to my face and she holds me like that, her eyes gazing into mine. This is how I enter her. Looking straight into her soul. She gasps as I fill her up, once again digging her fingernails deep into my flesh.

I want to fuck her hard. I want to make her moan, and whine, and keen from my rough handling.

But even though that sounds fun—and I'm sure it would be something Pie would enjoy—I would rather make it something more. Something meaningful.

So I slow down and let Pie catch her breath. "What's wrong?" she whispers.

"Absolutely nothing. I'm just gonna take my time, if that's OK."

She smiles at me in the yellow-orange glow of candlelight. Then she reaches up to my horns and gently strokes them as I carefully and slowly attend to her needs. I push up inside her—deep inside her—but I take my time and let her fully experience the sensations. Her hands grip my horns and she slides them up and down the same way she did my shaft a few minutes earlier.

This friction heats them up and they begin to glow with bloodfire. New shadows of red and black play across Pie's face as I ease back out of her, just leaving the tip of my dick in that glorious pool of wetness. Her hips thrust up against mine and I smile.

"Go faster," she says. "You're teasing me."

But I decide to give her one better. I wrap my hands around her waist and roll us over, so she's on top.

I decide to give her control.

Pie chuckles as she lifts up her hips, pressing her palms flat on my chest, and then sinks down.

I slide inside her and she throws her head back. This makes her breasts perk up and nipples tighten. I thrust up, making her tits bounce. Then I grab them with both hands and squeeze. Pie's excitement is building and she begins to bounce on her own, allowing me to slide deeper and deeper inside her.

My fingers trace down her stomach and land right between her legs. She opens her eyes, watching as I flick the tip of my thumb back and forth across her sweet nub.

There is a moment when she goes still. Her face tight, biting her lip.

And then it's like an explosion. She moans out into the darkness, her body tensing up, then falling forward on top of me as her pussy squeezes my cock. It's an irresistible invitation—much like that moment when she took my dick in her mouth. And even though I would like this to go on forever, I can't help myself.

I wrap my arms around her waist, pulling her tightly to me. Her mouth finds mine and we kiss as I come inside her.

It's a moment that seems to last a lifetime but also goes by far too quick. We linger there in the afterglow of sexual heat, sweaty and panting hard.

I trace a finger up and down her spine as her body becomes relaxed and lazy on top of me.

Her breathing slows, and so does my heart.

Finally, she says, "Pants are kinda dumb."

And I laugh into the night.

At some point, we must've drifted off. Because the next thing I know I'm waking from slumber. Pie is sitting up next to me. And there is a new kind of glow all around her. My movement makes her turn and when I see her face, I see her smile. "Look, Pell," she whispers. "Look at them."

I look up at the air just over her head and find the source of the new glow.

Then I sit up, rubbing the sleep out of my eyes. "What are they?"

"Fireflies," she says. Then she opens her palm and points it at me. Tiny orange fireflies burst into the night, growing bigger as they get further away. And then they light up a golden yellow and flicker dark and light. Dark and light.

"What happened to the moths?"

"I dunno," Pie says. Then she tips her head up and grins at the change in her power. "I don't know, but I like the fireflies better."

She lies back, fitting into the crook of my arm like we were meant to be this way.

We watch the flickering glow as the swarm of lights disperses into the tops of the giant trees, then finally merges with the sky, becoming pinprick stars in the night.

CHAPTER TWENTY-FOUR – TOMAS

The feed store is closed when I get into town, but there is a note on the door so I get out of the truck and walk up to it.

Tomas—I'm running an errand for my uncle. I'll meet you at Big Jim's at seven.

She signs her name Madeline with a heart over the 'i.' I stare at the note. Enjoy the way my name looks in her loopy cursive handwriting. Then I fold it up, tuck it into the front pocket of my flannel shirt, and get back in the truck so I can drive down to Big Jim's.

When I walk inside, he's at the counter, messing with something. The bell jingles over the door and he looks up. "Yep," he says. "Madeline said you'd be by. How are the generators working?"

I walk up to the counter and casually lean against it, taking a moment to realize where I am and what I'm doing. And how, one year ago, I would've never guessed that this would be my new life. Wouldn't even have dared to dream it.

"Hello?"

"Sorry. I was lost in thought."

"Yeah. I gathered that about you."

"Gathered what?" I ask, my face scrunching up in confusion.

"You're one of those thinkers. A deep thoughts kind of man."

"Hmm." I consider this, not sure if he's right. Pell would definitely not agree. But then again, Pell doesn't know me very well, does he? He thinks he does, but... he's wrong. "Maybe I am," I finally decide.

"Yeah," Big Jim agrees. "But that's the problem."

"Problem? What problem?"

"With you and Madeline?"

"What are you going on about?"

"She's not your type, Tomas. Can't you see it?"

"Not my type? I'm not sure I have a type." In fact, I'm positive I don't. Because I've been in the company of exactly two women in my entire existence. But I don't tell him this. Maybe I'm not an expert in this new, modern world but I know a man who appears to be my age—which Pie says is somewhere around twenty-eight—and with my physique and handsome good looks would've been with dozens of women by now.

I try to picture that, what it would feel like to have had dozens of women in my bed, but find that I can't.

Madeline is the girl in my fantasy bed.

The only one I need.

"She's... different," Big Jim says.

"Different how?"

"You know. *Off.*"

Off. I say that word in my head, trying to understand what he means.

"She's... weird, Tomas. You can do better than her."

"*Better* than her?" I scoff. "My dear man, your niece is perfect in my eyes."

He points at me. "See? That's not right, son. It's very weird. And if you feel that way, fine with me. None of my business. But don't go saying that around town if you want people to like you."

"What?" I'm just about to ask him to explain when the bell over the door jingles again, making me turn.

And there she is.

My Madeline.

Smiling, and happy, and covered in a layer of feed store dust that I find both alluring and sweet.

"You're here," she says, walking up to me. "I hope you weren't waiting long."

I smile back at her, enamored. "I literally just walked through the door, luv."

"Hope my uncle wasn't bending your ear off. He has a tendency to do that with my friends." She eyes him. But it's not with suspicion, even though it should be. It's affection, I realize. She loves her uncle. Then she drops a paper bag on the counter and says, "It's all there. See ya tomorrow, Uncle Jim."

She waves at him, grabs my hand, and tugs me towards the door.

Big Jim calls out, "Better heed my words, son."

I look over my shoulder just as Madeline pulls me through the door and find Big Jim walking off with the paper bag she delivered.

"What was that about?" Madeline asks, once we're standing by my truck.

"What?"

"Heed his words? Was he fillin' your head up with a bunch of crazy conspiracy theories about monsters?"

"Um…"

"Don't listen to him."

"Oh, don't worry about that. I won't. He has no idea what he's talking about."

"Where should we go? Are you hungry?"

"No. I'm really not. But if you are—"

"Nah. I ate a late lunch. I know we planned on going out of town tonight, but… would you rather go into the woods?"

"The woods?" I glance at the forest around us.

"Not these woods." She playfully slaps me on the chest. "It's a nice night. And we won't get many more of these since it's gonna be full-blown winter soon. We should make the most of it while we can. There's a state park not too far from here. It's got a good trail and at the end, there's a waterfall and a little pavilion where you can sit. That waterfall freezes in January, but it won't be frozen yet. We used to go up there in high school all the time."

I think about this. It sounds nice, actually. There's a chill in the air tonight and that's not something I'm used to, since the weather inside the sanctuary is almost always mild and sunny. But I've got a coat on. Still, I worry about being around too many people. "Won't there be kids up there now?"

"Nah. They stopped going up there a few years back." Madeline rolls her eyes. "Monsters. They're all afraid of the monsters."

"Hmm."

"Don't worry, Tomas. They're not real."

"I know. As my good friend, Pie, would say, your uncle is full of shit."

Madeline giggles. "Well. No. I mean, he is weird and everything. But he actually knows a lot about the monsters. He wrote a few books about monsters. And whenever they have those conspiracy conventions, he's always invited to be a speaker. So he's legit. But"—she presses an open hand at me—"not about these woods. I've been all over these woods. Trust me, Tomas. There are no monsters here."

I smile and realize she's even more of a delight today than she was yesterday. I have no idea what Big Jim was going on about, but whatever it was, he's wrong about Madeline. "To the woods we go, my dear lady." Then I take her hand, lead her over to the other side of the truck, open her door, and put her inside.

She is wonderful, I decide.

Simply wonderful.

We chat the entire drive up to the trailhead. She tells me about her day, and her customers, and her lunch break at the Honey Bean diner.

I tell her about mine, as well, describing the sanctuary and the monsters—minus their monstrous bits. Her eyes go wide when I describe the breakfast Cookie made this morning. And then she laughs out loud when I tell her how they reacted to Big Jim's show last night. "They are all into this," I say. "They want to hunt monsters now too."

"Are they gonna go with you?"

"With me?"

"Aren't you hunting monsters with Uncle Jim and Sheriff Roth tomorrow night?"

"Oh. I forgot all about that. No. I had better leave them home." Then I laugh at the thought of showing up for a monster hunt with the actual monsters being hunted.

Except Big Jim and Russ Roth aren't hunting those monsters.

They are hunting Pell. They just don't know it yet.

"Has your uncle ever caught a monster?"

"Yeah. Plenty of them."

"What?"

She giggles. "I swear. He catches them for real. But like I said, they're not around here. He never found any around here."

For a moment I wonder if I will need to rescue these captive monsters and take them home to the sanctuary. "Where does he keep them?"

"Keep them?" Madeline looks confused.

"The monsters. When he catches them, where does he keep them?"

"Oh. He doesn't catch them in that respect. He… hunts them."

"He kills them?"

I'm appalled. And I'm pretty sure this shows on my face because Madeline says, "I know. I don't like it either. Even though I'm like a hundred percent sure these monsters of his are just deformed deer, or whatever. I don't like the thought of killing them. He should just let them be."

I frown, picturing what this hunt might turn into tomorrow night.

"If you don't want to go with them, you don't have to, Tomas. You don't need to impress my uncle. He will like you because I like you. Because he likes me."

I reach for her hand and squeeze it just as we pull into the trailhead parking lot.

She is sweet. Maybe too sweet. Not for me—I love sweet.

But she's misguided about her uncle. I don't think he cares about her the way she cares about him.

Why would he say those things to me? Why would he call her 'weird' and 'off?'

I don't like it.

I don't like him, I decide.

I am going on that hunt tomorrow night. He won't be finding any monsters, but… perhaps it's time for the monsters to find him?

"Here we are," Madeline says. Then she lets go of my hand and opens her door. "Come on. I'll take you up the trail and show you the waterfall."

I get out and meet her at a sign for the trailhead. I read it out loud. "Saint Valentine's Falls. One point five miles. Who's that? Saint Valentine?"

"Oh. I dunno. I guess I never thought about it before."

She reaches for my hand and our fingertips touch. It startles me for a moment, and when I don't immediately grasp on to her, she pulls back. "Sorry."

"What are you sorry for?"

"I guess I was being presumptuous. By trying to hold your hand."

I reach for her hand and lace our fingers together. "You weren't." This makes her smile. And shyly look away from me. Perhaps hiding a blush.

"Come on. It's not a far hike."

We begin walking up the trail, our hands swinging a little. And it's quiet. Which I don't really mind because I'm usually alone. But it feels a little awkward when I'm with a woman in the dark. So just to make conversation, and because it's still fresh in my mind, I ask, "Are there any other things with the name Saint around here?"

"Hmm. Yeah. I guess I never thought about it before but lots of places around town have the name Saint in them."

"Really?" I look down at her, confused. Because is it odd that the sanctuary is called Saint Mark's and this waterfall is called Saint Valentine's? "Like what, for instance?"

"Like what?" She sighs. "Well, there's the bar. Savage Saints. And the laundromat. Spinning Saints. And, of course, there's the church, Saint Augustine's."

"Is it normal for places to be called after saints?"

"Normal?" Madeline thinks about this for a moment. "I'm not really sure if it's normal. I guess it is. I never thought about it much. And I haven't been very many places to compare the names of local things. Not any farther than Pittsburgh, actually. Sad, right?"

"Why would it be sad?"

"Well, I'm so… unworldly. Ya know. Hick."

"Hick? What does this mean?"

"Backwards. Dumb. Simple."

Her face has changed, going from bright and excited to… I'm not sure. Possibly sad. "I like simple," I say. "And you're certainly not dumb. You know everything there is to know about hay."

A laugh bursts out of her. "I'm not sure that's a selling point, Tomas. But thank you."

"Oh, it's a marvelous dataset to possess. I had no idea what I was doing the other day. And Pell"—I chuckle—"he was quite perplexed as well. I love seeing him off his game. He's always walking around the sanctuary like he's the King of Beasts."

"The sanctuary?"

Oh, shit. I should not have said that.

"What's the sanctuary? That's the name of your camp?"

"Ummm. Part of it, yes."

"Why do you call it a sanctuary? Is it a religious place?"

"Mmm. No. Not quite."

She giggles. "OK. Now you're being cryptic. And that just makes me want to know more. Tell me about it. You live up there with no power. It's like… what? An off-grid community of oddballs?"

"That's a good way to put it, I guess."

"Does your family live there with you? Are you related to that other guy? Pell?"

"No family. But Pell and I are like…" I let out a breath. "Friends."

"Good friends?"

"Well, for most of our lives we've simply tolerated each other. But lately, after Pie came, we've gotten closer."

"Pie?"

I really need to shut up. "She lives there too."

"But she's new?"

"Yes. Very new."

"So you take on new people?"

"Well… technically, yes. We do. We've taken on a lot of new people lately. But it's a recent thing as well."

She stops walking and turns to face me. "Do you think I might fit in up there?"

I just blink at her for a moment. "You want to come up to the sanctuary?"

She nods.

And I hesitate. Which is the wrong thing to do, because it only takes her a few seconds to backtrack.

"Never mind. It was stupid of me to ask. I mean, we don't even know each other. And I'm the town weirdo." She drops my hand, turns around, and starts walking back to the parking lot.

"Where are you going?"

She stops. Her shoulders slump. Then she sighs. "You don't have to pretend, Tomas."

"Pretend what? I don't understand."

She turns to face me. Her mood... not dark, not angry. Sad, I think. "You don't have to pretend that you like me."

"Why would I be pretending?"

"Are you kidding? Look at you."

I look down at myself. I'm wearing a blue and red checked flannel, a black t-shirt underneath, a pair of light jeans, and work boots. Pie helped me choose clothes from the hallways a couple weeks ago. She said it would make me blend in with the people in town. And she was right. Madeline is wearing a flannel as well. Brown and scarlet. But she's wearing a heavy canvas coat too, since it's chilly out. "It is quite a nice outfit, but I don't understand what this has to do with pretending."

This makes her chuckle. "I don't get you."

"What's not to get?"

"Tomas. You're... hot. Like... supernaturally hot. Like..." She cannot find her words, so she just shakes her head.

"When you say 'hot' you mean figuratively. I'm not on fire, right?" I look down at my arms to make sure.

This makes her guffaw. "Oh, man. See? Are you fucking with me?"

"Fucking with you? Like… pulling your leg or teasing you?"

"Yes."

"Why would I do that?"

"Because… *look* at you. And then… look at me."

"I am looking at you. And I like what I see."

"This." She points at me. "Why would you like *me*, Tomas? Why are you even here with me?"

"Because you're… simple." I smile. "I like simple." She doesn't know what to say. But thanks to the conversation with her uncle earlier, I'm starting to understand.

You could do better. That's what he said. And he must've said something similar to Madeline and that's why she's unsure of my intentions tonight.

I take her hand once again and squeeze it just a little. "I think you're very pretty, Madeline. I like your sparkling eyes, I like your plaited hair, I like the way you dress, and talk, and laugh. I like the dust and the smell of sweet feed on your clothes. I like how you know everything about hay." Then I shrug. "I just like you. I'm not teasing you. And if you want to come see my sanctuary, well… I can make that happen. And if you want to stay there, I can make that happen as well."

She lets out a breath and her smile slowly creeps back. "You can? You will?"

"Sure."

"Are they all like you?"

"Who?"

"Your people at your camp?"

"Well…" I bob my head back and forth a little, thinking about this. "We do all have one thing in common. Two, actually."

"Really? What are they?"

And now I'm in trouble. Because my answers are 'we are all monsters' and 'we are all cursed.'

But I don't say that. I say, "We were all alone... until we found each other."

Her brightness returns. Her cheeks might even blush pink, but it's hard to tell in the moonlight.

"Come on." I tug her. "Let's find that waterfall."

We're quiet after that. And it's not awkward or too silent, either. It's just right.

We hear the waterfall before we turn the corner and see it. It's not big, like the ones I've visited in the upstairs hallways. It's rather small, actually. But it's fitting for this place. Just the right size, actually.

Madeline leads me over to a picnic table and we sit, our backs to the table, and gaze out over a pool of silver water.

"I like to swim up here in the summer," she says.

"Not afraid the monsters will get you?"

She chuckles. "No. But if there are monsters up here, then I love that."

"Why?"

"Because. That's why no one comes up here anymore. And the only reason I can."

"You didn't come up here with the other kids, did you?"

"Nope. I'm a loner. And before you feel sorry for me, don't bother. I like being a loner."

"Hmm. I like being a loner too. Especially when we're alone together."

She turns to look at me.

And I turn to look at her.

And then... there it is. She moves towards me, and I move towards her, and I have my first *real* kiss.

A kiss that is not a dare from Pell or a peck on the cheek to say goodbye.

A kiss that is... something else entirely. Something so very, very much more.

I don't even know how it happens. One moment we're alone together and the next we're... just... together.

It only lasts for a few moments and then we pull away and sit there in silence.

And nothing about this is awkward.

Eventually we talk. And walk back to the truck. And I drop her off near her uncle's store and watch her walk into the woods and disappear.

And then I spend all twenty minutes of my drive home replaying that kiss in my head on repeat.

I have a girlfriend.

A *real* girlfriend.

I want to invite her up to the sanctuary, and give her a place of her own, and sleep with her at night the way Pell and Pie do. And wake up to her. And kiss her good morning, and good afternoon, and good night.

I want to bring her into my world and I want to keep her forever.

CHAPTER TWENTY-FIVE – PIE

Pell stirs next to me. Then it's as if we both awaken at the same time and cling a little tighter to each other. He pulls me closer, his large palm flat against my lower belly. His… "Oh, God."

"What?" he mumbles. But I can hear the smile on his face.

"You know what. Your giant package is poking me."

He buries his face into the back of my neck and a rush of warmth floods my body. Last night was fun.

"Last night was fun," he says, reading my mind.

"Wanna do it again?"

He lets out a long breath. "Woman, if we get started now you will not be going to work today. Morning sex is for weekends, remember?"

"Throwing my words back at me," I huff.

He squeezes me. "Tomorrow is the weekend. We'll have morning sex."

"Oh. Shit."

"What?"

"I forgot to tell you. It's not a seven-day workweek there. It's ten."

"Ten?" He sits up a little to look at me. "What kind of fucking monster has a ten-day workweek?"

"Right?" I sigh. "You have to work eight and then you get two off. So I won't even get my first day off until late next week."

"You should go on strike."

"I'm a hundred percent on board with that."

He presses his lips into my neck. "Ya know... if you can open one door you can open many doors."

I turn, trying to face him. Pell fights this, unwilling to stop clinging, but I win. And when we're eye to eye, I place my hands flat on his cheeks. "I was thinking the same thing. I have a feeling I'm good at this shit, Pell."

"You're finally admitting the obvious?"

"The obvious?"

"That you're a witch."

"Oh, no. I'm not a witch. I'm just a girl who can spell. Actually, I think it's all about the rhyme. Don't you think?"

"'A wood, a buck, a nymph, and stone. A way into a satyr's home. A door appears, the nymph walks through, and now their lives begin anew.'" Even I think this is good. And I'm really not the kind of girl who brags. "It's very catchy, Pie."

"And you know what?" I sit up and prop my elbow under my chin.

"Tell me."

"It was easy, Pell. I feel like this spelling shit might be my thing. I'm gonna try to spell you into my new job world."

He puts his hand behind his head and looks up. "I would love that. It would just be so nice to be with other people like me."

"There are fifty other monsters here now."

"It's not the same."

"They're not Tarq."

"Exactly."

I lie back too, also looking up. There's a tree up there. It's kind of a willowy tree with thin boughs that have wispy trails of leaves. "Fireflies."

"Yeah. How about that."

"Better than moths. But why do you think they changed?"

"I think it's about emotions."

"Oh. That kinda makes sense. So my moth power is dark and dangerous. And my firefly power is soft and sexy."

He slowly turns his head, grinning. "You're the best."

"*You're* the best."

We both laugh.

But I get what he's saying. And he gets what I'm saying too.

We're not alone anymore.

And it's nice.

Something catches my eye off to the left and Pell must see it at the same time, because he sits up a little.

"What's that?"

"I dunno," I say. But no sooner are those words out of my mouth than I realize what it is.

Pell sits all the way up. Rubs his eyes. "Am I seeing things?"

"No. I see it too. It's a fucking door." And no sooner does that come out of my mouth than a noise off to the right catches my attention. "What's that?" I look over at our pile of clothes. They're moving. "Please tell me that's not a rat. I will burn those cute pants and silk blouse."

"Listen," Pell says.

We both lean forward to hear the tiny sound. "What is it?"

"Shit." Pell gets up—his morning-wood package dangling between his legs—and walks over to our clothes.

"What? What is it?"

He lifts up his pants and points to the pocket. "That fucking bag of rings." Then he reaches in, pulls out the bag, and yep. Sure enough, they are moving around in there. In fact, they are moving around so much, the bag is leaning to one side. In *mid-air*.

And not just any side, either. They are leaning towards the shimmering new portal door.

"Uhhhh... what's happening?" I get to my feet.

"I'm not sure." Pell stares at the bag, then at the door. He opens the bag and he's about to look down into it when a ring flies up and starts spinning in the air.

Then it comes straight at me—like a frickin' bullet!

But instead of taking me out, it slides onto my finger!

"Oh, fuck this!" I shake my hand, trying to get the ring off. But when I look down, it has melded with my other ring. Like... like... *melted into it* and now I'm wearing a completely different ring!

"What the hell!" I hold my hand up so Pell can see.

"Well... that's weird."

"Weird? A magic ring just assaulted me!"

He chuckles. Then he side-eyes the door. "Hmm."

"What?"

"Why is this happening now? I mean, you've been around the rings for weeks. Why now?"

I already know. So I sigh out the word. "Great. That's just great. This is about that stupid door, isn't it?"

We both look at the shimmery portal, and then it just fades away as we watch.

Pell and I stare at each other. Then he throws up his hands. "I have no clue."

"Hmm." I look down at the new ring. It used to be silver with little leaves and tiny acorns on it. But now it's kind of a brassy gold with a loop of moths.

Pell comes over and takes me hand, studying the ring. "Moths." Then he looks at the empty space where the portal was. "Hmmm."

"Hmmm what?"

"That ring is a key to that door."

"How do you figure?"

"What do you mean? Clearly it opened the door."

"No. It *closed* the door, Pell."

"Hmm," he says again. Then he peers into the bag of rings. "I wonder what the other ones do?" And then he actually reaches in, like he's gonna grab one.

"Well, don't bring one out! I don't want, or need, more ring magic!"

"I don't think these rings are for the monsters, Pie. I think they're for you."

"Well… what should I do?"

He shrugs. "Learn to use them?"

I squint my eyes at him.

"What? You were just bragging about your spelling ability. Why are you getting so upset about a bag of magic rings?"

"Because I'm in control of the spelling, Pell. I'm not in control of these rings. Like at all."

"Well... write a spell to control them."

I think about this for a moment. "Can I do that?"

"Why *couldn't* you do that?"

"Oh, I dunno. Perhaps there's some rulebook called *Pie and Her Magic Rings* out there somewhere and if I fuck around and find out, it's gonna trap me in some magic debt for a bazillion years."

"Alternatively," he says, in his I'm-the-calm-one-here voice, "you might just grab that bull by the hornjob and take over the world."

I crack a smile. "It's not funny."

"It was a little bit funny."

I let out a long breath. "Well, what should we do with the bag?"

"You can take it with you, if you want."

"Why the hell would I do that? I walk through portal doors to get to work, Pell. This sounds like a bad idea."

"Yeah," he admits. "You're probably right. I could keep them here."

"What if another portal door opens and they just... fly through?"

He shrugs with his hands. "Problem solved?"

I narrow my eyes at him. Tap my hoof. "You don't seem very concerned about this."

"I've lived in this tomb for two thousand years, Pie. I've never seen a portal open like that before today."

"So it's me." I try to say this calmly, but I don't entirely succeed. The shock of the portal door and ring attack has worn off now and panic is setting in.

"I'll just keep them with me. I'm finishing the new bag today, anyway. It's not a big deal."

"But... should I put a spell on it? You know, to keep them from doing anything weird?"

"Should you? Couldn't hurt. But can you?"

I bite my lip and think, tumbling words around in my head. "What would be the goal?"

"Keep them hidden? That's a good start."

"And keep people from finding them."

"Perfect. Give it a whirl." Then he grins at me.

"What? Why are you looking at me like that?"

"Because I get to watch you do your thing."

I swell a little with pride. "My spelling skills are gonna impress the fuck out of you."

"I can't wait."

"OK. Let me think. It needs to start with A. Talina told me that. And it needs to have the right syllables. And the rhyme, of course."

"Of course."

I bob my head to a beat, trying to get the cadence right.

Pell says, "Don't forget about the bag. Bag magic is a thing. I'll even lend you some of my breath to seal the deal."

"OK. Let me think." It takes me a few moments, but then, all of a sudden, there it is. The spell is in my head and the words on the tip of my tongue. "'A bag and rings to hide inside. Keep them safe from... prying eyes. Invisible they will be. Cloak them up, no one can see.'"

I do a little poof with my fingers in the direction of the bag because... that feels necessary. Then Pell brings the opening up to his mouth and breathes inside it.

"Done," he says. "But we'll probably have to do it again tonight."

"How come?"

"I'm gonna finish the new bag today. It's a magic bag. More magic is better, right?"

Is more magic better? I'm not sure I agree. But I don't want to spoil his contribution. We feel like a team right now. So I say, "Right."

"OK." Pell extends his hand to me. "Let's get you some work clothes, young lady. And I have to get the forge started."

We put yesterday's clothes back on, and then Pell leads me back through the tomb forest. It's still as dark as it was last night and I'm very glad I'm not in here alone because it would take all of ten seconds for me to get lost. But pretty soon we see light leaking through the tree branches and then we're at the edge of the inner chamber.

We don't stop. Pell just tugs me towards the exit. But I look over my shoulder at the statue on the throne.

It's Pell, but not Pell. And to be honest, the whole Egyptian vibe is a little bit unsettling. I have never liked ancient Egypt. In school, kids were all fascinated by the writing, and the pyramids, and the mummies. But it always weirded me out. And they had tombs. With... curses.

Hmm.

Now I am interested. And I want to go back and study it. Learn every line and curve of that thing. Peer into its stone eyes and run my fingertips along its stone horns.

But Pell is tugging and then I'm outside and the inner chamber is nothing but a wall.

Batty is waiting for us and Tomas is just coming around a tomb, heading this way.

"There you are," he calls. But I think he's talking to Pell. "I have to talk to you, Pell. There's some shit going down tonight and you need to know about it."

Pell lets out a long breath. Like he wants nothing to do with Tomas and his problems. "Later, Tomas. I'm walking Pie down to her cottage to get ready for work. And then I have important things to do at the forge."

"But—" Tomas protests. "It's about the town. And the sheriff."

"Russ Roth?" I ask. "What about him?"

"I met him," Tomas says.

Pell is annoyed. "Why are you talking to the sheriff, Tomas? What the actual fuck?"

"I didn't. Not on purpose. He was in Big Jim's shop when I went looking for Madeline. They're going into the hills tonight to hunt a monster called a squonk buck."

"A what?" I ask.

"Don't ask me," Tomas says. "Madeline says it's some hideous conspiracy monster. But it sounds suspiciously like Pell."

"What would I have in common with a hideous monster?" Pell growls.

And this makes me giggle. "Thanks, Tomas. But we'll all be safely behind the walls tonight. So they can hunt this thing all they want, right Pell?"

"Right." He squeezes my hand. "Come on. Let's go."

"But—" Tomas protests.

But then Batty is right in front of me, trying to hand me another sandstone rock. I take it and nod. "Thanks, Batty. I'll bring it back tonight."

"He's doing magic with those, ya know," Tomas says.

"Good for him," Pell says.

But I'm curious. "What kind of magic, Tomas?"

"Time magic," Tomas says. "And it's risky. Like sands through the hourglass. Hmm? Sound familiar?"

"'These are the days of our lives?'" I snort.

All three monsters just stare at me.

"It's a joke. That old soap opera—never mind. Anyway."

"What's he doing with the time?" Pell growls.

Tomas shrugs. "How should I know? I'm not the monster-keeper around here."

"Wait. Was that a dig at me?" I ask.

"No, no, no," Tomas says. "Sorry. Pell's indifference is always infuriating."

"We don't need to worry about the hunt, Tomas." Now Pell is defensive. "They can't get in. Pie banished the sheriff. And that spell was powerful. It will take decades for it to wear off."

But I suddenly get a really disturbing thought. "What if there are more of them, Pell? What if his whole family is like that?"

"What family?" Pell asks.

"I dunno. He once mentioned a sister's mother's brother-in-law or something like that. Eileen? The dispatcher?"

Even Tomas is confused. "What the hell are you talking about?"

"He must have family. Hell, the whole town could be of the same bloodline for all we know." Then

I get an awful idea. "Tomas!" I turn to him. "You be careful around that girl you're seeing."

"Oh, she's harmless," Tomas says. And he gets a dreamy look in his eyes. "Trust me. She's not like the rest of them."

"Why do I suddenly feel like this is turning into something bigger than it needs to be?" Pell asks.

Then we just stand there in silence. Because maybe this is a bigger deal than we first thought? And maybe we're too busy with our new lives to see it?

Pell must be reading my mind because he says, "OK, tonight, when you get home from work, Pie, we're going to do another banishing spell. This time, we'll cast it for the whole town."

"Um." I put up a hand. "That sounds like a horrible idea."

"Why?" Pell asks.

"Well, correct me if I'm wrong, because I'm just a new student here, but didn't you tell me that banishing spells were dark magic?"

He did. And he knows this. So Pell's face falls.

But before anyone can say anything, Batty is suddenly very talkative.

"What's he saying?" I ask.

"Yeah," Tomas says. "He says don't do it, Pie. Magic is another way into debt." Then Batty points at his wings.

"Oh," I say. A chill shoots up my back and makes the little hairs on my neck stand up. "Is that how he got those wings?"

Batty nods, but holds up his little rock and says something else.

Tomas translates. "He says the sands of time— ohhhh. Well, you get the idea."

Hmm. Yeah, I do get the idea. He's paid a price for his magic. I look at Pell, suddenly feeling a little panicked. "Wait a minute. Every time I do magic, I go into debt?"

"It's not in your book," Pell says. "So I would say no."

"But that's weird," Tomas says. "Don't you think?" He's talking to Pell, not me.

"Shit." I look up at Pell, eyes wide. "Well, this sucks! My entire job is doing magic for Tarq!"

"Tomas!" Pell growls.

"What?" Tomas says. "I'm not saying it's true, I'm just saying it's weird that Pie has magic inside her that no one controls!"

"Wait, what?"

"You have previously said," Tomas explains, "that you don't ask any of the gods or goddesses for help when you do magic, correct?"

"Yes. That's right. I don't. I just... yell things and it works."

"Well, then... this means you're special, Pie." Tomas is beaming at me. Like being special is a good thing.

I'm just about to open my mouth and set him straight when Pell tugs me away. "Forget about them," he says. "We can think about this tonight. It's... it's... it's all fine, Pie. Don't worry."

I sigh. A break? Got one for me? Anyone?

We don't say anything else until we get back to the cottage, then Pell says, "Go get dressed. I'll make sure Cookie has a lunch ready for you."

And then he kisses me and walks away.

But when I go inside the cottage, Cookie is already there. I almost turn back and call for Pell, but then decide not to. He wasn't going to look for Cookie. I don't think so, anyway. I think he wanted to talk more about this new debt idea with Tomas and Batty, but he didn't want me around.

Cookie is busy in my kitchen, presumably making me something for lunch. And he's talking, but of course, I don't understand him. So I just go upstairs and find a new outfit on the bed, courtesy of Eyebrows.

It's a skirt, but not a miniskirt. In fact, it's a very fancy skirt. With layers. Like tulle, or chiffon, or whatever the hell that fluffy fabric is called that adds volume to skirts. It's kind of a mustard-yellow color and there's a lot of embroidery along the hem. And now that I look closer, there's gold thread weaved into the top layer of fabric. So that when I tilt my head, it shimmers.

"Fancy," I say, sliding the skirt up my long legs. Of course, it fits perfectly. Eyebrows makes these all custom for me.

Then I look at the top. Which is... much more than a top. It's a silky blue camisole with a short jacket made of thick fabric embroidered with a blue and tan floral pattern. Again, there are a lot of gold threads woven into the jacket.

"Hmm." I tap my lip with my finger as I look in my full-length mirror. "This outfit looks suspiciously like the fashion Tarq was wearing that first day."

I'm not sure what this means. And when I go downstairs and try to get answers from Cookie, he babbles on and on, but of course, I have no idea what he's saying.

Then he tucks my lunch into my messenger bag and hangs it off my shoulder, proclaiming me ready for work.

"Thank you." I blush a little. Because at no time in my life has anyone ever taken care of me like... well, a mother. And Cookie, though he is not female, feels very much like a mother in this moment.

Then, before I tear up, I leave and go looking for Pell.

I find him waiting for me at the top of the hill. He's standing on a tomb, hand up to his eyes like a visor, looking out over the cathedral.

"What are you looking for?"

He looks down at me, surprised. Like he was distracted and didn't see me coming. "That black tomb." Then he jumps down, landing in front of me. He takes a moment to study my outfit.

"Love it or hate it?"

"I kinda love it. It's... very pretty."

"It really is. Eyebrows has outdone himself this time."

Pell offers me his hand. I take it, and then we walk like that through the maze of tombs. Not talking. Just kind of strolling. I want to do this with him forever. Take long walks, and lie on a blanket in front of the lake, and kiss, and have sex, and just generally give him a hundred percent of my attention.

But I have work.

And Pell has to finish his magic bag.

We stop near Tarq's tomb and face each other.

Pell smiles at me. "I'm gonna miss you today."

I lean up and kiss him, then turn in the direction of the tomb. Because I do not want to leave and if I say anything else, I might just change my mind and never go back.

Pell must feel the same way, because he doesn't call out for me. And then there's my door. So I know he walked away.

I step into the doorway and start a brand-new day in a whole new world.

CHAPTER TWENTY-SIX – PELL

I get my fire going and work on the bag. And even though these tasks are important, it's not enough to distract me. I think about last night. Run it over and over in my head. Smile, almost continuously, as I fully internalize that Pie was inside my tomb.

No one has ever been inside my tomb.

And that's great. I love it. I love her being there. But it's more than that—it feels like she belongs there, too. Like it's a place for both of us. Which is a new experience for me. Even though, for as long as I have been a prisoner inside Saint Mark's, I've had a slave caretaker, I've never really felt like I have a partner.

Pie being in my tomb feels like a partnership.

But. There is always a but in the world of cursed things. But that portal door. And the fireflies. And was the black tomb a dream? Or something else?

This is also what I'm thinking about as I finish weaving the rings into a chainmail bag and forge an iron plate to put on the front. It needs some kind of sigil. No. Words. They are so powerful and Pie seems to be mastering them quicker than anyone expected, so this bag requires a spelling.

And, conveniently, she has already composed one. So I get a tiny chisel and start tapping letters onto the plate.

Obviously, her spell last night to enter my tombs was a game-changer. But after her spell this morning, I'm starting to get a feeling about all these new changes. A *good* feeling.

However, that portal cannot remain a mystery. We need to figure it out. And the rings, too. I like the idea that they build upon each other to create powerful magic. But the way that ring practically attacked Pie and melded into the one already on her finger disturbs me.

What the hell was that all about?

I can take a good guess. I've been around long enough to understand where this might be headed. And here's where I land:

The entire bag of rings is about Pie. And somehow Pie is connected to that door. And that ring that slipped on her finger is also connected to that door. That ring is a key to the portal, same way the first ring was a key to the sanctuary. So this bag of rings—which I am currently trying to add magic to— is a bag of keys through portal doors, and so far, at least, I think they are meant for Pie.

Pie says Tarq can't get through the doors. And she thinks it's my bloodhorn that makes all the difference. Because while Tarq is the one with the all-powerful spellbook of Ostanes, he doesn't understand that the bloodhorn—in the spell he gave Pie, at least— isn't the common flower, but is a code for... well... me.

I am the key ingredient.

This makes sense to me. In fact, after all these thousands of years, this little puzzle piece almost pulls the whole shit show together in a new way.

We all got something powerful from Ostanes. Tarq got the book. That part has always been clear. But my part has never really lined up. Yeah, I am the master of Saint Mark's. And inside Saint Mark's are tombs. But what's inside the tombs?

All this time I have just assumed that there were monsters like me inside them. I mean, based on the statues outside, this is a perfectly logical conclusion.

But after last night, I'm having doubts.

About all of it.

Like maybe I've had it all backwards this whole time.

Maybe I'm not the master of Saint Mark's?

Maybe I'm a key too?

I can see how I might be. My bloodhorns are unique. I don't have a great cross-section of monster civilization to compare things to, but there are fifty-three monsters inside these walls at the moment and I'm the only one with bloodhorn inside me.

I'm not the only one with hooves, or wings, or fur, or horns.

I'm the only one with *bloodhorn*.

And I was made by Ostanes—one of her last creations before she shut that whole chimera breeding program down. So why wouldn't she do something special with me?

Tomas is unique here too. Aside from the fact that before Pie came, he used to be… an apparition, or whatever, and now he's wearing a physical body, he's also the only dragon chimera.

Not just that, either. Before he was the only dragon chimera, he was the only dragon.

Maybe even the last dragon anywhere.

At the very least, he's the only one with dragon scales.

And Pie as well. She's the only one with moth hands and, of course, this new bag of rings seems to be part of her magic.

I mean, I could say we're all unique. Eyebrows is some kind of fashion designer. Cookie is some kind of chef. And Batty is a rock mage.

But that's not what I'm getting at here. Everyone is unique in some way. And that's not unique. That's just a truth.

The way in which we three are different feels important. The bloodhorn, the portal doors, the rings, the dragon scales. Not to mention, we are all *here*. Stuck in Saint Mark's. *Together.*

It feels intelligently designed. Like we're part of a plan. And even though the last two thousand years have been pretty boring, with almost no progress whatsoever, the last few weeks feel like a whirlwind of growth.

It feels like a storm coming and we're all gonna get swept up.

Like we're on the verge of a precipice.

This is how I pass my morning. Deep in thought about our place here, and in the grand scheme of things at large. And when I look up and realize that the sun is high overhead, I also realize that the bag is done. I have chiseled Pie's entire spelling onto the metal plate.

"'A bag and rings to hide inside. Keep them safe from prying eyes. Invisible they will be. Cloak them up, no one can see.'"

I hold it in my hand, my clawed fingertips passing over the smooth, soft iron rings. It bends like fabric—supple, but also strong.

I braided wire together to make a drawstring ribbon that can open and close the bag with small tugs on each end. I check this relentlessly, opening and closing it. Watching for the wire to weaken and break, because that's the nature of wire under stress.

But it doesn't weaken, even though it does soften and the motion becomes smoother.

That doesn't make sense, but neither does the bloodhorn inside me.

If I'm the key to walking through portal doors, then perhaps I'm also the key to making magic bags?

Puzzle pieces are everywhere.

And I'm close, I think.

I've very close to cracking this curse and getting the hell out of this place. With the help of Pie, of course. And probably Tomas too.

But one thing at a time. The new bag is not quite done. It needs rings, obviously. But also magic words from Pie, dragon fire from Tomas, and my breath to seal it up.

I take the bag of rings out of my pocket, shake them out onto an old wooden table, and pick them up one by one. I hadn't really looked at them before now. Before this moment, they were a collection. Not individual things.

But I now notice details about the rings. They are all very different. Some are pewter. Some are silver. One is platinum. About a dozen of them are copper. There are dull, almost brassy ones. And one very soft high-content gold ring that, when I slip on my finger, expands to my monster-size hands.

I quickly take it off and set it back onto the table because that feels weird. These rings are not for me, they are for Pie. I'm sure of it. They are part of her magic, not mine.

This realization leads me to a new thought. What if we don't want to seal them up? What if we want to use them?

My eyes wander over to another table where the book I took from the apothecary lies open. I walk over, sit down, and read the section on bags and rings. Then recite the poem out loud:

> *"Rings and bags are hard to tame*
> *They must be sealed with dragon's flame*
> *Blackened iron, ammolite*
> *Nuts and bolts and smote and smite."*

It's a spelling, obviously. And now I'm wondering if my breath is necessary. The poem doesn't say anything about breath. It says 'sealed with dragon's flame.' And that's Tomas.

I should maybe not fuck with this spelling by adding something new. I will need to talk this over with Pie. But this bag has to be better than the old one so I get back up, walk over to the rings, push them all into a little pile, scoop them up, and sprinkle them inside the new iron bag.

The bag is different when full. It's even more supple, and smooth, and soft. It feels heavy and substantial now that the rings are inside. Like by itself it was one thing and filled up it is something else.

I stare at it, holding it in my hand, tilting it this way and that to get every angle, to see every tiny ring of chainmail, and smile. Surely more than a thousand years have passed since I've made something so beautiful.

A glint of firelight sparkles off to my right and my gaze wanders to the table where a single gold ring is sitting.

Did I miss it?

No. I picked it up. I saw it in my cupped hand. I watched it fall into the bag.

But there it is. The soft gold ring I had slipped onto my finger.

I pick it up, put it in the bag, and look at the table. Where it still sits.

"Fuck," I mutter. I, of all people, should know better than to put rings on. "No," I growl at it. "No." I point at it. "I'm not interested in ring magic. Get back in the bag."

It, of course, does nothing.

I pluck it up, drop it into the bag, then look back at the table.

"Ha!" It's gone.

But then I notice a glint of light coming off my hand and—"Fuck."

There it is. On my finger!

I'm about to start tugging it off when a shimmering portal appears off to my right.

I take a step back, momentarily startled. Then squint my eyes, trying to see past the door's frame.

Is that my tomb?

I walk towards it, but not through it. I know better than that. And sure enough, it is the woods inside my tomb.

Maybe this door and the door we saw this morning are the same one?

This thought intrigues me. Because it means that Pie and I both control the same door.

What are the odds of that?

Then I get a new idea. What if I can wear more than one of these rings, the same way Pie can?

What if I can make more than one door?

What if these doors lead all over the fucking world?

And... what if I can walk through them, the same way I walk through the gates of Saint Mark's?

Well. There's only one way to find out.

I step through and then come out inside my tomb.

CHAPTER TWENTY-SEVEN – TOMAS

Batty is going on and on about his plan for tonight. He squawks at me. "Yes, yes," I tell him. "But are you sure—"

He cuts me off with some growling.

"Well, I know that, Batty. I'm not an idiot. But I have concerns about your lack of empathy for the humans."

He goes off, ranting and raving. Hands waving in the air. Wings flapping.

"All right, all right." I push my open palms at him, giving in to shut him up. "I understand that part. But if anyone gets hurt, I'm holding you responsible."

He sighs. Smiles. Wins.

"Good," I say. "Now"—I look around—"where did Eyebrows go?"

Batty squawks at me again.

"I know his name is Clarence, thank you, *Darrel*. But Pie calls him Eyebrows and you Batty, so now his name is Eyebrows and yours is Batty. Anyway. I need to find him. I would like an outfit for tonight. So I will see you later. Do not"—I say these words sternly, then repeat them for emphasis—"do. *Not*. Leave here without me."

He shoots me a coy look. And babbles on and on about how he's trapped here like everyone else.

But it's not true.

I caught Batty flying over the wall earlier this morning.

Turns out there's a zone high above the sanctuary walls where the curse doesn't work if one is a magic flying thing with rock mage powers. He has been out in the woods every single night since Pie brought that little sandstone rock back from Tarq's tomb.

If I had known about this loophole from the beginning, I could've left Saint Mark's eons ago.

But then I would be a dragon forever and not this handsome specimen of a man who could attract a perfect woman such as Madeline.

So I think it all evens out.

"We shall have another chat before I leave, do you understand?"

Batty is already walking away, so he makes a dismissive motion in the air with his hand that probably isn't agreement.

But what can one do? I am not in charge of anything here. I am but a simple dragon chimera who would rather leave this place for good and be a human man with a human wife—named Madeline, of course—and never think about monsters again.

I push Batty out of my mind and go searching for Eyebrows. I must have a new outfit. Something worthy of both a hunt, and a date. Because I envision this hunt taking about an hour, and then I envision going to town and meeting up with Madeline so we can practice our kissing.

Perhaps we might even practice other intimate things?

I find Eyebrows up in the hallways in a room filled with luxurious fabrics and sewing paraphernalia.

He's making a coat for Pie, but when I tell him I have a date, he claps his hands and tells me to climb up on a stool so he can fit me up.

He chats non-stop while he pins flannel to my chest and denim to my legs, talking all about some long-ago party he went to in another world. This party is filled with monsters like us. Dressed in elaborate finery. Gold threads woven into luxurious skirts, and waistcoats, and pantaloons.

And the food! At one point during the fitting, Eyebrows sends a small monster on an errand to the kitchen, asking Cookie to make him a snack right out of his memory. When the boy returns just a few moments later—the time in here is weird—he is holding a whole tray of pastries made of pastel-blue dough with gold icing.

I eat seven of them.

Several seamstresses appear at one point. But they are from the other time, so they flit around us like we are not here. Because to them, we are not. I like watching them though. It takes my mind off how much I yearn for Madeline.

I think I love her.

I think I will marry her.

I think I will get Batty to whip me up a magic rock spell that will let me leave forever.

Or, at the very least, a few decades. That's all I want. Just twenty or thirty short years to myself. To have a real life, and maybe a real family.

Not that I don't love my Saint Mark's family. I do. Very much. Especially Pie.

But when I picture my Madeline with small children who may or may not breathe fire and shed scales, I just… I don't know. I get this overwhelming feeling of… satisfaction and happiness.

This is what I want, I decide. And I deserve it. More than even Pell. I have been trapped in this place for millennia. I have paid my dues. I even helped with Pie's banishing spell.

My reward has been earned.

This thought is still floating around in my head when Eyebrows snaps his fingers at me and tells me to leave so he can sew in private. He will be quick and deliver the garment to the back patio where we listen to the radio at night.

I leave through a door, end up in medieval somewhere just in time to place a bet on a joust, then continue on my journey home by way of a Venice canal. You have to love magic hallways.

When I finally arrive back at the stairs, I descend into a large gathering outside near the radio.

I lean in to a shoulder. "What are we doing?"

This monster tells me that Big Jim is doing an interview with the Love Doctor. Talking all about the hunt for monsters.

When this last word comes out, there is hushed mumbling.

They are afraid. "Oh, come on now, monsters! He's not looking for you, he's looking for Pell! And I'm going to be there. They will never find this place. Batty and I have made sure of it."

But they are not convinced. Not at first, at least. They tremble and fret about Big Jim and Sheriff Roth. Batty doesn't help, either. He hypes up their fear, cajoling them into more fretting.

It gets so bad that I have to whistle with my fingers and yell, "Shut up, all of you!" in order to get their attention. "No one is coming over the walls. The only monsters the hunting party will find tonight are me and Batty. We're going to scare the shit out of them and they will never come back into these hills. Tell them." I look at Batty and narrow my eyes.

I have taken care to nurture an air of innocence and a personality of meekness over the past several weeks with these monsters. Because even though I am no longer a dragon, I am still the remnants of one.

And yes, Batty's kind are quite… terrifying. Ugly. Violent. Somewhat mad.

But the dragons—though there is only me here, now—are several hundred thousand levels of frightful above the batty things.

And while this human world outside the gates hasn't seen a dragon in the skies in over two thousand years, these monsters don't come from this world. They come from worlds that are something else altogether. Places where the massive heavy wingbeats of giant creatures are still a common thing. Where fire from a mouth can blister entire cities and make whole mountains shake and tremble from the wrath of things like me.

So when I look at Batty and instruct him to soothe them, he sees these cruel things behind my kind eyes.

And he does as I say.

CHAPTER TWENTY-EIGHT – PIE

I'm one step through the doorway when I realize something fairly critical.

I forgot my dragon scale.

And just as that thought manifests, I'm in Vinca. Standing in the lobby, as per usual, as many, many office workers pass by me.

And three things hit me all at once.

One. Wow. I didn't need the dragon scale. What's that about?

This is a fairly big realization which, under normal circumstances, would occupy quite a bit of time and space inside my brain. But these aren't normal circumstances because…

Two. Instead of the office workers being mostly humans with a smattering of monsters, it's all monsters. Which leads me to…

Three. They are all naked.

Gone are the pretty fashionable clothes and now, front and center, is… well. A full-frontal of everyone.

"What the fuck," I mutter.

And just as these words come out of my mouth, everyone in the entire place stops what they are doing and just looks at me.

That's weird thing number four. Because all the other times I've come through, no one really noticed.

They just acted like the whole walking-through-a-portal thing was normal.

Then I hear a voice calling me. "Pie!"

I turn and find Luciano rushing towards me. "Hey—"

"What the hell are you doing?"

"What?" I'm so surprised by his angry tone, I take a step back. "What do you mean?"

He grabs my arm—kinda hard—and tugs me into a nearby hallway. It morphs as we walk. And I'm a little bit distracted by this because I've never actually seen a hallway move like that. Not in real time. "What are you doing?" Luciano growls again.

I yank my arm from his grip and stop walking, forcing him to stop too. "What are you talking about? I'm not doing anything. It's a work day, right?"

"Work day? This has nothing to do with a work day. What the hell are you *wearing*?" He's looking me up and down and then his eyes stop on my hand and he gasps. "Holy shit!"

I hold my hand up to see the ring. "What the—"

"Where did you get that ring?" Luciano is seething.

The ring isn't my ring. It's not even the new, double ring that was just there on my finger a few moments ago. It's a wide band of gold covered in pavé diamonds, with one ginormous center stone that I cannot identify. It's not a diamond because the facets shimmer like a rainbow when my hand moves. But it looks more expensive than some fake heat-treated quartz crystal.

And from the look Luciano is shooting me, it must have more meaning too.

"Why are you so angry?"

"Because you are wearing the queen's jacket and"—he lifts up my hand—"the queen's ring! How did you get these things? Were you in the palace? Did you make a door into the palace?"

Once again, I yank away from his grip. And one more time I ask for clarification. Only this time, I'm just as angry as he is. "What. The fuck. Is happening?"

"What's happening?" Luciano is practically squealing. It's not a good look for him. "You're wearing the queen's clothes and flaunting the queen's ring! On *Fireday*!"

"Luciano." I force myself to stay calm. "I'm new here, OK? I don't know what any of that means."

"I'll handle this, Luciano."

Luciano and I both look down the hallway— which is still morphing and changing in real time— and find Tarq—also naked!—standing between two shimmering, almost shapeless, walls.

"Go back to the lobby and convince everyone that they did not see what they thought they saw." Tarq flicks a finger at him. A very dismissive, and regal, gesture that implies absolute power.

And this right here, yeah. This is the Tarq I expected on day one. A massive monster with polished ebony horns, polished ebony hooves, and nothing but fur and skin from top to bottom.

"Holy shit," I say. "Where are your pants?"

"Come with me." Tarq grabs my arm, even harder than Luciano did, and drags me down the still-morphing hallway. But just a few steps into this abduction I find myself in Tarq's office.

There is a nymph woman on the other side of his glass walls, also naked, who stops whatever she is doing with a stack of papers to gape at me, but then jumps when Tarq growls, "Get out!"

She practically runs away.

Something I would also like to do.

Tarq lets go of my arm and walks to the other end of his office. He pauses and my heart begins thumping wildly inside my chest.

Fear, I think.

This feels like fear.

He takes an exaggerated breath, then turns back to me and lets it out. "Explain."

"Explain what? I don't know what I did!"

He walks over to me so fast I don't even have a chance to run. I just cower as his claws reach for my jacket. The next thing I know, I'm missing a sleeve.

He holds that sleeve up and bellows, "What is this?"

I am so stunned by this turn of events I can't even manage words. I can't even think.

"Where did you get this jacket, Pie?"

"F-f-from Eyebrow Monster!"

"What the hell is an eyebrow monster?"

"He's my t-tailor!"

I watch, almost ready to piss myself, as Tarq breathes loud and heavy. Is that steam coming out of his nostrils?

"I need to go."

But I don't even make half a turn before he grabs me again. "You're not going anywhere. I need answers, Pie."

I whirl on him because now I'm mad. Mad Pie is good, because she's stupidly fearless. "I don't even understand the questions! But I'm not staying here so you can manhandle me and scare me into submission! I don't like it!"

He and I stare at each other for a moment, our eyes locked. Then he lets go of my arm and walks over to his desk, putting space between us. He takes a seat and points to a chair. "I'm sorry. I didn't mean to scare you. Please have a seat so we can figure this out."

But I don't feel like sitting. And my heart is still galloping inside my chest. My hands are trembling and my legs feel weirdly weak. So I shake my head no. "I'll stand, thank you."

He leans back in his chair, trying to appear relaxed. But the way he steeples his fingers under his chin is still very unsettling. "I said I was sorry. You might as well sit."

I want to be brave here. I want to be Mad Pie. But honestly, I think my legs might give out if I don't sit, so I pretend to be annoyed by his offer, yet accept it anyway. It takes a lot of energy to walk over to that chair and I don't exactly sit. It's more like a collapse. The adrenaline is still coursing through my body and even though the moment of fear is over, I'm still shaken up over the sudden violence in his voice.

He tricked me, I realize. This whole week he's been pretending. Wearing clothes and being all considerate and shit. But this is the monster I met that first time through. The naked, powerful, urban minotaur.

"What?" he snaps. And he's still annoyed.

Which just makes me angry. "You," I say, sneering the word. "Pretending this whole time."

"Pretending this whole time what?"

"To be… some… reasonable… whatever you are."

He lets out another long breath. "I said I was sorry."

"Sorry for what? For scaring me? Or lying to me? Why am I here?"

"I didn't lie to you."

"You did. You tricked me into thinking you're… misunderstood, or something. But this is the real you, isn't it? All naked and shit. Why did you even bother wearing clothes to begin with?"

"What?" And now he's laughing at me.

"You wore clothes to make me feel more comfortable around you." I don't know why I feel so… lied to, but I do. Because Pell refused. Pell showed me the real him first. Then he showed me how he would be different to make me comfortable. Not the other way around.

But Tarq laughs again. Louder this time. "You think… oh. Oh, I get it. The clothes. No. It's *Fireday*, Pie."

"I don't know what that means!"

"Monsters and people, Pie. It involves a degree of trust. We're far more powerful, and cunning, and unpredictable. So we have Fireday to honor the queen's power."

I've got a really dumb look on my face, I just know it.

"We could," Tarq continues, "simply take Vinca for ourselves, don't you think?"

I don't know what to say to that, so I just shrug.

"We could," Tarq reiterates. Minus the question mark. "So once a week we bow to her authority and show our true selves or"—he pauses. Maybe for dramatic effect, maybe just because his next words are dramatic—"we face the consequences."

"You do this by being *naked?*"

"Yes. We remove the pretenses, work on our tasks all day and show up for her party as our true selves, and we bend the knee and pledge allegiance."

"Every week? You have to do this every *week?*"

"She's not very trusting." Tarq sighs. "No royals are."

"Well, that explains you, I guess." My eyes are narrow when I deliver this dig. And Mad Pie is back, if only for a moment. I relax a little bit when I realize the fear is gone now and my heart is slowing down.

"All of us are bare today. And *you*"—this is a very insulting 'you'—"you show up wearing the queen's jacket, when you're supposed to be bare, and flashing the queen's ring, which you are not supposed to have!" He leans forward on his desk, palms flat on the dark wood. "Where did you get these things?"

"I told you. My tailor made the jacket for me. I didn't know there were fashion rules here."

"And your tailor is a monster?"

I nod. "Eyebrows. That's what I call him. He's been making me special clothes. I didn't have any nymph clothes. I haven't been a nymph very long, so..."

"I understand. But this jacket—the gold thread, the pastel blue—Pie!"

"What!"

"This is all illegal! And it's Fireday!"

"Will someone please tell me what the hell Fireday is?"

His anger fades and turns into a snort. "She has a dragon, Pie. What the hell do you think Fireday means?"

I just blink at him. "She... it... fire day?"

He's nodding. "You're not allowed to wear those clothes. They are for royals. And if this monster of yours made these things, then he was a royal tailor. And he was *banished*."

Well. This day has gone completely sideways and I'm not any kind of Vinca-monster expert or anything, but I see where this is going. "I don't know anything about that."

"Forget him for a moment. We will come back to that. Did he give you that ring?"

I look down at the ring. It's heavy. Like… heavier than a gem this size should be. Heavy like it's got magic in it. "No. I have a bag of rings back at the sanctuary. It was left in place of the Book of Debt, which you ended up with, obviously. I don't know where the rings came from, but I was sure they were for all the new monsters."

"What do you mean? Why would you think that?"

"Because… well. Rings, in my world, allow you to go through doors. There were fifty rings and fifty new monsters, so…" I shrug. "I just assumed that these were for those monsters and they would enable them to walk out of the sanctuary. And I couldn't have that, so I hid them, and, well, it didn't work out the way we thought."

"Explain." He's still growling.

"Well, this morning one of the rings in the bag came at me like a fucking bullet, slid onto my finger, and melded into… well… this." I hold up my hand to display the ring. "Except it wasn't this ring. It was a different ring. And then I walked through the portal and it turned into this."

Tarq stares at it for a few moments. Then a few more. And a few more. Until it's completely awkward.

"What?" I ask.

"I don't know what to make of that. I think you should just go to work."

"Agreed." I stand up and turn, ready to get the hell out of here.

"You can't go like that, Pie."

"What?" I look over my shoulder at him.

He nods his head towards me. "You can't wear those clothes. You can't wear *any* clothes. It's forbidden. It's Fireday. You must surrender yourself to the queen."

I make a face.

"I'm sorry," Tarq says. "If you walk out of here in those clothes, you'll be arrested for treason. And I don't think you'll like what happens to monsters in the palace dungeon. Luciano saved you back in the lobby. Next time you see him, you should convey gratitude."

"How come he wasn't naked? He looks like a human, but he's not. He practically admitted it, so I know."

"He's a no-breed. Even lower than a half-breed. He has no citizenship here. He's a *slave*, Pie. Slaves don't count."

"What? But he's your friend."

"He is. A good one, too. But I don't make the rules."

Something comes over me when he says this though. A memory, first. About the spellbook. And then a sense of certainty that he's lying to me. "Funny," I say. "You are the one with the source code, though, right?"

Whatever he's feeling when these words come out of my mouth, he hides it. And his tone is calm when he replies. "I control the book, that's true. No one else can open it. But the magic is another thing entirely."

"What do you mean? You literally told me it was a cheat! That you were the ghost in the machine!"

"I don't know what that means, but now that we're here, at this point, I will tell you the truth. I don't control the magic in that book. Not completely. I was missing one very crucial thing."

He doesn't have to say it. I already know what comes next.

But he says it anyway. "You, Pie. I was missing you. This is why you're here. This is why the queen wants you. And this is why you will be mine."

Wow. Yeah. This is starting to make sense. Not good sense, though. But sense, nonetheless. "You need me to get things done."

"I do."

"You want out of here. This bitch of a queen has you on a tight leash, doesn't she?"

Tarq snarls at me, baring sharp teeth. "I do and she does."

"And you want to take the book with you."

"Correct again."

"Why?"

"Why what?" he snaps.

"Why do you want to leave?"

"Would you want to supplicate yourself to a selfish, backstabbing bitch you don't believe in every week?"

"I suppose not. But why didn't you tell me this in the first place? And what about all that princess bullshit?"

"Oh"—he nods to my ring again—"it's not bullshit. You're definitely her."

"And if I'm her, who are you?"

He smiles at me. "You get right to the point, don't you?"

"When I have one, I try to."

He stands up, flashing me his full frontal, and stands there. Almost proud. "You're mine. We will be together because the magic foretold it. It's been done and it can't be undone. I'm not going to force it because I don't have to, Pie. You're just mine. So whatever." He flips his hand at me the same way he flipped it at Luciano back in the hallway. Dismissing me.

No. It's different. He's not dismissing *me*. He's dismissing the idea that I will *reject* him.

But I don't have time to think more about that because Tarq says, "I need that jacket, Pie. Please take it off."

His segue into this new subject is abrupt and offputting. But I don't object. I just want to get out of his office. So I slide the jacket down my arms and shiver as his eyes follow my movements. I hold it out to him. "Here you go," I say, then realize my mistake.

Because he walks out from behind the desk and over to me. Close enough to take the jacket dangling from my fingertips. But he doesn't walk away or put it down, he just stands there. Way too close.

I look up at him. "What?"

"You need to take off all the clothes. You can leave them here and change on your way home tonight."

"Do you mind, then?"

"Do I mind, what?"

"Can you leave? So I can take them off?"

He smirks at me. "I've already seen you naked, Pie. And everyone will see you naked when you leave my office. The whole point of Fireday is to expose yourself. So why bother with the pretense?"

He's right. I get it. And it's not really that big of a deal to be without clothes when I'm a nymph. My hair can cover my breasts and I have fur—light and velvety as it is—covering pretty much everything else I typically cover up.

But it's different.

And even though he's standing here naked in front of me, with no shame at all, he knows it's different. Because he knows it's weird for me, even though it's not weird for him or anyone else.

He's putting me on the spot, on purpose, and that makes me want to be Mad Pie.

But I'm not going to give him the satisfaction.

I unzip my skirt and let it fall down my legs. It floofs into a puddle of fabric at my feet. His eyes travel that distance right along with it. And they linger there—at the pool of chiffon, or tulle, or whatever the hell it's made of—on the floor at my hooves.

Then they travel back up. Slowly. And he watches me take off my camisole. I drop that to the floor too, then arrange my hair to cover my now very perky nipples.

"Happy now?" I ask.

He just grins.

I begin to turn away from him. But once again, his words stop me.

"The ring, Pie. I need the ring."

"You can try, if you like, but the ring won't come off." I regret those words even as they are leaving my mouth. Because he reaches for my hand.

I want to pull back. But I force myself to hold my ground. He has power, yep. That's true. But he doesn't have power over this. This is *my* power. And I want him to know that.

So I don't even shiver when he holds my hand in his and tries to pry the ring off my finger.

It doesn't budge.

"Hmm."

"Yes. Like it or not, this ring is mine. And there is no way you can get it off. But trust me, if you could, I would let you. Because then I'd be free of all these curses and magic."

His eyes flash. "And then you wouldn't be mine? Is that what you think?"

I shrug. Because I wasn't really thinking that. I was thinking about Pell, and the sanctuary, and how he can walk through the gates now and look like a human in a human's world. But I'm stuck there, being a monster in a monster's world. And it's all very unfair. Like the fricking universe is conspiring against us.

"Talina's latest report said you were progressing."

"Progressing?"

"With your spelling?"

Oh, shit. She's his little spy.

"Pie."

"What?"

"How do you feel about your progress?"

"Who cares what I think? I don't know anything. What did Talina say?"

"It was a written report, so she didn't say anything. But she mentioned—" He reaches over to his desk, grabs a folder, opens it up, and scans the contents. "Here we go. Yes, she was raving about your first attempt. 'A wood, a buck, a nymph, and stone. A way into a satyr's home. A door appears, the nymph walks through, and now their lives begin anew.'" He looks up at me, beaming. "It's *very* good."

"Umm… thank you?" I don't know what else to say. He went from dark and evil to… smiling and… what? Proud?

This whole meeting feels like… abuse.

"What was this spell for?"

"To get into Pell's tomb." Tarq just stares at me, so I go on. "So we could sleep together in his forest."

If I was hoping that would—what? Piss him off? Make him jealous?—well, it does neither. He just looks excited. "Did it work?"

"Yep. It worked. We had a very nice time last night."

Tarq smiles at me. "I'm glad." Then he holds up the written report. "This is a very good start, Pie. A very good start. I'm extremely pleased. This afternoon, we will meet the queen. But today. Today, I would like you to work on opening another door. One for me."

"Which door?"

He ignores my question. "I have a list of key words I would like you to use." He removes a small piece of paper from the file and offers it to me. "They're on here. I like what you did with that first line. 'A wood, a buck, a nymph, and stone.' It's so close. But not quite what I'm looking for. So use these words for your first line instead. And please have something ready by the end of the day. I'll stop by the lab after lunch."

I take the little piece of paper and tuck it into the front pocket of my bag. "You're the boss." Then I hike my bag over my shoulder, turn, walk to the office door, open it up, and leave.

And this time he lets me go.

As soon as I enter the hallways, they begin to change. I picture my lab, fully expecting to be taken somewhere I don't want to be, but after I turn the first corner, there they are. The double doors to my lab.

The semi-opaque glass gives me a distorted view inside. After being told that Talina is writing up reports on me, I'm in no mood to see her. But there's a shadow moving around on the other side of the doors, so unfortunately, she's already here.

Even though I did learn some very useful magic yesterday, I don't like this job. I don't want to be here with these people. I just want to go home.

This makes me pause, then smile. Because the sanctuary feels like home now. I like the protective walls. I like my magic cottage and I love Pell's forbidden tomb now that I can go inside it. And I like my monsters. All of them. Even weird Batty.

At first this place was kinda cool. The city is pretty and the magic is interesting. But I don't like Tarq and I can't trust Talina. That second part makes me a little sad. I was looking forward to Zantha's celebration tomorrow. It would be nice to have a real friend. And everyone in Talina's group is so intriguing.

But here's the problem with this place—it's just like the outside world back home. It's a bunch of people clawing their way to the top. It's just another rat race. Just the same old, same old that feels… very, very old.

And this whole royalty thing is not what I thought. Not that any monarchy is good—I'm not that naïve. But I guess I expected more of this place. A queen who is so suspicious of her monster subjects that she needs them to supplicate themselves weekly by wearing no clothes or punish them with dragon fire is… just… well. A bitch.

I don't want any part of that.

But I have a debt. And I must repay it. So I open the doors to my lab and enter.

Talina has her back to me, working at her bench. There is a line of glass beakers on the stone table top, all different shades of purple. Some of them glowing and some of them are smoking.

She turns and smiles. "Hey. There you are."

So innocent. Like she didn't write up a report on me last night.

But I don't have space in my head to think about that because I'm actually kind of stunned at how pretty she is without clothes. She looks a little bit like a dairy cow. Mostly chocolate brown, but with white spots on her shoulders and stomach. Even a long swatch down one thigh. It's a striking pattern.

"I'm so glad you didn't wear clothes today," Talina says. "It didn't even occur to me that you might not know what Fireday was until late last night, and then it was too late."

I walk over to my bench and set my bag on the floor. "Well, I did come in clothes but Luciano pulled me aside and took to me to see Tarq." I narrow my eyes at her. "You're writing reports about me."

She looks a little surprised. "You didn't know that?"

"No, I didn't know that."

Talina shrugs. "It's just my job, Pie. And it's not a report. It's just an update. Anyway, I didn't say anything bad. I told him you were doing amazing."

"I'm a private person, OK? I don't like people talking about me."

Talina chuckles. "Well, duh. No one does. But you can't stop people from talking about you."

I can't say I disagree. And I don't have anything else to say, so I take my notebook, pencil, and list of words Tarq gave me out of my bag and take a seat at the table without answering.

I open the notebook up, tap my pencil on the table, and stare at the key words.

Hoof. Horn. Eye. Bone.

"Oh, fuck," I mutter.

"What?" Talina asks.

"Nothing."

Talina sighs. "Look, I'm sorry I have to give progress reports. That doesn't mean we can't be friends."

Yes, it does. But I don't say that out loud.

"I'm here to help you, Pie. So if you've got a problem—"

"I don't have a problem."

But I do. I have a very big problem. Because the spelling that Tarq is looking for is the very one that is written above all the freaking doors in the sanctuary.

Not only that, there are two of them now. And both have these four keywords. In fact, the first two lines of both poems are the same.

A horn, a hoof, an eye, a bone. A man, a girl, a place of stone.

Both of them say that.

I've always kind of assumed that the man was Pell and the girl was me.

But… what if the man is Tarq?

Maybe it could be any man?

Hell, maybe the girl isn't even me?

And maybe the place of stone isn't the sanctuary?

A memory flashes through my mind. That dream place when Pell and I were in the upstairs hallway. The woods and off across that meadow—the temple.

A place of stone.

Hmmm. This is starting to get interesting.

Then I turn my attention to the third and fourth lines.

The first spelling talks about time, a mistake, and being safe behind the gate. But the second one talks about a fight, a fall, and a brand-new dawn.

What if the first two lines are mandatory? Maybe all the magic is about a man, a girl, and a place of stone. And maybe the way you change the spelling is by changing the third and fourth lines?

"Pie!" Talina yells.

I look over my shoulder at her. "Huh?"

"Are you even listening to me?"

"Sure." But my mind is still on that last thought. It feels right. The power is in the first two lines, but the change is in the third and fourth.

There's just one problem with this theory: The spelling I wrote yesterday also worked and I didn't use these keywords. So what's so important about a horn, a hoof, an eye, and bone?

"Hel-*lo*!" Talina is yelling at me again.

"What, Talina? I'm thinking hard about shit right now!"

"So fill me in! I'm here to help."

Uh. Yeah. No. I don't think so. But I force a smile. I even try my best to make it real. Because I think I just might have the freaking answer to everything. And there's no way in hell I'm gonna share it with anyone from Vinca. I don't trust these people. They're kinda creepy, actually. Queens, and Firedays, and ten-day workweeks. It's all very what-the-fuck.

I close my notebook and stand up. "I need coffee. My brain isn't working yet. It's just a jumbled mess up there."

Her whole forehead crinkles up in… what? What is that? Confusion? Irritation? I'm not sure. I barely know her. But it's definitely something. Then she says, "You're doing this on purpose."

"Doing what on purpose?"

"I can't go to the coffee shop today."

"Why not?"

She huffs, then points to the white spots on her shoulder and thigh. "Moonspots? Hello?"

"I don't know what you're talking about. What the hell is a moonspot?"

Her mouth goes tight and her eyes go narrow. "This is a real question?"

Confusion, I decide. I'm doing something wrong here, but she's not sure if I know I'm doing something wrong, or if I'm just acting ignorant. "Yeah. Real question. I have no idea what you're talking about."

"We're not allowed out in public until the clock strikes Fire Hour, Pie."

I throw up my hands. "What the hell does that even mean?"

"You really don't know?"

"I really don't, Talina. So if you could just spell it out for me, I'd be eternally grateful, thank you."

She relaxes, then sighs. "The moonspots." She points to her beautiful white markings. "They're a mark of lower class."

"What?"

"You know. Social class. All the monsters of Vinca have moonspots." She looks me up and down. "Except you, and Tarq, of course. But that's because the two of you, you're royal beasts—pure-bloods—and we're just… half-breeds. Common freaks."

Royal. *Beasts*. And I thought I had heard it all. "So let me get this straight. Everyone with beautiful spots on their bodies is… what? A peasant?"

Talia shrugs. "We serve at the queen's pleasure. But it's not so bad."

"Not so bad? You can't wear clothes on Fireday and you can't go outside until the clock strikes Fire Hour?"

She nods. "Well, we're allowed to go to work, of course. But we're not allowed to leave until Fire Hour."

"And Fire Hour is what time, exactly?"

"What do you mean?"

"What time is Fire Hour, Talina? Four o'clock? Five? Six? When?"

"It's just… Fire Hour."

I shake my head. "Nope. Nope, I can't do this."

"Do what?"

"Ten-day workweeks? New hours on the clock? I can't, OK? My brain is not smart. In fact, I'm sorta slow. I don't have space in my head to learn these things right now. What time is it *now*?"

Talina looks at the watch on her wrist. "It's Earth Hour."

"How many more hours until Fire?"

"Six. We have Earth Hour, and Wind Hour, and Breath Hour—"

"Stop." I close my eyes and breathe. I don't want to be here anymore. The culture shock, it's a real thing. But I force myself to deal and open then back up. "I don't have moonspots."

"Nope. You don't."

"So I'm allowed to leave this building and go get coffee?"

"Technically—"

"Technically?"

"You could, but then everyone would see you, Pie. And they would know you're real. So far, it's just a rumor. The humans are going crazy. It's all over the gossip channels."

"And the monsters?"

She smiles big. "Oh, they already know you're real. I'm not really known for being discreet. I blabbed to the girls yesterday. Plus, you're part of our prophecy and we all believe in the prophecy."

Great. The P-word. She just used the P-word. I can't do this. Especially before coffee. "Talina?"

"Yes, Pie?"

"How can I get coffee?"

"There's a break room. I'll get it for you." And her entire attitude has changed. Like she's happy I finally need something from her today. "BRB."

"Yep." I sit back in my chair and sigh. None of this is good. In fact, this news might be worthy of a panic attack.

I need Pia. Where is she, anyway?

I need to find her.

My chair scrapes on the tiles when I push back, then I get up, and I'm walking towards the door when

Talina is suddenly back, holding a cup of coffee. "Here you go."

"That was fast."

She hikes a thumb over her shoulder. "The break room is right next door. And on Fireday, we always have pots going."

"Because we're not allowed to leave."

"Us, but not you. I know it sucks being locked down like this. But at least it's only temporary for you."

"What do you mean?"

"Well, Tarq has to let the queen in on his secret eventually. And then you'll... well." She frowns. "You won't be here anymore. You'll be in the palace. And Tarq will return to the palace and..." She pauses. Frowns deeper. "Wow. I guess I never really thought this through. If Tarq leaves to live in the palace with you, then who will be our boss?"

"I'm going to assume that's a rhetorical question. Also, I won't be living in the palace. I don't live here, Talina. I live in my own world and I have my own home."

"Yeah, but..."

"But what?"

"You're the royal beastess." Again with the B-word. It's almost as bad as the P-word. "She's not going to let you leave once she knows, Pie. Tarq didn't mention that?"

"Nope," I say. "He sure didn't."

"Well, you've got a whole day of anonymity left. He doesn't plan on telling her until just before the gala."

Yeah. This news is definitely worthy of a panic attack. My heart is thumping, my pulse is racing, and I have a sudden urge to get the fuck out of this world and never come back. Because he's going to trap me here, isn't he? He was all agreeable yesterday. *Oh, don't worry, Pie. You don't have to go to the party this week.* Bullshit! It was all bullshit! Like… literally, when I think about it. Because he's an actual bull!

A giggle bursts out of me. It's one of those uncontrollable, inappropriate giggles that actually aren't about anything funny.

"Pie?" Talina sounds worried. She should be. I'm definitely losing my shit. "Pie? Are you OK?" But I can't answer because now I'm starting to hyperventilate. She takes my arm, leads me over to the table, and helps me sit. Then she sets my coffee down in front of me. "Drink it. Fireday coffee is always good for calming nerves."

Nerves? This isn't nerves. This is full-on I'm-about-to-be-kidnapped-out-of-my-world panic going on here. I need a whiskey to process this one.

But all I have is coffee, so I gulp it down.

Funnily enough, this does seem to help. A sense of well-being floods through my body as the hot liquid hits my stomach. And I actually do relax.

"That's better," Talina says, her voice all calm and her fingertips petting my hair. "Now. Just… concentrate on your task today, Pie. Tarq wants a portal spell. Just sit there and think up a good one. Just like you did yesterday. And when he comes to check on you later, he'll be so pleased."

"Ooookaaaay," I mumble, so happy now.

Talina giggles. "Yep. You really did need that coffee. But it's good stuff for spell writing. You'll see."

The next thing I know, someone is tapping my shoulder and I'm snapping back to attention. I blink a few times, focus on my notebook and then realize it's filled with spellings I don't remember writing.

I quickly close it up.

"It's nearly Fire Hour, Pie," Talina says. "Tarq is on his way to talk to you. He said not to let you leave until he gets here. He wants to check your work. And, oh! He's going to be so pleased with all you've done today!"

All I've done? I don't remember doing anything after I took a sip of that coffee.

Did she drug me?

"Ooop! Speaking of the royal beast himself! She's all yours, Tarq. I'll see you tonight, Pie." She pats my shoulder again, then I listen to her tapping hoofsteps as she leaves the lab.

"Talina tells me you've been busy, Pie. That's great. I want to see all of it. But first, I want you to look at this book."

I snap out of my coffee-induced stupor and look up at him, forcing myself to unsee his dick—which is pretty much impossible, since it's eye-level and he's standing right next to me.

Thankfully, he plops a huge book down in front of me and takes a seat to my right. Then he opens the book.

It's a page of twelve pictures with names and other information below each one. They are all pictures of monsters.

"What is this?" I ask, my voice husky and deep from my coffee-induce trance. She did drug me. I have to blink a few times to let this realization settle in.

She. *Drugged me.*

"It's a list of defectors."

"*Defectors?*" Wow. That's not a good word under any circumstance. Especially one in which I'm a long-lost royal beast who might never go home again. "What the hell are you talking about?"

"You mentioned your tailor earlier. The one who made that royal jacket."

Oh. Shit. I think I fucked up. Like... *royally.* No pun intended.

"I want you to look through this book, Pie. And let me know if you see him. Or anyone else who might be at your sanctuary."

Yep. I fucked up. This is not good.

"Pie?"

"Yeah. OK. Sure." I force a smile and scan the page. Then shake my head. "Nope. None of these guys look familiar." He flips the page. I scan again. "Nope." He flips it again. And again. And again. And each time I deny, deny, deny even though I have already recognized Eyebrows, Cookie, Batty and all of Batty's questionable friends.

I say nope for every single page.

Tarq isn't buying it. At all. He closes the book, gets up, and starts pacing in front of the window. "You're protecting them. I get it."

"I'm not!" But my protest is overly shrill and there's no way in hell he believes me.

He stops pacing. Looks at me intently. "You don't trust me."

"I don't even *know* you."

"Fine. I accept that. But I need you to listen to me, Pie. I need you to hear me, OK? I need you to *hear me*. I'm on your side."

I want to argue with him. I want to say all kinds of things like, *How can you be on my side if you don't know what my side is?* But I don't because my mind is wandering back to a conversation Pell and I had in my Jeep that time he drove me around the block to the lake gate. He said those same words. *I need you to hear me, Pie.*

This awakens something inside me. A realization, perhaps. The idea that I might be putting off a vibe here. A vibe that says I'm not listening.

So I just let out a breath and take a moment.

Tarq waits me out. In fact, the silence goes on so long, it becomes awkward. So then I feel compelled to explain. "OK. I hear you."

He shoots me a look. "Do you?" It's a doubtful look.

"You have... plans. To save this girl, right?" I kinda pull this out of my ass, but he did mention this a couple days ago, didn't he? He has a woman and he wants her back? And I didn't really hear him, did I? I wasn't paying attention. Because if I had, I would not be surprised at his... desperation right now. "How will you save her?"

"What?"

"Tell me how, Tarq. If you want my cooperation you will fill me in or I swear to God, I will fuck things up in spectacular ways."

His eyes narrow. "Is that a threat?"

"You can take it any way you want."

"Fine." He lets out a long breath. "The queen needs us."

"Go on."

"To be together."

"Together how?"

"As… you know. A couple."

"A couple? Like… an intimate couple?"

"Intimate is a strong word. And not the right one, either. This is a negotiation. A contract. A deal, OK? It's a short-term thing, Pie. It's not about *feelings*. But…"

His pause goes on for too long. "But what?" I snap.

"It's not entirely wrong, either."

"What do you mean?"

"Intimate, Pie. It will be a little bit intimate."

I try to read between the lines. The queen needs us. And he needs me. But there is something more to it.

He's desperate. He wants his woman back. He will do… *things*… to get her back.

He will *use* me.

And if we need to be a couple in order for this to happen… "Oh, fuck that," I say.

"Just listen," Tarq breathes. "It's not what you think."

Maybe it's not? Maybe my imagination is running wild right now and he's not going to hand me over to the queen, and she's not going to put us together so we can do things that couples normally do.

Maybe he's really not saying that.

But then again, maybe he is.

Hold your shit together, Pie. This is a negotiation. You will not freak out, you will not overreact, and you will not be weak.

So instead of screaming, *You're going to hand me over to the bitchy queen, who will force us to breed like animals, and then give her our child in exchange for your woman*, I say, "You are extremely loyal to this woman you're looking for, correct?" And my voice is calm when these words come out.

Now Tarq squints at me. Distrustful. Because yep. I'm going somewhere with this. "So you *did* recognize the monsters in the book."

"I'm not saying that. I'm not saying that I have a plan either. But I have people I care about too. And I'm not going to give them up to you—a man who kinda scares me, and has plans that involve me, which I am not aware of, nor do I consent to, nor do I have any say in. At least I don't have plans that involve you. I'm not out to flip *your* world upside down, Tarq. Because you've got nothing to do with my life. I'm only here because you're making me be here." I leave out my suspicions about the queen, and the breeding, and the baby because if it's true—if that's why he needs me—then I'm not ready to have that conversation. Like… at all.

"And you know what?" I pause. Like maybe this isn't a rhetorical question and he has a chance in hell of guessing what I will say next. But he's really good at remaining silent and just stares at me expectantly. "I think I'm gonna leave now."

He chuckles like this is funny. Like I'm joking. Like I have no power here, like he's the owner of my debt book.

But I'm not joking, I do have power here, and maybe he is the owner of my debt, but he hasn't been gifted the ability to walk through portal doors by making up poems.

"A horn, a hoof, an eye, a bone."

Tarq's whole face lights up. Like this is the miracle he's been waiting for. "Wha—"

"A beast, a nymph, a place called home."

And it *is* his miracle. Because I have figured out the magic of doors.

Too bad I'm not going to take him along for the ride.

Tarq's face scrunches up. Like he's catching on. "Pie?"

"A lab in Vinca becomes a door—"

"Pie. What the fuck are you doing?" Yep, he's definitely starting to understand because he comes towards me now.

But I scoot away and get the big conference table between us and quickly yell the final part of the spell. "The nymph goes through, her boss no more!"

A door appears.

A bright, shimmering, violet door appears. Right in front of me. Like inches away. Like it was meant only for me. I look over my shoulder. Tarq is yelling. Something about security, something about debt books, something about—

Well, I don't hear the rest because I step through my door and Tarq, and his crazy world, just disappears.

CHAPTER TWENTY-NINE – PELL

I am in my tomb.

I started out in the smithy, then I made a portal, and now… I am in my tomb.

I just stand there for a moment, relishing this new feeling of power.

It has been so long since I had power.

I turn in place, look behind me, but the door I came through is already gone. I like that. A lot. Because it means the doors are temporary. If it was permanent, then people could follow me through. I will have to test these boundaries, make sure I have the magic straight in my head before I really start using this new power, but it's a very good sign.

When I look around, I realize that I'm well inside the interior of my tomb. The forest. In fact, it's the same place where Pie and I slept last night.

My favorite spot under the canopy of lush green boughs is just a few feet away so I sit down and lean my back against the thick, leathery trunk and sigh.

Life is so weird.

A couple months ago I was stuck here with Grant. Nothing to look forward to. Nothing to reminisce about, either. It was just thousands of years of stagnation and stupidity.

And now, everything has changed.

It's Pie. I know it's Pie. She was the catalyst for everything.

And how ironic that Grant was the one who set it all in motion.

I reach into my pocket, pull out the bag of rings, and stare at the metal plate on the front. Pie will have to say these words and put her stamp on it. Then the magic will be both of ours. Something meant only for us. Maybe I'm not the smartest monster in the sanctuary, but I'm not bad at finding a connection when I try hard. And I think this bag of rings is our power.

No. It's more than that. It's our future and we need to protect it.

I look down at the gold ring on my finger and just stare at it for a moment. My idea back at the smithy comes forward again. What if I can wear two or more rings? What if this is just my base ring and this door that I just walked through is my base door, but each time I add a ring, a new door opens for me?

I open the bag, dump the contents out on the smooth dirt, and poke through them with a clawed finger.

One of them sparkles. A sign, I think. I pick it up—but it's tiny. So tiny there isn't a chance in hell that it will fit on my finger.

But just like last time, it wiggles and hovers, taking on a life of its own. And then it's slipping onto my finger, widening, until it bumps into the one I'm already wearing. Then there is a small flash. Like a chemical reaction just took place. And the two rings become one.

"Huh." I hold my hand up close to my eyes so I can get a better look. The new, melded ring has a winged lion motif. "Huh," I say again. Because I've seen this lion. It's the same lion on the banner of Saint Mark. Not Saint Mark's the sanctuary, but the actual person, Saint Mark. The winged lion was his symbol. There are many lions carved into things here at the sanctuary too. But they are just a face. And it is always wearing a crown.

The winged lion is different. Though they could be the same lion, I suppose. It wouldn't be a far leap to come to that conclusion.

Pie found a book about Saint Mark in the apothecary a couple days after everything went down with the sheriff and Grant. It was thick and beautifully illustrated with many pages illuminated in gold leaf. But neither of us could read the words. It wasn't Latin, or any of the other languages Pie had magicked us into understanding.

A door appears, startling me. I scramble to my feet and wait, wondering if something will come through.

But no.

The door is mine. A new door because I'm now wearing a new ring.

I walk towards it, peering through, trying to get a look at where it might lead. But then there's a small commotion behind me and I turn, fangs bared, ready to fight.

But there is no one there.

It's just the rings. They are hovering in mid-air. Lined up, one by one. And one by one they spark and shimmer.

Then other doors appear.

But it's not like a pop. It's not like one moment they are there, the next they aren't. It's more like a smooth transition from empty air to something solid.

I watch, transfixed, as the rings begin to float towards the doors. I have a moment of panic that they will travel right through them and disappear forever. Which is ironic, since I've spent the last few days wishing they would do just that.

But they don't go through the doors. They just hover in front of them. Like keys.

I smile. Then chuckle. Then laugh heartily.

Two thousand years I've been powerless.

Two *thousand* years I've been stuck here.

And now I have keys to more places than I could've ever imagined.

There is a loud, crackling sound behind me. And when I turn, another door appears. A bright, shimmering, violet door. And who comes through?

"Pie?"

She sees me, smiles, then there's panic on her face as she whirls around to look at the door she just came through. But it disintegrates into empty air as we watch.

She turns back to me. "Holy fucking shit!"

"What are you doing?"

Then her wide, blue eyes find the doors just over my shoulder and she points. Speechless.

"Doors," I say. "The rings are all keys to doors, Pie!"

She gasps, clutching at her chest with a hand. "Oh, my God. Oh, my fucking God, Pell."

"What are you doing? Why are you here? And why are you naked?"

"I just spelled my way out of Vinca and I'm never going back. Like, ever, Pell. Tarq." She shakes her head. "No. I can't do it. I don't like it there. It's weird, and there's a book filled with pictures of all our monsters, and some low self-esteem queen who makes us be naked on Fridays—excuse me, *Fire*days! *Firedays*, Pell! And I'm not saying I'm some kind of expert on this Vinca place, by any means, but this bitch is crazy! She will sic her dragon on us if we wear *clothes*!"

"Calm down, you're OK." I walk over and place a hand on her shoulder. "Start from the beginning. Tell me what happened."

She takes a deep breath and it all comes spilling out. I have to stop her like eleventy million times because she's talking so fast, I can barely keep up. But finally, I get the whole story.

"He wants you to make doors?"

She nods.

"Like these?" I point to the new doors.

"Exactly."

"What does he want to do with them?"

"What do you think he wants to do with them, Pell? He wants to rule the universe!" I can't stop the laugh. Which just pisses her off. "Go ahead. Laugh all you want. I get it. It's some… far-fetched comic book plot. I'm not blind, I see that. But he's seriously trying to take over worlds, Pell!"

"Come on now."

"I swear! I know this because he's lying to me. And why do people lie, Pell?"

I shrug. "Because they don't want you to know the truth?"

"Exactly! His stupid story about—" But she stops.

"About what?"

She takes a deep breath. "Here is my point. He wants power. And he's planning on using me to get it. Then..." She throws up her hands. "Who knows what he'll do with it? All I know is that I don't want to be a part of this. The queen, Pell! She's insane! The whole place is crazy! I'm not going back. Plus, he has Ostanes' spellbook! The fucking book!"

She's really freaked out. "OK, OK," I calm her. "I believe you. I trust you. If you say it's a bad idea, then it's a bad idea."

She squints her eyes at me. "This is platitudes."

"It's not. I do trust you. You're the key to everything, Pie. I mean, look." I wave my hand at the seemingly never-ending line of magic doors. "This is all because of you. And I have power too! We're like... a super-team!"

Pie is not enthusiastic. "I don't think I like this, Pell."

"Just look at them," I say. "Come look at them with me."

I take her hand, but she balks. "I don't want to walk through them."

"I said *look*, Pie. You can see the other side."

She narrows her eyes, now trying to get a better look at the doors. "You can?"

"Yeah. I was just looking through the first one when a whole bunch of others appeared. But I think it's Granite Springs."

"Which one?" She's looking at them intently now.

"That one right there. Come on, I'll show you."

We walk over to the first door and lean forward, trying to see what's beyond the shimmer.

"It's woods," Pie says.

"Yeah, but see that?" I point. "I know that tree."

She shoots me a dubious look. "You know that *tree*?"

"Pie, I've spent nearly five hundred years in Pennsylvania. I *know* these woods."

She lets out a long breath. "Fine. You're the resident expert on woody PA. Where is it?"

"It's just up the hill from Granite Springs. See, look between those two branches." She leans forward, squinting. "That blue thing, see it?"

"Yeah, OK. I see it."

"That's the sign to that stupid candle shop."

I feel her relax next to me. "I really like that shop. I burn their lavender candle every time I take a bath and even though I had to sell my soul to get all that cute stuff, sometimes, when I'm surrounded by goat's milk bubble bath, sniffing that lovely lavender candle, I think it was worth it."

This makes me smile. Pie, man. She's a gift. The best ever. "Wanna go down there?"

"Down *where*?"

"There. To Granite Springs."

She points to her naked nymph body. "Like this?" And her words are bitter now. Like she has regrets about being a nymph.

I shrug. "We don't have to go into town, but it would be nice to get out of this place for a little while, don't you think? We could take a walk in the woods." It's kinda lame. We're already in the woods. But these are magic woods and those woods, beyond that door, are the real woods in the real world.

And a little bit of real might go a long way right now.

Pie sighs. "I should put some clothes on?"

"Why?" This makes her snicker. "I mean, wood nymph chimeras don't wear pants, Pie."

Now she chuckles. "But... what if we get stuck there?"

"So? We walk back. No. We *run* back." I'm not a mind reader, but I can read her mind right now. Running in the woods. That was our first shared memory. She liked it. She was her true nymph self in those hallway memories.

"Well, where do the other doors go?"

"I don't know. I haven't looked yet."

She takes a few steps to her left and looks into the next one. "It's nothing. Just... shimmering."

We look at a few more, but they are all the same. "Huh."

"Maybe..." She pauses.

"What? What were you gonna say?"

"I'm just spitballing here, but maybe they're blank slates?"

"What's that mean?"

"Like... they need a spell to activate them. Like maybe they're just... nothing until we make them into something."

"They can go anywhere."

"Exactly."

"You have somewhere else you want to go?"

"No. Not yet, anyway." Then she smiles. Because she's warming to the idea that we are not prisoners anymore. She turns back to the Granite Springs door. "How come this one has a destination?"

"I think this one is attached to my ring." I hold the ring up.

"Oh, shit!" Her eyes go wide. "You have a ring!"

"Yep. Forgot to mention that, I guess." Then I tell her my story and how I got here. And how the rings reacted.

"So they are keys," Pie says.

"I think so."

"OK, but before we jump into some unknown trip to the PA woods, I wanna try something." She walks back over to the closest door and plucks the hovering ring right out the air. Then slips it on her finger before I can stop her.

The door does nothing. "Huh," I say. "What do you think that means?"

"I think my theory is right. They need a ring *and* a spell."

"Then why did Granite Springs appear to me?"

"I dunno. It's different, I guess."

"Hmm. It's possible that this isn't my power. Not completely, at least. It's possible that I have limits."

"It's possible I have limits, too. Let me check." She takes a deep breath, rolls her eyes up like she's thinking hard about something, and says, "A horn, a hoof, an eye, a bone. An open door, a place unknown."

I point at her. "Oh, that's good."

"A trip to town, a candle shop. There and back in one quick hop."

The empty door in front of us is no longer empty. Instead, it opens up to the stupid candle shop.

"Oh, fuck!" Pie takes a step back. "People!"

But it only takes a moment to realize that they can't see the door, or us.

Pie and I look at each other. I take her face in my hands and stare into those water-blue eyes of hers.

"Holy shit, you magnificent wood-nymph beast! You did it!"

"Oh, my God. This is crazy!"

"We have doors, Pie! Doors that can take us anywhere!"

"We're free, Pell! Free!"

We both sigh and look at the door. Then she slips the ring off and the candle shop disappears. We look at each other again, smiling so big.

"Wanna go on a date to the PA woods?" I ask.

Pie giggles. "I would love to."

I take her hand, lead her over to the door, and we walk through.

When we come out on the hillside, our hooves crunch in a layer of pine needles. But I look down at them—

"Holy good luck, Batman!" Pie exclaims. "I have feet!" She stomps them. "And shoes!" Then she pats down her body. "And clothes!"

She is dressed in the clothes she arrived in. Even the flannel. And this makes both of us snort. "You're a slutty schoolgirl, Pie. A naughty, slutty, schoolgirl."

"Pell! I'm human again!" Then her eyes go even wider. "And so are you!"

And yep, sure enough. When I look down, I am human.

"I wanted to burn this outfit," Pie says. "But right now, I'll take it. And you!" She points to me and her lips suddenly become pouty. "Is this how you always look when you go into town?"

I look down at my black leather jacket, white thermal shirt, jeans, and boots. "Yep. Pretty much. No one gave me a clothing spell. Is it horrible?"

She studies me, frowning. "No. You look fuckin' hot."

"Then why do you look so upset?"

"Because you're not supposed to look hot when I'm not around!"

I guffaw. "What's good for the goose…"

"Yeah, yeah, yeah. But I like the jacket. This flannel isn't enough. It's much colder out here than it is at the sanctuary. I wish I was wearing something warmer."

"Like fur?"

She giggles. "I have grown fond of my fur."

"Here." I slip the leather jacket down my arms. "Take mine. I have this thermal on and to be honest, this is way too much clothing for me."

Pie smiles and accepts my offer, slips her arms into the jacket and tugs it tight around her body. It's way too big for her. While I am not my typical seven-foot-tall beast without the hocks, the new conformation of my leg bones only shaves off about seven inches of my original height. Human Pie, on the other hand, is petite. Almost diminutive. So the jacket covers her all the way down to mid-thigh. I like this look. Not only does the jacket hide her too-tight bustier and postage-stamp skirt, it also sends signals. Anyone who checks her out will immediately understand that she is wearing *my* jacket.

They will know that she is mine.

"What's this?" Pie asks.

She's fished a pen and paper out of one of the pockets. "Spendin' money." I wince. I hate that she is the one who supports us all. It's… kind of demoralizing. I should be providing for her, not the other way around.

Pie shakes her head at me. "Don't worry about it. We have doors now, Pell. The curse doesn't matter. We have loopholes. So we might as well enjoy it, I guess."

"I will find a way to get rid of this debt. I promise, Pie. I will."

"All things for other times. Tonight, we're on a date."

"Yeah," I say, letting out a breath. "All right." I take her hand and look around for a path we can use for our walk.

"Wait," Pie says.

I look down at her and notice that her eyes are the color of moonlight right now. "What?"

"We're both human. For the first time since the hallways. And you know what this means?"

There is a hint of deviousness in her tone. I love it. "Tell me. I'm dying to know."

"Our date plans have changed. Forget the walk in the woods. We're going to the bar and we're gonna get shitfaced drunk. On something good, too. Not some cheap-ass beer. Something I've never had. Like... bourbon."

"You've never had bourbon?"

"Nope." She's grinning wildly up at me. "I'm a keg girl. I never really had the money to drink in a bar so all my party moments come from crashing keggers. I want a real drink tonight. Something expensive. Then it will be a moment I never forget and it will have happened with you."

A drink, in a bar, with a woman.

No. A drink, in a bar, with the woman I *love*.

This is the best day of my two-thousand-year-long life.

"Your wish is my command." I take Pie's hand and we make our way down the side of the hill. It's a foggy, December night, but there's a full moon out, and no wind, so everything is lit up in a silvery mist that almost gives the town an air of mystique.

The bar is called Savage Saints. Which an interesting name for these parts considering our home also has the word 'saint' in the title. I kinda want to think more about this coincidence, but we're already approaching the bar, so real life can wait. This is date night.

When I pull the door open and we walk into the dark, atmospheric room, I find that I'm excited in a way that I had almost forgotten was possible. I let out a breath and relax as we pause in the little entryway and take it all in. Rock and roll is blaring from a jukebox, but in between beats, the crack of a cue ball draws our attention to the far end of the room where a group is playing pool. The flickering neon beer signs above the top shelf behind the bar light the bottles up pink, and yellow, and blue.

A few people near the door stop what they are doing to look at us, but it's just a casual look. We are just regular people tonight. People who fit in. Nothing special about us at all.

"It's kinda busy," Pie says, her voice almost disappearing into the rumble of a song I actually recognize. Something about a ball and chain from decades back. "There's a table over in the back." She points to a table. Which is technically empty. But the pool players are crowding it, so I point to a section of the bar near the jukebox.

"There," I say, then lead her through a short maze of tables.

She settles onto her stool, smiling and spinning a little, her cute little combat boots tapping on the stainless-steel footrest attached to the bar.

I hold up a finger to get the attention of the bartender. He nods at me from the other end of the bar, then I take a seat as well.

"How long has it been?" Pie asks.

I have to think back pretty far. "Maybe since this song came out." I chuckle. "Decades. This place has been a bar for seventy-five years, at least. But I've never actually been in here. There was another one Grant and I came to back in the Eighties."

"Holy shit," she giggles. "I can't believe you were alive in the Eighties. What was that like?"

"Bad music, ugly clothes, and lots of seedy pot."

She laughs. "You smoke pot?"

I shrug. "It was a thing back then."

"I'm pretty sure it's still a thing now."

"Yeah. We were growing it for a while."

"What?"

"Grant." I roll my eyes. "He was always trying to make money. Pot in the greenhouse was just one of his many get-rich-quick ideas."

"Hmm."

"What? What's that 'hmm' about?"

"I'm just remembering something he said to me that night I had a date with Russ Roth. He was very focused on money."

"Well, it makes sense if you think about it."

"How?"

"I don't know if he was always Saturn—it's possible that Grant was a mostly normal dude when he first stepped through the Saint Mark's gate—but he was definitely Saturn when he left."

"What's that got to do with money?"

"Oh"—I laugh—"everything, Pie. Money is the actual, literal root of all evil in this world."

"I don't know about that."

"That's because you don't have money. Or crave it. Once you have it, the craving just comes along for the ride. You want more. You get obsessed with it. And then, pretty soon, you're growing pot in a magical greenhouse and corrupting an entire generation of PA teenagers."

"I'll take your word on that." She chuckles. "But what's that got to do with Saturn?"

"Saturn is the god of money. And FYI—he also ate children."

Pie crinkles her face at me. "Gross."

"Oh, he's gross, all right. But forget him. It's time to drink."

The bartender is walking towards us. He's a young guy. Maybe the age I currently look, which is thirty or so. His hair is dark and he's got a shadow of a beard, lots of tattoos on all his visible skin, and the words 'good' and 'luck' spelled out across his knuckles. He taps all of those knuckles on the bar in front of us. "What can I get you?"

I glance at the top-shelf whiskey and actually recognize a bottle. "Give me that bottle," I say, pointing to the Blanton's.

"The *bottle*?" Bartender asks. "It's… top-shelf."

"Obviously."

The bartender hesitates. "It's a two-hundred-dollar—"

But Pie has already scribbled 'moneta' down on a bar napkin and is pushing it towards the guy. "Here. Keep the change."

The bartender's eyes light up. He looks at Pie, then at me. "Wow. Thanks guys. I really appreciate it. I'm Carl, by the way." He turns, grabs the bottle of Blanton's Special Edition, and sets it down in front of me. Then he reaches for two rocks glasses and pushes one at each of us. "Want me to pour?"

"We've got it," I say.

"If you need anything else, just let me know." He walks away staring at the piece of paper, grinning and shaking his head like he can't believe his good fortune.

"How much do you think we tipped him?" Pie asks.

I watch as the bartender puts the napkin into the drawer and then helps himself to some bills. "Looks like a wad of twenties."

Pie and I both laugh as I pour our first drinks. I slide her glass over, then we hold them up in the air.

"What should we cheers to?" Pie asks.

"*Audentes fortuna juvat*," I say. "Fortune favors the bold. And we are nothing if not bold tonight."

"I can get on board with that." Pie laughs. We clink glasses and take our first sip.

"Wow," I breathe out. "It's been a long time since I had a drink. And this one is smooth."

Pie makes a little face at the initial bitterness. But then she takes a deep breath as the bourbon hits her stomach. "Oh, yeah. This is nice. I like it." She takes another, bigger sip, then her shoulders relax. "I like this night already."

I just stare at her, wondering how I got so lucky. I mean, I guess it was bound to happen. Two thousand years of shitty luck can only last so long. But Pie, she's the perfect gift. She's everything. And even though I couldn't see it that first day, it didn't take me long. "That ride around the block," I say.

"What?"

"That's when I fell in love with you, I think."

She chuckles. "What are you talking about?"

"When you came home from your first trip to town and you were all excited."

"After I sold my soul for shoes and candles?"

We both laugh and take another sip of our drinks. "No. It was when you clapped your hands. All excited about finding a new magic person from town to take your place."

"Oh, my God. I was so dumb."

"Nah, that's not what it was. It was…" I go searching for the words Tomas used to describe her earlier that day. When she was sure she could talk to the sheriff through the gate. When she was positive that there was no way in hell that this curse would get the best of her. "Eternally hopeful. That's what you were."

"Oh, fuck," Pie says. "Slow, stupid—"

"Cute," I finish for her.

She looks up at me, her cheeks flushed pink now from the whiskey. "It's not a curse. Not if it's right where I want to be."

"Yeah." I let out a long exhale and agree. "That's how I see it now, too."

"And we have doors, so…" She shrugs. "We're not even trapped. It feels like…"

"Like a treasure chest of solid-gold good luck?"

She points at me. "That."

I reach down, grab the edges of her stool, and pull her closer to me. So close, our knees lock together like puzzle pieces. She giggles and grins. Leaning back in her seat. This makes her knee slide along my inner thigh and I'm suddenly feeling a little aroused.

She is too, because her eyes close a little as she looks at me. My jacket is no longer hugging her body the way it was outside, so I get a good look at her ample cleavage. And an urge to reach up and squeeze her round, soft breasts.

She leans forward. The leather jacket opening up even wider. Her blue eyes are locked on mine when I feel her warm palms on my knees. She slides her hands up my thighs, still looking at me, and when she runs into my cock she pauses to massage it with her thumb.

I tilt my head at her. "Pie…"

"Pell."

"What are you doing?"

"What does it look like I'm doing?" She squeezes my dick.

I put my hands on hers, forcing her to pause. "We're at a bar, Pie."

"I'm aware, Pell."

"So you're teasing me?"

"I guess I could be. Or I could be inviting you into the women's restroom for a little fun."

I look around, count up the females in the room, and come up with way too many to have a tryst in the bathroom. "That's… bold."

"Fortune always favors the bold."

"We'll get caught in the women's."

"So we go to the men's."

"Fuck that. If anyone walks in the men's I'll have to kill them."

Pie chuckles as she drags her eyes away from mine, then holds up a finger.

Two seconds later, Carl is in front of us. "What can I do for you guys?"

"Do you have an office here, Carl? We"—she points to me, then her, then back at herself—"need to have a conversation and there needs to be a door that locks."

"Oh, sure," Carl says, his face lit up and bright with the opportunity to help us out. "It's right back there. Hold on." He goes over to the cash register, grabs something, then comes back. "Here's the key. Take your time."

He drops the key in Pie's waiting palm, then turns and walks away.

I lean into Pie's neck. "Damn, woman. You're like... a fucking enchantress."

Pie's grin is both devious and innocent. An invitation and a challenge. She stands up and grabs my hand. When I rise with her, a pink blush rises in her cheeks. I grin back at her, totally accepting her challenge. Then she leads me through a maze of tables, down a long, dark, hallway, and to a door where the key fits in the lock.

She opens it, pulls me in, and I kick it closed behind us.

And now, a decision has to be made. A quick, dirty fuck? Or a slow, intimate lovemaking?

Pie leans up on her tiptoes. Her hands on my shoulders. Her knee between my legs, pressing up against my cock. "You never know how many doors will lead us to chances like this. So you better make it good, monster. You better make it something to remember."

Oh, I plan on it. I slide one hand under her skirt and caress her ass. The other one is pulling her panties aside so I can flick my finger back and forth in the growing pool of wetness. She tilts her head back, eyes closed, and I lower my mouth to hers. We kiss slowly. Our lips taking their time. Our tongues performing languishing twists as I slip my finger up inside her. She gasps a little, but it's a pleasurable gasp.

So I guess I've made up my mind. Slow, intimate lovemaking.

Pie's hand is suddenly flat on my thigh. Pressing and rubbing over my cock. It's mostly hard already, but it grows bigger with her attention. Her fingers pop the button on my jeans and drag the zipper down. I push up inside her a little deeper and she goes up on her tiptoes with her mouth wide open. Pressing against mine.

Our kissing becomes more frantic as she shoves the front of my jeans down, reaches in, and pulls out my dick. I pause our kissing so I can look down and watch as her small hand wraps around my thick shaft, her fingertips not quite meeting up to form a circle because of my wide girth.

"This is a pretty good start," Pie whispers, her eyes open now. She throws me a lopsided grin. A devious grin. And then she slowly begins to bend down. My finger slips out of her pussy and drags a line of wetness up her belly, hidden under her miniskirt until she's down on her knees.

She wraps both hands around my cock—eyes still locked with mine—and I growl, "Oh, fuck," when she opens her pouty lips and slides her tongue back and forth along the underside of my cock.

I hold my breath with anticipation. Waiting, watching. And when her lips close around my head, I grab her hair and pull back, watching as my dick begins to disappear inside her mouth.

I encourage this action and her movements become faster and more deliberate. Her head bobbing in front of me now.

Pie looks up at me with a grin. She knows she's killing me here. She knows exactly what she's doing to me. And then she does it more. Her legs open—knees wide apart—and one hand slips down between them. I can't really see her playing with her pussy because of her little skirt, but my imagination can fill in the blanks.

I press her head forward and she opens her mouth wider, trying to take more of me. I grit my teeth as her lips tighten against my shaft, and then I can't just stand here anymore.

I grip her head with both hands and hold her still as my hips begin to move forward and back. She makes little gagging sounds that drives me nuts. And her hands let go of my dick and grab my thighs. Even through the thick denim of my jeans, I can feel her fingernails digging into my flesh.

This drives me crazy. I don't want to come like this, but I let it go on for another minute or so. I just let myself enjoy it. Enjoy this one moment. This pause in our crazy curse. Pie and I haven't had sex like this before. It's been amazing. Mind-blowing, even. But it hasn't been dirty until tonight.

I step back, watching my huge dick drop out of her mouth. Threads of saliva run down her chin as she looks up at me with those wide, blue eyes.

There is only one light on in the room. A small desk lamp in the corner. It throws a nice, warm glow across her face. Making hazy, romantic shadows.

Pie smiles. "Done already?"

"Woman, we're just getting started." I offer her a hand and she takes it, allowing me to help her up off her knees. Then I spin her around, press her back up against the door, and slip my hand back between her legs. "Your turn now."

She sucks in a deep breath as I lower down, flipping her skirt up as I descend. I pull her panties down her thighs a little. Just enough to give me access. And then I tap her inner knee and say, "Open your legs."

I watch her face for a reaction and she doesn't disappoint when she bites her lip, and then obeys. Her eyes are sparkling and dancing with questions and anticipation. This movement pulls her panties tight and she stops, but I say, "Wider." Until the thin cotton fabric is biting into the outer flesh of her thighs. Then I look up at her. Smile. And push my face right between her legs. When my tongue flicks against her clit, she gasps and thrusts her hips forward. Her hands reach for my head, the same way I did. Then her fingers are rubbing the velvet of my cropped hair.

I open my mouth and eat her pussy like I'm starving.

It's not the first time I've done this for her, but it feels like the first time.

It feels different.

It feels like we are new people now.

And it's got nothing to do with our bodies or being out in public.

It's got something to do with our souls.

Pie begins to moan. "Holy shit." Then her fingertips are grasping at my head. If I had hair of any length, she'd be pulling it right now. Twisting it up in knots. But I don't have hair, so she has nothing to transfer that excitement to.

This thrilling sensation builds, making her wiggle. Making her back buck. Making her hips move forward and back. And I know she's close.

"Pell," she whispers huskily. "Pell, stop!"

Oh, fuck that.

I grin as my tongue sweeps across her clit and then I push my thumb up and give her little nub a swirl.

"Pell!" She's close. "Pell, stop!"

I draw back a little. But I do not stop. "Come," I command her. "Come right on my face, Pie." Then I resume my ministrations. Both tongue and thumb. And there's no way she can resist me.

Her legs clamp together, her knees locking against my face. Her fingertips dig into the flesh of my neck. Her back curves, and her breath gets heavy, and then she is *moaning*. Loud. My name is coming out of that pouty mouth of her hers. "Pell, Pell, Pell." And then she quiets and goes limp. I stand up and catch her, slipping my hands under her knees so I can lift her up and press her back against the door.

Then I move my hips forward, press the tip of my cock against her gushing, wet opening, and slip inside my love.

She wraps her hands around my neck. Burying her face into my shoulder. Like she's holding on for dear life.

And then I fuck her slowly.

I fuck her like we have all the time in the world.

I fuck her like she's mine and mine alone.

CHAPTER THIRTY – TOMAS

I'm jittery with excitement as I drive the truck into town for the hunt. Just thinking about it makes me practically cackle. I'm just about to pass the feed store—my plans were to go straight to Big Jim's—when I notice that my dear Madeline is in the parking lot. I swing the truck in and come to a stop along the side of the building.

When I open my door to hop out, the dear girl is already there. Waiting for me.

"I thought you were going on the hunt tonight," she says.

I step down from the truck and take her in my arms, pulling her close. "I am. But I was passing by and saw you, so I stopped here first."

"I was just helping a customer load some wood shavings."

"Are you coming tonight?"

"Nah." She reaches up and pushes a wayward lock of dark hair away from my face. "It's a guy thing. They don't want women there. And even if they did, I still wouldn't go. I can think of nothing less fun than traipsing around in the woods during a full moon, looking for monsters. I mean, who does that?"

"Me?"

She laughs and playfully slaps my chest. "You're only going because you think you have to in order to fit in. You don't, by the way." She lowers her chin a little, and looks at me coyly. "Need to fit in, I mean."

"I can't recall a single time in my life when I did fit in." This would've been a true statement a couple weeks ago, but tonight it feels like a lie. "Well, that's not true. I actually do fit in."

"Ya do?"

"Not here." I wave a hand around to indicate Granite Springs. "But back at my sanctuary. I mean, I have always been at home there. My only home, actually. But recently there's been a lot of changes."

"What kind of changes?" Madeline's eyes are bright and curious.

"New… people. Mostly. Lots of them, actually."

"Family? Or friends?"

"Both, I think."

"Your place sounds nice. I really would like to see it some time."

"I would love for you to see it."

"Maybe tomorrow?" She's lit up with excitement.

"I'll see what's going on. Maybe I can swing it. What are you doing tonight, Madeline?"

"Oh, I'm just going home."

"I would love to see your home as well. Maybe I could stop by afterward?"

"Oh"—she laughs—"trust me. Big Jim and Russ Roth will be out there in those woods until they find their monster or until the sun comes up. One of the two. And, well, you know. Finding monsters is kind of a needle in a haystack thing."

"Maybe they'll get lucky? Maybe they'll run into their monster early and this whole hunt business will be over in a matter of hours?"

Madeline chuckles again. "Doubtful. But… tonight is probably not a good night to come by my place."

"Why not? You have other guests?" There's a little hint of jealousy in my voice. Which surprises me.

But Madeline laughs. "No. We don't really do guests. My family is kind of… reclusive. Maybe private is a better word."

"Mine as well," I admit. I really do want to bring her to the sanctuary, but of course, I would have to fight a mighty battle to win that argument with Pell. Still, I don't want to dash her hopes, so I keep quiet about the potential complications.

A horn honks, startling us both. And we turn to find Big Jim yelling from the window of his tuck.

"Hey, you sorry son of a bitch. We've been waiting on you!"

The bed of the big red truck is filled with local men all holding shotguns.

"Welp." Madeline pats my chest one more time. "That's your cue. Tomorrow, though, right? I can come see your house?"

This is probably not going to happen, but there are many hours between tonight and tomorrow, and you never know when fate will intervene. So I agree. "Absolutely, dear Madeline. Tomorrow." Then I place my hand on her cheek, gaze lovingly into her eyes, and kiss her. Right on the lips and right in front of everyone.

She lets out a hurried breath when I step back. Like I made her swoon. Then her fingertips touch her lips. Like she's reliving the kiss that just happened a moment ago.

Big Jim honks his horn and yells, "Let's go!" Then honks again.

Madeline twiddles her fingers in the air and I twiddle mine back.

Then I force myself to turn away and walk towards Big Jim. "Shall I follow you?"

"Hell no, boy. We're going up in Big Red here." Big Jim taps the outside of his door. "Grab your gun and get in the back with the boys." He hikes a thumb over his shoulder to indicate that 'the boys' are the men crowded in the bed of his truck.

"I don't have a gun."

"Well, why the hell not? This is a huntin' trip, son!"

"Right. Right. But this is not a let's-kill-them hunt, correct? We're just flushing them out?"

Big Jim laughs. Everyone laughs. Then Big Jim growls, "Boy. Get in the back of the truck."

All those warm feelings I just had—all those thoughts about fitting in and feeling at home—they disappear when I climb into the back of the truck and take a seat on the edge next to a man with a blond beard and crazy green eyes.

I don't look at him. I don't look at anyone. I don't recognize a single face. The only two people I know are Big Jim and Russ Roth. Big Jim is driving, obviously. And Russ Roth is up front with him. So I just smile nervously as we all jerk from side to side as Jim takes us up into the hills.

It's very dark once we enter the woods, but every now and then I catch a glimpse of the full moon.

The timing of this hunt suddenly makes more sense. The full moon has always been a signal of some sort to various monsters and gods. Why should these people be any different?

We stop at a trail head and park. All the boys get out and I follow along. We gather in a group in front of a sign that proclaims this trail to be the Trail of Beasts. I'm squinting my eyes, trying to read the little paragraph of information underneath the title, when Russ Roth says, "Ready, Tomas?"

"What?" I snap to attention.

"You're in the lead, son," Big Jim says. "Show us where the monsters are."

"Well, then." I look around to get my bearings, then point in the direction of Saint Mark's. We are miles and miles away, so there is absolutely no chance of us actually finding Saint Mark's tonight, but a good lie always has a sprinkle of truth in it. "This way, lads. Follow me."

This hunt does not go the way I figured it would. In my mind I had imagined that we would traipse through the woods, clambering about. There would be some shouting, and excitement, and many, many false positives.

But that's not how it goes at all.

These men are silent. Even though they are all wearing heavy boots, they barely make a rustle. It's like they are tiptoeing across a carpet. They communicate with some secret sign language—which I do not understand, obviously—and there is almost no talking. When they do talk, it's in a hushed whisper. It strikes me that getting a big group of men to be this quiet implies some training. And somewhere around mile marker number three, I realize… I might've underestimated them.

A hand grabs my shoulder and pulls me to a stop. When I turn, it's Russ Roth looking back at me. I shrug—my own version of silent language—because I have already been yelled at for talking almost a dozen times.

"How much further?" he asks, his tone hushed and serious.

"Further to where?" I ask back, my tone equally hushed. "I'm not taking you somewhere specific. Just guiding you through the woods in the dark."

Russ doesn't answer me. Instead, he turns to Big Jim and they have their own hushed conversation. I catch the gaze of one of the other men, then smile at him. But he does not smile back. They are not a friendly bunch. In fact, they are very, very serious and I'm just about to start worrying that maybe this plan wasn't one of my better ideas when from above there is a great flapping of wings.

The group of men lets out a collective gasp. And there is a rattling as all their guns are aimed at the treetops.

But the flapping has stopped and there is no shadow across the full moon above us.

"What was that?" someone asks.

"An owl," Russ Roth whispers back.

"That wasn't no owl," Big Jim mumbles. "It was huge."

"Let's keep going," Russ hisses. "They're here, I can feel them."

"Them?" one of the other men asks.

"And why are they flying?" yet another says.

"Yeah," the first one says. "You said squonk, Jim. You didn't say nothin' about no Mothman."

"Mothman?" another man says. And do I detect fear in his voice?

"I didn't sign up for no Mothman," another grumbles.

"What's the difference?" Russ says. "A monster is a monster, right?"

"Well," I say good-naturedly, "that's not really true. I've heard of this Mothman. He seems formidable. And even though I am a stranger to the squonk, that beast comes off as... well... the opposite of formidable."

"Yeah, I don't think we're prepared for a Mothman, Jim," one of the men objects.

"And it's getting late," another says.

"And it's kinda cold," yet another adds.

"What's wrong with you pussies?" Jim barks. And his voice is so loud compared to all the other hushed whispers, everyone does a little jump. Even me. "We're here to catch a monster! If you do not want to be here, then go the hell back!"

There are several seconds of awkward silence as the men and I look at each other, picturing ourselves anywhere but out here in the dark, cold, Pennsylvania woods.

"That's what I thought," Jim growls. "Now let's—"

But that's as far as he gets. Because a great winged beast is suddenly coming at us from above!

Everyone screams.

Well, mostly the pussies scream. Russ shoots at it. Then Big Jim is shooting too.

Bang, bang, bang! All sorts of firecracking is happening. Smoke in the air, the smell of gunpowder, and ringing in my ears.

And when the dust settles… one of us is missing.

"Where's Mark?" one of the pussies says. "Where's Mark!" He screams it.

While I am not quite sure which one was Mark, I do know where to find him. So I point up and yell, "Up there! He's up there!"

There is a commotion, and screaming, and Mark is futilely kicking his feet in the empty air because he has been strung up by the nape of his jacket on a tree limb.

"Get him down!" Big Jim yells.

And there is a sudden burst of teamwork as I position myself in just the right way so that the next time Batty comes swooping down, he picks me up.

I scream. As loud as I can!

Then I kick, and fight, and he drops me.

I'm not going to lie, the fall is overkill. And it bruises my hip.

But the men are all riled up, yelling and screaming. And Mark has been freed, so several of them are running away, right back down the path towards the truck.

I just lie there on the ground until Russ Roth offers me his hand. "Are you OK?"

I accept his hand and let him pull me to my feet, then stutter out, "I-I th-think so," with a fake, trembling voice.

"What the hell was that thing?" Big Jim barks.

"A Mothman," I say. "I saw his wings. And his claws got my shoulders." I pull my flannel down to reveal claw marks. There is even blood.

"Good Lord above," Big Jim says, his eyes wide as he looks at me. "You've been poisoned."

"No," I say. "Just a scratch. But I think I've had enough for one night. Do you think the hunt is over?"

"Over?" Russ says. "Boy, we're just getting started."

I'm just about to sigh with weariness when Big Jim objects for me. "No. He's right, Russ. I think we've had enough for tonight. The boys have all run off. Look." He points his gun to… well. An empty space where the rest of our hunting party used to be.

"Bunch of pussies," Russ yells. "You can go, but I'm staying. We're close, I can feel it."

"Now, come on, Russ," Big Jim says, slightly irritated. "You do this every time."

"Because every time we get *this* close"—Russ holds his thumb and forefinger quite close together—"and then the pussies puss out and we never make no progress! I'm not leaving tonight. I'm going after that thing. I *know* there are monsters up here." Then he eyeballs me with a look of…

"W-w-why are you looking at me like that? I don't know anything about monsters."

"Don't you?" Russ says, his tone very accusatory. "Don't you, Tomas? You live up in these hills. Off-grid. Say you've been living here your whole life, but we've never seen you before. How's that happen?"

"Russ," Big Jim says, putting his formidable body between me and the sheriff. "Don't be like that. This boy is…" He looks over his shoulder at me. I squint my eyes, waiting to hear him finish. "You know. He's… like Madeline."

Sheriff Russ Roth scoffs. "No, Jim. He's nothing at all like Madeline."

"Look at him."

"What do you mean, 'like Madeline?'" I ask.

"Slow," Big Jim says. "She's a simple girl. Not all there." He taps his head. "Like you. He doesn't live off-grid, Russ. He lives up at that sanitarium."

"What's a sanitarium?" I ask. But neither of them is paying attention to me.

"What are you talking about?" Russ barks. "This boy here, Tomas?" He sneers my name. Like maybe it's not my name. "He's part of that *other* place, Jim." Then he points at me. "I remember you."

I make big eyes. "Me?"

"Yeah, you." Russ is getting mean. I can hear it in his voice. And his eyes are squinty. "You live up at that..." But he stops. Stutters a little. "Th-that... that..." He cannot get the words out. Probably because Pie put a powerful spell on him. Which also seems to be wearing off.

"All right," Big Jim says. "We're done for tonight. Let's go."

He doesn't wait for Russ to agree or even look over his shoulder to make sure he's following. He just goes back down the trail in the direction of the pussies.

I hurry after him so I don't get stuck alone with Russ. He's going to be a problem and as soon as I get home, I will warn Pie and we will have to spell him again.

Russ Roth follows me, grumbling the whole way back.

When we reach the parking lot, all the pussies are in the back of the truck, ready to go. No one says anything. Big Jim gets in the driver's seat, Russ Roth gets in the passenger seat, and I climb into the bed and give Mark a sympathetic pat on the shoulder as I settle next to him.

We end up back at Big Jim's store, but no one hangs about. Everyone gets into trucks and I walk back to the feed store to pick up mine. The whole way there I think about Madeline. And then there she is. Sitting in the truck, listening to the radio, waiting for me.

She quizzes me about the hunt. But not in a serious way. And then we are practicing our kissing, and letting our hands wander, and making promises to meet up tomorrow.

I wave to her as I pull out of the feed store parking lot, then grin with blissful joy as I make my way back towards Saint Mark's.

I'm only a few miles out of town when a formidable winged figure lands in the road in front of me.

I reach over, open the passenger door, and Batty slides in.

Laughter is a universal language.

And we speak it all the way home.

CHAPTER THIRTY-ONE – PIE

"Beautiful Pie. My beautiful Pie."

Pell is driving me crazy, whispering these sweet things in my ear. His grip on my thighs is tight as he pushes me against the office door and he slowly moves forward and back.

It's the slowest, most intense, most absolutely erotic sex I've ever had in my life. And even though he's already delivered the goods once, I'm ready again.

"Pell." My face is pushed into his neck so I breathe these words right into his ear.

He growls a little, thrusting just a little deeper inside me. Just enough to make me gasp, and then… yeah. I can't hold it in. So I let it out.

I moan, and wriggle, and writhe against his hard chest. He bites my earlobe, making me squeal, and then I feel his release inside me.

After that we relax a little. His arms tremble slightly as he slowly lowers my legs, and then we're holding on to each other, a bit weak.

He pulls my panties back up my legs, straightens out my skirt—while shooting me a devious, satisfied grin—then leads me over to the office desk. He sinks down into a plush leather chair, pulling me into his lap. I position myself sideways so I can cling to him and rest my head on his shoulder at the same time.

Then we sigh.

"This is nice," he says.

"I have no complaints."

"Good." He laughs.

"Really though." I sit up a little, just enough so I can find his eyes. They're not beastly yellow when he's a man, but they're not brown either. It's something in between. "I needed this night out. I guess I didn't realize how much I missed the outside world until we got here."

"I have to agree. There's no point in dwelling on what you can't do when you're in the middle of a terrible, endless curse. But just this little taste of freedom these past few weeks is enough to make me remember what I've been missing. I guess I'm a little jealous, too."

"Jealous of what?"

"You. Going to work every day. In that new world where you fit in."

"Yeah." I kinda sigh this word out. "I get that. And I thought that too. At first. But there's something wrong with that place, Pell."

"There's something wrong with every place, Pie. Perfection doesn't exist."

"Agreed. But it's more than that. Tarq is up to something and—"

But before I can finish, there's a great commotion out in the bar.

"What the hell is that?" Pell stands up, setting me down on my feet as he does this. He tucks his giant dick away and buttons and zips his pants.

"I dunno." We both kinda lean towards the door, trying to hear what's going on. There are a lot of voices now. Excited voices. And then the music cuts off and we can hear them better.

Pell and I look at each other. He says, "Did I just hear the word 'monster'?"

And at the same time, I whisper, "Is that Russ Roth out there?"

"Shit," Pell says. "We need to get out of here."

"Like. Now."

"Come on." He takes my hand and we walk to the door, pressing our ears up to it, trying to hear more.

"Order!" someone is yelling. "Order!"

There's mumbling, then total silence.

Pell looks down at me. "What the fuck?"

I just shrug.

He reaches for the handle of the door, but I stop him. "No! I don't want to go out there! Not with Russ Roth in the bar! He's an eros! He'll... arouse me!"

Pell chuckles. "You're completely satisfied. So I'd like to see him try."

I smile. Can't help it. "You know what I mean."

"I just want to hear what they're saying." He opens the door, just a crack, and we both press forward.

"The Order of the Savage Saints is now in session," an ominous voice declares.

"Who's that?" I whisper.

Pell shrugs.

"We have a major development," another man says.

"That's definitely Russ," Pell growls.

It definitely is.

"We ran into a winged one tonight, men," the first voice says. "It attacked Mark, and Madeline's new man, Tomas."

"Oh, shit," I moan.

Just as Pell says, "I'm gonna kill him."

"I don't trust that new guy," Russ says. "Tomas, or whatever? There's something wrong with him. We need to talk to Madeline, Jim."

"Now calm down—"

"No," Russ growls. "No. I remember him. I've seen him. I'm tellin' you! You all think I'm crazy, but those people up in the woods, they did something to me. Something to make me forget. Remember when we were kids, Anthony? 'Member?"

Someone, presumably Anthony, says, "He's right, Jim. We were up there as kids and we saw—"

I turn to Pell. "He told me this story that day he came when we were in the hallways. He's not lying. He did find the sanctuary as a child and Grant must've put a spell on him."

"And if he's remembering—"

"Yeah," I say. "My spell is wearing off too. We need to go. We need to get home and start making a new spell. I'm pretty sure—"

Pell covers my mouth and then taps the door quietly closed. *Someone's coming*, he mouths.

I hold my breath as loud footsteps approach. But then let it out when whoever it was goes into the bathroom instead.

"Let's go now," Pell says. He's got the door open before I can answer, sticks his head out, nods to me, and then he's tugging me down the hallway towards the emergency exit.

He pushes through, but the fire alarm goes off.

We panic and stand there for a moment just staring at each other. Like deer in headlights.

And then the bathroom door swings open and who is in the hallway staring at us?

Who else?

Former high-school quarterback Sheriff Russ Roth.

He squints his eyes. And he's about to open his mouth and say, *Pie?* I just know it. I just fucking know it. But then we're outside and Pell is dragging me through the parking lot.

"Run," he says. "Run!"

And that's what we do. We run. We run like we're kids again. Leaping over shrubs, ducking under branches, scrambling up the hillside towards the portal.

And at some point, I realize two things at the same time.

One. I am no longer human and neither is Pell.

We are monsters.

And two. Russ Roth sees us. Because he yells, "I see you, Pie! I see you! I see those horns, and those hooves, and—"

But the portal is right there. It shimmers and quakes in the dark woods. Giving off a silvery light.

"I see that too!" Russ yells. "You're one of them! I knew it!"

And even though we are monsters with long, strong hind legs meant for escaping things, Russ Roth is not very far behind us.

And for a moment—one eternal, time-bending moment—I know in my heart that he will catch us.

But then Pell says, "Jump!"

And we leap. We leap right through that portal and as soon as we slip inside, they're gone.

CHAPTER THIRTY-TWO – PELL

Pie and I fall into my tomb, tumbling and rolling head over heels until we both come to a stop in the grassy clearing. All the doors and rings lined up in front of us.

I get to my feet, help Pie up, and then look her over. "Are you OK?"

"Holy shit!" she yells.

I chuckle. "I'll take that as a yes?"

"He saw us, Pell!"

"I know. But it's fine. We're here. He can't get in."

"He can too! He's a frickin' eros!"

"Oh." I deflate a little. "Fuck. I forgot about that."

"We need to do a spell. Like right now, Pell!"

"All right, all right. We can do that. Can't you just…" I shrug. "You know. Whip up a little poem?"

"A *poem*? No! That's for *doors*, not hiding things. We need"—she points to my horns—"that."

"And a dragon scale," I add.

"Yeah. Good thing we have plenty of those."

"Do we though?"

"What do you mean? I have a whole box filled with portal keys."

"Yeah. That's what I mean. *Portal keys*, Pie. They've already been used."

"So? Can't they be repurposed?"

"I don't think it works that way."

"Well, that's dumb."

"Hey." I put up my hands in surrender. "I don't make the rules. And as far as I'm concerned, they're all stupid."

"Agreed." She huffs. "Well, we need to find Tomas, then. He needs to get us a real freaking dragon scale."

I don't contradict her, but I don't think there are any more real freaking dragon scales. I know I said he could pull some fire out of his ass, and I'm pretty sure he's got a puff or two hidden in there. But fire and scales are two different things.

"What are you doing?"

I look at Pie. "What do you mean?"

She twirls a hand in the air. "You're having a whole internal conversation with yourself. What are you saying?" I open my mouth to deny it, but she points her finger at me. "Don't lie."

God, she really is cute. "All right." I sigh. "Do you want the bad news? Or the bad news?"

"Bad news, please."

"I don't think Tomas can get another scale. He cleaned the dungeon out and he took every single scale to the apothecary. Those small ones were shed."

"So? What's the difference?"

"A scale that falls out because it's no longer useful is... well, mostly no longer useful. It's obviously enough to do a portal spell, but there's no way it can do a banishing. I really don't think we have any real dragon scales left."

Pie sighs. "Then what do we do?"

"Well, we do have an entire apothecary filled with those apothecary monsters. Why don't we just get them to do it?"

"We can do that?"

I shrug. "Why not?"

"Rules?"

"I've read that rule book thousands of times. Nothing in there about not using other magical creatures to banish each other."

She plants her hands on her hips. "Huh. I wonder what else they can do?"

I walk over to her and place my hands on top of hers, then spend a moment thinking about the amazing sex we just had, and get the urge to kiss her. And even though we just ran through a portal wearing our monster bodies, and were seen by our current archenemy, she kisses me back.

It's a nice, long kiss too.

I smile all the way through it. And when she leans back, forcing us to part, I miss her immediately.

"Pell, we have to go get this whole banishing thing taken care of."

"I know. But can't it wait until tomorrow? It's the middle of the—"

"Nope. I cannot sleep tonight knowing that Russ Roth could roll up at any moment and come through our gate!"

"Fine. I know. You're right." I back off, take her hand, and lead her out of my tomb.

When we get outside all the monsters are gathered around the radio they keep on the patio near the cathedral. Tomas and Batty are talking excitedly, but we only catch Tomas's parts, because, of course, we don't understand Batty.

"And then," Tomas says, his voice animated and loud, "they ran like pussies!"

All the monsters laugh.

Then abruptly stop when they see Pie and me coming towards them.

"Oh, good," Tomas says. "You're here. I was telling them how we scared the shit out of Big Jim and his boys on the monster hunt tonight!"

"Is Russ Roth one of his boys?" Pie asks.

"How did you know?" Tomas replies.

"I wonder," I deadpan.

Tomas's face falls. "Oh, no."

"Oh, yes," Pie says. "We ran into him at the bar."

"At the bar?" Tomas is confused. So we spend a few minutes going over what we found out about the doors and the keys.

There's a sudden commotion amongst the apothecary monsters.

"What are they saying?" I ask Tomas.

He puts up a hand, still listening to them, then turns to me. "They say we need to hide the sanctuary. That's the proper protocol when outsiders want in."

"Oh, hey!" Pie says. "That's a good idea. Instead of banishing the sheriff, we can just hide the sanctuary!"

"How do they propose we do that?" I ask, already annoyed by the change in plan.

"Oh, it's very simple, they say. There's just one thing they need."

"I can't wait to hear it," I deadpan.

"The book, Pell. They need a spell from the book."

"The book?" Pie asks. "As in Tarq's book?"

"That's correct," Tomas replies.

"Forget it," Pie says. "I'll do a banishing." She looks at me. "We'll find a way to make those used scales work." But when I don't agree immediately she says, "Pell. I'm not going back. He's getting weird. I'll get stuck there!"

It's not that I think she's lying, I don't. I just think she's overly dramatic when it comes to Tarq. I blame it on his giant dick. She's just uncomfortable around his cock. Which I am OK with. She should not be looking at his dick. I'm even on board with her never going back. But the Book of Debt doesn't work that way. If you fight it, life gets hard. Still, I can see that she really doesn't want to go talk to Tarq about this, so I say, "I'll go."

"You?" She shoots me a look.

"Yeah. Why not? You know how to open the doors now. And clearly, I can go through them. So I'll go, talk to Tarq, get the spell they need, and we'll be good."

She shoots me another look. "You're sure?"

"Of course I'm sure. What could go wrong?"

"Don't tempt fate, mister," Pie chastises me with a pointy finger.

I hold up both hands. "Promise. No tempting."

Pie shrugs and lets out a breath. I believe it is a breath of relief. "OK. If you say so. Give me a minute to come up with a spelling."

I take her hand. "You can walk and spell at the same time?"

"Umm…"

"Great. Let's go. I want to get this over with. I do not want that sheriff coming out here and I'm tired of thinking about this. The sanctuary needs to be hidden from everyone."

"Shh," she chastises me. "I'm walking and spelling."

When we get back inside my tomb and we're standing in front of the row of portal doors, I say, "How do you think this works?"

"I think I just take the ring"—she plucks one from the air—"and then give it to you."

She offers it, and I take it.

"Put it on."

"You're sure?"

"I'm making this up as I go, Pell."

We laugh, but it's one of those... this-is-probably-not-a-good-idea laughs. But what else can we do? "OK." I put the ring on. It gets stuck at my first knuckle because my hands are far too big. "Now what?"

"Now." She thinks for a moment. "You stand here." She shoves me in front of the door. "Then I'll say the spell. 'A horn, a hoof, an eye, a bone.'" She says these words quickly, like they're not special. "The sleek and shaggy now both grown. An office via portal door. The satyr exits, prisoner no more."

"Hey, you're really getting good—"

But before I can even finish my sentence, the ring slides all the way down my finger and the door sucks me through.

CHAPTER THIRTY-THREE – TOMAS

As soon as Pie and Pell leave to go do their portal spell the new monsters are both ecstatic and agitated. But there is one reaction that catches my eye immediately. Batty is arguing with Eyebrows. And while Batty is the more frightening monster in appearance—he has that leathery black body and bat wings, and Eyebrows has a grandfatherly look to him—it's the latter monster's low, even words that change the dynamic between the two. Eyebrows is giving off a boss vibe. Like he's in charge here. And I hadn't noticed that before.

Even so, I expect Batty to win this disagreement because he is young, and obnoxious, and wild. So when he firmly shuts up and gives in to Eyebrows, even going so far as to exhibit an almost submissive posture, I take more notice and walk over to them.

"What's going on now?" I ask. Because I'm getting the feeling that there's more to this story.

Batty opens his mouth and he's just about to enlighten me when a sing-songy voice calls out from the forest beyond the walls.

"*Mon-sterrrrrrrrrs. We* know you're *innnnnnnn therrrrrrre.*"

"Oh, shit," I mutter. "How did they find us?"

But no one even hears my question. All the monsters are suddenly on the move, hopping up onto tomb rooftops, jumping like goats from one statue to the next, and growling like they are watchbeasts.

"*Mon-sterrrrrrrrs*," the sing-songy voice repeats. "Come out and plaaaaaaay-aaaayyy."

"Come out and play?" I'm not following. I turn to Eyebrows, the only monster who is still standing near me. "I don't understand. Is this an invitation or an attack?"

Eyebrows is looking right at me, straight in the eyes, when the first flaming torch comes flying over the walls and hits a tomb.

Of course, the tombs are made of stone, so it should just go out. But then another projectile comes flying over, landing in the same place. This one shatters because it is a glass bottle. But not only that, the fire ignites and a small explosion occurs. Lighting up the night with orange and yellow flickers.

I turn back to Eyebrows, who is scowling now. "Well, that was exciting, wasn't it?"

He yells something at the others, but I don't quite catch all his words, because another dozen flaming arrows and explosive bottles come flying down upon us.

And this time, they set one of the apothecary monsters *on fire*!

CHAPTER THIRTY-FOUR – PIE

"Um…" I blink. "Pell? Fuck! I didn't mean to…" But I stop talking because obviously, I'm talking to myself. "Shit." I stomp my hoof. "I really hope I sent him to the right place. I wasn't ready. I was just telling him the spell. I was gonna get input, for fuck's sake!"

Note to self: Spelling has a hair trigger.

Good to know.

But shit! "Pleeeeeeeease," I beg to whomever listens to this kind of begging. "Please, please, *please* do not lose my Pell in the… ether, or whatever! Please make this work. *Properly*. For once."

The funny thing is—well, it's actually not funny at all—but the weird thing is, the door is gone. Just… poof!

One magic portal, now missing.

"Is this normal?" I look up. Which is so dumb. Even if there's a god—who is not a trickster asshole like Saturn, or whoever—they don't live in the sky.

Also, why am I still wearing these slutty schoolgirl clothes? I stomp my hoof again. Can't I catch a break? Ever? "This is old now, OK? I have lots of other clothes!"

Again, I'm yelling to the sky.

I sigh down at my skimpy skirt and too-tight bustier. I think I've gained weight, actually. Either that, or a cup size. Because my nymph tits are so squished, I almost can't breathe.

This is great, just great.

I look back at the empty space where the portal was and try to make sense of it. Maybe, when a portal is in use, it can't be used by anyone else?

This is actually kinda handy. And makes sense, if you think about it.

But only if the portal is still there where Pell is now.

Oh, my God. What if it's not? What if he's stuck there? And what if 'there' isn't where I was trying to send him?

"Please," I beg again. "Please, please, *please* don't lose my Pell."

I pace a little. Then I get an idea. Maybe one of the many, many, many monsters I have at my disposal outside can tell me how portal doors work?

Part of me wants to stay here and wait, wait, wait. But I don't know how long this will take and I'm in desperate need of some reassurance.

So I make my way back to the opening of Pell's tomb and even from way across that foyer area, I can see that something is not right outside.

Because it's lit up like a sunset and it's the middle of the night.

"Oh, shit!" I yell, then run towards the door and leap through.

There are flames all over the tombs, and the ground, and the statues!

And my first thought is—fucking Tomas!

But then I remember Tomas isn't a dragon anymore.

My heart thumps once in my chest. It's a hard, singular thump that is loud enough for me to hear.

Something has just gone terribly wrong.

And that's when I hear a voice calling me from the woods on the other side of the wall.

"*Piiiiiiieeeeeee*! I know you're *innnnnn therrrrrrre*."

It's Russ Roth's voice.

Sheriff Russ Roth is here. Right now.

And we do not have a spell to keep him out.

I run through the maze of tombs towards a commotion near the back of the cathedral and find all the monsters gathered there. Several of them are charred, like just moments ago they were on fire.

"Tomas! What is going on?"

He turns to me, his face a panic. "There're here!"

And I'm just about to open my mouth to say, *Who?* when another voice pierces the night.

"Tomas!" A faint scream comes from the other side of the cathedral. "Tomas!" the girl screams again. "Are you in there?"

"Who the hell is that?" I ask.

But at the same time, Tomas says, "Oh, shit."

"Oh, shit, what?"

"It's Madeline." Then he brightens. "She came to visit."

I blink at him. "Tomas. Please. She's not here to *visit*." Sometimes he's so… obtuse.

"Why else would she be here? I live here. She is my girlfriend. She is here to see me. It's so obvious."

I press my lips together, trying to find a polite way to tell him he's an idiot, when another voice pierces the night.

"Tomas!"

"Now who the hell is that?" I ask.

"Oh." Tomas's brightness dulls. "It's Big Jim."

"Big Jim?" I have only casually been paying attention to what's been happening with the solar generator and the radio this past week, so my confused self-answer is more of a question. "He's the guy who hunts monsters?"

"Exactly." Tomas takes a deep breath and yells, "Madeline! I'll be right there, love! Don't leave!"

Don't *leave*? I just kinda stare at him. "Tomas. You do see what's happening here, right?"

"It's a complete mess."

"Exactly."

"I'll be right back. I've got to get Madeline."

I get it. I'm not the not the sharpest tack on the bulletin board either, but his level of delusion is impressive. And I mean that in a bad way. So I'm just about to pull him aside and spell this whole thing out for him—i.e. 'your girlfriend has been kidnapped by a talk-radio freak and is being held hostage until you go out there and give yourself up'—but he's already inside the cathedral, blindly running towards his woman.

I let out a sigh and follow him.

CHAPTER THIRTY-FIVE – PELL

For a moment I feel like I am nowhere. I don't exist. There is nothing but that eerie grayness of the fog that lingers outside the sanctuary when I'm in between slave caretakers.

But at almost the same instant that I realize this, it's gone and I'm standing in an office made of mirrors. But no, they are not mirrors. They are windows and it's night outside, so I can see myself in them. There is a large desk at the far end of the room—something executives use. And while the lights are on, they are dimmed.

I stand there, listening for voices. But only hear footsteps.

Before I can take a step forward, the office doors open and in walks my friend, talking on some kind of phone device. He's naked—as any respectable satyr should be—and agitated.

"I'm sorry. What do you want me to say? She made a portal and disappeared. I've told you this a thousand times—"

He holds the phone away from his ear. The talking on the other end continues. It's a woman's voice. And it's shrill. She's pissed.

Tarq rolls his eyes and I grin. But then he takes a few steps forward and walks right through me. Like I'm some kind of apparition.

I turn, still in the doorway, and watch him mess with a bookcase. Then watch the bookcase turn into a door.

This is when I realize he can't see me. "Tarq?" I say, testing this theory.

He sighs and turns back my way, but he walks through me again and ends up by this desk. The irate woman on the other end of the phone is still talking.

He puts the phone back to his ear. "I know what I agreed to. It's not like I gave her permission to spell herself up a doorway, Callistina. I'm not in charge of—"

More shrieking. And this time, I can make out words. "I am the queen! You will address me as Your Highness! And you are literally her boss!" The woman has one of those posh accents that used to be common in the Old World before my sanctuary was moved over to Pennsylvania.

"In *title*," Tarq enunciates. "I have no power, remember? You took it away."

Well. A clue. Maybe.

"I said I would," Tarq continues. "Yes, by tomorrow. Good night, *Your Highness*." He ends the call and throws the phone across the room. I watch it sail right through my body and crash into the bookcase. When I look back at Tarq, he's got his palms pressed flat on the desk and he's looking down, like it's been a rough day.

I step out of the door, then look back at it just to make sure it's still there. It is. And I breathe a sigh of relief because if it wasn't, I don't know what I would do. Getting stuck here—without Pie—would be the line in the sand for me. I would be done at that point. And I would probably do stupid things. Stupid things like how Tomas burned everything down to get rid of the sheriff a few weeks ago.

Luckily, I don't have to think about that. So instead, I say, "Hey."

Tarq looks up, startled. His eyes narrow on me. And I'm not sure if it's anger, or confusion, or something else. "Pell?" he finally says.

I throw up my hands. "It's me."

"W-what are you doing here?"

"Well, that's a long story. You don't seem very surprised though."

"Well." He smiles. And it feels genuine, so some of the uneasiness I had about him—thanks to Pie—fades. "For someone who claims to 'not be a witch' your woman does appear to have a pretty good command of magic doors."

I chuckle. I can't stop it. "I hear that."

Tarq comes out from behind his desk, crosses the room in a few strides, and the next thing I know he's pulling me in for a hug. I just kinda stand there, arms at my side—not because I don't want to hug him back, but because he's got my arms pinned, so I can't.

I would say this hug lasts for about five seconds too long. And then I start to push him away.

He backs off, his head down. "Sorry." He lets out a long breath. "Really." And when he looks up at me, his eyes are sad. "It's just—I really thought I was fucked. When Pie lit out of here like that, I really thought I was fucked."

I'm not sure what to say to that, so I don't say anything.

And Tarq is talkative, so he just goes on. "She's coming back, right? I know I can come off a little... strong, Pell. I get it. But whatever she told you, I'm just doing my best to mitigate things, OK?"

Hmm. Pie didn't mention this. She did say he made her uncomfortable, but this feels like more. Like something... intimate. "What are you talking about?"

"The baby and the marriage." He shrugs. "You love her, she loves you. I get it. I get that—"

"Hold. The fuck. On." I put up a full-stop hand. "What are you talking about?"

His eyebrows go up. "She didn't tell you?"

"Tell me what?"

He shakes his head and laughs. "Of course she didn't. Of course she didn't. And of course I have to be the one to explain it." I don't think he's talking to me. I think he's talking to himself. I think my friend is... broken. At the end of his line. At his wits' end, as they say.

He has been through something. And of course he has. It's been two thousand years and he's been living here, in this... somewhat real world. While I've been spending my unreasonably long life in a place called *Sanctuary*.

I could go on and on about my hardships, but even I have to admit that there was never any real chance of anything hurting me. I have been protected behind charmed walls. Under the care of a slave— slaves who were never really on my side until now— but under the care of people, nonetheless.

Tarq has the look of a man on the run. He has the look of a man who is always behind and can't seem to catch up. He has the look of a man who needs a moment of peace and there isn't a chance in hell of that ever happening.

No. Wrong. That last part is wrong, isn't it?

He does have a chance to catch his breath. And that chance is a woman called Pie.

Tarq has the look of a man who has been hurt.

No. A man who is currently *hurting*.

And I hate this. "Tarq."

But he won't look at me.

"Tarq?"

"What?" He's still not looking at me.

I place a hand on his shoulder and finally his eyes meet mine. "How about we sit down and you start from the beginning?"

For a moment I see the suspicion in his eyes. Maybe he thinks this is a trick? Maybe, in this world, when a man hears another man use the words 'baby' and 'marriage' in a sentence that refers to his woman—and he's not the one being referred to—he expects violence and outrage.

And I'm not gonna lie. Once I get this story I will probably be filled with rage and threatening violence. But Tarq is my friend. And yeah, I can be a dick. I'm selfish and, at times, obnoxious. I care little for most people—monsters included. But I am nothing if not loyal.

Tarq not only gets the benefit of the doubt from me, he gets a chance to explain.

He points to one of two chairs in front of his desk. "Have a seat then. You're gonna need it." As I sit, he walks over to a counter, which I realize is a bar, and then pours us each a drink. It's dark green. The color of moss. And it doesn't look very appetizing to me, but when he hands it over, I accept it to be polite.

Tarq drinks his down in one gulp, then pours another and takes the other chair. He stares at me for a moment, then says, "I've done some things."

I have no doubt. "Spill. Get it all out. I won't judge you, brother."

"You will," he says. "You *will* judge me, Pell. Because you and I, we're very, very different men."

"OK, then. I won't presume to know what you're going to say or how I'll feel about it, but I know a man at the end of his rope when I see one. And you are that man. You gotta tell someone, no matter what happens after. It might as well be me."

He gulps the second drink down and breathes out, setting the glass down on his desk. The air is suddenly filled with the scent of… I look down at the drink. "Is this…"

"Wood wine."

I sniff the drink, then take a sip. "Holy shit. I have not had wood wine in—"

"Two thousand years?"

"Yeah. Where… how…"

"Like I said. I have done things." He sighs again and leaves it there.

Waiting to see what I will say to that, I guess.

"What have you done, Tarq?"

Wood wine is made from wood mud. And wood mud is what wood nymphs use to make their nests in the forest. It's a nourishing thing for the wood-nymph daughter she will soon have. But it's also a magical thing. At least, it *can* be. If you make it into wine.

Once the daughter is three days old she can no longer digest the mud. Some mothers just let it rot. But others make wine. They don't get magic from the wine, but other monsters can. So it is a special thing. A precious thing. A *rare* thing.

More than rare, actually. Because there are no more pureblood wood nymphs.

There are only chimera.

So it is a non-existent thing.

Or, at least, it should be.

But obviously, it is not.

Tarq is watching me as I work out the logic. And maybe he's a bit of a coward for letting me do this instead of just telling me what's going on, but I can't say I blame him. Because if he's doing what I think he's doing, he is a despicable man. "You keep… wood nymphs *prisoner* here."

It is a drink you do not keep in bottles in office bars. There would never be enough for that. It's so rare.

Unless… "You have… what? A *farm*?" It's a really ugly word. But it's the only one that fits. "You have a farm of pureblood wood nymphs here?"

He nods and I have to sink back in my chair a little. The idea that he is keeping nymphs prisoner is bad enough. But if he is forcing them to make wood wine… I can't even conjure up the number of atrocities that would fit this reality.

"How? They're gone. There were no more—"

"I hunted them," he says. His tone is low. His voice a rumble. Almost a growl.

"You *hunted* them." And even after hearing him say this, and repeating his words, and looking at the drink in my hand, I'm still unable to fully grasp what he is saying.

"I *hunt* them," he corrects. Present. Tense. "I have a lab filled with alchemists who can open doors."

My eyebrows go up. "They have opened all the ones they can. And I have taken all the wood nymphs I can. But there are more doors, Pell. Doors that we cannot open, but…"

There is a beat here. A pause. A small moment for me to work out the reality of what he's saying. Because Ostanes diluting bloodlines at the request of gods wasn't the only reason wood nymphs went extinct. They only give birth once. They put everything into one girl child. The mother raises her, teaches her magic, and then, once the child has reached maturity, the mother wood nymph gives her magic to her daughter and withers away until she is dead.

But aside from that—because that's just nature. So aside from that, there is another, darker, grosser part of what he's saying.

"How many?"

"How many what?"

"How many are left?"

He huffs a little here. And it's funny, I know what he's thinking. He's thinking… two minutes ago you thought there were none. Now you're concerned with their possible extinction?

And the answer is yes, I am.

"How many are left, Tarq?"

"Twenty-five. But we have a problem."

"What do you do with the wine? What kind of magic do you get from it?"

He sighs. "Listen, I get where you're going—"

"Good, then answer me."

"But there are extenuating circumstances. You see—"

"Just answer the question. What kind of magic do you get from the wine?"

"It's portal magic."

"So let me get this straight. You use the wine to open doors, where you hunt down and kidnap wood nymphs. You bring them here?" I point to the floor and he nods. "Then they make nests, have babies, make wine. You open more portal doors…" It's a cycle. And it doesn't make much sense… unless… "What are you *really* looking for, Tarq? When you go through those portals?"

I already know what he's looking for. There is only one possible answer to this question. So I wait, and make him say it.

"Pie, Pell. I'm looking for Pie. But it's not what you think. The queen, she's insane, OK? In. Sane. And she knows who I am. She knows what I can do. Or, rather, what I can *produce.*" He turns his head away from me. Takes a moment. Then side eyes me. "She wants *my child.*"

"I don't get it. You have a kid?"

"No. Not yet."

I laugh. Loud. "You want *my* Pie to give you a child?"

"Not me," he growls. "Her. The fucking queen!"

"You think you're going to steal my woman and use her to make a baby to hand over to your queen?" I guffaw. There is nothing else to do but laugh.

"Not exactly." I must look very confused because he puts up a hand. "Yes. The queen wants a baby. But not just any baby. A prince, Pell. A *godling.* The only way to get a royal beast is to make his parents for this purpose, and this purpose alone. This is my purpose and Pie is my mate. You *know* this."

"How the hell would I know this?"

He stands up. Roars at me. "Because you were *there*!" I open my mouth to respond in kind, but he puts up another hand. Two full-stop hands. "You don't understand! I don't want to do this! I haven't wanted to do any of this. But my woman is one of those twenty-five nymphs, Pell. My true love is one of these few special creatures. And if I—"

"If you give her Pie's child—"

"*My* child."

I scoff at him. "That's even worse. But beyond that, you are going to take Pie prisoner, rape her—"

"What the fuck is wrong with you?"

"Me?" I guffaw again. "Dude!"

"I didn't ask to be a royal beast any more than Pie did! And I'm not going to go through with it, you freak! Pie is powerful. I was going to talk her into helping me once I knew she could open doors. I want to take her to the palace where my woman and the other nymphs are and ask her to make a door so we can get the fuck out of this place!"

"Oh."

"Yeah. Oh. For fuck's sake, Pell. You must really have a low opinion of me."

"Well excuse me for jumping to the obvious conclusion. But you're the one who's been hunting wood nymphs to extinction for two-thousand years!"

"Yeah, well, so what? How was I supposed to stop that? I was fifteen years old. I came here with a magic book that I didn't know how to use. That book? It's special. We all know that. But it's complicated. And it's got its own magic. It was able to hide itself from the queen until I had enough power to hide it myself. But this queen, she's relentless. She wants her godling. She will stop at nothing to have that child. He blows out a breath, making his nostrils flare. "I just want Pie to help us *leave*. That's all."

"That's it?"

"That's it." He throws up his hands. "That's really it. I just want out. I want to get us all out. Get us somewhere safe."

Somewhere safe. Like… a sanctuary. Now it's my turn to blow out a breath. Because maybe this is my purpose? Ostanes sent Tarq into that tomb with the book so Saturn couldn't get his dirty hands on it. And then she what? Just assumed that I would… save him?

We were best friends. And if I had known that was my job, I would've done my best.

I would've worked harder.

And this leads me back to my forgetting, and my apathy, and my… submission.

What if Pie wasn't sent to me as a caretaker slave? What if Pie was sent to break the spell someone put on me? And what if I am supposed to save Tarq the same way Pie saved me?

Maybe Saint Mark's really is a sanctuary for monsters?

It could be right. But I'm worried about this crazy queen. How does she fit into the picture? "If you leave, and take her precious wood nymphs, won't the queen come after you? And us?"

"She can't open the door to your realm. Only Pie can open that door."

"Why is that? Why is Pie the only one? It makes no sense." And it's actually not true, either. I can open doors. This whole thing—the sanctuary, the curse, the doors, the debt—all of it is starting to become suspicious. I feel like I just fell into a mountain of clues, but I will need lifetimes to figure them out.

Tarq shrugs. "Ask Ostanes. This is all her doing. I would kill that bitch if I ever saw her again."

"Seems to me the bitch you should be killing is the queen."

"Yeah, no shit. But..." He pauses again.

"Now what?"

"She doesn't just have nymphs, Pell. All the monsters here, *all* of them. She has opened doors, and conquered worlds, and taken slaves. They are *all* her slaves. She uses every one of them for something. There are millions of us who live under her tyranny. If I killed her, they would suffer."

"Suffer how?" I snort. "She'd be dead."

"She has us all working against each other. The water nymphs have put curses on the satyrs. The gorgons have put curses on the cyclopses. The satyrs have put curses on the minotaurs—"

"Hold on. Are you saying... everyone here is pure?"

"No. Not all of them. Hardly any, actually. But all the purebloods, like me, we're being blackmailed. She's using us to get to each other."

"So again, just kill her and end it."

"We can't."

"Well, why not?" I'm losing patience with him. I don't understand anything and it's starting to piss me off.

"Because if *she* dies, the *magic* dies. It's the queen's magic that binds the purebloods. It's the only thing stopping them from destroying everything. Trust me when I say this—they would torture me for eternity if they could. And maybe I deserve that? He sighs. "And if that's what happens, fine. But before I die, I'm gonna save my woman."

"Who is this stupid queen, anyway?"

"You think Ostanes is powerful?" He scoffs. "Just wait until you meet her daughter."

Daughter! The word echoes in my mind. "But... Pie is her daughter."

"Yes. Pie is Ostanes' daughter. One of them, anyway. Ostanes did big magic on us, Pell. Big. I'm still trying to unravel it."

"You and me both."

"I'm pure, you're pure, and Pie—she's pure too."

"How does that work? That would mean she comes from a pure wood nymph too. And Ostanes was not a wood nymph."

"I've been thinking about that. The queen isn't a wood nymph, yet she is Ostanes daughter too. I don't know what you were told about the 'big divorce' but she told me that I'm Saturn's son. That I am powerful and I am pure."

"She told you that, huh?"

"What did she tell you?"

"I don't think she told me anything. I can't remember her telling me anything."

"What do you remember? Because... it's weird, Pell. How you don't remember that Pie was made for me."

I blow right past that and just answer the question. "I remember the fight. Ostanes put all the chimera monsters into tombs, gave you the book. Then Saturn sent in the eros, and Juno made it so the eros couldn't get inside the tombs. Only I could. Then Saturn made the tomb doors invisible to me, so I couldn't get in, either. Then Juno made the Book of Debt for the caretakers. That's all I know."

"Well… don't you think that if I'm Saturn's son, and Pie is Ostane's daughter, that maybe… you are the offspring of a god as well?"

I sigh. Kinda tired of this.

"Anyway." Tarq must see that I'm done because he doesn't wait for my answer. "Pie doesn't understand her power and claims to be just a normal girl, but she's not a normal girl, Pell. She's got magic inside her that could do extraordinary things. You see it, right? Even if she doesn't?"

He's right. Pie is extraordinary. She can do big, big magic. Bigger than Grant could ever dream of. Hell, bigger than Saturn, obviously. Because we took him on and we *won*. So I say, "I do. I see it. But you can't save millions. Not if the other purebloods are working against you. So you're just gonna what? Get your girls out and leave everyone else here?"

"You have a better idea?"

I pause to think. "Maybe. But I'm actually dealing with a load of bullshit back in my world as well. That's why I'm here. I need the book. I need a spell to hide my sanctuary. The locals are starting to get all pitchforky. We need to make them go away and then we can pool all our resources and get you and your people out of this."

Tarq gets up, walks over to the open bookcase, and disappears inside. I don't follow him. But he's only gone a minute or so. And when he comes back, he's got the book. He hands it to me.

I take it, but cautiously. "You're giving me the whole book?"

"I'm tired of hiding it. If she knew…" He shakes his head. "If that bitch queen knew I had this thing— I don't even want to think about what she'd do."

"Who is this fucking queen? And why are you so afraid of her? Look at you, Tarq! You're magnificent."

"Thanks," he says. "Hopefully, you will never understand, my friend. But we're making a deal here, right? I give you the book and you convince Pie to help me open a portal door so we can escape."

I know better than to make deals with anyone. I'm no fool. I have two thousand years of experience telling me all deals are bad.

But he's my friend.

And he's trying to do the right thing.

So I agree. "I will."

Now I just need to convince Pie.

CHAPTER THIRTY-SIX – TOMAS

I throw open the front door of the cathedral and I am immediately blinded by headlights. I cover my eyes with my forearm and move towards the gate. "Madeline?"

"Tomas!" But that's all she is able to say because a large man has placed his huge meaty paw over her mouth.

I squint my eyes, trying to see through the gate. "Big Jim? What are you doing?"

And then it suddenly hits me what this is.

The fire, the threats, the sheriff.

But this… he can't… she's his niece!

"You're not serious?" I ask, approaching the wrought-iron barrier between us. "You've taken your niece captive? For what?"

Big Jim clicks his tongue. "Son, I can't even begin to explain how disappointed I am in you."

I point to myself. "You're disappointed in *me*?" Then I scoff. "I'm not holding anyone captive!"

"You're a monster!" Big Jim bellows. "You lied to me, boy. I don't take kindly to liars."

I tip my chin up in indignation. "I did not lie. I am not a liar. You never asked me if I was a monster."

"Oh, I have to ask, do I?"

"If you want information, you do."

"And you would've told me the truth?" He's side-eyeing me now.

I chuckle. But don't answer. Because I *am* a truth-teller. So if I get an uncomfortable question, that's all I can do. Just... don't answer.

"That's what I thought," Big Jim says. Then he squeezes Madeline. Manhandling her! Pushing her! And even through his meaty paw I can make out her muffled screams.

"Stop that!" I demand. "Right now. You will let her go—"

"Oh, will I?"

"If you know what's good—"

But he cuts me off again. "Boy, you're gonna listen to me now. Because while this girl might be my niece, there's no love between us."

He's wrong. I understand that he has no feelings for her, but Madeline has genuine affection for her uncle. And this disproportionate love makes me angry.

Because that's how I've been treated my whole life as well.

I might not be the smartest monster. I'm not clever and cute like Pie. Or cunning and charming like Pell. But I am a loyal beast. Dragons are nothing if not loyal.

My love for others far exceeds the love given back. It has always been this way. And up until now, it was fine. I am a dragon and that is part of our curse.

But Madeline is not a dragon. She is an innocent, beautiful, pure soul who sees the good and never the bad. And this jerk is her kin. And he is using her—

"I'm waiting, beast!"

"Waiting for what?"

"Are you gonna come with us? Or do I have to hurt her?" And when he says hurt her, he *does* hurt her. Because she squeals. I don't know what he did. Pinched her, maybe. Kicked her. Squeezed her.

But it doesn't matter. Because I am starting to get pissed.

"Don't be stupid, boy," Big Jim says. My anger must be written all over my face. "You have no idea how long I've been searching for you monsters. You have no idea how many decades I've been ridiculed for *believing* in you monsters. So you have no idea what it feels like to be mocked for stating the truth about you monsters. You think you can make a fool out of me, son?" He shakes his head. "No, boy. You cannot."

Now I'm starting to get bored. Humans. They have so much ego, it gets on my last nerve. "What do you want?"

"You are gonna come out from those walls, allow me to tie you up, and then we're gonna go into town and you're going to jail."

"Jail?" I blink because I'm confused. Not because I don't understand what jail is. But because… *jail?* Really? That's the best he can come up with? So I shrug and walk towards the gate. "Fine. But you will allow Madeline to stay here behind the safety of these walls."

Big Jim laughs. "Like hell. She's the only leverage I have. No deal. Either you come with me, and I keep Madeline, or she's done. She never makes it home ever again."

I pause at the gate and run a few scenarios through my head. How might this end?

How, indeed.

Well, there are many possibilities. Some better than others. But all of them end with Madeline in my arms.

So once again I say, "Fine."

But at the same time, from behind me, comes a voice.

"No." It is a very firm no.

And it is coming from Pie.

CHAPTER THIRTY-SEVEN – PIE

"No!" I say it again because I'm not sure they heard me. For a moment I wonder if I'm invisible again, like that first time I talked to Russ Roth through the gate. But when I check my finger, the ring is still there. "No!" I yell it louder now.

Tomas turns and I have a small rush of relief that I am, indeed, still here and visible.

But in that same moment comes a voice from behind me. "Well, well, well. Aren't you a vision in plaid."

My heart skips a beat. Then it thumps wildly as I turn and face him.

Sheriff Russ Roth.

And he is *inside* the walls of Saint Mark's.

We haven't seen each other since I banished him. And can I just say that a spell that required me to open a portal door, go into slave-debt to a minotaur, and cut off my man's horn to make it work should last longer than a few weeks?

I tip my head up because deep down I know he can't hurt me. And I'm actually not afraid of him anymore. "Hello, Sheriff."

"I think you owe me an explanation."

"I have to disagree."

"We can do this later," that Big Jim guy says. "Come on, Russ. We got what we need."

"Not so fast," Russ says. And now he's walking towards me. And as he gets closer, I realize how much bigger than me he is.

And that scent.

Oh, shit.

I put my hands up and take a few steps back. "Stay away from me. Don't come any closer!"

He just grins. "What is it about me, Pie? Hmm? Why can't you be near me?"

Tomas practically snorts. "Oh, come on now, Sheriff. Surely you're not going to tell us that you don't understand what you are?"

"What I am?" Russ laughs. "Why don't you enlighten me?"

"Tomas!" I caution. "Do not—"

"Why not?"

"Because." Which is not a good reason, but my head is suddenly swirly and light. "Fuck," I mutter. Then take a few more steps back. But Russ Roth is still coming towards me, so there is no relief. I feel myself… smile. Then I'm twisting my hair between my fingers and swinging my hips and… holy fuck! I'm flirting with him! But I manage to yell, "Stay away from me!" one more time.

I bump into Tomas and he puts his arm around me. "Stay back, Sheriff. What you're doing right now is tantamount to assault."

Russ Roth laughs. And oh, my God, it's *such* a beautiful laugh! And those green eyes! Wow. They are so beautiful! Then I notice his lips and I want to kiss them. I lean forward, but Tomas pulls me back.

"Stay here, Pie."

But I don't want to stay here with Tomas. I want to go with Russ Roth. I don't even care where we go, I just want to touch him. Kiss him. Feel him inside—

A sharp stinging across my face snaps me out of it. I place a palm on my cheek. "Ow, Tomas! What the hell?"

Tomas doesn't answer me. Instead, he points at Russ, then at the gate. "He leaves. *Now.* Pie stays here and Madeline and I will go with you, Big Jim. But the sheriff needs to get away from Pie immediately."

I want to pay attention. I really do. I want to hear all the little details being discussed right now. But I can't stop looking at him. I can't stop *wanting* former high-school quarterback Russ Roth.

I am in some kind of fog that makes me dizzy, and stupid, and…

The next thing I know, I'm standing by myself on one side of the gate and Tomas and Russ Roth are on the other. Then they are in their truck. Men come from the woods, piling into the back. Seconds later, they are all gone.

CHAPTER THIRTY-EIGHT – PELL

When Tarq and I step out of my tomb, the sanctuary is pure pandemonium. Monsters everywhere. Yelling, and pointing, and waving their hands around.

I grab one as he runs by, jerking him back. "What the hell is going on?" He tells me, but of course, I don't understand him. "What?" Then I'm just frustrated. "Dammit! Speak Latin!"

"He said something about a sheriff?" Tarq offers.

"What?" I look around, frantic. "Where's Pie?" No one answers me. They just keep freaking out and running by. So I roar it. "Where the fuck is Pie?" And this time, my words shake the ground, reverberating off the nearby tombs, making them tremble.

"Here!" Her voice is distant. "I'm over here, Pell!" It's coming from the cathedral. I take off in a run, bounding over crumbling ruins, my hooves slipping on wet grass as I weave my way through the maze of tombs and statues.

When I come out from the tombs I see her, standing in the middle of the back patio, surrounded by monsters. "Pie!" Relief washes through me.

"Pell! Oh, my God! They took him, Pell! We have to go!"

I reach her. Pull her into my arms and hold her tight. "Thank the Gods you're OK. Someone said the sheriff was here—"

"Pell! They took him! We have to go!"

I don't want to let her go, but her voice. It's filled with panic. So I push her back and hold her at arm's length. "What's going on? Took who?"

"Tomas went on some hunt tonight looking for monsters and… I don't know what happened, but something bad! They know, Pell! The town knows. They were here! And Russ Roth came inside! They took Tomas! We need to go save him!" Suddenly her eyes dart over my shoulder and she actually gasps. "What's he doing here?"

She's pointing at Tarq.

"We can't save Tomas, Pie. We need to help Tarq."

"Fuck him! He's… he's… not one of us! And Tomas is!"

I grab her shoulders and give her a small shake. Because her panic is real and I haven't seen her this freaked out since the day she arrived. She's looking at Tarq the same way she looked at me that first day. "There are things you don't know, Pie. Circumstances you don't understand."

"I'm sorry that I scared you," Tarq says. "I was upset. And confused. And I was really, *really* hoping that you were gonna help me, and then it became quite clear that you weren't, so—"

Pie puts up a hand to cut him off. "Oh, I'm not." Then she looks at me. "Did he convince you to bring him here and talk me into this?"

"Umm…" I don't know what to say, because he kind of did.

"Pell!" Pie's eyes are wide and crazy. "What the fuck?"

"Pie, listen. You need to hear the whole story—"

"We don't have time for fucking stories! We need to save Tomas! They have him! They're gonna hurt him, Pell!" I scoff at this. Which just pisses Pie off. "What?" she snaps.

"Tomas is fine, Pie. He can take care of himself, trust me."

"What's that mean?"

"It means he's a fucking dragon, Pie. He doesn't need our help."

"But no! He's not! He's a dragon chimera and—"

Now it's my turn to put up a hand to stop her. "He doesn't. Require. Our help."

She looks at Tarq, then over to Batty and Eyebrows. Both of them nod at her, agreeing with me. So she lets out a long breath. It sounds like relief. But a moment later, her face is all scrunched up and angry. "If he's not fine..." She lets the threat dangle.

And while Pie is a very powerful... whatever she is, she is not mean. Or spiteful. Or... well, anything other than cute, to be honest. So no one takes this threat seriously.

Still, it's my role as her man to reassure her. So I put my arm around her and pull her close. "He'll be fine, I promise. But we need your help, Pie. You don't understand what's really going on in Tarq's world. But once you do, you'll agree with me."

We all—me, Tarq, Pie, and the monsters—go into the cathedral and up to the upper great hall, which is now the monster dining room. We sit. Tarq talks. Everyone listens.

And by the time he's done, even Pie has to admit, she must help him.

She slinks back into her chair and closes her eyes. Like she's tired.

I get it. This place, and the magic, and the curse, and the debt—it's a lot. And now we want her to save a whole bunch of wood-nymph strangers who literally live in another world.

Finally, after several minutes of anxious silence, Pie lifts her eyes to meet mine. "I don't know if I'm even capable of doing this, Pell."

I look around the table at the monsters and Tarq. "Can you give us a moment?"

They all push their chairs back and wander away. Not out of the hall, but far enough away to give us the illusion of privacy.

I turn in my chair towards Pie, then grab hers and pull her as close to me as I possibly can. I take her hands. Look her in the eyes. "Pie, you are the most powerful person in this room. You have skills we don't even understand yet. But you and I both know that you *can* do this. You *can* make up a spelling, take us through a door that leads to the palace, and then bring us back. That's all this is."

"That's it? That's all I have to do? Just open and close doors?"

"That's it."

She sighs. "Fine."

And just as she says that, Tarq calls out, "Hey. What is this?" We both look in his direction. He's standing in front of the apothecary looking up at the words over the doorway. "'A horn, a hoof, an eye, a bone. A man, a girl, a place of stone. They fight, they fall, they rise again. A brand-new dawn, a new domain.'" Tarq turns to look at us.

Pie and I get up and walk over to him. "It's the curse," Pie says.

And even though before this moment I didn't realize that. It suddenly makes so much sense. "Holy fuck," I say. Turning to look at Pie. "It is, isn't it?"

She nods. "Yeah. I only just figured it out myself. The curse is a spelling. And it changes. I don't know how, or why. But it's definitely the curse."

"Huh," Tarq says. And he's in a little bit of a daze. But then he snaps out of it. "OK. So? We're on the same page now? We're going to go save my woman?"

"And the girls!" Pie snaps.

"Yes," Tarq snaps back. "All of them." But then he mumbles, "But most importantly, my woman."

"Fine," Pie says. "But do we have to do it tonight? So much has happened and—"

"Yes," Tarq barks. "Tonight. They are all at the palace for the Fireday gala. They will not all be in the same room for another week and there is no way in hell I can keep you secret from the queen for one more hour, let alone one more week."

I take a softer approach. "Pie, it really does have to be tonight. But look at it this way. In a few hours, it will be over. And your debt to Tarq will be cancelled. Plus, he gave me the book. We have the source code now. We can do all the magic we want. And we end this curse for good."

Pie perks up. "You have the whole book?"

I nod. "It's in my tomb, safe and sound with all the rings."

Then she looks at Tarq. "And my debt to you is cleared?"

Tarq nods. "After this one favor, it is."

Pie blows out a breath, which makes her hair fly up over her face. "All right. Where do I need to take us?"

Tarq describes the palace and the harem room. But we decide not to enter directly into the harem room. Instead, we will come out in one of the kitchens, where his allies are waiting and keeping it secure.

"OK," Pie says. "Give me a moment to come up with the right words." She paces in the grand hall, back and forth for several minutes, kinda mumbling to herself. Then she looks over at us and nods. "I've got it."

I take her hand and we walk back to my tomb, enter, and find our way to the doors and rings. Pie plucks a ring from the air and slides it onto her pinky finger. She looks at me. "This one's for the second door. So we don't have to take them all the way back to the door we come out of."

"Brilliant, Pie." I'm so damn proud of her right now.

"Yes, that's a good idea," Tarq says. "Smart thinking, Pie."

Pie blushes a little from all the praise. But then jolts herself out of it, walks to the next door, plucks another ring from the air, puts it on her ring finger, and starts her spell. "'A horn, a hoof, an eye, a bone. A palace gala, time unknown. The kitchen help is who we need, to help us get the nymphs all free.'"

The door appears and Pie turns to Tarq. "Are we in the right place?"

Tarq squints and moves forward, peering through the doorway and looking around. Then nods. "Yep. There's Talina and Mikayla."

We all take one final look at each other, then I grab Pie's hand and we walk through.

CHAPTER THIRTY-NINE – TOMAS

It has been quite some time since my heart thumped wildly inside my chest, but it does so now. And I like it. It makes me feel alive again. Unlike all those centuries locked up inside Saint Mark's dungeon where I was literally withering away in the dark, my only escape a bit of leftover magic I scoured up from discarded eggshells and my human-like apparition of a body.

But since Pie came everything has changed about me.

I am human, I am chimera, I am… in love.

I gaze over at my gagged and handcuffed girlfriend. Her blue eyes are wild, like her tousled strawberry hair. She is panicking. A little. Her breath is coming quick and shallow.

But I send her good vibes. *All will be fine, my lovely Madeline. Do not fret.*

We're in the back of the truck with 'the boys' and on our way to town. I can hear Russ Roth ranting and raving about Pie and Pell even through the closed window of the truck cab. Big Jim is trying to calm him down, but the sheriff is pretty pissed off about being made a fool of.

We go slow down Main Street. It's empty—it's the middle of the night now—and Big Jim pulls into his parking lot where several young men are waiting with baseball bats.

Madeline looks even more panicked when she sees this group of new young men, and then I realize—they look like her. Same strawberry hair. Same blue eyes.

But not the same gentle soul.

Her brothers, I deduce.

Lovely. I get to meet the family.

Strong hands grip Madeline and pull her from the truck. She is shrieking through her gag. Even stronger hands pull me up—I am not bound, they didn't bother. But there are no fewer than a dozen shotguns pointed at my face.

"Don't make any stupid moves, monster," Russ growls. "Or we'll just get this over with right now and blow you to pieces."

He's not a very nice man. In fact, he's a dick, as Pie would say.

So I decide to start there.

"Sheriff," I say, my voice light and congenial. "If I'm a monster, then what are you?"

"What?" he snaps.

"What's he talking about?" one of 'the boys' asks.

"Gibberish, that's what he's talkin'," Big Jim says. "Don't listen to him. Everything that comes out of his mouth is lies."

I scoff. Loudly. "I assure you, I do not lie. Ever. Ask me anything and I will give you the truth."

Big Jim narrows his eyes at me. Then he snatches Madeline from another man's grip and pulls her in front of him. "What's wrong with my niece? Did one of those monsters seduce her mother? Is that why she's this way?"

I don't understand what he's talking about, but I am decidedly sure that no monster from Saint Mark's ever got Madeline's mother pregnant. So I say, "No. That's not it. In fact, there is nothing wrong with Madeline at all. She's perfect."

"Perfect?" This comes from one of the strawberry-haired brothers. "Dude, I don't know who you are or where you come from, but my little sister is not perfect."

"How so?" I ask. "Please." I look at all of them. "Explain this to me. How is she not perfect? Just look at her!"

We all turn our attention to a gagged, thus quietly sobbing Madeline. Her face is streaked with dirty tears, her hair all mussed from riding in the back of the truck. And now that I take a good look at her, she's wearing pajamas. I'm about to admonish them for this when I see something unusual on her arm. "What is that?" I ask, leaning forward in the grip of my captor to get a better look.

Another brother walks up to Madeline, pulls up her sleeve, and all 'the boys' gasp.

"What the hell?" one says.

"Is that…" another tries. "Is that… a *scale*?"

"I knew it!" I exclaim. And if my arms were free, I would be pointing my finger high up in the air like a man proclaiming 'Eureka!' "I knew you were my soulmate, dearest Madeline! I *knew* it!"

She looks horrified, her eyes darting wildly from one man's judgment to the next. And I just want to soothe her. But Russ Roth shakes me furiously. "See! See! What is that?"

"Is she a reptile?" one of her brothers asks me. He looks to be the youngest. Maybe… fourteen human years. His eyes are softer than the others. And his voice is low.

"No," I say. "She is not a reptile."

"She's a monster!" Russ yells. "A monster just like the others! Look at it! It is a scale! And it's red and orange. Like hellfire."

"Huh," I say. But no one hears me. They are in an uproar over Russ's accusation. And now I see that something must be done here. They are going to get out of hand and that's never good. Especially the first time people are confronted with their true monster nature.

I need to take their attention off Madeline and put it somewhere else. So I say, "Russ Roth is a monster too. Didn't he tell you that? He's an eros! A love-stealing, swoon-swindling, dirty, filthy eros!"

There is an uproar over this proclamation. A big commotion. And suddenly Russ is dragging me backwards with him, gun pointed at the brothers, and Big Jim, and 'the boys', who now have the look of mad pitchfork-holding villagers. "He's lying! Stay the fuck away from me!"

I always love this part of the stories. When the bad man gets his comeuppance. It's such a satisfying way to end things.

But we're not done here just yet. I yell, "You're all monsters! You're *all* eros!" And then I growl, "Or worse." Because it's very plain to me that Madeline is not an eros. They do not have ammolite scales on their arms.

Only dragons have those.

I should've known.

Well, technically, I think I did know. It was the strawberry hair. Even if I didn't see her scales, I would know in my heart that dear Madeline was born here, in this time and place, just for me.

Madeline is my Pie.

And this time, the curse will not just change—it will be broken.

Meanwhile, back at Big Jim's parking lot, the commotion has turned into a pre-riot. Everyone has a gun out, pointing every which way, and Russ Roth is screaming at the top of his lungs for them to stay back.

And that's when the thundering sound of wingbeats fills the air.

Monsters descend, wings flapping. Mouths open. Teeth bared. Voices shrieking.

And I take a moment to think… ut-oh. This was not in the plan. Well, I didn't really have a plan. I was just going to snatch Madeline away from this terrible town and take her back to the sanctuary where she belongs, obviously.

But now—

Guns go off. Smoke fills the air. People scream.

And when the dust settles, there are bodies on the ground. Two brothers, four 'boys', and…

My heart stops.

My eyes do not blink.

"Madeline?" I say, my voice soft.

She has fallen backwards on top of Big Jim. And they have both been shot. Crimson blood pours out of her. He's clearly already dead. One bullet got him in the head. Russ's bullet, I think. He was the only one who could've done it. He was the only one facing the mob.

And Madeline. Still alive, but dying right in front of my eyes. Blood slowly seeping out from the tape over her mouth and dripping over the shoulder of her brown canvas jacket.

I whirl around, searching for the eros who shot my soulmate.

"You!" I growl at Russ Roth.

And the moment this word comes out of my mouth, I feel the rage inside me.

I feel the blood boiling in my veins.

The burning of it as it pumps through my heart.

And then the change comes quick.

Scales, and wings, and teeth. Oh, the teeth!

I black out from the fury and the anger and the next thing I know, I am high above the town and my wrath is on full display down below.

The town is on fire.

Bodies in the parking lot.

Batty and his winged friends, hovering next to me.

My dear Madeline, limp in my not-so-dragon-chimera-anymore arms, *dead*.

CHAPTER FORTY – PIE

We enter a pastry kitchen, empty, except for Talina and Mikayla. Both are wearing only their fur. Talina's brown and white dairy-cow pattern makes her look approachable and fun. But Mikayla. She's... well, I would not call her plump, but I *would* call her both voluptuous and buxom. Not to mention exotic. Her fur is sun-streaked, almost golden. She looks like she belongs on a beach in Fiji. No. Not a beach. Maybe... a desert. Standing on top of a pyramid.

Mikayla looks like a freaking goddess when she's naked. That's the only word to describe her.

She came across a little shy back in the coffeeshop that first day. But nothing about her naked body has anything to do with shy. Mikayla, I realize, is the cupcake version of Marilyn Monroe in Vinca. And she has very nice tits. Which I have a great view of, because her hair is piled up on top of her head, in between her stubby horns, and not trailing down her front to cover her nipples like Talina's white mane.

A jolt of jealousy surprises me for a moment, and I chance a glance over at Pell to see if he's admiring their wood-nymph chimera bodies, but he and Tarq are huddled close, talking about their plan.

We are stealing wood nymphs.

"Pieanna!" Talina whisper-exclaims, then comes towards me, hands out. When we are about a foot apart, she takes my hands in her and smiles. "I'm sorry I wasn't able to tell you everything."

"Eww. Just please. Call me Pie."

"But you *are* her. You are a royal beast, Pie. Even if you weren't naked, showing off your flawless fur, I can see it in your bone structure. In your eyes. In your horns. And even your hooves. It's all... genetically perfect."

"The queen is too," Mikayla says. "But not the same way you are. She's horrible. Just... horrible."

"Hmm." Tarq says that this queen is my sister. And now I'm curious. "Does she look like me? Does she have fur, and horns, and hooves like mine?"

"No," Mikayla laughs. "She has fur and horns. But she doesn't have hooves. She has *paws*."

"Paws?" My eyebrows shoot up. "Then how are we related?"

"Pie!" I look over at Pell. "It's time. Are you ready?"

I take a breath, still slightly disturbed that my sister has paws, then bob my head a little as I silently go over my spelling. "I think so. I don't know if it's great, but it should be good enough."

"Let's hear it," Tarq says. "Talina can give you her opinion. We only get one chance to do this right. If we don't get them out of here tonight, we're all fucked."

"OK." And even though I was just told how dangerous and cruel our current nemesis is, I actually feel better about this plan. I think Tarq is on the up and up. I think he really is trying to make up for past sins and be the good guy now. And Talina's spying was necessary so Tarq could make sure we were ready for tonight. So I turn to her and spit it out. "'A horn, a hoof, an eye, a bone. A pack of nymphs enslaved at home. They paid their debt, they now are free. Take them back to sanctuary.'"

"Hmm." Talina considers my words. "It's good."

"But not great," I admit.

"The syllables are off at the end."

"I know. 'Sanctuary' is a tough word. But that's not only where we're literally going, it's also a mechanism of implied safety."

"Yes, that part is brilliant. Still. The extra syllable bothers me."

"I have an extra ring, too." I hold up a hand and wiggle my pinky finger to show them the iridescent pearly-pink stone ring that goes with the new door I will make. "That's the key."

"*Will it work*?" Tarq demands.

"Yes," Talina says. "It might not last long, but it'll get them there."

"Then that's all that matters." Tarq is looking at me now. "Ready?"

I look at Pell, and he nods. So I do too.

"Let's go." And then Tarq turns to the door, opens it up, and we go out into the party.

Tarq leads, holding on to Talina's hand. Mikayla clings to her with one hand, and me with another. "Stay close," she whispers. Pell is last, protecting us from behind.

The hallway is narrow and very dark. We walk for a while, past many other kitchens, and a beat thumps through the walls. We come to a door and when Tarq throws them open, the party hits us in the face like a wild southern wind. Obnoxiously loud music, strobe lights flashing across the walls and ceiling. People laughing, and dancing, and... being very intimate. In fact, the new hallway is lined with groups of naked monsters. All in the middle of sex acts.

I look back at Pell and mouth, *What the fuck?*

He just smiles at me.

But there's not much time to worry about the royal orgies because I'm tugged forward by Mikayla and we are on the move again. We pass many, many rooms—none of which have doors, but are instead outfitted with great, long swaths of rich pastel velvets. Light blues, and pale pinks, and muted yellows. Which is completely at odds with the almost techno party going on all around us and I absently wonder what the palace really looks like when there's no Fireday sex party to muck it all up.

I'm trying to imagine it when we stop. "This is it," Tarq says. "When we get in there just keep them calm so Pie can work her spell, OK?" He looks at us, like he's waiting for confirmation, so we all nod. "We need to get the fuck out of here before the sun breaks and all the spells wear off."

"Spells?" I ask.

"The whole party is charmed," Talina says. "It keeps everyone in kind of a hazy state of apathy."

"Wow," I say, thinking about the sex happening in this place. "That's... gross."

"Yeah," Mikayla says. "But it's not like they give us a choice. The only reason I'm not drugged is because I'm the on-duty pastry chef. And Talina here, she's immune to the spells."

I cock an eyebrow at her. "That's handy."

"Years and years of lab work." Then she looks up at Tarq and they both grin at each other.

This look they share sparks something inside me. Something familiar. And I'm about to ask them what that's all about, but it's really not the time. And anyway, Tarq says, "OK. Ready?"

Pell squeezes my hand and we all nod in agreement.

Ready as we'll ever be, I guess.

Tarq throws open the door, barges through—we follow—and… stop.

"What the fuck?" I whisper. "Why is it so dark?"

Because it is dark. I'm talking pitch-freaking-black dark. I can't even see my hand in front of my face.

"Something's wrong," Talina mutters.

And just as she says that, lights click on. Bright, white, blinding spotlights shining right in our faces. I put my hand up to shield my eyes just as a posh, bitchy voice says, "You always were predictable, Tarq."

I block the spotlight with my hand, trying to peek around it so I can see the woman who is talking.

But I don't need to see her to understand who she is.

Obviously, she is the queen.

And double obviously, we have been caught.

All the lights come on and even through blinded, squinted eyes, I can see that we are not just caught. We are fucked.

Soldiers surround us on all sides. Tall, muscular monsters armed with swords. But they are not satyrs. They are not any kind of monster I've ever seen.

The only word that makes sense to me is… *griffon*.

They stand on two legs but they are not human. They have the face of lions, or eagles, or some hideous amalgamation of both those things. They have thick thighs covered in feathers—or fur. They all have massive talons on their feet and hands. But they are not feet or hands, they are paws. And they tower above me. Taller than even Tarq and Pell. Maybe a solid eight feet in height.

And they are growling.

I shrink backwards, bumping against Pell's chest. He grabs my hips with his hands and whispers, "Stay calm, Pie."

That's when I see the queen and I actually step around Pell in surprise.

She is like her guards. Only... *gorgeous*. Like... so fucking beautiful, I don't ever want to stop looking at her. A long, wavy, golden mane of hair surrounds her whole face and literally looks like it's made of spun gold. Her fur covers her whole body, even her stomach and breasts. Short velvety fur, like the kind I have between my legs and on my butt. And it too, is golden. Her eyes sparkle, light and devious, when my gaze finally lands on them. Then she bares her teeth at me. Long, sharp canines. But somehow this only makes her more alluring instead of scary.

She is bare on top, but she's wearing a skirt, something straight out of a Roman gladiator's closet. Multilayered lappets made of woven gold line her upper thighs and split apart, allowing anyone who cares to look a glimpse between her legs. Her shoes are simple pads of leather with straps, and straps, and straps for days going up her calves—all made of gold chains.

Her head is topped with a magnificent set of golden antlers. Jewels dangle from them. Rings, and chains, and bracelets. And at the top of each antler is a crown.

Wow. Two crowns. That's something.

She is sitting on a golden throne that is intricately carved with mythological creatures. Which, now that I'm a little further along into this whole new world, probably aren't mythological.

A *throne*, though. This makes me pause.

How did we get to her throne room?

I'm just about to admit to myself that Tarq set us up when he sneers her name. "Callistina."

She pounds a golden scepter on the floor and roars, "You will address me as Queen!" Then she rises and I find myself taking another step backwards. Even Pell takes one. When she points her scepter at Tarq, I see that it's topped with a stone. And my eyes narrow and focus in on it. Because while it is a very unique stone, it is also familiar. I look down at the ring shoved up to my second knuckle on my pinky and mumble, "Huh."

At the same time, the queen yells, "*Kneel!*"

There is a small commotion behind me, a rustling of clothes and feet, and when I turn, I realize that both Talina and Mikayla have dropped to their knees and they are pressing their foreheads to the floor.

I almost do the same, but Pell grabs my hand, squeezing, and I catch a small shake of his head. *Do not kneel for this woman*, that shake says. *No matter who she is, we will not kneel.*

This small act of rebellion infuriates her. "You dare!" And she's pointing her scepter. I'm so focused on that pink top stone that it takes me a full two seconds to understand that she's talking to me.

I point to myself. "Me?"

"You will kneel down for me, sister! Or I will—"

"You'll what?" This comes from Pell. And it's not his normal voice. It's much deeper. Very throaty. It's actually a growl and it comes with a rumble. The threat is clear. "You're going to do *what?*"

My mind is hovering between two things in this moment. One. She called me her sister, which is not really a surprise because Tarq and I talked about this, but it *is* jarring. And two. I get that Pell is pissed off, or being protective, or whatever—but what is with this air-shaking, floor-rumbling growl he's suddenly showing off?

The last time he did this I was coming out of the cathedral after Tomas was taken. And I wasn't close. But I heard him call for me. His voice was like a quake through the air. A vibration, maybe? I think it might have something to do with his breathy power.

"Well, look at you," the queen taunts. She stands up—and wow. I thought she was something else when she was sitting. Her full height with those multi-tined antlers almost makes her tower over Pell.

Her throne is situated on a kind of pedestal or something, and even when she takes two steps down, she still feels gigantic and imposing from my perspective.

She saunters—yes, saunters—up to Pell. A smirk on her face, her fingers extended so the tip of her nail is pointing. It's a claw, I realize. A long white claw that taps Pell on the cheek and then slides along the skin of his jaw as she passes him and redirects her attention to Tarq. "Aren't you going to introduce me to your friend?" Her posh accent is softer now. Like… is she flirting with my man? What the fuck?

"There is no need," Tarq says. "This isn't a social call."

There is an audible gasp in the room. Some of her guards shift their feet.

I take it Tarq isn't supposed to be talking back like that.

So I watch the queen as her face almost goes pink. Maybe with embarrassment. But she must be well-schooled in the art and science of aggressive altercations, because that blush fades so quickly, I almost think I imagined it.

"Enough of this. Guards—"

Tarq grabs her by the throat, pulls her in to him, and whispers, "I don't think so, Callistina," into her ear. It's not a subtle whisper, either. We *all* hear it.

The guards snap to attention and then there are swords, or staffs, or spears pointed at us from all directions. We are surrounded.

"Do it," Callistina snarls. "Do it and see what happens, dear Tarq. You can't kill me. I cannot be *killed*." Then she looks at me and smiles. "Not even you can end this."

End what? I wonder. I have no clue what's happening.

"You will give me those wood nymphs," Tarq demands. "Or I will have Pie remove you from power, imprison you in the Bottoms, and then I will replace you and rule this kingdom the way you never could."

"*What?*" Callistina, Pell, and I *all* say this at the same time.

Because that was not the plan. I'm not even sure what he said.

But also, I'm thinking… that was a good burn!

Tarq shoots me a look. "You don't need to keep it a secret anymore, Pie. It's done. It's out. Everyone knows who you are."

Except for me, I don't add.

"She is no one," Callistina barks. It's almost a laugh. "She is the *discarded* sister." Her eyes dart to mine, Tarq's large, clawed hand around her throat seemingly of no consequence. "They threw you away, Pianna."

"Oh, gross," I mutter. "Don't call me that. My name is Pie."

"They threw you away and never even bothered to tell you. Just wiped your mind, set you loose amongst those lowly, pathetic humans. With no magic, and your beastly royal blood so contaminated, there would be no chance of you amounting to anything."

"Well," I say. "That escalated quickly. Look. I don't know who you are, and I don't care. There is no point in getting mean. I'm not Pianna, I'm Pie. I'm not your sister, and I'm not here for you. I'm here for him." I hike a thumb towards Tarq. "He wants his wood nymphs—"

"Oh, does he?" The queen's laugh bursts through the room, echoing off the high ceilings.

"Where are they?" Tarq asks.

"Oh, they're fine. I would never hurt a hair on their heads. You, on the other hand…" She narrows her eyes at me, even though she's talking to Tarq. "Him," she growls. "*He's* the one who hurts them. And he can blame me all he wants. It's simply not true. I do *nothing* with those girls."

"Except profit off their death." This comes from Pell and once again, the room vibrates with his words.

What is going on with him?

The queen laughs again. "But isn't that the point of death?" And once again, she's looking at me. "I profit off all death, dear Pianna. Even yours."

"All right," I say, bored. "I'm done with this witch." I direct my gaze to Tarq. "Can we just get on with this, please?"

"Don't you even want to know how?"

"How what?" I ask her.

"How I profited from your death?"

"Well. I'm not dead, so I'm pretty sure you didn't."

"Aren't you?"

"Oh, please." I sigh. "Have you been talking to Grant? It's not going to work. I called Jacqueline from the gas station. Hello? I'm real."

The queen smiles, then tries to turn her head to see Tarq. She barely manages. His grip on her throat is tight. "No one told her?" The queen laughs. "So I get to be the one to break the news? Oh, that's perfect."

"Stop playing games, witch!" Again, Pell's reverberating words stun me. "And tell us where the wood nymphs are. We're not leaving here without them."

"Fine!" the queen says. "Take them. Why would I care? I already told you, it's not me hurting them, it's him." Then her gaze shifts from Pell to me and I get one of those really bad, sinking feelings in my stomach. "But you can't leave so soon, dear sister. It would be such a waste to have gone through all that trouble—the whole charade with the bonus and the—"

"What? What did you just say?"

"—and the new home. You're not a very clever girl, are you?"

"What are you talking about?" But that sick feeling is curdling the acid in my stomach. Something is very wrong here and I'm on the verge of finding out what it is.

"Why would I care if they leave? Why would I care what any of you do when I have you in a cage?"

"Me?" I look at Tarq. "What the hell is she talking about?"

"Look over there," Callistina says, nodding her head in a direction across the room. My eyes follow and find a weird dome-like object on a stand next to her throne. "Go pull the cover off, *Pie*. Go pull it off and see what I'm talking about."

"Don't do it," Tarq says. "It's a trick."

"Not a trick," Callistina snickers. "Not a trick at all. There is a cage under that cloth cover, Pie. A cage just big enough to fit something very specific." Her smile is pure evil.

"No." I shake my head and say it again. Louder this time. "No."

"Oh, I'm afraid so, dear. It was a piece of bad luck, your gifts. It made you so vulnerable. I mean, look at how long it took you to get here. And this is but the first stepping stone to your goal."

I'm walking towards the throne as she talks, only half listening. But still, I want to stop and ask her questions. How long it took me? And what goal?

But these are floating thoughts. My eyes are on that covered cage.

"Pie!" Pell says, running up and grabbing my arm. "Don't do it. Stay here."

But I jerk free. Not even his rumbling, breathy words could stop me now. I know what I'm going to see under that cover. I know, I know, I know...

And still, when I pull the cover off, I almost fall to the ground when I see her lifeless body limp on the floor. "Pia?"

Pell catches me before I actually collapse. He holds me as I just shake my head. "No. No, no, no. This is *not* happening." I pull free of Pell again. Then whirl around and yell, "You can't kill her!"

"Oh, but I can. And I have. And that is you in that cage, dear sister. Your magic is gone now. What a dumb thing to ask for. To put your magic all in one place. It's so—"

But I can longer hear her. Everything has gone red for me. The entire room is nothing but red.

This is what Pie's anger looks like, I think to myself.

This is what Pie's despair looks like.

No. This is what Pie's *rage* looks like.

And then my mouth is moving. And words are spilling out. Like a stream, they come from me. Without thought, or reason, or fear of the consequences. She is wrong. My magic is still very much alive. I am walking towards Callistina with every intention of clawing out her eyes. "A horn, a hoof, an eye, a bone."

The queen squints.

Tarq says, "Yes!"

Pell says, "Pie?"

"A bitchy queen on her makeshift throne."

"Do it!" Callistina yells. "I dare you to try to dethrone—"

"Her sins are mine to keep and *hold*!" Now it's my turn to make words tremble a room.

"Pie!" Pell yells. "No! You don't want to—"

But I *do* want to. So I yell the last part and it shakes the windows until they break. "In debt she goes in my control!"

The portal opens. A door with a purpose. Just one, and one alone. To enslave this bitch to me.

It's a sliver of shimmer wedged between her back and Tarq's chest. Like it's part of her, and part of him.

I rush forward, push her backwards with two flat palms to her chest, and even though Tarq is directly behind her and he should maybe fall through the door with her—he doesn't.

She goes tumbling through, disappears, and I go in after her.

CHAPTER FORTY-ONE – PELL

Stunned silence is the only way to describe the room.

"Um…" one of Tarq's girls says. "Where the hell did Queen Callistina go?"

Which might not have been the right first question, because all the palace supplicants, who are still kneeling on the floor, quickly lift their eyes up.

"Tarq?" I whisper. "What the fuck just happened?"

"She's your woman. You tell me."

"I think," Tarq's other girl says, "Pie just kidnapped the queen."

Which is most definitely the wrong thing to say. Because all the guards snap to attention and all the supplicants get back up on their feet. There's one last moment of confused silence and then all hell breaks loose. The guards are coming at us, and the supplicants are screaming, and Tarq's two women are pushing us in front of them, and Tarq is leaning down into my face growling, "*Do something.*"

"Me? What the fuck am I supposed to do?"

"Magic," he says. "Do it, Pell. Do it now, or this whole thing ends here and no one gets what they want!"

I'm about to make a bullet-point list of all the reasons why I will not be of any help whatsoever, when the realization hits me.

I *can* do something. I *do* have power. I am a magical monster. I can freeze people. Not only that, I am a maker of magic bags and a breather of magic breath. I'm not quite sure what's going on with my new earth-quaking word power, but it has to mean something. All three of these things have to mean something.

So… I 'pull a Pie'.

When you don't know what you're doing, make shit up.

I put up both hands in a palms-out full-stop motion, sweep the room with them, and yell, "Stop!"

Everyone in the room stops.

Even Tarq. Even his two girls.

And maybe for the first time in my very long life, I feel… in control.

Not gonna lie. It feels good.

"Now," I say, facing one of the guards. He's in full charge, his pointy sword directed out in front of him like he was planning on being stabby with that thing. His uniform is slightly different from the rest and I interpret this to mean he's got some kind of rank. "I'm going to unfreeze you and you're going to answer my questions." I wave my hand to unfreeze him and he falls forward, hitting the marble floor with a loud grunt.

He's still for a moment, almost supernaturally still, and I start to wonder if he fell on that sword and killed himself by accident. But no, he rolls over, panic in his eyes.

"We came here to save some fucking wood nymphs," I tell him. "We're not leaving until we save the fucking wood nymphs. So you had better tell me where they are!" I roar these words, making the whole room shake. The chandeliers up above swing wildly from the reverberation of my threat and the guard scrambles to his feet, covering his head and looking up, like he's afraid they might crash to the floor and take him out in the process.

He points to a set of double doors near the far corner of the room and stutters out, "Th-th-they're in there! In their bedchambers!"

I turn to Tarq and his girls, wave my hand and unfreeze them, then point. "Get them. We're leaving."

"But the queen!" the pastry-kitchen girl says. "What happened to the queen?"

I want to grab her by the shoulders, shake the fuck out of her, and yell, "Who cares!" But I don't. She's not mine to discipline.

So instead I look at Tarq to see if he's got this answer. But he shakes his head. "Don't ask me. Pie took her somewhere. Where did she take her? Will she bring her back?" Then he chuckles a little, shaking his head. "No magic, my ass."

"Right?" I say, calming down a little now that things are almost in control. "She drives me nuts."

"If the queen is gone," Tarq's assistant girl says, "then who is in charge? Are they going to come after us? Will they start a war?" She grabs the other girl's hand. "We can't stay here!"

"You'll come with us," I say. "We'll all go, just like we planned." I glance at Tarq for confirmation, but he's got a weird look on his face. "What?"

"I'm just thinking—"

"Not a good time for that, Tarq."

"Hear me out. If we leave like this—if we run away—then the queen is still the ruler of Vinca. Her guards will hunt us—"

"Tarq, we'll be in another world. Unless they can make portals, they can't follow us."

"Right, but things will go bad here."

"Who cares?"

"I care," Tarq says. "I care. Like it or not, this place *is* my home. And Talina's. And Mikayla's. If we leave it like this, we can't ever come back."

"So what do you suggest?"

He grins. And I can't help myself, I grin back. Because this grin of his takes me on a trip through time. When we were kids, and he always had a crazy plan, and I was always his unwilling accomplice. "Tarq?" I say, caution in my voice.

Tarq puts up a hand. "Just hear me out."

"If I have to hear you out, I already know this is a bad idea."

"Seriously, it's not. If the queen is gone, then the line of succession needs to be followed."

"Ohhh-kay."

"She doesn't have any children," the one called Talina says.

"And she's practically immortal," the other girl says. "So there's never been a need for a successor."

"Hence her desire for a godling," Tarq says. "But"—he's still holding up that hand—"I am a royal beast. I will be the father of her godling, should that day ever come, so it stands to reason—"

"*You* want to be king?" I ask.

"Why not?"

"I mean…" I can honestly think of about a thousand reasons why I would never want to be a king, but I am a rather antisocial monster.

"Someone has to do it," Tarq says.

"What about the wood nymphs?" I ask. "And your woman?"

"You take them out of here. And my woman goes too. Take them back to the sanctuary. They'll be safe there. You'll all be safe there. Stick with the plan. I'm sure that's where Pie went, anyway." He adds that in to sweeten the pot because he knows she's really my only concern once we're out of here.

But he's also right. Where else would she go? Saint Mark's is her home now. The world outside those walls is a strange place where she never fit in. She *would* go back. I think.

"I heard her spell," Talina says. "Did you hear it? She said, 'Her sins are mine to keep and hold, in debt she goes in my control.'"

"Wow," Mikayla says. "That's good."

"She put a debt spell on the queen?" This ungodly shriek comes from the unfrozen guard, who I had actually forgotten about.

"Holy shit," I chuckle. "She did. She put a debt spell on the queen."

"And where do debt spells live?" Tarq asks.

"Saint Mark's, apparently," I say.

"Exactly. Take my woman and the wood nymphs to the sanctuary and you will all be safe. Talina and Mikayla will stay here with me and I will be king."

"I love how you say, 'I will be king.' Like it's just that easy."

"Not only am I the logical successor, but it can be that easy, Pell. All you have to do it make it so."

"How do I make it so?"

"Spell me."

"Spell you *how?*" It's really not a laugh-out-loud moment, but then again it kinda is.

"Recite a poem and make me king."

"I don't do that, Tarq. I... make bags, and... slam doors, and freeze people."

"Wow," Talina says, planting her hands on her hips in a way that reminds me of Pie. "I can't decide if you're simple, stupid, or charming."

"What?" I turn to look at her.

"You're roaring out commands, Pell. You are a natural commander of words. This is very high magic. It's maybe even more powerful than Pie's. Surely you didn't miss the fact that you shook the room?"

"No, I noticed. I just don't know what it means."

"It's very simple," Tarq says, "It means you have power, Pell. Power to do very exciting things. So make up a spell to proclaim me king and take the nymphs back to your sanctuary so you can keep them safe until I get things under control here."

"This is not going to work!" We all turn to look at the shrieking guard. He's got one of those freaked-out looks on his face. Like he's about to lose his shit. "You monsters are all crazy! Who the hell do you think you are? Coming in here, stealing our queen, proclaiming yourself *king!* It's preposterous! I will have you all arrested! I will put you in prison! I will—"

Yeah. He's annoying. So I just pull another Pie. "A horn, a hoof, an eye, a bone."

"No!" the guard screams. "No! I will not allow—"

"I take the power of this ring." I hold up my hand to show it off, wiggle my fingers a little. "My best friend Tarq is now the king!"

I make a little 'poof' motion with my fingers just to give these words a little extra.

Then we hold our breath, waiting. The asshole guard is looking at me, eyes wild and wide, his mouth open, like he's about to shriek more objections. Then his gaze redirects over to Tarq and he drops to his knees, pushing his face into the floor. "My liege! My liege has returned! All hail the king!"

"Holy shit," Talina mutters.

Holy shit, indeed.

And when I look at Tarq, he's wearing a fucking crown.

CHAPTER FORTY-THREE – PIE

I don't exactly fall through the portal, even though it feels that way. It's different than all the other times I've done this. It's like… a world shift. Like I don't move at all, but everything else does.

It's weird. But I force myself to pay attention, to be alert. Because I just kidnapped a queen and put her in debt to me.

That's when I notice I'm holding a book. "Now what is this fresh hell?" I read the spine, which is written in some language I don't understand, but then, right before my eyes, the lines and loops of the unfamiliar letters rearrange and turn into English.

The Royal Beasts: A Book of Family Debt.

Ho-lee fuck. It's legit. I made a Book of Debt. And even though I don't have time to look, I am certain that Callistina's name is in there.

Did I really mean for this to happen?

I don't think so. I'd like to think it was more a circumstantial accident than a purposeful revenge scheme. But then the image of Pia's lifeless body lying at the bottom of that cage conjures the rage back up and then… yeah. I'm certain that I did.

I whirl around and find… well. Not the queen. "Who the fuck are you?" I look around, searching for Callistina.

"What the—" The woman is looking down at herself. She is human. Kinda dirty and wearing rags. Her hair is long and greasy. Maybe light brown, maybe blonde. It's hard to tell because it's so filthy. In fact, everything about her is filthy. She looks up at me and snarls, "What did you do?"

I just squint at her for a moment, trying to force this to make sense. Because it does make sense, it's just—"Callistina?"

Her face goes all rage-y and she screams, "You will refer to me as Queen!"

Uh. Yeah. That bitch and this bitch? Same bitch. I laugh, I can't help it. "You're human. And I'm not trying to be mean, I swear, but…" I shake my head. "It's really not a good look for you."

Her face goes red with anger. And I'm once again reminded of Pia. Then she yells, "Where is my scepter? Where is my—"

But that's as far as she gets because a wolf-whistle, of all things, makes her shut up.

I look around, searching for the source of the whistle.

We're the only ones here. And here is… well, let's just call it interesting. Because it's the sanctuary. It's Saint Mark's. I recognize the tombs. But then again, it's not the sanctuary. It's dark, for one. Foggy too. I quickly look down at my finger to make sure the ring is still there, because it's the same kind of meandering tendrils of fog that tried to get me those first two days when I refused to put it on.

The whole place is… like… an opposite world. Where the Saint Mark's I'm used to is always sunny and warm, this place is dreary and cold.

"What the hell?" I mutter, mostly just talking to myself. Then I notice that I'm human too. Wearing that same slutty schoolgirl skirt. It's haunting me, this outfit. It's got to mean something, I'm just not sure what.

"Hey, hey!" a man's jovial voice calls.

Then another whistle. And another. More calls.

"Hey, girl, come this way!"

"Open the gate!"

"No, open mine first!"

"Let me out! Let me out! Let me out!"

I turn in place and really see what's happening here. The tombs, they're all the same as I remember them. Exactly the same except for one thing. The black, shadowy doors have bars across them and on the other side of those bars are… well, men. Human men. But they have a scary resemblance to the monster statues in front of each tomb.

"Ohhhhhhhhhhh," I say. Because… this can't be good.

"Open the doors! Open the doors!" one demands.

"Over here, sweetie! Open me first. I'll make it worth your while."

"Oh, shit," I mutter.

"Oh, shit is right!" human Callistina says. "Now you've done it! We're prisoners!"

But are we? Are we really?

That's when I notice something else, too. Another tomb. A new tomb. We're not near the cathedral, but I can see it. So I know that I'm kind of in the northwest corner of the grounds. It's an older part of the sanctuary. A lot of these tombs are crumbling and look much worse for wear than some of the newer ones. But this tomb in particular has caught my eye because, although it too has a shadowy entrance, and the door has bars, this door is open.

For a moment I panic, thinking that one of the monsters has gotten out, but then I see the statue in front of this new tomb.

It's her. The queen. It's Callistina.

I guffaw so loud, it echoes. And riles up the residents, too. Because they start screaming, and roaring, and laughing with me.

I point at the tomb, then look over at the filthy, dirty, ragged former queen with a sudden sense of pure satisfaction I've never had the pleasure to feel before.

"No." She even stomps her foot as she says this. "No. I will not—"

But then there she is. On the other side of the door, behind the bars. Like I put her there with my mind! I almost clap. Like I seriously have to control my glee. Because this is... well. Kinda awesome.

"I told you," I tell her. "I told you I would get you back!"

But in fact, I never did say this.

At least, not in this lifetime.

Then a rush of realization comes to me. Like a long-forgotten memory. Like a rush of reality, actually. Callistina and I are children in a land I almost don't recognize but instinctively know that it is home. I'm older than in the dream, or whatever it was, that I had with Pell in the woods. I'm a woman, not child, not even a teen.

She and I both are.

And we are both royal beasts. Her, the same form she was back in Vinca. A lioness, a sphinx, a griffon or something in between. Regal, and powerful, and stunning.

But me... I am still me, I recognize myself in this person, but I am glorious. Golden, everything is golden. Just like she is. I don't have paws. I'm not a sphynx. I'm still a wood nymph chimera. But I have the wings of a moth and the light of fireflies.

The memory blinks and shutters, and then I am human. I am a small child with an imaginary bird. I am being yelled at. I am being discarded. I am left powerless and plain.

This is when it starts to make sense. I jerk my gaze over to Callistina and say, "You're stuck, aren't you? You can't get out of that tomb, can you?"

"Welcome to the club," some monster man yells. His voice is deep and angry.

Then they all start yelling again. Screaming obscenities, and threats, and offers of sex, of all things.

But I tune them out and concentrate on my sister.

"What do you think? You bitch," Callistina screams. "I will get you back for this!"

"Oh, I have no doubt. But it won't be today, will it?"

My smirk is smug. It's... elation. It's... pride, and ego, and all kinds of very negative things that don't typically describe Pie Vita.

And even though I am still Pie Vita, I'm not only Pie Vita. I am someone else, too.

"You're not going anywhere either!" Callistina threatens. "You're stuck here too!"

But she's wrong.

I know this in my soul, she is wrong.

I look around to make sure, but I'm right. There is no tomb for me.

And it suddenly all makes sense.

My life as a human child has meaning. It's not a good meaning, but still, it's an answer to questions that have always plagued me.

Who am I?

Why am I like this?

Why does nobody love me?

Where is my home and why don't I live there?

Where is my family and why have they abandoned me?

Well, my answer is clear now. They put me here on this earth. In this world. As this freak of a girl. On purpose. To... what? So I could stumble into Pell's curse? No. That's not why.

Humans are weak and have no magic.

Someone turned me into a human to steal my power.

Ostanes? She's the logical conclusion because she did come to me in that magic-induced dream state and spill all kinds of cryptic info. And I was so sure she was good, and honest, and had my best interest at heart when we had that talk, but right now... right now I'm not even sure that talk was real.

I'm starting to think it was part of my curse.

Yes. My curse. That's what this is about. Me.

I look at the men in the tombs and it all makes so much sense.

They are all human here because they are all in prison. And they are all powerless here because they are being held against their will. And they are all stuck here. They have been stripped of their monsterity to hold them in place.

And so was I.

I was a weak, pathetic human girl with no power.

Until I met Pell and started turning back into the monster I really am.

Just as I think these words, I hear a scream. For a moment, all the men shut up—even Callistina stops her threats. We are all listening to the wailing that soars through the maze of foggy tombs.

And I recognize it.

It's not the voice of the man I know, but it is the voice of his monster.

"Tomas!" I yell. Then I am running, weaving my way through the tombs, trying to find the source of the scream. "Tomas!" I yell, over and over.

But I won't find him here.

He's not in this bottomless pit of a place.

He's up top, where the sun shines.

I need to get back. And to go back, I must find a door.

That's when I see a ray of sunshine pointing the way. I run in that direction—towards the light—and find that Pell's tomb looks exactly the same way it does on the other side. No shadows darken the doorstep of his tomb. No foggy tendrils threaten to strangle me into submission. My spelling poem is even scribbled over the entrance in black Sharpie. I slip inside the tomb and Tomas's cries get louder and louder the deeper I go. Until I reach the little clearing where Pell and I sleep.

There is only one door there, so I don't even hesitate, I just step through, then run. Retracing my steps through an opposite world. A world of sunshine, and seventy-degree weather, and green grass, and... damaged gods.

Because that's what we are.

The damaged gods aren't Saturn, and Juno, and whoever the hell else is involved in this whole twisted story.

We are the damaged gods. Pell, and Tomas, and me. And these people here in this world—these humans, the town of Granite Springs and its eros protectors—those savage saints—they are the ones meant to keep us down. Meant to throttle our magic, keep our monsterity in check.

I come out of Pell's tomb to darkness, but with a glow of orange in the distance. It flickers over the tops of tombs and trees and lights up the sky with a color that can only be called bloodhorn.

Tomas's screams echo through the sanctuary. He is wailing, calling a name. "Madeline, Madeline, Madeline!" And when I step out onto the path that leads up and down the hill in the middle of the tombs, I see the monsters dragging him towards the cathedral.

"Tomas!" I yell, running towards him. My monster body is back. My hooves thump on the pathway as I skim the ground and I feel powerful. "Tomas!"

This time my call makes them turn. Tomas is wriggling and protesting, trying to break free. But he is surrounded by dozens of monsters holding him back.

"Look what they did!" he yells. "Look what they did to her!"

He is in tears, I realize. And my heart breaks as my gaze finds Madeline's lifeless body limp in a monster's arms. "Oh, Tomas." I want to cry with him. Because even though he just met this girl, Tomas is the kind of man who gives his love away to everyone. He seems like he doesn't have an evil bone in his body, though I know instinctively that this isn't true. He's here for a reason. He's here because he has done bad, bad things. He had to be punished, but they can't kill the last dragon, can they? Where would they get their precious scales? So they put him here.

"They killed her!" Tomas says.

But then Batty is between us. He's talking, furiously. Pointing at me, then Tomas, then Madeline.

"What is he saying?" I ask.

But Tomas isn't listening to me. "Do it!" he commands Batty. "Do it or I swear to gods, I will—"

Batty stops the threat with a hand. He's holding something up in the air and Tomas breathes, trying to calm himself.

I squint to see what Batty has and realize it's a rock. A little sandstone rock like the ones he gives me to take to Vinca.

Magic rocks.

Batty squeezes the rock between his fingers and it disintegrates into a puff of glittering sand. It blows over Madeline's lifeless body and I kind of lean in, waiting for something to happen.

But nothing does. And then they are on the move again, Tomas still wriggling and yelling Madeline's name. But more monsters appear and they drag him into the cathedral.

I know where they're taking him. To the dungeon. They're going to lock him down there. With a key, or a rock, or some other kind of magic.

There is a part of me that wants to stop them, but then I turn and look at the blood-red sky over the top of the trees.

I'm like a hundred percent sure that Granite Springs is up in flames and Tomas did that. And then

I am equally as sure that the dungeon is exactly where Tomas belongs.

"What the hell is going on?"

I turn and find Pell coming up the path, leading a huge group of monsters. And this suddenly feels like a life on repeat. Because didn't we just do this?

Well, almost a life on repeat.

Because these new monsters are all female.

I chance a glance at our monsters and despite the absolute shit-show of drama happening all around us, I find them grinning like wild beasts.

Things are about to get a lot more interesting around here, that's for sure.

Pell walks up to me and takes my hand. "Are you OK? What happened? Where's the queen? Why is Tomas screaming? Where are they taking him?"

I don't answer right away. I just look over my shoulder where Tomas is being shoved through the cathedral doors. Then I turn back to Pell and explain everything in a few simple sentences. "We can't break the curse, Pell. Because it isn't a curse, it's a blessing. Saint Mark's really is a sanctuary and it's the one place in all the universe where we will always be safe."

CHAPTER FORTY-FOUR – PELL

THREE DAYS LATER

I lie in bed, drifting in a half-dream state. Pie's breathing is still even and slow. She's still asleep. I don't want to wake her. Yet, anyway. I have big plans for this bed before we leave it, but we've had kind of a big week and she needs the rest.

So I let my thoughts wander and I ponder all the things that have happened since she stumbled into the monsters of Saint Mark's. That was what, two months ago? She's done more for this place in two months than anyone else did in two thousand years.

This is cute, and awesome, and says a lot for Pie's magic.

But there's more to it.

I don't want to think about that 'more' part just yet. When there's more to the story it's usually details, and what's that old saying? The devil's in the details?

There's a devil waiting for us. I can feel it. But he's not waiting for us here. Because this is sanctuary. And Pie is right—this is the safest place in the whole universe for people like us.

I have a lot of questions about the Bottoms, as she called it. She described it as an upside-down copy

463

of Saint Mark's, but it wasn't upside down. I look over at her now and chuckle.

Cute.

But it's kinda crazy that she actually solved the mystery of the tombs. They are prisoners. I mean, I guess I always kind of knew that. I've certainly felt like a prisoner over the centuries. But they are not monsters in that prison. They are human and they have been stripped of their magic.

So this makes me... what? A warden?

It feels right but I can't be sure.

I've tried to get into the dungeon to see Tomas so he could be my translator when I ask some of the more sociable monsters if they know anything about this Bottoms place, but that smell is back. Which is not a good sign for Tomas. He's reverting back into his dragon form. I'm not sure why he was suddenly a chimera and able to leave the sanctuary these past several weeks, but this privilege has obviously worn off. I'm thinking it's best to leave him alone. He was new to the whole 'human' thing. He got attached to one and she died. That's not going to be easy to deal with and I don't want anything to do with him when he's in that kind of emotional state of mind.

Granite Springs did burn. But when I went over there yesterday to see what was left, all of it was still there. No sign that a fire ever occurred. I might be worried about this if I hadn't already seen the sanctuary rebuild itself after Tomas burned us down too. The one thing that did make sense was the fog surrounding the place. I know that fog. So I have a sneaking feeling that Granite Springs is just as much a part of Saint Mark's as Saint Mark's is a part of Granite

Springs. I don't really understand how that connection works, but I'm convinced it's there.

I drove down Main Street just as the sun was setting last night. The whole place was dead. Not like in 'dead' dead. But quiet and dark. No one in the shops, no one in the diner, no one on the streets. I even went inside a few places—including the sheriff's station—and they were all empty of people.

But nothing was a mess. Everything was neat and orderly. It almost looked like it was lunchtime, or something, and everyone was in the breakroom getting coffee or eating a sandwich. Like they could appear at any moment.

Of course, they didn't appear and then the sun went down and the whole place went dark.

I left the sheriff's station and when I got outside the darkness really sank in. It was a lesson in contrast because Main Street was nothing more than foggy shadows with the exception of one sign over the bar that flickered 'Savage Saints' at me in crackling orange and red neon.

I could hear music in there too. Rock and roll. Old-time rock and roll. Like that ball and chain song that was playing the night Pie and I had our date.

That's when the whole details thing first came to mind.

If there was a devil in this story, that's where I would find him. And this lit-up sign in the winter darkness of Pennsylvania was an invitation to negotiate.

I went home.

I have no doubt that I will find out who's really running Granite Springs soon enough. I don't need to speed things up.

First, we deal with Tarq, and that Vinca world, and our newest prisoner.

Then we can think about the town.

But I couldn't help but wonder about my own role at Saint Mark's on the drive home. Why am I really here? To protect Tarq's tomb so he can protect the spellbook? Well, I've got the book now and I'm also privy to a pretty amazing apothecary, greenhouse, and a whole team of magical monster alchemists.

It kinda feels like I'm expected to do something with all these advantages.

And Pie has erased her debt to Tarq. She's still in debt to me. I have her book too and her name is still in there. But every time we kiss, or hug, or even do the simplest things that make me happy like hold hands or laugh—her debt is erased.

This makes me happy in a way I don't think I've ever felt before. And if none of the other shit had happened, this would actually feel like victory.

But now she's in control of a book too. *Royal Beasts.*

We've looked at it. It's a breeding registry of some royal family.

Her name is in there and so is mine.

So... yeah.

One step forward, three steps back.

But we're closer now. I can feel it. We're gonna solve this mystery and then—

"Oh, my God. What are you thinking so hard about?"

I grin and turn my head to find a sleepy Pie cracking one eye open for me.

"You," I say. And it's not even a lie.

She reaches for me, her hand touching my cheek in a way that makes me feel cherished. She leans up and kisses me, her hand sliding down my face to my shoulder, then my chest, then... "Fuck yeah," I mumble. "But I thought you were over the morning sex?"

She kisses me between her words. "No more job, no more restrictions."

"So your new plans are... what? Lying around in bed all day?"

"It's like you're a mind-reader, Pell."

I flip her over, position my body over hers, and then lean down and kiss her back.

I know this isn't over.

I know there's more to come.

I know my future isn't going to be a life spent in bed with my woman.

But I've always been good at pretending.

EPILOGUE – TOMAS

There has only ever been one reason for a dragon to have a den.

And maybe a dungeon isn't the best place, but it's all we have.

The fire inside me is back. And for a moment I get lost in that request of Pell's. Could I make some flame for him? Could I seal his bag with fire?

I will do that, eventually.

When this is over.

'This' refers to Madeline and her present state.

My sweet, sweet Madeline with her ammolite scales on her arms, and legs, and torso, and breasts.

They are everywhere now.

She is changing.

She has changed.

Yes, of course she was dead. But dead, to dragons at least, has several levels.

I had forgotten about my early days. All these centuries in this place takes a toll on a person. They make you tuck things away, and neglect to see the big picture, and pretend that this day is the only day that ever mattered.

But of course, this day *is* the only day that ever mattered. None of the others that came before are of any consequence at all.

I rise up, my leathery, red wings spreading out until they push against the walls on either side, and I take it all in.

My beautiful Madeline and her new blood-orange body flickering with magic, and desire, and instincts.

Because, of course, underneath her new body are her eggs.

So many eggs.

They are everywhere. Filling up the space just like my wings.

And soon we will once again be everywhere too.

END OF BOOK SHIT

END OF BOOK SHIT

Welcome to the End of Book Shit. This is the part of the book where I get to have opinions and generally say whatever I want. And I have to be honest – on this particular day I feel like ranting. I have complaints. I have complaints about readers, and corporations, and family members, and taxes, and governments, and assholes, and all sorts of things and people.

I want to make statements about these things. Maybe intellectual statements. Maybe petty statements. Maybe unnecessary statements.

But the world is SO messed up right now, I feel like I should try and give a fuck or two.

So I'm not going to make any of those statements. Instead I'm going to make this one instead:

BE KIND.

I know, it's not that easy. I get it. There are all these people to hate. People who don't agree with you, people who don't like you, people who don't respect you. And that's not all, there are all kinds of organizations to hate too. Organizations that want to control you, and stifle you, and bully you, and make you feel responsible for all the world's problems so they don't have to take any responsibility. Then there

471

are the governments. The lying, cheating, good-for-absolutely-nothing governments. I can't stick to my BE KIND message and say any more about governments, so we'll leave it there.

The point is, hate is everywhere. Literally everywhere. Every time you turn around someone is shouting about how this person hates you, or that person hates you, and they seem to have made it their life's mission to make sure that you hate them back. There is a real push around the world to divide humans into camps, and once you're in the camp your job is to hate those outside the camp.

I don't have to list the camps, you know what I'm talking about. And nothing about this EOBS is about specifics, so it doesn't matter what camp.

There's nothing inherently wrong with dividing people into camps. People like to form clubs. People like to associate with others who agree on certain topics, or live in a certain area, or go to the same school. Families are an example of camps. Everyone has a family. Even if you have no blood relatives, you probably have a family.

So camps are not all bad.

But when the camps are super big—like a government, or a corporation, or some other powerful organization—well, we've got a problem.

Because the bigger one camp is, the smaller another has to be.

I am not a fan of big camps.

Someone once asked me if I was going to 'such-and such' march. Pick your favorite social/political awareness group and insert their march here. This was several years ago. And it was pretty unpopular to say no, I don't do that. But that's what I said. I don't do that. I don't march for anyone. And the reason why I don't march for anyone is because not only are those marchers a 'camp', they are a large camp.

They are a group.

And I don't get behind 'groups'.

I get behind people.

And if I'm going to get behind people, they will be people I know, people I trust, and people I respect.

You're probably wondering what this has to do with BE KIND. And I'm gonna tell you this—you don't have to march for someone to be kind to them. You can be kind to people you don't like, or respect, or agree with.

Being kind has nothing to do with agreeing with someone.

Being kind actually has nothing to do with someone else.

Being kind is about you.

You can be kind and not be invested.

You can be kind to someone who hates you.

You can even be kind to someone you hate.

You can be kind to everyone.

You're not agreeing with them if you're kind.

You're just being good.

When I die I want people to remember a few things about me.

I would like them to remember that I wrote good books. They are books that maybe aren't everyone's cup of tea, but I write good books.

I would also like to remember that I don't lie. I do not. Lie. Ever. I will shut the fuck up really fast if I'm asked a question I don't want to answer. If it's a question about me, I will just say I'm not answering that question and that will be the end of it. But if it's a question about someone else, and I can't say the truth without hurting them, I will shut up. I'm not gonna lie about it. And there are situations where the truth is not welcome. Thousands of situations where telling the truth can make things worse. So I get that. But I won't lie.

And because I do not lie, and I live in a world overflowing with liars, I think this is pretty special. So I'd like to be remembered for that.

But most of all I would like to be remembered for being fair.

I will ALWAYS stick up for a helpless stranger who is being bullied or hurt.

I will never cheat. I will never take money for something I didn't earn or believe in.

I cannot be bought. There is no price high enough to buy me.

And I will never hurt anyone on purpose.

Now, with that said, I *will* fight back. I'm not a pacifist. And if I fight, I fight hard so someone's getting hurt if I fight back.

But I am fair.

And maybe—I'm not sure—but maybe this is enough to be considered good.

I have had many goals in life throughout the years and I've written about a lot of them in the End of Book Shits. But being good is not a goal. It's a constant battle.

And I do mean battle. Because you have all these camps around you—vying for your hate.

They need your hate, guys.

They need it.

Because it takes absolute hate to get this insane world we're living in right now.

In the Sick Heart EOBS I talked about emotions and how these camps need your emotional response. They feed off your emotions like vampires. Negative emotions are powerful things. Likewise, so positive ones. But the vampires know that is so much easier to hate.

So they are very successful.

Hate is so easy.

Because hate is nothing but raw emotions and emotions are what make us human.

Emotions are powerful.

You must be careful with them.

That old saying "Sticks and stones will break my bones but words will never hurt me?" Yeah, that's fuckin' bullshit. Words are powerful. This is what I do for a living so I know better than most the power of words. (and don't you love that Pie just discovered this magic?)

I wake up every day with a new reason to hate. There's so much to hate.

I'm not being facetious here, either. There are thousands of things to hate in the world right now and quite a bit of them are justified.

So every day I have to make a very conscious decision not to do this.

I'm not perfect by any means. Some days I fail.

But the important thing is that I know I failed.

Some people just go around throwing their hate around. And they are so used to this—have been conditioned to do this—that they don't even realize they're full of hate. They're overflowing with hate. That's why they have to pass it on. They have too much. It's gotta go somewhere, right?

So they hand it out.

That's the easy thing to do. Get rid of your hate (and your self-loathing for the hate) and make yourself feel better by making someone else feel worse.

This is the absolute coward's way to live.

Strong people are kind. They fail at it, of course, because they are human. But strong people make a conscious decision to be kind. They put their emotions away, ask for strength, and be kind.

It's such a hard thing to do. So I respect everyone who tries. Even if you fail ninety-percent of the time, I respect you. Because if you *know* you fail ninety-percent of the time, you know the difference between kind and hate.

And if you know the difference, then you can get better at it.

All of us have anger and hate issues. Everyone.

But what matters is the battle you wage with yourself, every day, to get past it.

When I came up with the idea for Saint Mark's Sanctuary I didn't really have a reason to call it that. I've mentioned my writing process in lots End of Book Shits at this point, so ya'll probably know that I just let the muse take over a lot of the time. But with this story it was 100% of the time. I didn't have a reason to call it a sanctuary. I plucked that out of "the river" and gave it a home in my story. That's all I did.

But when I got to the end of this book I realized that these monsters were lucky. So. Lucky. Because they were protected by walls and when they are inside those walls, they are OK. No matter who they are, what they've done, or what they look like. They are all safe.

This is what I love about Saint Mark's Sanctuary. It's a place where everyone can be themselves. Where you don't have to worry about the hate, you just get to work on being kind.

And I love that Pell is just starting to figure this out. He's been a rage-y monster for thousands of years. He's been an asshole.

But even monsters can do better.

If only we all had a Saint Mark's to protect us.

Wouldn't it be great to have your camp people inside protective walls so no one could hurt you?

It would be great.

But as great as it is, it's not really practical. Because who has money for a wall, right? Good god, I'm building a fence for my goats right now and it's freaking expensive.

Still, everyone needs a sanctuary to retreat to when being kind becomes overwhelming.

Find your sanctuary, guys.

Whatever it may be.

Because this world is a shit show right now and it's not getting any better.

You need a sanctuary.

I know a lot of you will probably say your sanctuary is books. I can relate to that. I did not have a bad childhood. We were poor, but I had a pretty amazing childhood. Still, books were my sanctuary.

But if books aren't enough, find something else.

Lots of people will say their pets are their sanctuary. I totally agree. Nothing makes me feel as good as when I hug Blue. He's my Alaskan malamute and he LOVES to be hugged. By the family, anyway. If a stranger tries to hug Blue, they will lose their face.

Blue goes crazy if he doesn't get his hugs every day.

And he's a dog.

So people really need hugs.

Find your sanctuary, guys.

The world is a cold, hard place right now. But even if it all goes to shit and we get to a place where there's almost nothing left, we can still be kind and make it better.

Thank you for reading, thank you for reviewing, and I'll see you in the next book.

Julie
JA Huss
April 18, 2022

ABOUT THE AUTHOR

JA Huss is a New York Times Bestselling author and has been on the USA Today Bestseller's list 21 times. She writes characters with heart, plots with twists, and perfect endings.

Her books have sold millions of copies all over the world. Her book, Eighteen, was nominated for a Voice Arts Award and an Audie Award in 2016 and 2017 respectively. Her audiobook, Mr. Perfect, was nominated for a Voice Arts Award in 2017. Her audiobook, Taking Turns, was nominated for an Audie Award in 2018. Her book, Total Exposure, was nominated for a RITA Award in 2019.

She writes Sci-Fi Romance and Paranormal Romance under the name KC Cross.